Terror Island

Rakie Keig

hadesgate

publications

Published by:
Hadesgate Publications
PO Box 167
Selby
YO8 4WP
Email: hadesgate@hotmail.co.uk
www.hadesgate.co.uk

Terror Island

Rakie Keig

© Rakie Keig 2007

First published November 2007

Rakie keig asserts the moral rights to be identified as the author of this work.

Mailings to: Rakie Keig
c/o Hadesgate Publications
PO Box 167
Selby
North Yorkshire
YO8 4WP
www.hadesgate.co.uk
www.hadesgateforums.co.uk

ISBN 978-0-9550314-9-6

Cover design by Martin Blanco at www.pitbrosproductions.com

Prepared and printed by:
York Publishing Services Ltd
64 Hallfield Road
Layerthorpe
York
YO31 7ZQ

Tel: 01904 431213   Website: www.yps-publishing.co.uk

DEDICATION

To Dad and Yasmin,
who wrote the original, much scarier
"Terror Island", and let me steal the title

Chapter 1

It was five nights before the full moon. The sky was bright enough that even beneath the trees there was more than enough light to see by.

Privately, the young doctor wished that it were darker. His mind might then have been able to gloss over some of the details regarding the body on the ground. Instead, the silvery light of both moon and stars perfectly illuminated the entire scene.

At least in this light the blood looked grey, not red.

'Has anyone moved the body?'

The doctor looked up to find Ehren standing over him, staring down at the body. A patch of shadow hid the older man's face, but his voice seemed unnaturally calm, as if it would take a lot more than violent death to faze him.

The young doctor shook his head, swallowing hard as the movement made his vision swim. 'No,' he said. 'No-one's moved him.' He could personally testify to that, because he had been one of the first people to arrive on the scene. The last thing that any of the others had wanted to do was to poke around in the mess of torn skin and pulped flesh that had once been a human being.

Ehren sighed heavily. 'Who was it, Seth?'

'He's wearing Sykes's passcard. If we want to be more sure than that we'll probably have to fall back on dental records.'

Ehren grunted noncommittally, then turned and strode away a few paces. Seth straightened up slowly, half-afraid that the world would start spinning again, and then followed him.

'How long were they missing?' Ehren asked him.

Seth checked his watch. 'Six or seven hours at least. No-one's seen them since the check-post reported them leaving this evening. Yesterday evening, that is,' he corrected himself, since it was now just after half past two in the morning.

'Alright.' Ehren stared down at the ground for a long moment, the corners of his mouth turning downwards in thought. 'Seth, I'd appreciate an honest answer to something.'

'Sure.' Seth already knew what the question would be.

'This was done by a wolf, wasn't it?'

Seth wanted to say no, to somehow find some other explanation, but he couldn't. Sykes had been torn open from throat to navel, his throat ripped out and half of his face chewed off, making him practically unrecognisable. There were obvious teeth marks on several of the exposed ribs, and the most cursory glance inside the open thorax revealed that many of the organs had been removed or partially eaten. It had been a wolf.

Slowly, Seth nodded. 'Yes, sir.'

'Alright.' Ehren straightened, as if Seth's answer had brought him to a decision. 'I need you to contact Brac. I want to know exactly where everyone was tonight. Everyone.'

Seth knew that that applied to him as well, and he nodded again.

'We're going to have to organise a search team,' Ehren went on. 'We've still got one person missing.' He looked up at the waxing moon above the black trees. 'The boat's going to be here in two days, and I want this all sorted by then.'

'I'll call Brac, sir.'

'Good. And we'll have to clear this mess up quickly as well, before it starts attracting more wildlife.'

Seth felt the bile rise in his throat again, and he turned away quickly. He didn't look back at the body of Sykes as he walked to the jeep, and he was glad that the shifting shadows hid his face from the other people.

He wondered if Ehren knew exactly how much the sight of the corpse had affected him.

He picked up the radio from the jeep and called back to base. Brac wasn't going to be happy to be woken at this hour, and he would be even less happy once he'd heard the news.

Seth glanced back at the body without really meaning to. The silvery quality of the light made the scene look unreal, and he could almost believe that the shape beneath the trees was just a tumbled mass of branches and rocks. Almost... if it hadn't been for the thick smell of recently spilt blood and offal, which still hung heavily in the air. Seth squeezed his eyes shut.

He wondered how Ehren would react if he knew the exact cause of the young doctor's discomfort. The smell of the torn, ruptured flesh had made Seth dizzy, because he'd wanted more than anything to plunge his face into it; to have that sweet, intoxicating smell surround him.

DAY ONE

Chapter 2

In her dream, Anna was back in her bedroom at home, as if she'd never left. The room was in darkness apart from the small amount of orange light from the streetlight directly outside her window. It cast just enough illumination for her to make out the furniture around her; familiar items suddenly made to seem dark and alien by the shadows of the dream. In the distance, she could still hear the sound of the sea.

She was sat silently on the bed, dressed in the faded blue t-shirt that she always slept in, her hands folded lightly in her lap. Her eyes were the only part of her that moved, following the shadows slowly across her bedroom walls as they formed and reformed like shapes on the surface of a bowl of water; shapes that could have represented anything or nothing. She could feel the calmness and the sadness of her familiar surroundings, because she had had this dream countless times before. It was as much a part of her as anything else in her life.

The dream was never exactly the same. The setting changed, usually altering to whatever place Anna had fallen asleep in, but sometimes when she was feeling the most lost and confused, it reverted back to the room she had slept in for fifteen of her twenty-two years. Only two things were always the same about the dream – the constantly shifting shadows on the wall, and the little girl.

In this moment of the dream, the girl was sat next to Anna on the bed, her short legs drawn up so that she could rest her elbows on her knees. The girl's eyes were the same dark blue as Anna's, although it was sometimes hard to tell in the dim light. Her hair was darker than Anna's, and it was always a frizzy, slightly tangled mess, falling to just short of her shoulders in a style that only a young child would wear. That night she wore a pale yellow summer dress, but the orange reflected light from the street drained the colour out of it and cast thick patches of shadow over her chest and arms.

'Why did he leave?'

The girl's voice was never more than an echo in Anna's mind. As usual, Anna found that she could not look the child in the face, and stared down at her hands instead. The shadows were moving across the floor as well, playing around her ankles like waves in the sea. She didn't have an answer to give to the girl, so she shook her head. 'Everyone leaves,' she said at last, her voice sounding too loud in her own ears. 'I'm sorry.'

The girl sighed, and the shadows moved with the sound. She reached over and took hold of Anna's hand, and her fingers felt warm yet insubstantial, like a breath passing over the skin. 'You'll find him,' the girl said then. 'Won't you?'

Anna wanted to nod, but in truth she didn't have an answer to that question either. She started to say that she'd at least try, but then the girl walked away and the dream faded back to nothingness.

Chapter 3

Anna Martin opened her eyes, blinking despite the fact that the sun wasn't particularly bright that day. She had obviously been more tired than she'd realised, since she'd drifted off to sleep when all she'd intended to do was sit down quietly for five minutes. The strain of the past few weeks was apparently catching up with her. She rubbed her eyes irritably. It had taken her a long, long time to get this far, and she couldn't rest now, not on what was hopefully the last leg on her journey.

The floor beneath her moved steadily up and down with the gentle swell of the sea. The air was filled with the racket of the battered outboard engine of the boat. Anna was sat on the small front deck of the *Narrenshiff*, protected from the wind and the spray by the wooden bow. One hand was gripped around the metal rail, instinctively steadying herself even in her sleep, and her fingers had gone numb from the cold.

There was a small cabin attached to the boat, but the noise of the engine was overbearingly loud in there, so Anna and the one other passenger had escaped up onto the open deck. The wind wasn't quite cold enough out there to force them back inside, and Anna had been content to curl up in the bows and drift off to sleep for a few minutes. A quick glance at her watch told her that the few minutes had actually been closer to twenty.

Bracing herself against the rolling motion of the boat, she stood up. The stiff breeze immediately whipped her long brown hair around her face, and she smoothed it back with her free hand as best she could. All around the grey sea rose and fell in fat, rounded waves. The sky was the same cold, empty grey, as if one was just a reflection of the other. Anna turned her eyes westward, and a small shiver ran through her body. There on the horizon, like a very dark and low-lying cloudbank, was the island.

Her first glance couldn't confirm any of her hopes or fears, since at that distance it was almost impossible to discern the details of the island. All she could really tell was that it was larger than she'd expected – maybe twenty miles from end to end – and that most of its coastline rose in steep, sheer cliffs. Rising above the cliffs, some distance inland, she could just make out the vague shape of mountains, concealed behind the thick and drifting cloud.

Anna wondered for a moment what she'd been expecting, and whether this was it.

Apart from the captain and the thin teenage boy who had sullenly helped them aboard, Anna and her friend Mike were the only passengers aboard the boat. The state of the vessel made it clear that it didn't usually cater for passenger travel.

As Anna was looking out at their destination, the teenage boy was standing on the other side of the boat, leaning against the rail and watching the grey sea with dull, flat eyes. He held a cigarette cupped in one hand, and the fingers of the other hand were idly twisting a section of rope. Occasionally, his gaze would drop to the man who was talking to him, and his lips would move in a quick, weak grin. Each separate movement – lifting his cigarette to his mouth; twisting the rope between his fingers; the short smile – was quick and jerky, and each was completed before another began, so that no two parts of his body were ever in motion at the same time.

The man talking to him, Mike Jeffreye, was currently sat on top of an upturned crate with his long legs stretched in front of him. In contrast to the boy, Mike was constantly moving, fidgeting and waving his hands to reinforce even the slightest point. He held a cigarette in his own hand, but seemed to forget all about it for long periods of time as he talked. Flecks of grey ash fell away and were carried off swiftly by the wind. His black hair had become ruffled by the same wind, and one hand made continuous, unconscious attempts to tug it back behind his ears.

He was a student at the same university as Anna, but apart from the fact that they shared a single class together and hung out with a few of the same people, they were acquaintances rather than friends. He was a media student, repeating his second year after failing his last set of exams – although that didn't seem to concern him any more than anything else in life. Mike was one of the most relaxed and easy-going people that Anna knew. Privately, she suspected that that was one of the reasons why he'd agreed to come with her on this trip, despite the fact that they weren't close friends. Just about everyone else she knew had been supportive… up to a point. Only Mike had shrugged his shoulders and said 'why not?' when she'd asked him.

At that particular moment, Mike was telling the teenager about something that had happened to him back home. Despite the animation with which he spoke, he was really just talking for the sake of it. He doubted that the boy was even slightly interested.

'You wouldn't believe what a stupid, small thing it all started over,' he said, his eyes moving over the surface of the sea as if searching for something.

'I bought a load of pills off this girl, but I didn't have enough cash on me. I figured she was going to sell them to me for two or three quid a piece, since we were friends and all, but the tight bitch charged me four quid each. Anyway, I bought twenty, but I only had forty pounds on me, so I told her I'd give her the rest after the weekend...'

The young boy nodded and smiled at various points of the story, his gaze still wandering vaguely. Across the boat from him, Anna wondered if he even knew what her travelling companion was talking about.

Mike didn't seem at all perturbed by the possibility. He kept talking, entertaining himself if no-one else. '...So then it gets to Monday and suddenly I'm getting all these texts off this girl asking where the hell her money is and threatening me with all sort of shit. I mean, let's be serious now – forty quid isn't that much, and it was only Monday. I couldn't see what her big problem was. Anyway, I took her the money that evening and she screamed all this abuse at me, saying that she hated me and was never going to help me out ever again, blah blah blah blah blah...'

Anna listened to Mike's voice with only half an ear, her attention distracted by the dark smudge of land on the horizon. So far, she'd heard him tell four different version of that story to different people, and she was fairly sure that none of them were the strict truth. Mike was a natural embellisher, and he would never let something as mundane as facts get in the way of a story.

Her eyes drifted again to the island up ahead. What exactly was Mike going to make of things there? Anna had only a garbled account of the island, and she couldn't be sure if even half of it was actually true. It had taken her weeks of research and questioning just to find out that the island really did exist, and then weeks more to gain permission to visit. The letters her father had sent had all been written in a strangely stiff, cautious style that had at first confused and then worried Anna. She was certain that the letters had been concealing something... or had been *forced* to conceal something.

She had brought the last of the letters with her, carefully folded up and kept in the top pocket of her jacket. She'd read it so many times in the last few weeks that she could pretty much have recited it from memory, but it still didn't make any more sense now than it had the first time.

As she watched the dark outline of the island draw slowly closer, Anna's mind went back to the words her father had used in that last letter to her; the letter that had finally convinced her to make this journey:

'The monsters everywhere... we study them and they study us... the living and the dead... and the undead too...'

Chapter 4

Mike was still talking, as if anybody apart from him actually cared what he was saying.

'Maybe I wouldn't be so mad about the whole thing if she hadn't started slagging me off behind my back over this all. She just turned into a total bitch, and I couldn't understand it. Anyway, the short version of the story is that I got pissed off, and then I got really drunk, and then I had the stellar idea of teaching her a lesson. So I called Crimestoppers on her.'

The younger man let out a snort of laughter, and Anna rolled her eyes. Almost every story she had ever heard Mike tell somehow involved him getting himself into trouble. And over the course of the past few weeks, she had heard a *lot* of his stories.

'Yeah, I thought it was pretty funny at the time,' Mike said with a smile. 'Of course, when I woke up in the morning with the world's biggest hangover and this huge feeling of impending doom, it didn't seem so great. That was about the time I figured a holiday wouldn't do me much harm.'

'What happened to the girl?' the teenager asked. Anna was surprised by the fact that he spoke with a barely perceptible accent. She hadn't heard him say two words during the trip and had assumed that he didn't speak English.

Mike waved a hand vaguely. 'Oh, the police found three hundred pills in her flat. That's more than enough to do her for intent to supply, so I kinda suspect she's in a whole lot of trouble. And if she ever finds out that it was me who called the cops, then I'm going to be in approximately five million times more trouble. Rather than learning to live without my kneecaps, I accepted Anna's kind and timely offer of a few weeks vacation.' Grinning, he settled back in his seat, the smoke from his cigarette being dragged away by the breeze. He caught Anna's eye and winked.

Anna rolled her eyes a second time and turned away.

The island on the horizon was closer now, and she could make out the first details of it. The most noticeable thing was the absence of human habitation.

A cluster of white buildings stood on the shore directly in front of them, standing out like a patch of pale fungus on a dead tree, but apart from that Anna couldn't see any other buildings or signs of life. She'd already guessed that the small town they were heading for was the encampment that her father had mentioned in his letters. The term "encampment" had always implied to her something less permanent in appearance though. From what she could see, there seemed to be several dozen white-painted buildings spread out over an area maybe half a mile across. All around the buildings dark forest stretched out on both sides, covering most of the rest of the island.

As they drew closer, Anna examined the makeshift town. She saw that the forest had been cleared all around the buildings, with many stumps and broken trunks still littering the ground. The clear ground extended for quite a distance away from the town, and it took Anna some moments before to work out why this was. Completely surrounding the buildings and reaching all the way down to the sea was a large perimeter fence, with an area of clear, empty ground on either side of it.

'This is it?'

Mike's voice made her jump, because she hadn't heard him approach. He leaned on the rail next to her, flicking the stub of his cigarette into the grey water. 'I'm assuming it'll look more interesting when we get ashore, right?'

Anna shrugged. 'I've no idea. I assume so.'

Mike grunted noncommittally, then went back to take his seat. The teenager had by now found something more important to do, so Mike put his feet back up and lit himself another cigarette. Privately, he wondered how exactly he'd come to find himself on this floating heap in the middle of the ocean, nearly a hundred miles off the coast of Norway.

In half an hour or so, the boat chugged its way in towards the harbour. Anna realised that the fence surrounding the town not only reached down to the shore, it had also been built out into the sea on small breakwaters made of concrete blocks. Each arm of the fence reached out a couple of hundred feet, curving in protectively around the bay.

The *Narrenshiff* steered between the two breakwaters and drew up alongside the small dock. Anna had already observed a jeep driving up close to the shore and two men getting out. Her heart had jumped, but then settled in disappointment as she realised her father was not one of them.

'Welcome ashore.' The first man who stepped up to meet them was in his fifties and smartly dressed in a grey suit with a heavy padded overcoat on top. His greying hair had been combed flat with obvious care but was now being ruffled up by the stiff breeze off the sea. 'You must be Anna Martin. I'm Doctor Ehren.'

Anna smiled automatically and let him take her hand as she stepped off the boat. Behind her, Mike and the teenage boy were complaining loudly about the weight of her bags. She ignored them. 'Good to meet you,' she said to Ehren. 'I remember my father talking about you.'

Ehren returned her smile brightly, and a small amount of the tension inside her eased. 'He spoke of you a great deal as well. Can I take your bags?'

Mike had just passed her the heaviest of her luggage, a large sports bag that contained enough clothing for several weeks. At least half of them were dirty by now. 'Sure. Thank you.' Anna passed the awkward bag over to the man. 'Is my father here?'

Ehren tested the weight of the bag, then shook his head. 'Not at the present moment, no. He went out of the encampment a couple of days ago, but he's not returned yet.'

'Oh.' Anna frowned, partly from disappointment and partly from surprise. She was sure that her father would have known she'd be arriving that day. 'Do you know when he'll be back?'

'I'm afraid not, although we wouldn't expect him to be too much longer.'

Mike was struggling to get onto the dock with his three bags. The one containing his camera and recording equipment was slung around his neck, and he was making sure to keep a tight hold of it. It didn't matter if his clothes got dropped in the sea, but it would've cost him several thousand pounds to replace everything in the camera bag.

The second man, the one who had been driving the jeep, walked over. His hair and eyes were very dark, and the corners of his wide mouth turned upwards slightly as he watched Mike struggling. 'You want a hand there?' he asked.

'Um...' Mike had managed to get one foot onto the dock, but the boat had shifted under his weight and he was trying to decide whether it would be a better idea to jump back into the boat or make a dive for the safety of the dock. 'Yeah, a hand would be good.'

Grinning openly now, the man took the other bag off Mike. Without the added weight throwing him off balance, Mike was able to get onto dry land safely. 'Stupid goddamn boat,' Mike muttered. 'Next time you decide on one of these trips, Anna, buy me a plane ticket, okay?'

Anna wasn't listening to him, her mind preoccupied by what Ehren had said. They followed the men down to the jeep and Anna threw her other bags into the back, looking out over the island. The encampment was mostly hidden from this angle behind a slight rise in the ground, but she could see the dirt track winding up away from the docks, and in the distance the outline of two or three of the white-clad buildings.

The driver slung Mike's bag into the jeep as well, then held out his hand. 'I'm Ramone, I'll be your driver for today. And probably for several more days after this.'

Mike shook his hand and introduced himself, shifting the camera bag on his shoulder. 'Where the hell are we, anyway?' he asked, his eyes running over the landscape and not being greatly impressed with what he saw.

'About seventeen miles from the exact centre of goddamn nowhere,' Ramone told him, grinning. His teeth stood out whitely against his dark skin. 'The Island of Laranosk. Also known as the Island of Madness, if you're feeling particularly superstitious.'

'Is that so?' Mike suspected the guy was winding him up. He probably treated all new arrivals this way. 'Why's that then?'

'Oh, just to freak you out,' Ramone said cheerfully. 'If that's too melodramatic for you, you can just call it Terror Island like the rest of us. Throw your bags in the back there, then grab yourself a seat.' He vaulted over the driver's door and started the engine, drumming his fingers on the steering wheel while he waited for the others to get in.

Mike glanced over at Anna as she climbed into the back seat of the jeep. 'Are you alright there?' he asked her.

'I don't know.' Anna stared out at the island, chewing on her lower lip. 'I'll let you know once I've found out where my dad's got to.'

Chapter 5

'What's the fence for?' Anna asked.

The jeep was taking them the short distance over to where the white buildings clustered together. Anna was sat in the back with Mike, who had his camera bag open on his lap. He was carefully checking over the equipment he had brought and was not paying much apparent attention to the surroundings. Anna, on the other hand, was trying to take everything in at once and make it fit with what her father had told her. Her eyes kept being drawn back to the surrounding fence.

Ehren smiled at her question, the same way he'd smiled politely at everything she'd said so far. 'How much did your father tell you about our work out here, Miss Martin?'

'Not very much.' Anna didn't feel like mentioning at that point that her father's final letter had been pretty detailed, albeit barely comprehensible. 'He said you were running research on… some of the local wildlife.'

Another patronising smile. 'Wildlife. That's a good way of describing it. This is a very unique island we have here, and our wildlife isn't exactly the type you'll be used to. Did your father tell you what he was specifically working on?'

'Um. No. Not really.'

Ramone the driver bounced the jeep carelessly up the dirt track, taking a wide circling route that brought them round in between the white-clad buildings. He was obviously used to driving the uneven ground and was cheerfully oblivious to the discomfort of his passengers. Even Ehren winced a couple of times as the jeep struck a particularly deep pothole.

Ehren half-turned in his seat so he could look directly at Anna. 'Miss Martin, do you believe in the supernatural?'

Without meaning to, Mike let out a snort of laughter. 'Sorry,' he said, when both Anna and Ehren looked at him. 'I just thought for a moment that I'd slipped sideways into an old Hammer movie.'

Anna hid a smile, but Ehren didn't seem fazed. 'I apologise,' he said. 'I didn't mean to over-dramatise the issue. It was actually a genuine question – do either of you two have any belief in the supernatural world?'

Mike shrugged. 'I'm open-minded. I've done a few video projects on ghosts and stuff like that, and I'm prepared to believe in anything I can catch on camera.'

'That's a good answer,' Ehren smiled. 'Miss Martin?'

Anna hesitated, then shook her head. 'No. I don't think so.'

'Meaning that you personally have never seen anything that could make you believe in the supernatural, right?'

'Um.' Anna thought about it. 'Right.'

Ehren nodded, apparently satisfied. 'Since our group of people came to Laranosk seven months ago, I've had to change my opinion on a lot of things I'd believed to be solid, irrefutable facts. But no, I don't believe in the supernatural either. If anything, this island has reinforced my belief that everything in this world has some kind of rational explanation.'

Mike would have been happy to argue the point – he was always happy to argue, and this happened to be a subject he was particularly vocal on – but at that point Ramone swerved sharply to the right. The jeep lurched over the rough ground and skidded to a halt in front of one of the larger, two-storey buildings. Mike automatically clutched his camera bag protectively to his chest, which meant that he wasn't able to brace himself and ended up smacking his head hard on the seat-rest in front of him. 'Ow! Fuck!'

'Sorry.' Ramone pulled the handbrake on and shut off the engine, then turned to grin at him. 'Brakes are a little sharp on this thing.'

Muttering under his breath, Mike looked up at the building. The paint was already looking scrappy in places, probably due to the harsh wind and rain on the island, but there was still a sense of newness about it. At several of the large windows, faces had appeared, looking down at the people in the jeep. Mike wondered how often they got to see visitors, and he waved sourly up at them.

'This is our main accommodation block,' Ehren explained. 'We've set aside a pair of rooms for you – Ramone will show you where they are.'

Ramone climbed out of the jeep. 'Technically that's not in my job description.'

Ehren ignored the comment, turning to smile at Anna again. 'The rooms are unfortunately fairly basic, but hopefully you'll find them adequate. Take as much time as you need getting settled in. When you're ready, Ramone will bring you over to our main lab.' He indicated another large building a short distance away. 'That's where your father has been working, Miss Martin.'

Anna stared over at the building, as if she could somehow glean the details of her father's whereabouts from it. It was a single-storey building, square and featureless and giving off the definite impression of being solid and functional and not much else.

Mike climbed out of the jeep and slung his camera bag around his neck. He seemed to be showing little interest in the lab building, but his quick eyes missed nothing. He pulled his other bags out of the back of the jeep, eager to get into their rooms and find out where he'd be sleeping that night. After the amount of travelling they'd done recently, it was always a pretty important question.

Ramone helped Anna with her bags, then lead the way inside. Ehren waited until they had disappeared before making his way across to the lab building.

Inside the accommodation block, Anna and Mike were surprised to find it well furnished and comfortable-looking. The lobby looked like the entrance to any hotel in the world, with pastel shaded wallpaper and carpets, and framed prints decorating the walls. Two young women, both dressed in jeans and t-shirts, were standing at one side of the lobby talking, and they looked up with interest at the new arrivals. Ramone waved pleasantly to them but made no attempt at introductions, instead leading Anna and Mike up a flight of stairs on the left.

At the top a corridor stretched off in both directions, broken up by windowed fire doors. It looked even more like a hotel, with identical numbered doors set at regular intervals along each side.

'Not a bad set-up,' Mike noted as he followed Anna and Ramone along the left arm of the corridor. 'Has that lovely corporate feel to it. So, who funds this place?'

Ramone shrugged. 'Government.'

'Yeah? Which one? Who does this island actually belong to?'

The man shrugged again. 'Not the sort of thing I worry about. I just carry the bags and drive the cars.' Ramone flashed him a quick grin. 'Try asking Ehren – next time you feel like having him evade the question for twenty minutes.'

Halfway along the corridor he stopped and set down Anna's bags. 'These are your rooms, twenty-three and twenty-four. Not the best rooms, I'm afraid, but they've got a view of sorts and all the better ones are currently occupied.'

'How many people are living here?' Anna asked.

'Fifty or sixty. If you want exact numbers, again you'll have to ask Ehren. Most of them have been here pretty much since the place was set up. Ehren's very proud of the fact that he doesn't have much staff turnover – you're the first people to have come over on the boat for weeks.'

'What about you? How long have you been here?'

Ramone shrugged vaguely. 'I'm not counting. A few months, I guess. If you start counting days it starts feeling like a prison sentence. Here you go, one key each.' He passed them over.

'Please tell me we have showers,' Mike grinned, pushing past the others to unlock his door.

As promised, the room was fairly basic, with a bed, a flatpack wardrobe and a sink unit with a square mirror positioned above it. To Mike's annoyance, there was no shower. Opposite the entrance, a screen door opened out onto a small balcony, just big enough for two or three people to stand on if they didn't mind being fairly friendly. Mike wandered out there and leaned on the railing, looking out at the view Ramone had mentioned. It didn't seem that remarkable. Directly in front of him, about two hundred yards away, was the perimeter fence, looking much larger and more solid than it had from a distance. Behind it the forest spread out as far as he could see.

There was a noise to his left and Mike looked up to see Anna coming out onto her own balcony. He waved to her and she gave him a wan smile.

'How's your room?' he asked.

'Alright, I guess.' Anna folded her arms across her chest, staring out at the forest.

'Some view, isn't it?' Mike searched in his pockets and found his cigarettes, wondering if he had time for a smoke before they went back to find Ehren. 'Hey, Anna?'

'Yeah?'

'How much did you know about this island before we came here?'

Anna shrugged. She seemed very distracted at that moment. 'Very little. I told you what I knew.'

'Yeah, I just wondered… do you know what exactly they're researching here? What these labs are for? Didn't your dad say anything about this?'

The girl shook her head, still staring out at the forest.

'Did you know anything about this Ehren guy?' Mike asked, not really expecting any answer. 'Or any of the other people here?' He took out a cigarette, then changed his mind and stuck it back in the packet. 'Hey, Anna? Why do you suppose Ramone had a rifle stashed on the floor of the jeep?'

She looked sharply at him then. 'What?'

Mike shrugged, smiling at her. 'He had a rifle by his feet. And most of that fence out there – apart from the bits over the sea – is electrified. Just an F-Y-I there.' He pushed away from the railing, heading back into his room. 'Anyway, I'd better put the spare camera batteries on to charge, now that I've finally found a plug point. Then do you feel like going and asking Doctor Ehren a few of these questions instead?'

'Sure.' Distracted, Anna's eyes roamed over the forest and the nearby fence. 'Give me a minute to get ready.'

Chapter 6

Brac looked up from his book as there was a polite knock at the door of his office. 'What?' he asked irritably.

The door opened a few inches and Ehren's head appeared. 'Have you got time for a quick word?'

'Sure.' Brac sighed to himself and slid a scrap of paper between the pages of his book to mark his place. 'Come in, take a seat. What's the problem now?'

There was nowhere to sit in the crowded and untidy office apart from the one chair that Brac currently occupied. Ehren remained standing. 'Have we made any progress on what happened the other night?' he asked, getting straight to the point. Ehren wasn't big on wasting time or words when he wanted something, although at other times he could be the most long-winded person in the world. The habit always annoyed Brac for some reason.

'Not particularly, no,' Brac told him. 'As far as I can see, no-one was out in woods that night that shouldn't have been. No-one left the village or the encampment apart from your own search party.'

'You've spoken to everyone?'

'Yes, Ehren, I've spoken to everyone.' Brac looked up at the man with thinly veiled exasperation. 'Maybe you should take your questions to Luca. It wasn't any of us, so he'd be the next best person to ask.' He picked up his book again.

'I've already talked to Luca,' Ehren said. 'He knows nothing.'

Brac snorted derisively. 'So he says.'

'Brac, think about it logically. It wasn't one of Luca's people that did this.'

For a long moment, Brac just stared at him. Then his eyes flicked back down to his book. 'Doctor Ehren, do you really think it was a good idea to invite visitors to the island at this time?'

Ehren answered smoothly. 'They were invited by Doctor Martin, not by me. And besides, that was before this whole problem arose.'

'That's a convenient answer… although I'm sure that someone in your position would've been able to stop them from coming here. I'm just not convinced that it's such a great plan to have Allister's daughter come here while he's missing presumed dead.'

'We're not presuming him dead, Brac…'

'If you say so. But tomorrow night is the full moon, and you know as well as I do that if you don't find him by then, you're not going to find him at all.'

Ehren kept his expression pleasant and calm, but his eyes hardened. 'Brac, Doctor Martin's daughter is going to be coming over to talk to Seth and myself in a moment. I'd appreciate it if you would keep those sort of opinions to yourself. Understood?'

'Sure.' Brac turned his attention back to his book, hiding a smile. 'I won't say a word out of place.'

'Thank you.' Ehren smiled again and backed out of the room, closing the door behind him.

The doctor's smile faded as soon as the door was shut. Brac's moods had been becoming more and more unpredictable recently, and the disappearance of two of his work colleagues hadn't exactly helped. Right now Ehren could really have done without the added problem of the visitors.

Ehren walked down the corridor and turned right into one of the labs. Usually there were three people working in there; at present there was only one. At least one of the absentees was not going to be coming back to his workstation.

Seth looked up from his work with a slightly guilty expression as the door opened. Ehren paid it no attention. The young doctor constantly looked guilty for no reason that Ehren had ever been able to discern. He put it down to Seth's innate nervousness and shy nature. Even now, as Seth looked up and saw who was coming in, he was automatically tugging down the sleeves of his shirt and bracing himself to have to speak to another human being.

'Morning, Seth.' Ehren took a seat next to the man. 'How's things in here?'

'Fine, going fine.' Seth nudged the mouse of his computer, another nervous habit caused by his dislike of the overzealous log-out system. 'Is the boat in? I thought I heard it earlier.'

'Yes, it's in. I've sent a crew down to the dock to unload the supplies and everything, so no worries there. Oh, and our guests have arrived.'

Seth nodded, having been expecting this piece of news. 'Okay. Where are they?'

'At the moment? Ramone's showing them to their rooms. Then they're going to be coming over here. I'd like you to talk to them.'

'Me?' Seth looked up, making rare eye-contact. His blue eyes always seemed weak and watery, as if he needed glasses but didn't wear them. 'Why me? And about what?'

'Don't worry, Seth.' Ehren smiled reassuringly. 'Normally I'd get Brac to do it, but his temperament isn't very reliable right now. So I'd like you to do it instead. Doctor Martin's daughter will want to speak to you anyway, since you've been working directly with her father.'

'Do you think…?'

'Yes, I really do think it's a good idea, Seth. Just tell Miss Martin about the research you've been doing.' Ehren raised his hand to silence another objection. 'All of it, yes. It's not going to be the easiest thing in the world to explain everything that happens on this island, so we'll just tell her and her friend the bits that we want them to know. Anyway, with any luck they'll only be here for three days until the next boat comes. So you tell them the basics of what we're doing and then I'll take them down to the southern enclosure. Maybe if Brac's feeling more co-operative tomorrow then we can take them up to the village as well.'

Seth's face had been getting gradually paler as Ehren talked, but he swallowed hard and nodded. 'Okay. If you think it's the best idea. So, what do you want me to say?'

'Well, first things last – don't mention anything about her father's disappearance, or what happened to Sykes either. Oh, and you'd better know that Miss Martin's friend has brought a video camera with him, so I'm assuming they might want to video in here.'

Seth's watery eyes bulged. 'You… you're going to let them *film*… in *here*? And at the enclosure? And…?'

'Seth… don't concern yourself with that. I know what I'm doing. They won't get anything on tape that we don't want them to see, so don't worry about it. Just let them come in here and sit down and set up their little camera, and you'll answer their questions in a friendly, polite way. As far as you know, Doctor Martin has gone out of the encampment for the time being, but should be back any time soon.'

The young doctor nervously shifted his mouse across the desk again, frowning as he saw that his computer had logged out regardless. 'So… you want me to tell them what me and… and the others were working on?'

Ehren nodded, smiling again.

Seth stared down at his hands, tugging at his cuffs. 'And you want me to tell them about the wolves.'

Ehren's smile widened. 'Yes. That's it exactly.'

Chapter 7

Ramone was waiting for them just outside the accommodation block. His hands were clasped in front of him as if he was unsure what to do with them. The gesture reminded Anna of the way she had used to keep her hands still when she'd quit smoking.

The man looked up as they came out, his wide mouth turning up at the corners. 'All sorted?'

'Pretty much.' Anna had changed out of her travelling clothes and was feeling a lot better for it, although her eyes still felt sandy from the brief sleep she'd had earlier. 'The rooms aren't as bad as you guys were making out.'

Mike wasn't quite so cheerful. 'Does this place actually have hot water, or is that just a myth?'

'It does,' Ramone told him, 'but you have to be a little patient with it. Most of the camp is powered by solar energy – the panels are up on the roof there – so it's occasionally a little temperamental.'

'I imagine it would be,' Anna noted, glancing up at the overcast sky.

'We also have a wave generator out by the breakwater for the times the sun doesn't shine. Which is about ten months of the year. Plus they've got a petrol generator that's used as backup.'

'Ah.' Mike carefully adjusted the lens of his camera, which was hanging on a strap around his neck. 'So, what do they use to power the fence?'

Ramone laughed. 'That runs off the backup generator, but only during the night. You'll hear it kick up this evening. But you should ask Ehren that same question – it'll piss him off that you noticed so quickly that it's electrified.'

'Really?' Mike looked sceptical.

'That fence isn't really so subtle.'

'No,' Ramone admitted, 'but Ehren is the sort of guy that would try and keep secrets from himself if he could. The more stuff you notice about this place, the more annoyed he'll get.'

For the second time, Anna wondered at the man's tone. There was a definite note of resentment present in his voice whenever he spoke of Ehren. For the time being she shrugged it off and followed him across towards the lab building. Mike hung back for a few moments, lifting his video camera to get a bit of footage of the outside area.

In general, Mike's attitude to filming on private property was that he would get as much done as possible before anybody came along and told him to stop. He usually worked by the assumption that everything was open to capture on tape unless he was specifically told otherwise. And even then the rules could usually be bent a little.

At that moment, he just wanted to get a few background shots of the area, with the lab buildings and especially the perimeter fence. Establishing shots. He had a pretty good lens fixed to his Canon XM2, and his hands were steady enough that he could get away with filming at full zoom. He liked to do it that way in certain situations, because most people didn't realise exactly how close he could zoom in. For example, right at that moment he was panning his camera over a short stretch of the fence, which was a couple of hundred yards away, but anyone who happened to be watching him would mistakenly assume that he was just scanning the closest buildings.

Through his zoom, it was easy to make out what Ramone had already told them – the fence was not electrified at that moment. But Mike could clearly see the plastic connectors that held the wires in place, and the currently unlit orange warning lights. His mind was already running over theories as to why the fence should only be used at night, which was another question he hoped to put to Doctor Ehren.

A short distance ahead, Anna was questioning Ramone. 'So, do you actually know my father?' she asked.

Ramone shrugged vaguely – a gesture that was already becoming familiar to her. 'Not really to talk to, no. You'd think that since this is such a small place with such a isolated population, everyone would know everyone, but it don't seem to work out like that. Scientists are very… elitist. They don't really like talking to anyone outside their own departments, let alone hired help like myself. So no – I know your father by sight and to say hi to, but not really much more than that. This lab is where he was working though, so you'll be able to speak to the people who *do* know him. A guy in there called Seth is probably your best bet.' The man stopped at the entrance to the building.

'Aren't you coming in with us?' Anna asked him.

'Nope.' Ramone's mouth turned up at the corners. 'Hired help, remember. Technically I do have lab clearance, but I don't take much advantage of it.'

'Oh.' Anna glanced round and found that Mike had caught up with them. His camera was resting on his shoulder and his eyes had taken on that slightly shiny look they always got when he'd found something interesting to film. Together, they pushed open the white door to the lab building and went inside, leaving Ramone behind.

Inside, the building looked very much like a hospital, its walls, floors and ceilings painted functional white. There was the faint hum of electrical equipment and the distant sound of muted conversation, but the corridor that Anna and Mike found themselves in was deserted. Unlike most public buildings, there did not seem to be any convenient signs to point out directions. There were two large windowed doors, one to their left and one to their right, through which they could see virtually identical lab rooms, but both seemed to be empty, and neither door was labelled.

'Did we catch everyone on lunch or something?' Mike asked.

The corridor turned to the right up ahead, and directly in front of them was a door marked 'Brac Schow'. Anna walked up to it, hesitated, then knocked.

A man's voice answered irritably. 'What is it?'

Anna glanced at Mike, who shrugged. Cautiously, she pushed the door open, putting on a smile that she hoped would mark her as "harmless-girl-who's-managed-to-get-herself-lost".

The office inside was small. Stacks of books and piles of paper took up all of the available desk and shelving space, making the cramped space appear even smaller. It also didn't help that the man who was sat in front of the cluttered desk was quite large. It was obvious that he was bulky rather than fat, as if he'd done a lot of weight-training earlier in life and age was now eroding his muscle tone. He was leaning back in a scuffed reclining chair with a paperback book in his large hands.

He looked up at Anna without raising his head, so that he ended up looking through his thick eyebrows. His hair was very dark and flecked with grey; his eyes piercingly blue in colour. He didn't speak, and there was a hardness to his face that made Anna immediately nervous.

'Um.' Anna cleared her throat. 'I'm looking for Doctor Ehren... or someone called Seth. Are they here?'

The man closed his book, keeping his thumb between the pages to mark his place. 'Seth,' he repeated slowly. His voice was as hard as his face, and there was a definite edge of distaste to his tone. 'Egyptian god of chaos and destruction, disrupter of my office and stealer of all my pens.' He opened his book again, his gaze dropping back to the pages. 'He's that way,' he said, pointing off down the corridor. 'Second lab on the right. I believe Ehren is in there as well.'

'Thank you,' Anna said politely.

'My pleasure.' The man didn't look back up as she shut the office door.

'Friendly,' Mike noted quietly as they made their way along the corridor. 'No wonder they get so many visitors here.'

Before Anna could answer, Ehren appeared in the doorway of one of the labs up ahead. He frowned in annoyance at finding them there, but his face quickly smoothed itself back out into a pleasant smile. 'I didn't expect you here so soon,' he said. 'I was just coming to find you. Come on in.'

He led them into the lab room, which was slightly larger than the other two they'd seen. The three windows looked out on a view down to the bay, which would have looked a lot prettier if the weather had been more inviting. The room was filled with workbenches holding an array of computer equipment, and here again there was the faint but distinct hum of machines at work. As well as the computers, there was a variety of scientific equipment, most of which Anna and Mike were at a loss to name. It all looked very impressive though.

Anna's attention went straight to the thin, nervous-looking man seated at one of the benches, while Mike's eyes roamed all around the room. He paid particular attention to a group of pictures that were stuck to the wall above one of the unoccupied desks, although he wasn't close enough to make out exactly what they showed.

'Miss Martin, this is Seth,' Ehren said, introducing the man at the bench, who stood up and offered his hand self-consciously.

'Good to meet you,' Anna said. 'Doctor Ehren said you'd be able to fill us in on the research you and my father were doing.'

'Uh-huh.' Seth sat back down, smiling weakly as if he wasn't entirely happy about this task. 'Well, mainly we… um… that's me and your father and Doctor Sykes…' He cast a nervous glance at Ehren, who smiled encouragingly. 'We've been researching one of the, uh, indigenous species of this island…'

Mike had moved away slightly, wanting a better look at the photos on the other wall. He shifted his video camera, thumbing the switch to standby, ready. There was an assortment of maybe a dozen photos on the wall, one of them a slightly degraded Polaroid of a group of middle-aged men in lab coats. He recognised Ehren in the centre and Seth off to his side, but before he could look closer his attention was drawn down to the other pictures.

Two at the bottom especially caught his eye – photos obviously taken in very low light conditions with a less than perfect flash. Some wild animal, larger than any dog he'd ever seen, but with the same elongated muzzle and deep lucid eyes.

'Wolves,' he said aloud.

Seth heard him and gave another weak smile. 'Not exactly,' he said. 'What we have on this island and in those pictures is *homo lupus*. Werewolves.'

Chapter 8

'I know this probably sounds a little strange to you...' Seth was saying.

Neither Anna nor Mike answered him. Anna was biting her lip, remembering the strange words that her father had written in his last letter. Mike was wishing that he'd thought to turn on his video camera sooner so that he could have recorded what the young doctor had just said.

'It's obviously a difficult thing to understand,' Seth went on, staring down again at his hands. 'But this is definitely a unique island, and there're things here that you'd never find in other places... certainly not in the numbers we have here. Some of the other people have theories as to why there's such a proliferation of... um... these creatures on this island. In this lab though, we've been mainly concentrating on, uh, the physiological side of... um...'

His voice faded out as he noticed the way that Anna was looking at him. Seth coughed uncomfortably, his face reddening. He glanced over at Ehren as if for support.

'What Seth is saying,' Ehren put in smoothly, 'is that we've long ago accepted that werewolves are fact, not fiction; they are natural rather than supernatural. Though we're no closer to understanding why they exist – any more than to knowing why we ourselves exist – we've made great advances into understanding how a human body can change and become something more than human. This is mainly because we have live test subjects, right here on this island.'

Anna answered slowly. 'And that's what the electrified fence is for, right?'

Seth looked up quickly at Ehren, but the older man just smiled and nodded. 'Pretty much, yes. We have a very different breed of wildlife around here, Miss Martin.'

Mike had unobtrusively switched the camera to ON, and was currently filming Ehren and Seth in close-up. Since he was all the way across the other side of the room, they weren't paying him nearly as much attention as they would if he were standing closer. He indicated the photos on the wall with his spare hand. 'That's what this is then? A werewolf?'

Ehren nodded, but Seth made a move like he was going to get out of his seat. 'Please don't touch those pictures,' the young doctor said. 'They belong to Doctor Martin.'

Mike moved his hand away from them and returned his attention to the camera.

'That is one of our regular test subjects,' Ehren told him. 'There are twenty-seven wolves living on the island at the present moment, although the population is a little transient. Many of them were born here, but a fair proportion come from other countries. They hear about this island – rumours that it's the place their entire species came from or something like that – and they come here. The most wolves that were ever on this island at any one time was seventy-nine, but that was about fifteen years ago, a long time before we got here.'

'And…' It was difficult for Anna to think, to take in the fact that this was what her father had been doing all this time while he'd been away. These were the things that he had hinted at in his letters. The first time she'd read those letters she'd worried that his mind had been going, but the truth was even harder to believe. 'And they live out there, in the forest?'

'Not exactly. There's a village up in the north of the island. We have a pretty good arrangement with them – they let us study them, and we provide them with food and supplies.'

'Food?'

Ehren laughed. 'I mean for the times when they're in human form. There's plenty of food out in the forest for them at the other time.'

'Right.' Anna felt a wave of unreality, as if she couldn't quite believe that this was happening to her. It all sounded so improbable. 'You'll obviously forgive me for being just the teeniest bit sceptical here…'

'Quite understandable,' Ehren smiled. 'Like Seth said, it's a difficult thing to understand, which is why we've always been very select about the people we've allowed to come to the island. Most simply wouldn't accept what they were being told. I assume it would be a little easier for you if you had some kind of proof…?'

Anna and Mike both looked at him. 'What sort of proof?' Anna asked.

'Well, if you were to actually meet one of the wolves and see the change manifest for yourself, then that would put most of your doubts to rest, correct?'

The two of them exchanged glances. 'Um,' Anna said. 'I don't know. Maybe?'

Seth was looking increasingly nervous. 'Doctor Ehren – '

Ehren waved him into silence. 'If it'll clear up any doubts, then it's a good thing to do right now, at the very start of things. Otherwise you'll be less than receptive to anything else we have here to show you.'

Anna wanted to ask what other things there were, but she didn't. The confident tone of Ehren's voice confused her, because he was saying these incredible, unbelievable things in such a matter-of-fact way. So she just nodded.

The smile on the older man's face broadened. 'Well, in that case you'll be happy to know that you've already been introduced to one of our wolves.'

Anna stared up into his benign face, her mind working fast. Before she could open her mouth, Seth started to speak.

'Doctor Ehren, I –'

Ehren waved him into silence a second time, but all eyes had already turned to the young doctor. Seth reddened further and mumbled something else that no-one else was able to hear.

'Miss Martin,' Ehren said, 'I'd like you to meet Seth MacColl, a member of the werewolf pack of Laranosk.'

The way he was smiling made Anna think for one wonderful moment that this was all a joke. But Seth's eyes seemed haunted, and he quickly dropped his gaze back to his hands.

At the back of the room, Mike grinned to himself. He'd had Seth's face framed perfectly at that exact moment, capturing the reaction for posterity. That gave him a much warmer feeling inside than anything Ehren had just said.

Ehren let the moment hang briefly, then pointed towards the photos on the wall. 'Those two at the bottom – those are you, aren't they, Seth?'

Mutely, the young doctor nodded.

'In his fully changed form,' Ehren explained. 'But maybe something less than that will be enough to convince you. Seth, perhaps you should give our guests a demonstration?'

Seth looked up at him, his watery eyes startled and almost scared. 'Uh... I don't know...'

'Come on. Just something small.'

Nervously, Seth tried to hold Ehren's gaze, but had to look away. He nodded slowly, then started to undo the buttons of the cuff of his shirt.

Ehren spoke to Mike. 'You might want to bring that camera a little closer for this.'

Mike did so, although he could have got a perfectly good shot from where he was standing. He carefully re-framed so that Seth took up the entirety of the picture.

The young doctor bit his lip as he loosened the cuff from his wrist. Both Anna and Mike caught a brief glimpse of several thin, silvery scars that snaked over the back of his wrist. He held up the hand towards them, palm outwards. Mike quickly changed the focus of his camera.

27

Seth looked up one more time towards Ehren as if silently imploring the man to change his mind, but Ehren only smiled and told him to go ahead.

The young doctor inhaled a deep breath and let it out very slowly. Then he held it there and concentrated on his hand.

It happened a lot faster than Anna would have expected. One moment it was just a hand, and the next the fingers seemed to flex inwards. Instead of curling in on themselves they stretched out, elongating as if the bones inside were growing at a startling rate. The skin moved and flowed instead of stretching, drawing back over the fingernails as they too lengthened and grew to points. The palm bulged outwards and the thumb twisted upwards and to the side, becoming more like an accessory digit than anything useful. The fingers bent over at the very tips, the nails like claws protruding from each one. The muscular change was so total that Anna barely noticed the fact that the hand had simultaneously sprouted a thick covering of coarse hair.

Her first coherent thought was that maybe she shouldn't be sitting so close while this happened. She backed away fast, almost knocking over a chair in her haste.

'It's alright,' Ehren told her. 'Stay calm.'

Seth flexed his hand, moving the wrist carefully as if trying it out for the first time. There was a sheen of sweat on his forehead, but his face appeared unchanged. No, not completely unchanged. The eyes were now sharper, no longer weak and watery but dark green like the forest outside. It made him look more sure of himself. And maybe something had happened to the bones of his face as well, or to the shape of his eyebrows, but Anna couldn't be sure… it was very difficult to focus on anything except the fact that man in front of her now had the paw of an animal where his hand should have been.

He met her eyes with surety for the first time. 'Is that proof enough for you, Miss Martin?' he asked, his voice a shade deeper than it had been before.

Anna nodded, unable to speak.

Chapter 9

For the third time that afternoon, Brac's concentration was broken by a knock at the door.

'Is a bit of peace and quiet too much to ask for?' he demanded. 'What is it now?'

The door opened and Ehren appeared. 'Brac, we need your help with something.' His tone was serious enough for Brac to immediately take notice. He quickly got to his feet.

Ehren didn't bother to explain, but led the way back to Seth's lab. Brac followed close behind him, his mind already going over the various possible ways that Seth could have got himself into trouble this early in the day.

The answer was waiting for him inside the lab. Seth was sat at his desk with the usual look of nervousness and mild panic on his face. The young doctor was partway through a change, although that in itself shouldn't have been too much of a problem. Neither was the reaction of the girl sat next to him, who didn't appear to be that shocked by what was happening. In fact, at the moment that Brac walked in, she was rather timidly stroking the hairs on the back of Seth's altered hand.

'You have to be a little careful of the claws,' Seth was saying. 'The virus is only really transmitted through saliva, but sometimes...' He trailed off, looking up sheepishly at Brac.

The older man let out an exasperated breath. 'Seriously, do I have to keep an eye on you every minute of every day, Seth? What have you done now?'

'I... uh...' Seth took his hand away from Anna's, attempting without success to hide it in his lap. 'I'm stuck.'

'Stuck?'

'I... I can't change back.'

Brac muttered something that sounded like "idiot", then crossed the room to where Seth was sat.

Anna watched the man as he crouched to examine Seth's hand and eyes.

He moved quickly now that he had a purpose, but there was still that blunt irritability that she had noticed in him during their brief meeting earlier. His dark blue shirt was creased at the back where he'd been sat down for too long, and his greying hair curled very slightly at the ends.

Brac took hold of Seth unchanged left wrist and held it between his fingers as if he were checking the younger man's pulse. 'So what happened?' he asked.

'I tried for a part change... y'know, just as a demonstration...' Seth's eyes glanced almost guiltily up at Anna. 'And now I can't change back. It's...' He closed his eyes momentarily and drew a deep breath, as if calming himself down.

Anna was still watching with an air of awed fascination. 'Does... does that often happen?' she asked.

Ehren answered her, his voice just as calm as usual. 'Not often, no. But then, not all of our wolves can do partial changes the way that Seth can. In fact, for many them, change is impossible at any time except for the night of the full moon, and then it's a purely involuntary change. It takes a lot of time and practice to be able to control it to the degree that Seth can...'

Brac interrupted, his voice conveying obvious annoyance. 'And even then it's not a very smart idea to attempt a partial change this close to the full moon. Because things like this can happen.' He sighed and sat back on his heels. 'Yup, you're stuck,' he agreed.

'I'm sorry.' Seth avoided meeting the older man's eyes. 'I guess I wasn't thinking.'

'No, I guess you weren't. Okay, you'll have to do a full change before you can come back out of it.' Brac got to his feet, smoothing down the front of his shirt. 'Come on, I'll drive you out to the village.'

Anna was standing as well. 'What's wrong?' she asked. 'Is he going to be okay?'

'He'll be fine in a couple of hours, don't worry. But lessons learnt for today – no matter how experienced or confident a wolf gets in their own abilities, it's always more difficult to control things as you get closer to the full moon.' His gaze flicked across towards Ehren as he spoke. 'Even the best of people forget that at times.'

Seth stood up, clutching his changed hand to his chest. He seemed a little unsteady on his feet, but Brac knew better than to offer him support. He motioned Anna out of the way, then manoeuvred rather than helped Seth out of the room. He was very careful not to make eye-contact with anyone else as they left, especially the young man holding the video camera. His priority right at that moment was to get Seth out of there and to a safe place.

At another time Ehren would probably have tried to follow them, but he obviously wanted to stay where he could keep an eye on his visitors. Good luck to him, Brac thought sourly. And good luck to his visitors as well, especially that poor girl.

* * *

Outside the lab building, Ramone was leaning against his jeep, talking quietly to a brunette girl who worked in the adjacent lab. Brac waved perfunctorily to him, leading Seth round the side of the building towards where his own jeep was parked. Seth kept his head down, his altered hand clenched into a fist and held tightly against his chest.

A few minutes later, the two of them were headed out along the dirt track that led to the main gate of the encampment. Brac's jeep was one of the noisiest in camp, due to the fact that he'd lost the muffler during an impromptu bit of off-roading a few weeks ago and was still waiting on a replacement to arrive from one of the neighbouring islands. Not for the first time, Brac cursed Ehren for lumbering them all with these army-surplus rejects for transport, and wished for something a little more reliable.

His temper was also not improved by the fact that when they got there, the main gate was unmanned again. He sounded his horn several times but no-one appeared, and he was forced to stop the jeep in front of the gates. There were supposed to be at least two people manning the gate at all times, and others at regular points along the fence, but recently Ehren had been letting these security measures slide during the day. Brac had tried to point out that on the island, being complacent was only one small step away from being dead, but the man had complete confidence in his security systems and wasn't to be convinced.

Swearing openly now, Brac got out of the jeep and hit the manual release button, then stood impatiently as the two reinforced gates swung awkwardly open. Then he got back in and drove through, automatically checking his rearview mirror to be sure that the gate was closing again, since sometimes it got stuck. This time, however, it swung shut relatively smoothly.

The journey to the village would have taken about ten minutes if the road had been any good. Unfortunately, the road was a long way from being good, and the journey usually took closer to half an hour. After the recent rains, every dent and pothole in the dirt road was filled with muddy water, forcing Brac to drive even slower than normal. His jeep was extremely temperamental when it came to water, and had an unfortunate habit of seizing up at the first hint of moisture.

After about ten minutes of bumpy riding, Seth began shuddering violently.

'You alright?' Brac asked him, cutting the speed immediately.

Seth licked his lips, a careful gesture. 'Yes,' he said after a moment. 'I'm fine.

I just… I'm gonna have to change very soon.'

'Just hold tight, we're nearly there.'

Seth nodded, leaning his head back against the seat and closing his eyes. 'This hasn't happened to me in so long,' he murmured.

'Try not to think about it.'

'I must just have got nervous.' Seth opened his eyes and stared up at the sky. If Brac had been watching his face instead of the road, he would have observed that the man's features had definitely altered since they'd left the encampment. 'Probably… probably because of…'

Brac laughed suddenly. 'Because of that girl, you mean? Seth, how old are you?'

Seth gave him a weak grin. 'Not old enough, apparently.'

'Well, you're going to be fine. We'll get to the village and – '

Seth shuddered again, leaning right forward in his seat as the spasm ran its course. Brac glanced at him, trying to decide whether it would be a better idea to stop the vehicle or to speed up as much as possible. Seth was shaking badly, the fingers of his left hand clutching the dashboard in front of him. Even as he watched, Brac saw the fingers elongate, fingernails growing and gouging deeply into the plastic surface.

He hit the brakes. The jeep swerved to a stop in the middle of the muddy track, and promptly stalled.

'Seth?' Brac took hold of the man's shoulder, hard enough to make him aware of his presence. 'Hold it together, alright? Take a deep breath and hold it in. Okay? Okay?'

Seth took a deep breath, let it out, then shook his head. 'I can't hold it.' His voice had changed as well, dropping a full octave and descending into something animalistic and barely comprehensible. 'I've got to go. Do you smell that?'

Brac didn't bother lifting his head to smell the air.

'What?'

'Deer.' Seth lifted an unsteady, hair-covered hand and pointed off into the woods. 'Went that way. Just a few minutes ago.' Another spasm shook his body and he moaned deeply. 'Let me go… I've gotta go…'

Brac hesitated for just a moment, then took his hand away from the man's shoulder. 'Go,' he said.

Seth looked up with eyes that were barely human. Then he was out of the jeep, awkwardly tearing at the buttons of his shirt.

'Hey!' Brac yelled after him. 'Throw your clothes back here at least! I'm not collecting them for you!'

Seth turned and grinned at him. His face had already stretched out into a muzzle, his eyes now deep-set and perfectly green like forest leaves after a heavy rain. Hair was sprouting all over his body, and his hands were more like claws than anything human. The grin revealed two perfect rows of sharp, pointed teeth, and it would have raised the hairs on any normal person's neck.

Brac wasn't a normal person, but even so he prudently restarted the engine at that point.

Ignoring the last command, Seth gave up on removing his clothes and simply let the change tear them from his body. His legs lengthened and the muscles swelled along the front and back. Bones stretched, hardened and reformed, pulling the skin with them. It took only a few seconds for the change to run its course once he let it have full control of his body, and by the way he struggled with it, it looked like it hurt.

When it was done, the creature that had previously been a man stretched, feeling the coolness of the air on his new body. He was no longer human, but not entirely animal either – something in-between, a state as familiar to him now as changing into a different set of clothes. His clawed hands and feet dug into the soft ground and he could almost feel the pulse of life flowing through it. The life of the forest. It was his to feel, to run with, to take. He raised his head and shouted, and it came out as a drawn-out howl of triumph.

Behind him, he sensed rather than saw Brac put the jeep into gear and start forward. Seth's mouth spread into an even wider grin, his tongue lolling out over his teeth. He turned his head, watching the jeep as it pulled away from him. He bunched his muscles. The deer could wait, for the moment at least.

He chased after the jeep in sheer exuberance, snapping at the wheels like a puppy. Even over the roar of the engine he could hear Brac swearing in a continuous stream at him. If he could have laughed in this form then he would have done.

He chased the vehicle for maybe a hundred yards before veering off into the waiting forest. Brac would be more than a little pissed off at him by the time they both eventually met at the village, but Seth couldn't help himself. This was what he lived for.

Chapter 10

Ehren continued to talk for some time after Seth and Brac so abruptly left. Although Anna was still paying attention, Mike was finding it increasingly difficult to focus on what the man was saying. He kept the camera running and steady, so he was able to justify his inattention by telling himself he could always watch the tape back later if he felt that he'd missed something. But right at that moment his mind kept going back to what they'd just witnessed, which was a whole lot more interesting than the technical details that Ehren was currently reeling off.

Mike had always been healthily open-minded. He was the sort of person who would quite willingly believe anything at all, so long as he was given some manner of proof. When Anna had first suggested coming out to this island, he was the only one of her acquaintances to have taken the idea even remotely seriously. But this was proving damn hard for even him to take in. He'd just watched an ordinary-looking man somehow change his hand into that of a monster, and now Ehren was sitting and talking quite rationally about the "virus" that caused it to happen.

'…One of the first things we had to realise was that the supernatural, as such, does not exist. On this island we've seen many things that defy regular categorisation, and the temptation will always be to file them all under the convenient heading of "supernatural". But everything we've encountered here has a natural explanation.' Ehren was smiling again. 'Lycanthropy is a virus, transmitted through blood and saliva, and causes in the host a sensitivity to the patterns of the moon and exposure to silver…'

'Silver?' Anna was also having a few problems keeping up with the conversation. The cool rationality of Ehren's tone was actually working against her, making the whole thing seem even more surreal. 'That's actually true?'

'You'd be surprised how much legend is based originally on fact,' Ehren said with another tolerant smile. 'Yes. Our wolves all have in common a violent reaction to anything containing silver. If you gave any of them a silver item to hold – for example, the cross around your neck, Miss Martin – then they would immediately break out in a very severe rash. If silver somehow got into their blood system, then yes, it could kill them. Any affected organs would quickly go into shutdown. In terms of other wounds though, our wolves have a very high regeneration rate – they can heal even the most serious wounds in a fraction of the time it would take a normal human, and the healed wounds very rarely scar, unless they were caused by something containing silver. This regeneration also affects the subject's life-span…'

'Really? How?'

'Well, Seth, for example, first contracted the virus approximately seventeen years ago, when he was in his early twenties.' Ehren paused for a moment, enjoying the look on Anna's face as she tried to work out what her own estimate of Seth's age would have been. 'Our best calculation is that a subject with the lycanthropy virus ages at about a third normal speed. The oldest resident of the island is roughly one hundred and seven years old and physically appears to be in her mid-fifties.' He smiled again, and Mike suddenly got the impression that this was not the first time the man had spoken like this in front of a video camera. 'Although, of course, it's not really polite to speculate on a woman's age. Hopefully, you'll get a chance to meet her yourself tomorrow.'

Anna sat back in her chair. Instinctively, she felt that she ought to have a notebook to hand so that she could be writing all this down, but she knew that Mike was getting it all on tape. She still half-wished that she had something she could be doing with her hands. It might distract her from the fact that the conversation seemed to be wandering far out of her depth.

'So…' she said at last, then laughed shortly. 'God, I don't even know where to start. Have there always been… wolves living here then?'

'To the best of our knowledge, yes. At least for the last century or so, although before that time records are a little sketchy. But according to Regina – that's the lady I mentioned – this island has always been considered the homeland of the wolves. Most of them can trace their lineage back here at some point. Unfortunately, we're still not entirely sure why or how the wolves came originally to be living here.'

'It seems like a bit of a weird choice of location.' Anna surprised herself by being able to think rationally about it. 'I mean… cut off from the mainland like this. You'd think there'd be a limited amount of food and stuff.'

Ehren nodded, accepting the point. 'This island is unique in more way than one. There's a surprising amount of wildlife native to the forests out there – more than enough to support our lycanthrope community.' He glanced at his watch. 'But all being well, as I say, you should get a chance to put all these questions directly to Regina tomorrow. If Brac returns tonight, I'll get him to organise a visit to the village in the morning.'

'Is that safe?' For some reason, Anna looked over at Mike as if seeking reassurance from him. 'I mean, I don't want to sound stupid or anything, but…'

'But it's the full moon tomorrow,' Ehren finished for her, his tolerant smile back in place now. 'Don't concern yourself – if we leave in the morning then there'll be plenty of time to be back here before nightfall. And even if we weren't, there's no real danger. In all the time we've been here, there has never been an incident between the wolves and us.' Again, he cast a look down at his watch. 'We've got a few hours of daylight left today though. If you'd like, I can show you some of the other work we're doing here.'

'Um. Sure.' What Anna most wanted to do was to sit down somewhere, close her eyes and take a few minutes to absorb everything that had just happened. Instead she forced a smile. 'Sure.'

Ehren got to his feet. 'Let's go find Ramone, in that case. There are lots of other labs we could show you round – introduce you to people, keep you inside listening to the technical side of things here – but I have a better idea. We'll get Ramone to drive us somewhere more interesting.'

Anna looked at Mike, but he was busy fiddling with the lens of his camera again. 'The village?' she asked, frowning.

'No, not the village.' Ehren was smiling, as if he knew all the secrets in the world and would happily share them with her… in his own sweet time. 'But there is more than one species native to this island.'

Anna and Mike followed him out of the lab. Mike had switched his camera back to standby and rested it on his shoulder as they walked. Usually he could stand for hours with the camera held steady as a rock, but today his hands had already begun to tremble. Privately, he blamed the boat journey and the slightly rough weather, coupled with the fact that he needed a cigarette. He could tell that Anna wanted to talk to him, but right at that moment he was glad they weren't getting the chance. His mind was working fast, going over everything that they'd been told, looking especially for the things that Ehren had glossed over or omitted. The first obvious question was what the other labs contained – Mike had not missed the way that Ehren was diverting attention away from them by showing him and Anna things that would deliberately shock and confuse them instead.

As the three of them stepped back out into the weak sunlight, Mike thought of another question. If Seth and the other wolves could change at any time, of their own freewill, then why was the fence around the camp only electrified during the night? Surely there could be dangers out there at any time of the day or night.

Unless… Mike was beginning to get the distinct impression that there was more to this island than just the wolves.

Ramone looked up as they came out of the building, and the girl he was talking to waved at Doctor Ehren. Anna vaguely recognised her as one of the women who had been in the lobby of the accommodation block when they'd first arrived.

'Doctor Ehren?' the girl said, coming over. She spoke slightly accented English, and Anna guessed from her features that she was probably from Norway or Sweden. 'I saw Seth leaving a minute ago. Do you know if he's going to be back this evening?'

'To be honest, I'm not sure,' Ehren told her. 'They might be quite some time. You'll have to radio up to the village and talk to Brac if you want to find out for definite.'

The girl nodded. 'I just wondered. I'm supposed to be helping Seth with a test subject tonight, but I've got to cry off, so he might have to do it by himself. Never mind, I'll radio the village.'

Ehren smiled dismissively at her, then turned his attention to Ramone. 'I was thinking that we could show our guests the southern enclosure. Any chance that you could drive us?'

Anna happened to be watching Ramone's face at that moment and saw the way that the man's expression hardened. He nodded, but his easy smile had become fixed. 'No problem, boss,' he said tightly. 'Are you sure you wanna go down to the graveyard?'

It took Anna a moment to realise that he was addressing her. 'The graveyard?'

Ramone nodded, his expression strangely unreadable.

Anna glanced over at Ehren, then at Mike. 'I guess we do,' she answered at last. 'Why's it called that?'

Ramone shrugged, ignoring the look on Ehren's face. 'It's where the dead live.' He turned away and climbed into the jeep. 'All aboard, then.'

Ehren took the front seat, and Mike helped Anna into the back then climbed in himself. He double-checked that he had enough tapes and batteries. Now more than ever, the last thing he wanted was to run out halfway through the day.

Anna was staring at the back of Ehren's head as if she could somehow see right through it and find the answers she was needing. On an impulse, Mike reached over and squeezed her hand. She looked up very briefly and gave him a tiny smile that made her look a whole lot younger than she really was.

Ramone started the engine.

Chapter 11

When they reached the main gate there was a young man standing beside it. He watched the jeep approach, standing up straighter when he noticed who was riding in it. He was dressed in a dark green shirt and trousers that would have looked military in origin if it hadn't been for the padded black jacket he wore over the top, in deference to the cold wind blowing off the sea. The jeep slowed in front of the gate and the man nodded to Ehren, then pressed a large release button set into a box on the fence.

The gate juddered open with a fair amount of noise, as if it had been a while since it had last seen maintenance. Ramone drummed his fingers on the steering wheel impatiently, then put the jeep back in gear and drove through, revving the engine harder than necessary. He hadn't said a word since they set off, but he was obviously not happy about something.

As they passed through the gate, Anna noticed that the area on the other side of the fence had been cleared, the forest cut back drastically for maybe fifty feet. There were dozens of tree stumps littering the area, and in several places the earth was blackened as if fires had been used to clear the undergrowth away. Another defensive measure, Anna assumed.

The track beyond the fence was no better than before, and Ramone drove angrily, with little regard for either his passengers or the jeep's suspension. Anna and Mike were forced to hang on tight, and abandoned all attempts at conversation.

As soon as the track passed into the forest itself, it split. Ramone took the left-hand fork, heading south. Here as well the trees had been cleared on either side of the track, and piles of felled trunks had been left at irregular intervals along the way. Beyond the cleared area the forest appeared surprisingly dark and impenetrable, the spaces between the close-set trees choked with bushes and other undergrowth. Anna had never been into an old forest like this one, and she couldn't help but feel unnerved by it.

The jeep struck a hole in the road, and Mike was almost unseated and thrown out. He clung on to the roll-bar with one hand and his camera with the other, swearing to himself. Ehren looked at Ramone as if on the verge of saying something, but then changed his mind. Ramone changed down a gear, over-revving the engine again, and hit several bumps in a row with unnecessary force.

After they'd been driving for maybe twenty minutes, Ramone abruptly hit the brakes, throwing all of them forward. Anna looked round but the forest here seemed no different to that which they'd been passing since they left the camp. The mountains off to their right had emerged from the mist and loomed up over the trees, their peaks black against the grey sky.

Ramone left the engine idling and turned to Ehren. 'You want to walk from here, or shall we drive up to the enclosure?' he asked, his tone coldly neutral.

'Drive on up.' Ehren waved his hand, ignoring the tone. 'It doesn't matter if they know we're coming today.'

Ramone nodded shortly and put the jeep back in gear.

Anna and Mike exchanged a look. Mike shrugged.

A few hundred yards ahead the track curved to the left, back towards the coast, and Ramone finally slowed to a comfortable speed as they rounded the corner. Anna sat up in her seat as she got a glimpse of another fence up ahead, one very similar to that which had surrounded the camp they'd just left. She got a brief impression of a handful of people milling around on the other side of the fence, and then the jeep was skidding to a bumpy halt and she had to concentrate on just staying in her seat.

Once the jeep was stationary, Ramone switched off the engine and sat staring straight ahead at nothing, making no attempt to get out.

Ehren turned to the two people in the back seat. 'This is our main area of observation for another species apparently native to this island. We've already introduced you to *homo lupus* – these are *homo mortis.*'

Anna and Mike were already standing up in their seats, and neither of them really heard what Ehren said. Their eyes were fixed on the fence in front of them, and Mike's fingers were automatically switching his camera to standby.

The figures beyond the fence had already begun to move closer, apparently drawn by the noise of the jeep's engine. Several were already at the fence, their fingers gripping the chain-link and their vacant eyes searching out the living people in front of them.

Anna opened her mouth, but it took her two attempts before she found her voice. 'They... those are...'

Ehren was smiling again. 'Those are *homo mortis*, also known as the living dead. Zombies.'

Mike raised the camera and pressed the record button without even thinking about it. He didn't bother looking through the viewfinder, his attention completely focused on the scene in front of him.

There were three of them at the fence, two men and a woman. The skin of their hands and faces was grey, and their staring eyes were tinged with yellow. One of the men was naked apart from a pair of khaki shorts, and every one of his ribs was clearly visible. His stomach was grotesquely distended, so much so that the skin appeared to have split in one place to show cut-flesh the colour of spoiled meat. The other man was missing an arm from the elbow down, the knob of bone poking out through tatters of flesh.

Mike's senses seemed strangely out of synch, and it was a moment before he realised that the air was thick with the stench of rotting flesh.

Anna had apparently already noticed, because her hand was held across her nose and mouth and she was making small moaning sounds as if she were in pain. Her other hand gripped the seatback in front of her so hard that her knuckles had turned white.

Behind the fence, more figures were making their way slowly towards them. A lot more. They were dressed in a variety of different clothes, and all were in various states of decay. Some seemed little more than walking skeletons, propelling themselves forward with the last vestiges of energy in their disintegrated muscles. Others could almost have passed for alive, if it weren't for the horrible blankness in their eyes and the sallowness of their skin.

No-one in the jeep spoke for a full five minutes as the dead slowly built up against the fence. By the end of that time, there must have been a hundred or more bodies. Fingers reached through the wire mesh, occasionally leaving tatters of flesh behind. The dead did not notice. Their eyes were all fixed on the humans just a short distance away from them. Mouths opened and closed in mechanical hunger, but none of them made any sound.

'Jesus.' Anna finally broke the silence, her hand still pressed against her mouth. She swallowed hard and then gagged as the stench of rot filled her throat. 'Are they seriously… dead?'

'See for yourself.' Ehren got out of the jeep, slamming the door behind him. The figures behind the fence followed the movement, pressing eagerly forward. 'This is our "graveyard" – although as you can see, our dead are not like the normal dead.'

Slowly, Anna forced herself to let go of the seat in front of her, fingers aching with the effort. 'Where did they all come from?' she asked. 'What are they doing here?'

'They've always been here, in small numbers. They used to be confined to a valley not far from this spot, and the wolves kept an eye on them to make sure none escaped. We've recently found out that most of them were originally from Reku – an island about twenty miles to the north. The islanders brought their dead here to be buried in the belief that there was some kind of magical force in the soil, which would enable them to return to life.' He smiled, although no-one at that moment was looking at him. 'On that point, they were technically correct. Anything human buried in the soil of this island will return to life, so long as they're buried not more than a day after they've died.'

'It's not life.' It was Ramone that spoke. He hadn't moved from his seat, and he was staring fixedly at his hands on the steering wheel. 'They move and feed, but they're not alive.'

Ehren ignored him. 'When we arrived here, we moved these subjects from the valley up to this enclosure where we could better observe them.'

There were now dozens of corpses lining the area in front of the fence, pushing and shoving against each other. Anna had to clench her teeth together to stop the rising feeling of sickness. 'Why?' she managed to ask. 'Why aren't they dead? Why the fuck did you put there all here?'

'They *are* dead, Miss Martin. They've died and been buried, but the earth around here won't hold them. And we put them here for two reasons – firstly so that we can study them, and secondly so that there is no danger of them escaping.'

Abruptly, Ramone got out of the jeep. Before he closed the door he picked up his rifle and slid the strap over his shoulder. Without looking anywhere except straight down at the ground, he walked some distance away, his hands gripping the rifle tightly. If Anna had been watching him at that moment, she would have realised what his hands had been missing earlier.

Anna, however, was still unable to take her eyes away from the living dead massing in front of her. When Ehren offered her his hand, she took it without thinking and let him help her out of the jeep.

Mike got out as well, hitting the zoom button on his camera and drawing the focus in on the walking dead pressed up against the fence. Looking through the viewfinder enabled him to stay more or less removed from what he was seeing, as if it had no more reality than a movie. 'Why are they so quiet?' he asked. 'Aren't they supposed to moan and stuff? I'd hate to think that TV's been lying to me.'

'The dead ones are unable to make any sound,' Ehren told him. 'The virus that animates them only maintains the parts of the body that it has need of. It doesn't need to make any sound, and so the vocal cords are one of the many parts that are quickly left to rot away.'

'How can it be a virus?' Mike asked. He zoomed in on a young girl at the front of the crush. Her blonde hair hung in dirty tresses down past her shoulders, and she had lost a large chunk of skin overlying her forehead and cheek, exposing the dirty skull beneath. 'You said they were dead, and then came back to life once they were buried. Viruses don't affect the dead.'

Ehren shrugged. 'As far as we can determine, the virus is carried in minute amounts within the soil itself, and does in fact affect dead flesh as well as living. At the moment, that's our best hypothesis. As far as we've been able to determine through tests, it *is* some form of virus, but further classification has been extremely difficult. Like the lycanthropy virus though it's transmitted through saliva and other bodily fluids...'

In his peripheral vision, Mike noticed that Ramone was walking away. Keeping the camera towards the fence, Mike turned and watched the man, who seemed to be heading in the direction of a group of Portacabins lined up a short distance away. On an impulse, Mike followed him.

Anna didn't see him go. She was unaware of him as she clutched unconsciously onto Ehren's arm. In fact, the only things she was aware of were the dozens of dead, unseeing eyes locked onto her own, and the words repeating in her mind:

'Gone to the graveyard, to visit the dead...'

Chapter 12

Ramone noticed Mike following him, but apart from a quick glance backwards he paid no attention. He continued walking towards the row of Portacabins with his eyes focused on the ground.

As they got closer to the cabins, Mike noticed that the sides were all reinforced with heavy slabs of timber and metal plates, and the windows were barred and covered by thick mesh. He glanced back towards the fence and saw with revulsion that a good number of the walking dead were following them at a slow, stumbling pace.

Ramone walked over to the metal door of one of the cabins and drew back the three large steel bolts that held it closed. As it was heaved open, Mike saw that it was plated with steel on both sides, and swung heavily on reinforced hinges. Ramone waited, holding the door open so that Mike could follow him, and when they were both inside he let it swing closed.

Mike found himself standing in a narrow corridor that seemed to run the length of the cabin. As soon as the outside door was shut, he caught the same thick stench of decomposing flesh that had been so noticeable outside, but in that enclosed space it seemed a hundred times worse. He gagged, his free hand coming up to cover his nose and mouth. Ramone turned to look at him, apparently unmoved by the smell. 'If you don't want to be here, then go wait outside,' he told him shortly.

Mike swallowed, almost gagged again as the thick smell caught at the back of his throat. He shook his head with an effort. 'I'm okay,' he lied. 'What the hell's in here?'

Ramone turned away without answering. If anything, he had become even more sullen and uncommunicative than before. Curiosity had Mike following him along the short corridor. It was obvious to him that the man had some kind of vast dislike of the zombies in the enclosure outside, but that didn't explain what he was doing in here.

At the end of the reinforced corridor was a second door, again plated with steel and held closed with three large bolts. From beyond it, Mike heard something shift; slow, dragging footsteps, as if something had been disturbed by the outer door closing. His mouth went dry and he glanced at Ramone, who was slowly drawing back the bolts of the second door.

'What's in there?' Mike asked again, his voice coming out faint.

As the final bolt was drawn back, the muffled noises from the next room got louder, a definite shuffle of expectant footsteps. Ramone put his hand on the door handle, his face resolutely set, as if performing an unpleasant but ultimately necessary task. His rifle was slung back over his shoulder.

Mike backed off instinctively as the man pushed the door open. The stink of rotten flesh flowed out in a wave, so overpowering that both men had to cover their mouths. Ramone pushed the door wide and then stepped through, not bothering to check whether Mike was following or not.

As Ramone stepped through the door there was a heavy thud, like flesh striking something solid. Hesitantly, Mike stepped forward, moving round so that he could see through the door without actually having to go through it. His fingers gripped the camera like a comfort object.

He edged forward until he was able to see into the next room. For an instant his heart leapt into his mouth as he realised that there was a zombie in there, barely two feet from the open door. It took Mike a moment to see that the creature was being held back behind a thick sheet of Perspex that ran the entire width of the cabin.

The zombie turned its feverish eyes towards him, and Mike felt his stomach heave again. Outside, it had been bad enough. At least there the dead creatures had been kept back behind the fence, and he had been able to almost convince himself that they were no more real than images on TV. But this was something else.

The creature drew back one half-rotted hand and struck the glass again with a heavy thud, hard enough to make Mike flinch backwards. Its jaws worked ceaselessly as if in anticipation of the food just beyond the partition, each movement making the loose and decaying flesh of its face flap and distort sickeningly. The hand pressed against the glass left a smear of yellow-tinged fluid as it clawed fruitlessly at the smooth surface.

'Relax, he can't get you.'

Mike's stare had been locked so totally on the zombie that Ramone's voice made him start. He had almost forgotten that the man was there. He looked over at him now, and saw that the man was standing very close to the glass with an odd expression on his face. Outside, Ramone had regarded the walking dead with revulsion, but now the look in his eyes was closer to absolute loathing. His dark eyes burned as he watched the zombie behind the glass.

Mike moved over towards him, breathing through his mouth as much as he could against the cloying smell of death. The zombie's eyes swivelled to follow him, living orbs trapped within a rotting skull. Mike felt bile rising in his throat and swallowed thickly.

'Why is he kept in here?' Mike asked. The initial shock of seeing the creature had faded a little now, and Mike's gaze automatically darted around the small enclosed area, taking in every detail. There wasn't much to see. Opposite the glass partition there was a door with a small hatch set close to the floor, presumably used for pushing in food. The floor of the cell was littered with bones.

'I got Ehren to put him here,' Ramone said, answering the question. Mike glanced back at him and saw that the man had moved even closer to the glass and now had one hand pressed against it. His dark eyes were unreadable now. 'Ehren had to give up something, since he wouldn't let me kill him.'

The dead creature was clawing at the glass again, its gaze fixed on the living hand pressed to the glass. Mike stared first at the zombie and then back at the man, his mind automatically searching for an answer. 'Who is he?' he asked at last.

'James.' Ramone's voice was soft. 'We worked together, over at the goddamn research facility. He was fascinated by these... these things.' His fingers, pressed against the glass, dug in until the fingertips stood out white against his tanned skin. 'We helped build a whole lot of this enclosure, me and him. He always had his doubts that the fence would be strong enough to hold them, but Ehren...' He broke off, shaking his head.

Mike was watching the zombie with a mixture of revulsion and fascination. The creature was dressed in the remains of a blue work-shirt and jeans, both badly torn and splattered with filth and old blood. Its skull was hairless and in many places skinless as well. It was impossible to guess what the man had looked like in life. Briefly, Mike considered switching his camera on, but even he realised the tactlessness of the gesture. Instead he stood silent and watched the creature, trying hard not to think about the fact that it had once been a living person.

Seeing that Ramone had lapsed back into silence, Mike voiced one of the many questions that had popped into his mind. 'Is it dangerous?' he asked. 'Is that why it's kept locked up?'

Ramone said nothing for a long moment, so long that Mike thought he hadn't heard the question. 'His name was James,' the man said at last. 'And no, he's not dangerous. At least, no more so than any of the others.' He smiled mirthlessly at his own joke. 'Ehren wanted to keep him because he's part of the experiments. He's the only subject that they've been able to observe both before and after death.' He let his breath out in a long sigh, then took his hand away from the glass. 'Ehren says they're keeping him here because they're working on a cure, but I know better than that. Once you're dead, you're dead. How can you cure that?'

Mike didn't have an answer, so he kept silent.

Ramone shook his head as if stuck for an answer as well. 'Some of those things out there have been like that for years,' he said then. 'If you keep feeding them, they don't rot so fast. Maybe they'll last forever, so long as they have fresh meat to feed on.' He pressed his hand once more against the glass. 'Hang in there, okay?' he said quietly, and Mike realised he was speaking to the dead man. 'I'll try to make sure it's not much longer.'

He turned and pushed past Mike with barely a glance, heading for the door. Mike hesitated, then switched his camera on long enough to film a few seconds of the creature behind the glass. The zombie watched him, its mouth still opening and closing automatically, hands scratching futilely at the partitioning glass.

Mike shut off the camera and walked out, making sure the door was closed and locked behind him.

Chapter 13

It was only after Anna had been standing watching the living dead behind the fence for nearly a full ten minutes that she started to notice differences between them. All of them were clawing futilely at the wire mesh, stretching their fingers through it towards her and Doctor Ehren, but only a few were actually looking at the humans. The eyes of the majority stared blindly off into the air or the forest, apparently unable to see anything at all. But there were maybe a dozen who were different, all of whom were right up at the very front of the crush. Their eyes were just as empty and dead as the others, but they moved and focused on the people in front of them as if they still had some vestige of sight.

She asked Ehren about this, interrupting the monologue that she'd been ignoring for some minutes now.

'Some of them are more alert,' he answered. 'They move a little faster and are able to respond to the outside world in a very basic way, which is something the others can't do. When the alert ones hear a car approaching, for example, they move immediately towards the fence or sometimes even the feeding gate over there. The others tend to follow them. They still have only a fraction of the intelligence of a living human – in fact, they have considerably less intelligence than ninety percent of animals – but the alert ones seem to be that little bit more aware of what's going on.'

'Why? What makes them different?'

'We're not sure yet. There seems to be no way of predicting the circumstances under which a body will regenerate in the more alert state. We've been trying to find out for some time now, with experiments on the test subjects here. The ones that show the most alertness are kept separate – ' Ehren lifted his hand to indicate the Portacabins, then stopped and frowned, finally noticing Ramone's absence.

Anna took several steps forward, watching the way that the more alert zombies followed her with their eyes. The rest sensed her movement with something other than sight and pushed forward with renewed urgency. An old man right at the front was being crushed against the chainlink with such force that the skin of his abdomen split open, and the rotten flesh was squeezed out through the holes in the wire.

Gagging, Anna turned quickly away.

The door to one of the cabins opened and Ramone appeared, with Mike following not far behind. He shut the outside door, taking care to bolt it securely.

As the two of them walked over, Ehren seemed to consider asking Ramone what he'd been doing, but decided against it. He turned back to Anna instead. 'I think maybe we should be getting back to camp,' he suggested with a tight smile.

* * *

It was over an hour later when the jeep drove back through the gate of the encampment. None of the occupants had spoken much on the return journey, and Ramone had driven at a more sensible speed. Anna had spent most of the journey with her head rested back against the seat and her eyes staring off into space. Mike sat beside her and checked his camera, playing back the footage that he'd just taken. He frowned to himself over a badly framed shot of a black-haired girl with half her ribcage missing.

The guy on the gate waved them through and they drove down into the camp. Once they'd pulled to a stop in front of the research building where they'd started, Ehren turned to his passengers.

'So, what do you think?'

Anna lifted her head and looked directly at him. She'd had plenty of time to think during the drive. 'I don't understand why you keep so many of them.' Her voice sounded tired, even to herself. 'How many do you really need for your research? Why do you keep the rest alive?'

'Miss Martin, it's not like they are a problem to us. It's as easy to keep a large number active as a handful...'

'That's not the point.' Anna would have put more anger into her voice if she hadn't been numbed by exhaustion. 'Those things are still human. You can't keep them locked up like that; like animals...'

Ehren's smile had begun to look a little fixed. 'You have to understand, Miss Martin, that these creatures don't have feelings, or emotions, or intelligence. They are almost totally oblivious to their surroundings. It doesn't hurt them to be kept in an enclosure where they're fed and looked after. And anyway, what would you rather we did with them?'

Anna didn't answer.

'I've got a question,' said Mike. 'Is it really a smart idea to have so many of them, from a safety point of view? I mean, what if they managed to get out?' He shrugged. 'I'm assuming they *are* dangerous, right? Unless you wanna tell me TV's been lying to me on that point as well.'

'The word here isn't really "dangerous",' Ehren told him. 'The undead are indeed carnivorous and will certainly attack humans without hesitation, but so long as they are in a closely controlled and monitored environment, there is no danger to us.'

As he spoke, there was the sound of a second jeep approaching. Mike turned in his seat and watched it drive along the bumpy track towards them, recognising Brac in the driver's seat.

The jeep pulled up next to them and Brac got out, frowning irritably. His passenger was fast asleep, his head leaning back and his mouth open, and didn't even stir when the engine was shut off.

Ehren got out to meet Brac. 'Good to see you back. Did you manage to get Seth sorted out?'

'See for yourself.' Brac jerked his thumb towards the sleeping man. 'He finally dragged himself back to the village a half-hour ago. I think he ate something while he was out, although he's a bit vague as to what it might have been. Then he started on at me that he had to come back here this evening and I had to drive him – apparently him and Tris have got a test subject coming in tonight and he wanted to be back for that.'

'Ah.' Ehren nodded. 'Tris was saying something about that earlier. Thanks for taking care of him.'

Brac grunted and walked around the jeep to the passenger side. 'Now I just need to figure out how to get him moving.' He poked Seth hard in the shoulder. 'Hey, wake up.'

Seth stirred and tried to push the man's hand away. Brac grabbed his shoulder and shook him.

'Get up – you're not staying here all day.'

Seth opened one eye and grinned up at him. His run in the forest had put him in a much better mood. 'Nah, I'm good here,' he said. 'You can just leave me, I'll be fine.'

Brac leaned down close to him and lowered his voice. 'I don't know if you've noticed, Seth, but Ehren's guests are right over there. Now, if you really want, I can pick you up out of that seat and throw you all the way back to your lab... if that's really the sort of thing you want those two to see.'

Seth raised his head enough to look over at the other jeep, where Ehren was speaking to Anna and Mike. 'Alright, fine. I'll move.' He sat up and stretched his arms, groaning at the aches in his muscles. 'I could really use another few hours sleep though.'

'Then go back to your lab and sleep there,' Brac suggested. He turned away but was caught by Ehren.

'Brac, I was wondering.' Ehren was smiling the way that he always did when he wanted a favour. 'Tomorrow I thought we could take our guests up to the village. Is there any chance you could clear it with Regina?'

Brac made an exasperated noise. 'I just spoke to her,' he complained. 'Fine, I'll get on the radio. Anything else you want while I'm there? Just so that I don't spend my *entire* day running around after other people, you understand.'

Ehren laughed, which just increased Brac's irritable mood. 'No, that's all, Brac. Thank you.'

'Any time.' Brac walked away quickly, wanting to get back to his office before anyone else could distract him. He'd lost almost the entire afternoon already and he was thoroughly sick of having to deal with people.

Smiling, Ehren turned back to Anna and Mike. 'Well, I think we've had enough excitement for one afternoon. It's almost time for the evening meal to be served, and then I guess you'll probably like to get an early night. I'm sure that today's been quite tiring for you.'

Anna would have liked to disagree, but the truth was she was feeling the effects of the long journey and the even longer afternoon, and there was a slow headache developing behind her eyes. As much as she wanted to find out more about what was happening on the island, the lure of a hot meal and a comfy bed was very appealing.

Chapter 14

From the balcony of his room, Mike could see along the fence for about fifty yards in both directions. Even if he leaned out, he couldn't see the gate or the generator, which was apparently some distance away. The generator had started up just before sunset, and now created a steady hum of noise in the still air. Mike stood out on the balcony and watched the sun going down over the mountains in the distance. His last cigarette of the day was half-smoked. The camera was on its strap around his neck, and he'd used it earlier to record the electrified fence with the orange lights illuminating selected patches of the dark forest beyond. Now he was content just to stand and watch the sunset.

He heard Anna's sliding door open, and a moment later she stepped out onto her balcony. Her hair was wrapped up in a towel, as if she'd just come out of the shower.

'Hey.' Mike waved over at her. 'Come to watch the sunset as well?'

'Sure.' Anna smiled wanly. She'd hardly spoken during the meal they'd eaten in the communal canteen, and there were dark bags developing underneath her eyes. Mike had been hoping that she'd already gone to sleep, because she really looked like she could use the rest.

'Did you find a shower?'

Anna shook her head. 'I washed my hair in the sink. The water's freezing, by the way.'

'I've never trusted solar power. Although I'm not sure if I'd trust that generator of theirs either – it took about five attempts to fire up tonight.'

'I know, I heard it.'

'Let's hope they never have to start it in an emergency, right?' Mike hoped to get a smile out of her, but he was disappointed again. 'Hey, are you alright? You're not looking so great at the moment.'

'Gee, thanks.' She smiled then, and it made Mike feel better to see it. 'Yeah, I'm fine. It's just been a lot to take in.'

51

'That's for sure. Incidentally, I think I've figured out why we got put in these rooms.' He waved a hand towards the dark forest. 'It's a nice view, but we can't actually see anything of any use. I've heard the gate open twice in the last hour, but we can't see who's going in and out. Likewise, we can't see anything of the camp. It's a very convenient way of keeping our attention away from anything that we might accidentally see.'

Anna nodded, as if the idea didn't surprise her. 'It's all just so weird, isn't it?' she said then. 'Werewolves and zombies… twelve hours ago those things were just myths. And now suddenly they're real, and they're right here.'

Mike nodded. 'You're right, it's weird. I think we both need to sleep on it.' He turned and smiled over at her. 'So, are you gonna be all right on your own? I mean, if you want someone to keep you company tonight…'

Anna laughed. 'Go to bed, Mike.'

'Okay, but I thought I'd at least offer.' Still grinning, he flicked the end of his cigarette away, then turned and went back into his room. 'Give me a shout if you change your mind, okay?' he called back.

She laughed again. 'Sure, I will.'

Anna stood out on the balcony for some time after Mike had gone back inside. The thrum of the electric generator and the coolness of the evening air was strangely soothing, and she lingered out there long after the sun had finally dipped below the horizon. Her mind was filled with the things she'd seen and heard that day, and as tired as she was she knew that she'd never get to sleep until she'd had time to get everything straight in her head.

A while after the sun had gone down, Anna heard the gate opening, but she paid it little attention. About ten minutes later it was opened again, and this time she heard the distant noise of a jeep leaving the camp. It circled round through the forest until it seemed that it was passing right in front of her, hidden by the trees. She watched the forest with slight interest, wondering if she would catch a glimpse of the headlights as it passed.

The noise of the engine got louder and then was abruptly shut off. Anna straightened up, staring directly ahead at the point the sound had been coming from. She could see nothing except dark and silent trees. She stood listening for a long moment, but heard nothing more and was about to shrug it off and go back inside.

Then a figure emerged from the trees on the other side of the fence. Anna blinked, leaning forward to try and see better. The shadows were so thick at that point that she couldn't even be sure that it really was a person standing there, and the longer she stared the less certain she was.

It was fully five minutes before the figure moved again, walking calmly out of the shadows and into the orange light cast by the warning signals on the fence. It was a young man, probably not much older than Anna, with thick black hair that was just long enough to reach his shoulders. He wore a plain black t-shirt and black jeans, and he walked towards the fence with his hands in his pockets, as serenely as if he were walking down the middle of a deserted street.

When he was within ten feet of the fence he paused, and looked directly up at Anna. She caught her breath and took a step backwards, her heart speeding up. The man's eyes were so dark as to appear almost black, and he regarded Anna with an expression that was unreadable at that distance.

He moved forward again, then bent his knees and jumped upwards. It was an easy, effortless jump, but it somehow carried him right up and over the fifteen-foot high fence in front of him.

He came down on the other side and landed like a professional athlete, as if he hadn't just jumped a clear twenty feet forwards.

Anna's breath was stuck in her throat and her heart was beginning to hammer. The man looked up at her again and she knew then that there was no way that he was human. He must be one of the wolves or… or…

'May I come up, please?'

It took her a moment to register that he had spoken to her. His voice carried perfectly clearly on the still night air, and his tone was friendly and pleasant, tinged with an accent that Anna couldn't immediately place. He stood underneath her balcony with his hands in his pockets and a look of polite expectation on his face.

'I…' Anna swallowed hard and tried again. 'Who are you?'

The man smiled. 'Can I come up? These things are easier to explain face to face.'

Somehow, Anna found herself nodding.

The man bent his knees again and made another effortless jump, this time landing squarely in the middle of the balcony. Anna backed away hurriedly, belatedly looking around for anything she could use as a weapon. There was nothing to hand.

'It's alright,' the man said, holding his hands up. He wasn't even breathing hard after the jump he'd just made. 'I'm not here to hurt you.' In the light that spilled out through the glass door, Anna could see that his eyes really were black; it hadn't just been a trick of the light.

'Who are you?' Anna asked again. She'd backed off so far that she bumped against the railing of the balcony, and it was only then that she realised she would have been a hell of a lot better off retreating towards the door. '*What* are you?'

The man smiled. 'When I heard that visitors had arrived today, I thought that it would be only polite of me to come welcome you to our island. I wasn't sure if Doctor Ehren would introduce us otherwise.'

'Are you one of the wolves?'

The man shook his head. His smile widened further, and for the first time

Anna caught a glimpse of his teeth. The incisors were abnormally long, like fangs. 'No. But in a way, they are my cousins. This island is our homeland just as much as theirs.'

Chapter 15

Anna shut her eyes and drew a deep breath. When she opened them again the creature was still standing in front of her. He was still smiling as well, although his teeth were hidden now.

'Y'know,' Anna said at length, 'I don't think I can take many more shocks today. Please, can you just explain who you are, what you're doing here, and how exactly you managed to jump that fence?' She pressed a hand to her temple, where she could feel a sick headache beginning to develop. 'You're a vampire, right? I mean, I'm just guessing, because of the teeth and everything...'

Luca inclined his head. 'You're a very prosaic person, if you can just accept something like that.'

'I'm not prosaic, I've just had too many surprises today.' Anna was watching the creature very warily. So far, he hadn't made any threatening moves, but that didn't mean she felt like relaxing. 'I mean, I only arrived here at lunchtime, and already I've met one werewolf and a whole bunch of corpses that are somehow still up and walking about. A guy with pointy teeth who can jump twenty feet straight up... you'll forgive me for not being as shocked as I normally would be.' She managed a faint smile. 'You caught me on a bad day.'

'Ah, so Ehren has been showing you around already. What do you think of our island?'

'Um. Well, the island itself is very pretty...'

'Do you like the mountains?' Luca nodded out over the forest, although the mountain peaks were now shrouded by darkness. The faintest outline, highlighted by the silver glow of the cloud-covered moon, showed their position.

Anna shrugged carefully. 'I'm not sure. We didn't really get close enough for a good look. I'm sure they're very nice though.'

'Oh, they are.' Luca took a step closer to her, being careful to move slowly so as not to panic her. 'We live up there.'

'We? You mean…' Despite her apparent acceptance of the point, it was still difficult for Anna to get her head around the fact that the man standing in front of her wasn't actually human. 'Others… like you?'

'Yes.' Luca smiled again. 'Other vampires. There're quite a few of us living up there at the present moment, and I'm the current leader of our little community.'

'Wow.' Anna was slowly getting over her initial fear, and her study of the man began to change from wariness to curiosity. 'That's incredible. I had no idea… I mean, Ehren didn't mention anything about… you living here.'

'Maybe he was planning on mentioning it later,' Luca suggested with a shrug. 'Or maybe he was hoping we would keep a low profile and you wouldn't find out about us. Doctor Ehren is occasionally too secretive for his own good.'

Anna nodded, remembering Ramone saying something similar earlier. 'So… um… I don't mean to be rude, but why are you here?'

Luca spread his hands. 'I wanted to meet you. I've spoken to your father on several occasions and I was curious to finally meet his daughter.'

'My father? When did you meet him?'

'I come into the encampment fairly regularly. Our community has an agreement with Doctor Ehren and his scientists, and we often come here to help them with research and tests and the like. That's why I came in tonight, in fact – I was dropping someone off.' His smile widened again. 'You should ask Doctor Ehren about us. He has a whole lab devoted to us, and I'm sure he'd love to show it to you. It's quite fascinating, some of the things they've discovered about our species so far.'

'Really?'

Luca nodded, still smiling. His voice with its faint accent was weirdly hypnotic, and his black eyes were almost completely flat and empty of any kind of emotion. It made for a faintly disturbing combination. The rest of his face showed plenty of expression, but the eyes were as dead and flat as those of a doll, even though the corners crinkled when he smiled. 'I'm sure that if you ask Doctor Ehren directly enough he'll be more than happy to tell you all about that. You may have noticed that he also likes to talk. Sometimes I'm surprised that he manages to keep so many secrets, considering how fond he is of his own voice. But anyway, that's not why I'm here right now. I came to invite you out into the darkness.'

He offered his hand and Anna instinctively shied away. 'Invite me *where?*'

Luca kept his hand held out to her. 'Up to the mountains, to meet the rest of my people. I thought you might be interested in that.'

Anna stared at him, then up at the darkened mountains, and suddenly wished that Mike would come out onto his balcony so that she wouldn't have to deal with this alone. 'I don't know. I don't know if that's such a smart idea.'

'There's no danger, I promise you that.' Luca smiled, looking a long way from any image of a vampire that Anna would have thought of. There was *something* about him, possibly his slightly formal speech and the slow, deliberate way he moved that suggested he wasn't entirely human, but if she hadn't been looking for it then she probably wouldn't have noticed.

Almost without realising she was doing it, she found herself reaching to take his hand. His smile was warm and welcoming, and his eyes were impossibly deep and dark.

She snatched her hand back quickly. 'Are you messing with my head?' she accused.

'Why would I do that?'

'I don't know… your eyes…'

'Even if I could do something like that, I promise you I wouldn't.' He offered his hand again. 'I'm an aberration of nature, I'll grant you that, but I am nothing supernatural.'

'Okay… but please remember that I just saw you jump up onto this balcony.'

The vampire shrugged. 'I have good muscles. So, would you like to come with me?'

Anna shook her head, but this time it was not a refusal but an attempt to clear her thoughts. Again, she glanced over at Mike's balcony and then back into her own room, but they were both still deserted. For the briefest of moments, as she was turning back, she caught a glimpse of her own face reflected in the mirror of her room, and the angle made it look like there was someone else there. A shorter person, because the mirror was lower than her head-height and angled out from the wall a little. It brought back sharply the image of the girl in her dream, almost like a reminder of why she was there.

'Do you know where my father is?' she asked.

Luca frowned, then shook his head. 'If he's not here in town then I don't know where else he'd be… other than the village. There's nowhere else that Doctor Ehren's people can really stay overnight on this island. And he's definitely not up in the mountains with us.'

'Ehren said that he'd left the camp for a while, but wouldn't say where he'd gone or when he'd be back.'

The vampire was silent for a moment, thinking. His black eyes seemed to stare off at a point somewhere behind her head. 'You're right, that's very strange. I don't know of any reason why he'd leave, especially this close to the full moon and knowing that you were coming. All I can think of is that there was an incident a few days ago – it's possible your father's investigating that.'

'What sort of incident?'

Luca shrugged. 'I don't know the details because it didn't involve any of my people, but I believe one of the humans got killed out in the forest.'

Anna blinked. 'How?'

'Brac spoke to me about it, and said that it looked like an animal attack, but none of his wolves were responsible.' The smile returned a little. 'Maybe Doctor Ehren knows more details and maybe he doesn't, but either way he's not saying anything to me or anyone else. The man who was killed was called Sykes, but I never met him.'

'I don't understand – if it wasn't your people and it wasn't the wolves, then what else could have killed him?'

Luca laughed softly, it's warmth belying the cold emptiness of his eyes. 'There are many dangerous things on this island, and most of them are much more dangerous than the wolves, or me.'

His hand was still extended, as if it were no effort at all for him to remain in that position all day long if necessary. Slowly, Anna reached out and took it.

'Alright,' she said. 'I'll go with you.'

The vampire's smile was just as warm as his laugh. 'Thank you. Would you like my promise that no harm will come to you?'

Anna laughed. 'And exactly what good would that do me if you really did mean to hurt me? Okay. I'll meet you downstairs.'

'If you wish, but there's an easier and safer way, if you don't feel like explaining to the guard on the front door where you're going to at this time of the night.'

Anna's eyes widened. 'There's a guard on the front door?'

'Entirely for your benefit, apparently. I'm guessing that Ehren doesn't want you wandering around on your own after dark.'

Anna was too tired to do anything but shrug it off. Maybe she could get mad about it tomorrow. After all, she'd only been here half a day and already she was tired of knowing only half the story and being caught off-guard every time she turned around. She looked into her room again, saw the altered reflection that made her look startling like someone else – someone who she had made a promise to. 'Alright,' she said then. 'What's your alternate idea?'

Luca smiled again. 'Don't panic now,' he said, and then he was suddenly moving towards her.

It happened so fast that Anna didn't realise what was going on until it was almost over. The vampire grabbed hold of her and lifted her right off her feet into his arms. Before she could even draw breath to scream Anna felt her stomach lurch sickeningly, the rush of gravity telling her that they were airborne. With her in his arms, Luca had jumped straight off the balcony.

Anna squeezed her eyes shut and didn't open them again until she felt the soft thud of Luca landing like a cat on the ground, fifteen feet down. She realised that she had caught hold of him instinctively, her hands clutched so hard into the material of his t-shirt that her knuckles were whitening. She opened her mouth to speak and Luca hushed her.

'Just hold on for a moment longer,' he said, his voice calm and reassuring. Then his arms tightened around her and he was running forward again. Anna got a brief glimpse of the fence in front of them and had time to wonder where the hell the supposed guards were at, and then she had to bite her lip hard to stifle a scream.

Another sickening moment as gravity seemed to release them for a scant half-second before reasserting its hold, and a longer drop that ended with a slightly harder landing on the other side. Luca didn't even stumble, moving forward quickly across the cleared ground towards the cover of the forest. As soon as they were amongst the trees he set Anna back down on her feet.

'Thanks.' Anna attempted a shaky smile, although she still had to cling to Luca's arm for support. 'Warn me before you do that again though, okay?' She looked back through the thin barrier of trees towards the illuminated fence, which suddenly seemed a lot less imposing than it had done an hour or so before. 'So much for security,' she laughed quietly.

Luca smiled as well. 'It's not much use against us, no. But we haven't quite got round to mentioning that fact to Doctor Ehren.' He shrugged. 'It doesn't matter, since none of my people would cross the fence without my permission anyway, and there are other things here that the fence *will* keep out.' He touched her arm. 'Come on, I've got a car waiting for us.'

Chapter 16

Underneath the trees it was very nearly pitch black, and Anna stumbled at almost every other step. Luca at her side moved through the darkness as easily as a cat, occasionally catching her elbow when she stumbled particularly badly. It would undoubtedly have been easier for him to carry her here as he had done before, but he kept a respectful distance now, letting her walk independently. Anna was too busy concentrating on not falling over to wonder about it.

As soon as they were away from the fence it was as if they'd stepped into a different world. If it hadn't been for the now distant racket of the generator, Anna would have found it hard to believe that the camp was so close by.

After only a minute or two of walking, the trees parted and Anna found herself standing at the side of a dirt track, although in the darkness it was difficult to tell where the rough ground ended and the track began. She stood there for a moment in a vain attempt at getting her eyes to adjust, and began to realise that the night was a lot colder than she'd thought. It maybe would have been a smart idea to pick up her jacket before allowing herself to be abducted like this. Then she noticed that the road wasn't as deserted as she'd originally thought.

There was a car parked not far away. From the vague outline that Anna could pick out, it appeared to be another of the open-topped jeeps that the men in the camp used. Irrationally, it made Anna smile to think of a vampire driving something so prosaic.

Luca led her towards it, and it was only as they got closer that Anna realised there was a young man sitting in the driver's seat. He appeared to be scanning the surrounding forest and not paying any attention to their approach. In the dim light, for one moment, Anna thought that it was Ramone sat there. The pose was so similar. Then the man glanced up, and Anna caught her breath. The man's face was pale, his dark brown hair cropped close to his skull, and his eyes glowed luminously in the faint moonlight. She knew at once that he was no more human than Luca. The irises of his eyes were so pale as to be practically colourless, and apart from the pinprick of black in the centre of each one his gaze looked almost blind.

The vampire glanced briefly up at Luca, then over at Anna. He ran his colourless eyes up and down her body, then smiled just wide enough to show the points of his teeth. 'Friend or food?' he asked Luca speculatively. He had a London accent, which seemed just as incongruous as his appearance.

'Friend,' Luca said with a trace of exasperation.

The young vampire turned his smile back towards Anna. 'He always says that,' he told her.

'Shut up and drive, Jason.' Luca swung himself into the back seat with a fluid motion, then held out his hand to Anna. Hesitantly, she took hold of it and allowed herself to be helped into the jeep.

The vampire called Jason started the engine and shoved it noisily into gear. Anna winced, glancing behind her in the direction of the settlement. 'Don't worry,' Luca reassured her. 'The men are used to hearing us moving around out here.'

The jeep lurched forward over the rough dirt track. Jason spoke over his shoulder. 'And even if they did wanna come investigate, none of them would dare come out here after dark.' The vampire flicked on the headlights almost as an afterthought, illuminating the road in front of them. The silent rows of trees kept their distance on either side of the track. Anna noticed that there was a cigarette tucked behind the man's left ear, and the fingernails of both his hands were chewed down almost as far as they could get. Apparently, being dead didn't necessarily cure you of bad habits.

Almost as soon as they got started, Anna began to feel the cold more acutely. The open-topped jeep meant that within minutes her face felt like it was frozen, and she began to shiver. Luca noticed and reached forward to pick up a jacket from the front seat, which he passed over to her.

'Sorry,' he said. 'We don't feel the cold, so I sometimes forget that others do.'

Gratefully, Anna pulled the jacket on. It was made of leather and was several sizes too big for her, but it was warmly lined and kept out the worst of the wind. It also smelled like old smoke, and she guessed that it probably belonged to Jason. He didn't seem particularly bothered with her borrowing it.

Jason drove along the dirt road at a similar speed to Ramone earlier, but either his reactions were a lot better or he was more considerate of his passengers, because he didn't hit nearly as many bumps and the ride was relatively smooth. Anna was able to watch the trees passing by on either side without having to worry about hanging on for dear life.

After roughly ten minutes driving, the road began to rise as they headed up into the foothills of the mountains. The trees thinned out and then abruptly stopped as if they didn't want the trouble of trying to climb any higher. As far as Anna could make out in the darkness, the landscape here was rocky and irregular, but it was impossible to see any details. Even in the twin beams of the headlights it was difficult for Anna to be sure of the road, but Jason drove with confidence, so much so that she began to suspect the vampire had the headlights on mainly for her sake.

The track ran over and between the smaller hills, then began a long and circuitous route around the first of the larger mountains. It started to slope upwards more steeply and the forest dropped away rapidly below them. There were no barriers at the side of the road, nor anything else to stop them bouncing and rolling all the way back to the bottom of the mountain if Jason made a slip. Anna frequently had to close her eyes as he swung the jeep carelessly around corners.

'How long have you been here?' she asked Luca, more to distract herself than anything else.

Luca shrugged, looking complete at ease with driving at speed next to a sheer drop. 'Me personally? Ten years or so. Jason's been here about… three months is it, Jason?'

The young vampire nodded. 'This'll be my third full moon,' he said over his shoulder.

'And how long have you been you been… um…' Anna hesitated over the right word.

'Dead?' Luca suggested with a slight smile. 'A little over fifty years.'

'Really?'

'I think so. Looking good for my age, right?'

Anna managed to return the smile. 'Are all the others as old as you?'

'Jason's only been changed about two years. Ciaran – the one who's at the camp at the moment – has about five years. Everyone else here is older than me. Erik's definitely the oldest, but he won't tell us his exactly age. Several hundred at least.'

Anna nodded, her mind struggling as it tried to take in the casual fact. 'God,' she breathed. 'That's unbelievable. Wait – if you're not the oldest, then how come you're the one in charge?'

Luca spread his hands. 'Being old is only the half of it,' he told her. 'Some of us are… stronger than the others. When the last leader left, I took his place, and no-one objected.'

Jason laughed. 'Not too much anyway.'

'There was no reason for them to do so,' Luca went on. 'I don't mind being the one to deal with Doctor Ehren and his scientists, and everyone else was quite content to leave me to it.' He sat back in his seat with another shrug. 'It's not much of a title really… I'm more like an intermediary, between us and the humans. I'm not sure what would happen if I tried to order the others not to do something that they really had their hearts set on.'

They were quite high up now, and Anna could see right out over the trees as far as the sea. Behind them, there was a cluster of lights which was presumably the encampment, and to the south a second cluster which could have been the zombie enclosure. There were no other lights to be seen, and Anna suddenly felt very cold and far from home.

'So, how did it happen?' she asked Luca then. 'How did you become a vampire?'

Luca glanced at Jason, but he was concentrating on the road and not paying them any apparent attention. 'It's a long story.'

'Oh. I'm sorry, I didn't mean to pry…'

Luca waved it away. 'It's alright, I don't mind talking about it or anything. But some of the others don't like speaking about their pasts, so you'd be as well not asking that question of anyone else.' He turned his head so that he was staring out towards the dark ocean, and he was silent for so long that Anna almost gave up on getting an answer. 'Doctor Ehren believes that we're the victims of a virus,' he said at last. 'Just like the wolves and the dead ones. With them, a bite or even a scratch is enough to transmit the disease, but ours is not so potent. A single bite will not do it. The body has to be weakened enough so that when the virus is introduced, it can take over easily. When it does though, it does so more fully – more completely – than with the wolves. They are still basically human and are forced to change only once a month, whereas we have to live in our altered forms constantly.'

Jason swung them round another corner, and up ahead on the mountainside a dim light came into view. It seemed to be perched on an outcropping with a sheer drop above and below it. The track led right up to it.

'That's why,' Luca went on, 'the new host has to be drained of blood to the point of death before the virus can take hold, and even then it takes a substantial amount of infected blood to complete the change. It's a difficult thing to do by accident, which is why most of our kind are deliberate creations.'

'*Most* of them?'

Luca smiled at her, widely enough to show the points of his teeth. 'I'm one of the exceptions – an accidental vampire.'

The jeep was coming up towards the light now, close enough for Anna to see that it was an electric bulb shielded by a protective box made of glass and metal. A cable ran from it along the rock face and disappeared into the entrance of a cave a short distance away.

Jason pulled the jeep to a halt alongside the light. 'Shall we go this far and no further?' he asked, turning to grin at Luca.

'Get out and shut up,' Luca suggested, climbing out of the back of the jeep. He walked round and held out his hand to Anna again. 'I'll tell you the rest later, okay?' he smiled. 'For now – come in and meet the family.'

Chapter 17

Ciaran sat in the small office, shifting nervously in his chair. He glanced up at the clock on the wall for the fifteenth time and chewed his lower lip, carefully so as not to draw blood with his incisors. It had been less than an hour since Luca had dropped him off in the camp, but he was still waiting for the two human scientists that usually dealt with him to arrive.

He hated coming in for these tests. There was a very good reason why he did it, but that didn't mean he had to enjoy it or anything. Ninety percent of the tests seemed utterly pointless and stupid to him, and he couldn't even begin to understand why exactly the humans had to take a blood sample from him *every goddamn time* he came in.

On average, Ciaran came in every two weeks or so. It was sometimes more and sometimes less, depending on how strong his will was. The longest he'd ever gone without coming into the camp was a month, and that had nearly killed him. Luca and the others could go on about the joys of living isolated out here on this goddamn island, but Ciaran knew that personally he wasn't cut out for it. He'd been there nearly a year now, and it was definitely time to start thinking about leaving. He needed to be in the city, amongst people and warmth and life.

He freely admitted to himself that the only reason he was still there now was because of Irae. And if she couldn't be persuaded to come with him when he left... well, then he'd just have to leave her behind. She was only human after all, and what the hell was a guy like him doing falling for a human girl anyway?

And now these son-of-a-bitching scientists were keeping him waiting again. Ciaran shifted in his seat, his eyes moving over the badly decorated interior of the small room. He hated waiting almost as much as he hated those goddamn pointless tests.

Eventually the door opened and interrupted his sour train of thought. Ciaran looked up with irritation as the nervous young doctor, Seth, came in. 'About time,' Ciaran complained. 'Have you any idea how long I've been waiting here?'

Seth tried to smile, but as always it appeared pale and watery. 'I'm sorry.' The apology was as automatic as the smile. 'It's been really mad down here today… our lab's seriously understaffed at the moment…'

'Yeah, alright. Whatever. Where's Doctor Trisha tonight?'

'Oh.' Another watery smile. 'Tris got herself double-booked again, I'm afraid.'

Ciaran laughed shortly. 'Double-booked with her boyfriend, is that?'

Seth's cheeks reddened slightly. 'Um. Yeah, I think so. I didn't really ask; you know how it goes. Uh, you want to come through?'

Seth led the way out of the small office and towards one of the labs. This one was kept aside specifically for the occasions when the vampires came in to help with the tests, and was fitted out with the necessary basics and not much more. There was a large chair that could be reclined back almost horizontal if necessary, and several cupboards that housed the medical equipment used for taking samples of blood and measuring blood pressure. There was a small sink and a yellow disposal box for used needles at the side of the room, and a button that looked like a lightswitch, coloured beige like the wall behind it. If it was pushed, it would trigger a silent alarm and bring every available guard to the room within minutes. None of the vampires knew it was there, just as they did not know the walls and doors of these rooms were all specially strengthened and could be used to contain the most violent patient, even one of unnatural strength.

It made Seth smile to know that Ciaran was oblivious to these safety measures. Yet another thing that Ehren had installed here and never quite got round to telling the vamps about.

'So, what're we doing today, doc?' Ciaran asked as he came into the room.

Seth smiled patiently, quietly amused by the nervousness of the young vampire. 'The usual tests, nothing special. But first things first – we'll take a blood sample.'

'I was afraid you'd say that.' Ciaran shrugged off his jacket and laid it carefully over the arm of the chair. Seth noticed that there was an almost imperceptible shake to the vampire's hands as he did so, and he couldn't help but laugh.

'I've never met a vampire that was scared of needles before.'

Ciaran glanced up at him and gave a quick nervous smile that flashed a hint of fang. 'Yeah, well,' he laughed. 'I never liked them before, don't see why that should've changed now.' He settled himself down into the padded chair as comfortably as he could.

Seth moved over to the cabinet next to him and picked up the freshly sterilised needle that was sitting in a metal tray on top. As always, Ciaran turned his head away and began studying the far wall intently.

'It just strikes me as odd, that's all.' Seth kept his tone deliberately light, since there wasn't any point in making the vampire any more nervous than he already was. 'It's like finding out that you're squeamish, or something like that.'

'I don't mind the blood, it's just…' Ciaran shuddered involuntarily. 'Look, I don't wanna talk about it. Just get it over with, okay?'

Sure, thought Seth, allowing his contempt to surface. *I'll hurry it up so that you can get out there and get your fix. You think I don't know about the deal you've got going with Ehren, but I do. You volunteer to help us out for one reason and one reason only – because on this island you can't get your blood-fix from a human unless it's voluntary.*

Sometimes he had to almost admire the way that Ehren had worked out the deal with the bloodsuckers. It had gotten Ehren his precious research materials, and it had allowed him and his human tribe the security to take up residence on the island. But at other times Seth felt little more warmth to Ehren and the rest of them than he did towards the vampires.

He turned back towards Ciaran, who still had his face turned steadily away. The vampire had rolled up the sleeve of his shirt to expose the vein at the elbow, and his hand was gripping hard onto the arm of the chair. The chairs in the labs were made of toughened plastic, but this one had padded steel arms to prevent it from splintering into pieces beneath superhuman fingers.

Since Ciaran wasn't concentrating at all on the person behind him, he had no idea that the needle Seth had picked up wasn't empty.

Seth swabbed the inside of the vampire's elbow, feeling him flinch slightly under the cold touch. The mild anaesthetic of the swab wouldn't numb the pain nearly as well as it would on a regular human being, but Seth shrugged that off. It was the creature's own fault for being the way he was. He gripped the vampire's arm firmly and slid the needle through the skin.

Ciaran caught his breath, then let it out slowly in a deliberate attempt to calm himself down. The scientist was right – it was stupid to the point of idiocy for him of all people to be scared of a little blood letting. Under no circumstances at all would he have admitted that the fear was always there with him, even when it was him doing the letting. It was the sensation of something solid piercing the skin that freaked him out, and as hard as he'd tried in his few short years amongst the undead, that fear had never left him.

He closed his eyes and thought hard about something else as he felt the familiar tugging in the vein of his arm. With his level of awareness he was able to feel every slight movement of the needle, and he had to really concentrate on not paying attention to it. If he had in fact being paying close attention, then he would have noticed that the feeling was slightly different from usual, and that a cold sensation was very gradually sliding up his arm.

Seth had counted on the vampire not noticing.

The doctor removed the needle and put it away quickly. Usually Ciaran remained staring fixedly at the wall for several seconds after it was finished, but Seth didn't want to take the chance of him changing his pattern today and glancing over at the now-empty needle. It was going to take at least thirty seconds for the sedative to take effect, and quite possibly longer. Seth had calculated it all on paper, but things had a way of working out very differently in practice.

He took his time clearing up and swabbing the injection site a second time. There was no need to put anything over it since the bleeding had stopped and the hole was already closing up. Inside his head, Seth began counting down from thirty.

He'd got to nineteen when Ciaran spoke.

'I don't feel so great.'

'Are you okay? Do you feel faint?'

'Yeah.' A puzzled frown formed on Ciaran's face – slowly, as if his movements were already becoming retarded. 'I do... a little.'

Seth pushed a lever on the chair that reclined the back and elevated the footrest. 'Just lie back and take it easy. Has this happened before? Back when you were alive, I mean.' His silent countdown was at fourteen, and his heart started to speed up as if in counterpoint. If the sedative failed, or if it was too slow to take effect and Ciaran realised what was going on, then Seth had no idea how the vampire would react.

'Yeah... a couple of times...' Ciaran's head flopped back against the headrest, his eyes filled with that same look of confusion as he stared up at the ceiling.

'Just rest for a few minutes, alright? It's quite normal to feel faint.' Eight seconds. He prayed that his calculations had been correct. 'Keep your head back.'

Ciaran's body was going limp, a piece at a time. His hands, which had been clenched into fists, abruptly released and hung loose over the armrests. Ciaran continued to stare at the ceiling, but his frown deepened. 'What...?' he started to ask.

Two seconds.

And then the vampire's eyes widened as if sudden realisation had hit him. He struggled to sit up, his mouth forming around the word, 'No'. His hands twitched uselessly as muscles failed to respond to the brain's commands.

Seth's mental countdown hit zero and he stepped backwards quickly. *Zero, zero, zero*. The vampire continued to fight, eyes wide and frightened and showing circles of white all around the pupils. The eyes swivelled, fixed on Seth as the body continued to spasm. With an act of supreme will, Ciaran forced his body up out of the chair, twisting like a broken puppet, his eyes now full of rage as well as fear. One hand stretched for the man, fingers splayed so wide that it would have been painful for any human person.

Seth backed off as far as he could, bumping against the far wall of the lab, and willed the change to rise in him. As a wolf he could take on the vampire. Ciaran's bloodstream was filled with a dose of sedative that was twenty times the LD50 for humans, and even if it didn't knock the creature out, then it should at least slow him down.

The change welled up through him like boiling water. He really hadn't wanted it to come to this.

Ciaran's feet touched the floor, his twisted hand still reaching out desperately. Bloodstained foam flecked the corners of his mouth, and his lips were drawn right back over his exposed fangs. His numbed feet skittered on the floor, refusing to support his weight, and abruptly he spilled to the ground.

The muscles in his arms twitched several times and then he lay still.

It took all of Seth's willpower to force the change back down. His skin felt like it was on fire, and as the change unwillingly retreated, his head started to pound with the mother of all migraines. Slowly, he sank to the floor and knelt there, staring at the inert body of the vampire as his own ragged breathing gradually came back down to normal.

Twenty times the lethal dose and the bastard had taken forty-seven seconds to even pass out.

Seth knew he didn't have much time. His calculations had already proved to be far enough out to be dangerous, so he had only the roughest of estimates as to how long the vampire would stay unconscious.

The first thing to do was to get the arms and legs pinned.

Chapter 18

Silver wouldn't affect the vampire the same way that it would a wolf, but it would still be hellishly uncomfortable. Seth had done plenty of tests on vampires and their blood, and he knew that while silver was toxic to wolves in remarkably small quantities, it was not fatal to vampires. Sufficient quantities of it did, however, provoke a severe allergic reaction. A wound inflicted by a silver bullet might take hours or even days to heal, as opposed to the scant few seconds required for a regular wound.

Privately, Seth wished that he'd had more opportunity to test this phenomenon, but he knew that wouldn't have been possible. The vampires would put up with a lot of tests in order to honour their deal with Ehren, but willingly submitting to torture under silver was not one of them. This was to be his test – his ultimate test, since if he failed it would almost certainly mean his death.

Seth had had the metal spikes made to exact specifications and delivered secretly on the *Narrenshiff* earlier that month. Each of the two spikes was twenty-four inches long and tapered at both ends. The silver ratio in them was as high as was possible without compromising the strength. Seth had to handle them through thick rubber gloves, and even then touching the cold metal made him feel like he was handling a particularly temperamental venomous snake.

Now, he gripped one spike tightly in his gloved hands and tried to ignore the way his skin felt like it was trying to crawl away from the metal. Ciaran was propped up in front of him on his knees, supported by the lab table. His head lolled to one side and his eyes were still shut.

The vampire's hands were stretched out in front of him as if in prayer across the table. The illusion was spoilt by the fact that both hands were held in place within a large metal clamp. Seth had spun the handle of the clamp until he heard the sharp cracking of the small bones in Ciaran's wrists. The sedated vampire hadn't so much as twitched.

Seth steadied himself, gripping the metal spike in both hands. 'Too far gone now,' he muttered, but it wasn't clear whether he was speaking to himself or to his unconscious captive. He took a deep breath and held it, then slid the spike forward.

The front point pierced the skin of the vampire's arm just above the wrist and slowly slid through. There was a slight hissing noise like water touching heated metal as the silver reacted with the undead flesh. Seth halted, checking that the spike was going cleanly between the bones of the arm, then pushed forward again. He saw the tip emerge from the inside of the right wrist and then press into the left one.

Again he halted; again checked that the point was sliding between the bones and not over them. The last thing he wanted was for the vampire to somehow free his arms. With the metal physically trapped between the arm bones, that would not be an option.

Another push and the metal tip emerged from the other side of Ciaran's left wrist. There was surprisingly little blood, but Seth reminded himself that the heart of a vampire beat very slowly unless they'd recently fed. He smiled at the thought that this vampire had taken his last human meal.

He still had to work quickly though. It was little effort for him to grab both protruding ends of the metal spike in his gloved hands and bend them upwards and around each other. Under normal conditions, it would have been equally easy for the vampire to escape this makeshift bond, but Seth's calculations were that the high silver content and the fact that the spikes were fastened not *around* the arms but actually *through* them would prevent this. Even if Ciaran did somehow wake up.

That part of the job done, Seth quickly released the hands and lowered Ciaran's inert body to the floor. It would have been difficult if not impossible to lift the body and get it in the right position to clamp the ankles, so Seth simply straightened out the legs, removed the clamp from the table and fastened it in place over the ankles. After all, he didn't have to hold the vampire still, just keep the ankles together while he inserted the second spike.

Once that job was done, it was a relatively easy task for Seth to drag Ciaran's body out of the back entrance of the building and into the jeep that he had parked there earlier.

* * *

The zombie enclosure was in more or less complete darkness, the only lights being situated at regular intervals along the perimeter fence. Seth drove up as close as he could to the fence, then parked directly underneath one of the lights. He shut off his headlights and the darkness swept down around him, sealing off everything except that thin illuminated line of fence stretching out in front and behind him.

Seth got out of the jeep and swung the door closed. The noise echoed loudly through the silent forest and Seth winced. Usually, his sensitive ears would have been able to pick up even the smallest sounds of the forest – leaves rustling, animals moving; just about anything like that – but around the enclosure nothing ever seemed to move. It was as if the forest around here was dead, or maybe holding its breath. Certainly nothing living was moving within a hundred feet of where he currently stood.

The undead were silent too. Seth had never fully understood the movements of the zombies – why sometimes they would congregate in one section of the enclosure, sometimes in another, sometimes altogether, sometimes spread out at random across the barren ground. The last time he'd been here at night, they had all been close to the fence, a slow moving group all walking together but apparently without a destination in mind. As soon as they'd seen the lights of his jeep they'd looked up and changed direction, shuffling right up to the fence and stretching desperate hands towards him.

Tonight though, they were evidently gathered in a different part of the enclosure. Seth was certain that they would be coming towards the fence soon, like Pavlovian subjects drawn instinctively to the possibility of food. Well, any that turned up tonight were not going to be disappointed.

The motionless body of the vampire was propped up in the back seat of the jeep. It had been impossible for Seth to keep an eye on his prisoner as they drove through the pitch-black forest, but as far as he could tell Ciaran hadn't moved so much as an eyelid throughout the whole of the journey. As Seth dragged the body out of the jeep, he noticed that the skin of the wrists and ankles where the metal spikes protruded was red and inflamed. He poked at the wrist and saw a small amount of clear fluid oozing from the wound. He'd been very careful to keep his gloves on at all times. He was glad to see that Ciaran didn't even twitch at the pressure on the obviously sore wound. The vampire was definitely still out cold.

Seth lifted the body and hefted it over his shoulder with only a slight effort. His heart was beating too fast from a combination of fear, excitement, and the fact that he'd forcibly suppressed the change earlier. He could feel the tightening of his body, signally that he would have to change tonight, and fairly soon. Otherwise he was going to start hurting a lot. The change wasn't something that he could hold down forever, even though he'd already gone through it once that day.

But he had one thing to do first. After it was done, his alter-ego could have the use of his body for as long as it wanted.

Ciaran's body was as lifeless as a sack of grain. Seth carried him from the jeep in a fireman's lift, being very careful to keep the pinioned limbs and the toxic bars that held them well away from his own body. He had quite enough scars already and didn't feel like picking up any more tonight.

The fence was ten feet high and extremely sturdy, but unlike the one around the human encampment, this one was unadorned. Zombies didn't have the necessary motor functions for climbing, so no-one had thought to put barbed wire along the top of this fence. The thick chain link had so far proved more than enough to keep the undead inside.

Tonight, Seth was very pleased that no-one had added reinforcement to the enclosure. It made it easy for him to hoist the body and throw it up over the top of the fence. It wasn't an elegant manoeuvre, and the body tumbled as it went over the top, but Seth managed it on the first attempt. Ciaran's shoulder hit the ground on the other side, with enough force to have splintered bone in any regular human. His body lay on its side like a broken doll, the head lolling forward so that the face was hidden from the man on the other side of the fence.

Breathing hard from the effort, Seth straightened up and dusted down his clothes, then carefully peeled off the rubber gloves. He could hear movement now from inside the enclosure. The soft shuffling of dead feet over dead ground, moving slowly closer. The more alert ones would be there first, Seth knew, and the rest would blindly follow not far behind.

He crouched on the ground directly opposite Ciaran, watching the vampire's half-hidden face intently. He was pleased that his victim had remained unconscious up until this point, but now that the difficult bit had been done, part of him wished that Ciaran would wake up so that he could be conscious for this last little bit of his so-called life.

A flicker of movement, and then the first zombie lurched out of the shadows of the enclosure. Seth immediately saw that it was indeed one of the more alert undead, although he couldn't have said for sure how he knew. Maybe it was something about the way that the creature's eyes immediately focused on him, displaying the last dying traces of human intelligence.

The first zombie shuffled forward and the rest followed.

Chapter 19

At first there were only four or five that Seth could see. Two alert ones, their eyes taking in both food sources – the moving one in front of the fence and the unmoving one on their side of it – and two or three others, their eyes blank and staring at the sky or the darkness around them. They followed the alert ones, sensing the presence of food by some instinct other than sight or smell, neither of which were available to them any more.

Seth watched them and shuddered. He couldn't understand why Ehren even permitted these monsters to live. They were nothing but decaying flesh that didn't have the good sense to lay down and be dead.

A low moan filled the air, raising the hairs on the back of Seth's neck. It took him a moment to realise that it wasn't one of the zombies that had made the noise.

Ciaran's eyes were open. He attempted to raise his head but fell back against the hard ground, his hair falling across his face. His eyes were round and wide and unfocused, and his lips moved as if trying to form silent words.

Seth couldn't help but smile. The shuffling footsteps increased in pace as if responding to the vampire's cry.

Ciaran must have heard the footsteps too. He twisted on the ground and tried to see behind him, but the sedative was obviously still paralysing most of his body. He couldn't do any more than raise his head and stare uncomprehendingly at Seth.

The doctor smiled pleasantly back at him. 'I'm not sure if you should be grateful or not that you can't see behind you,' he said. Personally, Seth was quite happy that Ciaran had landed facing this way, just so that he got to see the terror that was rapidly filling the vampire's eyes.

'No...' Ciaran tried to lift one of his hands, and his voice became a shriek of blind pain. The silver scratched against his raw wounds like sandpaper, and Ciaran screamed again, louder.

Seth wished that he could have had a video camera along with him, just to record these moments. Even the increased pressure of the change rising up inside his guts couldn't dull his pleasure. This was the best one yet.

With an incredible feat of willpower, Ciaran twisted himself over onto his back, his breath catching harshly within his throat. His staring eyes took in each separate element of his torture – the metal bars through his arms and legs; the slow dragging feet of the zombies implacably approaching him; the man crouched just on the other side of the fence with the smile of a small child watching feeding time at the zoo. Ciaran's eyes took these things in and his brain tried to throw them back out; tried to insist that this was all some nightmare brought on by his fainting fit in the lab. But the gnawing pain in his wrists told him otherwise.

Seth watched as these thoughts whirled through the vampire's mind. He watched him try to sit up, fail, try again, barely manage it. His smiled broadened as Ciaran struggled backwards until his back was pressed against the wire of the fence. It must have been quite an effort, since every movement would have brought renewed pain from his bonds.

'Hey, Ciaran,' Seth grinned. 'You like this? You like playing the victim for once?'

Ciaran twisted so that he could see him. 'Seth? What – ?' His voice cracked and gave out; Seth wondered if it was fear, or just a side effect of the drugs.

'It's okay – just another little test.' Seth gestured towards the zombies, who were barely ten feet from Ciaran's prone figure by now. 'I've always wondered if the dead ones would eat one of your kind, or if they feed exclusively on the living. You're making history, Ciaran; you should be proud.'

Ciaran tried to draw breath, choked, tried again. 'C'mon,' he managed at last. 'Seth… get me out… get me out of here…'

'Get yourself out.' Seth got to his feet. 'You're so tough – you and the rest of the vampires. You think you can do anything you like. So go ahead. Get yourself out of this one.'

'Hey – come on…' Ciaran attempted to turn himself round to face the fence, but the bars through his wrists and ankles prevented it. 'Get me out of here. Get me out!' The zombies were closing in on him, their grasping hands reaching for his flesh. 'Why are you doing this?' His voice took on a pleading note. 'I never did anything to you!'

'Not personally, no.' Seth stepped away from the fence, wanting to see if the zombies would follow him or continue advancing on the trapped vampire. He was pleased to see that they more or less ignored him. 'Sorry, Ciaran – as far as I'm concerned, you're just the wrong species.' He took off his jacket and dropped it on the ground.

'No…' Ciaran tried to draw his feet back out of the way as the nearest zombies stumbled over each other to grab him. 'No, get me out! Get me – ' His words broke off in a scream of terror. The first of the zombies had caught hold of his shoulder, dragging him forward. 'No!'

Seth watched with almost clinical detachment, carefully unbuttoning his shirt. His fears that the dead ones might reject undead flesh turned out to be completely unfounded. They were grabbing at Ciaran as if they'd not been fed in a hundred years, tearing his flesh in their haste to get it into their mouths. Ciaran screams got louder and louder, reaching the point where it seemed they had to stop or his vocal cords would burst. And yet they didn't. Even as the zombies were taking bites out of him, his undead body was attempting to heal the damage. It took a lot longer for his screams to be silenced than it would have for a human.

Seth dropped his shirt on top of his jacket, closing his eyes to savour the moment. The only thing that spoiled it was the fact that the moon was hidden behind the clouds and not shining down on him as it should be. But he could live with that. His body could feel the moon and responded to it instinctively.

The artificial light from the beacons on top of the fence illuminated the scene perfectly. Seth, now naked to the waist, smoothed his hands over the scars on his arms and smiled to himself. He watched Ciaran's body in its last stages of life, being pulled to pieces between the squabbling hands of the dead. He didn't take his eyes off the scene until one of the zombies finally silenced Ciaran's cries by tearing out his throat.

Seth let out his breath in a long, shuddering sigh. Then he finished stripping off his clothes, his body trembling with the continued effort of suppressing the change. His head pounded, making it difficult to think, and he knew that there was no way he could stay here and clear up as he had intended. Not until he'd let his alter-ego have its turn.

The change took him violently, as if angry at being held down so long, and his conscious mind was shoved out of the way with force. It was like blacking out, except his body kept moving without him. When he came to, he was in his wolf form and running through the woods, animal exuberance coursing through his altered body.

Chapter 20

Anna kept one hand on the wall of the tunnel, moving forward with shuffling steps through the darkness. Despite the fact that Luca walked confidently at her side, she couldn't help the feeling that at any moment she might walk into a wall or trip over something. The dim light at the cave entrance didn't shine very far inside, and within a few metres the darkness was nearly complete.

'Jason,' Luca said suddenly. 'Go on ahead and tell them to switch the lights on, would you?'

'Sure.' Jason moved past them like a shadow and disappeared. Anna slowed her pace still further, waiting for the expected illumination.

'It's just a little way ahead,' Luca told her. 'There's a bend about ten paces in front of you, and then another just after that. Then we're there.'

'Okay.' Anna closed her eyes for a moment, steadying herself. 'And where is "there" exactly?'

'Our home. It's too difficult and dangerous to build homes above the ground – we can never be completely assured that they'll be totally daylight-proof. So we went underground instead.'

Anna walked forward. Her guiding hand found that the tunnel did indeed turn to the right, and she followed it round. As she did so, she saw up ahead a faint glow of light, coming from around a second corner. She walked forward more confidently, anxious to get out of the darkness.

They came around the second corner and Anna saw where the light was coming from.

The tunnel ended about ten feet in front of where they now stood, opening out into a vast cavern. The floor sloped downwards then levelled out, and the walls swept up and outwards to a distance that was beyond the reach of the meagre light. On the flat plateau below, a dozen houses faced them in a semicircle. Behind those stood more buildings, stretching out nearly as far as the distant wall. Some of the furthest away seemed to be in a state of ruin, but it was difficult to tell from where Anna stood. Certainly, the ones nearest to her looked to be in good condition. They were all of a single storey and flat roofed, with narrow, slit-like windows and heavy wooden doors. From several of the thin windows came the glimmer of electrical light, and one of the nearest had a stubby chimney from which issued a thin trail of white smoke. Anna wondered if these lights were powered by solar generators as well, kept outside on the mountainside. It would be ironic if they were.

The main light was coming from what looked like an oversized street-lamp, its top fashioned into a stylised point like a glass blade. It glowed pale orange and illuminated the figures standing below.

There were five of them, two women and three men, one of them Jason. They stood there like a silent welcome party, their pale skin almost luminous in the dim light.

One of them, a tall man with blond hair that was so pale as to appear almost golden, spoke first. 'Luca.' His voice was incongruously deep, and held a Scandinavian accent. 'You're supposed to warn us if you're going to be bringing anyone back.'

'I didn't know if she'd come.' Luca put his hand on Anna's arm to guide her forward. 'This is Anna Martin – you might remember her father came up here recently.' One of the women nodded, smiling a little. The other woman was watching Anna as if something about her was deeply puzzling. 'Anna, this is Tyr.'

The blond vampire smiled and raised a hand in greeting. Anna caught her breath. His right arm was twisted round so that the elbow stuck out strangely and the hand faced the wrong way.

'Frances and Rebecca,' Luca said, indicating the two women.

Rebecca was the one who had smiled. She had black hair shoulder-length hair with a slight kink in it that made it flick up at the ends. Her eyes were incredibly green, as if a child had coloured them in with primary paint. The second woman was shorter and had a rounder face, and her dark, curly hair was cut very short.

'And Kristoff.'

The other man inclined his head towards them, a little sullenly. He hung back from the others, his arms folded across his wide chest, staying out of the light as much as possible.

Anna raised her hand tentatively. 'Hi,' she said.

'There're usually more of us here,' Luca told her. 'The others are all out hunting at the moment.'

Despite the fact that she was trying to take in all the details around her at once, Anna caught that one word. 'Hunting?' she asked.

'Not humans,' Luca said with a smile. 'Don't worry. There are plenty of animals out in the forest – we feed off them.'

Tyr shrugged. 'Mostly.'

Luca gave him an irritated look, which was ignored.

'Hasn't Doctor Ehren told you about the arrangement we've got with him?' the blond vampire asked Anna.

'She's not one of his workers,' Luca put in. 'And she only arrived today. Doctor Ehren hasn't even told her of our existence yet.'

'What arrangement?' Anna asked, looking between Luca and Tyr.

'Have you wondered why we're here?' Tyr asked her. 'It doesn't make much sense, right? Considering that Doctor Ehren and the others have only been here for a short while.'

'This is… some kind of homeland for you.' Anna glanced at Luca for confirmation.

'That's true.' Tyr came a few steps closer, folding his arms with the twisted one lying on top, palm up. 'The first vampires who ever lived were born here, and many of us made the return journey for that reason alone. But there's another reason to stay – it's an escape. An escape from humans, and from the constant temptation to feed on them. Here, up until recently, there was no option but to feed on animals.' He smiled, showing the points of his teeth. 'It's a nice change.'

Luca took up the story. 'When Doctor Ehren came here he made a deal with us – we help him with his research, and in return he provides us with willing volunteers to drink from.'

Without meaning to, Anna shuddered.

'It's not so bad,' Tyr said with a shrug. 'The option is there for us if we ever want to take it. It's like occasionally going out for a special meal, rather than eating at home all the time. But some of us still choose to feed exclusively on animals while we're here.'

Anna looked over the assembled vampires, the question obvious in her eyes.

Smiling, Tyr raised his hand in acknowledgement. The female vampire, Frances, did the same. None of the others moved.

'We should go inside and sit down,' Luca said smoothly, guiding Anna forward towards the nearest lit building. The others stepped aside as they approached.

Anna cast a glance backwards at Tyr. 'What happened to his arm?' she asked in a whisper.

Luca opened the door to the building and held it for her. She didn't realise that Tyr had moved up behind her.

'It was a gift,' the blond vampire told her. 'From my last master.'

Anna flushed and started to apologise.

'It's okay. I have good hearing.' Tyr led the way through the door into a large room. The walls were all painted white, and mismatched chairs were placed around a large wooden table. There was an arched stone fireplace in the far wall, and a fire burning comfortingly in the hearth.

'This is kind of a reception building,' Luca explained. 'For the times when we have visitors. Sorry it's not more welcoming.'

'It's fine,' Anna said, her eyes on the fire. She'd almost forgotten how cold she was. Smiling at the others, she picked up one of the chairs and sat down close to the blaze. The other vampires came filing in.

Tyr approached, bringing another chair and placing it opposite her. Without meaning to, Anna found herself staring at his arm again. The vampire noticed but smiled very slightly. 'It happened about twenty years ago,' he told her. 'Back in Oslo. Our master there was very old, and he… well, age and power did some strange things to his head.' He sat down, leaning forward to talk to her as if the others weren't there. 'It got to the point where me and the rest decided to confront him about it. Except, when it came to the time, I found that the rest had suddenly backed down about halfway through. The master took it all out on me, and broke my arm.'

Anna frowned. 'I'm not being rude but… don't you heal that sort of thing?'

'I did heal, that was the problem. He pinned me on the ground and twisted my broken arm round so that the bones were misaligned. Then he held me like that until they healed… except it was all in the wrong place by then.' He sat back, flexing the twisted arm out in front of him. 'I guess I could fix it, if I really wanted to break it again and move it back… but it doesn't hurt now and you kinda get used to these things.'

'So… how long have you been here?'

Tyr shrugged. 'I left Oslo that night. I met a couple of others, and they convinced me to come here. This has been my home since then.'

'What was it like, before Ehren and the others arrived?'

'Peaceful. Like a detox farm for the monsters.' He grinned up at the other vampires, who laughed. 'There were no humans; just us and the wolves and a few of the dead ones. More animal life than you can imagine as well – which was good news for us, unless we fancied going after the wolves for food.'

Kristoff laughed shortly. 'Fuck that for a game of soldiers.' It was the first time he'd spoken, and Anna was surprised to find that he had an American accent.

'Yeah,' Tyr agreed, smiling. 'But the animals aren't exactly a push-over either. Have you seen any of them yet?' he asked Anna.

She shook her head.

'There's something messed up about this place. It just seems to breed monsters. They multiply like crazy, which is why there's so much life here. Anything that lives or grows on the island – ' He made a vague gesture with his twisted right hand. ' – Evolution has gone nuts. Hey, Luca.' He turned in his seat to look for the other vampire, who had remained near the door and was watching the exchange with an unreadable expression on his smooth face. 'This girl's your guest – you should be the one doing the talking.'

'You seem to be doing just fine, Tyr.'

'Yeah, well. I'm tired now, it's your turn. Get in the hot seat and entertain your guest, Mister Leader Man.'

Anna watched the two vampires as they exchanged seats. The words were light in tone, and Tyr was still grinning broadly enough to show his teeth, but there was a certain tenseness in their movements and in Luca's face that suggested it wasn't all as friendly as it seemed.

A quick glance at the others confirmed it. They were all watching Tyr and Luca just as closely as she was.

Chapter 21

Despite the fact that she was in the most unusual situation of her life, Anna was finding it increasingly difficult to keep her eyes open. The warmth of the fire, plus the long and stressful nature of the day she'd just had were conspiring against her, and she was beginning to have problems keeping her attention on what Luca was saying. He'd been talking for some time now, with occasional unasked-for interruptions from Tyr, but Anna was frequently losing track.

When she unsuccessfully stifled her third yawn, Luca paused in what he was saying.

'I'm sorry,' he smiled. 'I forget that it's very late for you.'

'It's okay – it's just been a long day. In fact, it's been a long couple of weeks. We've been travelling for a long time, and we've been kinda short of sleep recently.' She smiled. 'But I am listening, honest.'

'It might be an idea to carry this on some other night.' Luca got to his feet, moving his chair back to its original position. 'We'll drive you back into the camp. Maybe you can speak to Doctor Ehren tomorrow morning and ask him about us – perhaps make the next visit official.' He smiled again. 'How long are you planning to stay on the island?'

'I... don't know; I'd not really thought about that part of it. I was assuming that my father would be here and we'd take things from there...' She trailed off.

'Well, the boat usually comes here once a week,' Luca said, covering the moment, 'but it makes an extra visit directly after the full moon. Just in case there's been any, ah, incidents or anything. So that'll be the day after tomorrow, and then the next one should be four or five days after that. Again, you'll have to double-check that with Doctor Ehren.'

Anna stood up as well. 'Thanks for letting me come up here,' she said to the others. 'It was great meeting you all.' It sounded like an incredibly inane thing to say, but she couldn't think of anything else.

They didn't seem to mind. Tyr got up and shook hands – left-handed – with her. 'You too,' he grinned. 'Y'all come back now, y'hear?'

'Sure.' Anna said goodbye to the others as well, although one of them, Kristoff, had disappeared at some point.

Jason was waiting by the door. 'You want me to drive?' he asked Luca.

'It's okay, I'll do it.'

Jason gave him a cynical look.

'Hey, I've been driving since before you were born,' Luca told him.

Tyr laughed loudly. 'Yeah, you were a personal friend of Henry Ford, weren't you?'

'I'll be back in an hour,' Luca said, irritably. 'Think you can keep an eye on things, Tyr?'

The blond vampire gave him a mock salute with his twisted right hand.

Anna followed Luca out of the building and across the open ground to the tunnel that led back to the surface. From this side she realised that there were huge wooden doors set at the entrance to the tunnel, which were currently pushed back against the walls but could obviously be closed to completely seal the entrance. She asked Luca about them, and he told her that they were closed during daylight hours, 'just in case'.

When they got to the jeep, Luca took the driver's seat and Anna climbed in beside him. She kept her doubts about his driving to herself. If he felt confident enough to navigate the twisting road back to the camp, then she would trust him. She briefly tried to work out what decade it must have been when Luca had been alive and learning to drive, but the thought disturbed her so she put it out of her mind.

Luca turned the jeep around in a very small space and headed back down the mountain.

'So, what did you mean earlier?' Anna asked.

'What did I mean about what?'

'You were saying… that you were an "accident" or something.'

'Oh yes.' Luca smiled. He was driving at a slower speed than Jason had done on the way up, but with just as much confidence. 'Actually, that's an overly dramatic way of putting it, I guess.'

'What happened?'

Luca was silent for a moment, frowning as if trying to collect his thoughts. 'It didn't make any sense at the time,' he said at last. 'For most of us, when it happens, there's some kind of preparation… or at the very least you're told what's happening to you. I was changed unintentionally, so there was no preparation or warning or anything.'

'But you were saying that for someone to be… changed… they have to –'

'Have their lifeblood almost completely drained, and then on the point of death to have the blood replaced by that of the attacker. It's a difficult thing to do by accident, but I managed it.' He flashed her another grin. 'Unintentionally on both our parts.'

'How?'

'I was young when it happened, and very drunk. Me and some of my friends were out celebrating, and at some point I managed to lose the rest of them. We were in a strange town and I was lost, and this woman stopped me in the street and offered to help me. Since I wasn't in any state to say no, I followed her. After that there's a period of blankness in my mind; I've never been able to retrieve it, and I've given up trying. Anyway, I passed out at some point and woke up in a bedroom somewhere with the woman's teeth in my neck.'

'That can't have been good.'

'No, it was quite a long way from good.' Luca's tone was still light, but Anna couldn't see his expression. 'I panicked – understandably, I suppose. I tried to throw her off, but she was a lot stronger than I was and she wasn't about to let go. So I grabbed the nearest thing to hand – which turned out to be a wine glass next to the bed – and hit her with it. It shattered and cut my hand but did the woman absolutely no harm, so I tried again, aiming at her throat with the broken glass. This time I managed to cut her open, and she let go of me in a hurry.

'But I had hold of her hair, and then it was *me* holding *her* down. I've no idea where I got the strength from, or what was going on in my head, but some kind of mad rationalisation hit me. All I could think of were the mosquitoes that I'd been subjected to during my time in Africa, during the war. That's how I saw her in that moment – filled with blood, but all of it mine. So when I cut her throat my first thought was, *that's my blood, not hers.* I clung to her and wouldn't let her escape, and did the only thing I could think of – I put my mouth over the wound and tried to take back the blood I'd lost.'

Anna shuddered, and hoped he didn't see it. 'Did you realise that...?'

'No.' Luca shook his head. 'I had no idea that she was a vampire, or that I was doing the one thing that would save my life. It was just some crazed instinct.' He sighed then. 'I didn't let go of her until the sun started to come up. That was very nearly the end of both of us. I still didn't know what was happening, but the first light of dawn started to burn me, so I ran out of there and down the stairs. I was fortunate enough that the building had a basement, and I was able to find the door. The woman was so weak that she couldn't move, and the sun burnt her up. When I woke up the following evening in my newly changed state I came back upstairs and found that her body and the bed she'd been lying on had been burnt to ashes. I've never been able to find out who she was, and if she told me her name then I can't remember it.'

They were back down among the trees now, driving along the uneven dirt track. Luca lapsed into silence and Anna didn't question him any further, so they drove through the black forest without any more conversation.

Once they got back to the point near to the fence, Luca parked the jeep and shut off the engine. They repeated their trek through the woods and the dizzying double-leap over the fence and back up to the balcony of Anna's room. By now Anna's legs were beginning to shake from exhaustion, and she wanted nothing more than to crawl back into bed and stay there for the rest of her life.

'I hope you sleep well.' Luca smiled at her. 'You've seen a lot today – I hope none of it will trouble your dreams.'

Anna shook her head. 'I don't think there's much chance of that, I think I'm too tired for dreaming.' The thought made her glance into her room, remembering the dream she'd had that afternoon on the boat. 'I hope so, anyway.'

'You have nightmares?'

'No, just…' She shook her head. 'It doesn't matter. You don't want to hear about stuff like that anyway.'

'No? It's the one thing I do like hearing about.'

'Really? Why?'

Luca shrugged. 'I don't have any of my own any more.'

'You don't dream at all?' Anna asked in surprise.

'I don't think any vampire does.' Luca's dark eyes were distant and impossible to read. 'At least, not any of the ones I've ever known. Maybe it's one of the side-effects of being dead.' He smiled then. 'Anyway, that's something else we can discuss at another time. You sleep well, Miss Martin.'

'You too… Luca.' It was the first time she'd used his name, and it made her smile. 'Good night.'

'Till we meet again.' Luca bowed to her with mock theatricality, then vaulted neatly over the balcony and dropped to the ground.

Anna watched as he walked unconcernedly back towards the fence, then she turned away and slid open the door to her room. It felt like a lifetime since she'd left the small room, but she guessed that it must only have been a couple of hours.

It was only when she got back inside that she realised someone was knocking at her door.

Chapter 22

Just after midnight, Mike went downstairs and out of the front door of the accommodation block. He'd been standing out on the balcony of his room for the previous half an hour or so and had finally got fed up of being able to see nothing from there but featureless black forest. He could still hear movement around the camp, although the gate had not opened again, so there were obviously things still happening. It had begun to bug him more and more that he couldn't see what was going on.

As he walked downstairs, he half expected the front door to be locked, but apparently Ehren hadn't wanted to start ignoring basic fire safety for the sake of security. Mike stepped outside into the cool night air, pausing to take a look around. The camp was brightly illuminated by ground level lights around each of the buildings and along all the sections of roadway, although the area beyond the buildings leading down to the sea was in darkness. The moon was still hidden behind the thick clouds and no light shone down on the surface of the ocean. Mike could just about hear the sound of the waves on the shingle beach over the noise of the generator. From where he stood, he couldn't see anyone moving around, and the occasional voices he'd heard earlier seemed to have stopped as well.

'Couldn't sleep?'

The voice came from startlingly close by and made Mike jump. He turned to find Ramone standing next to the doorway, leaning casually against the wall with his rifle propped up next to him.

'It takes some getting used to,' the man went on. 'The noise, and the darkness. It took weeks before I settled in enough to be able to sleep at night.'

Mike recovered from his surprise. 'What are you doing out here?'

'Ehren asked me to keep watch.'

Mike glanced around, confirming to himself that there were no guards on any of the other buildings. 'Because of us?' he surmised.

Ramone nodded without a trace of embarrassment. To him it was just a fact. 'He doesn't want you wandering around the camp at night.' He smiled wryly. 'For your own protection, of course.'

'Of course.' Mike considered bargaining with the man to let him take a look around the camp, then decided to remain where he was for the moment. He'd been after a view of the camp that was better than the one from his balcony, and he'd at least managed to achieve that.

He dug in his pocket for his cigarettes, offering them to Ramone. The man took one with a smile. 'Thanks.'

'No problem.' Mike lit his own, then passed the lighter to Ramone. They stood and smoked in silence for a while. 'Are you planning on standing guard all night?' Mike asked at last.

'No. Someone else'll be along in an hour or so to take over. If I'm lucky I might get five hours of sleep before Ehren finds something else for me to do.'

'Tough job. Hope he's paying well.'

Ramone laughed, but avoided the implied question.

'So,' Mike said, trying another tact, 'how did you scientist guys find this place?'

Ramone shrugged. 'Rumours. Stories. Fisherman's tales. As far as I understand it, a few parties came over here years ago to check out what sounded like a really dumb wild goose chase, and found out that this one was actually the real deal. Then the government stepped in kinda fast, took the whole thing over and started sending official investigating parties.' He exhaled blue-grey smoke, watching the breeze tug it away. 'All I've heard is rumours from that time, but apparently at least one of those parties arrived during the wrong phase of the moon and almost got itself wiped out by the wolves. Everything came close to going balls-up at that point – the government was this close to just sending the army in and wiping the island clean of all its inhabitants. It was Brac who stepped in and prevented that.'

'Brac?' Mike remembered the grey-haired man with the creased shirt and the irritable disposition. 'Why him?'

'He'd lived here in the past.' Ramone smiled, almost to himself. 'At the time this all happened, he was working as a senior executive in a hospital – up in Wales, I believe. He got to hear about what was going on and used his connections to intervene.'

'Wait.' Mike was frowning. 'Brac used to live here, before the rest of you guys came over? What was he doing here?'

'Living up in the village with the rest of the wolves, I imagine.'

Mike's eyes widened. 'He's a werewolf?'

Ramone looked at him, then burst out laughing. 'Oh man, Ehren is *really* intent on keeping you in the dark. Y'know, I've always said that we should make name-tags for everyone with name and species on them...'

'I had no idea.' Mike shook his head. 'Jesus, how many others have we met today?'

'I don't know, I don't know who you've been introduced to. But there are about eight wolves currently working here, and you've met at least two of them – Seth and Brac.'

'Seth I knew about.' Distractedly, Mike finished his cigarette and flicked the end away. 'Wow. So, you say that Brac was working in management before he came here? Didn't that kinda throw everyone a bit, finding out that their senior exec was a werewolf?'

'Yeah, well, no-one got to find out about it. He was tactfully transferred out and offered a job over here… on the grounds that he could persuade the island inhabitants to peacefully coexist with us human types.'

Something else occurred to Mike. 'Wait – he was working at a *hospital?* For how long?'

'Dunno. Ten or fifteen years, I think.'

'But… did no-one notice this? I mean, the guy goes hairy once a month… that's the sort of thing that gets noticed. Even in Wales.'

'I assume he kept out of sight at those times. There're plenty of others that manage it.'

'Oh my God, how many others? You mean there's werewolves all over the place?'

'Maybe not all over, but yeah.' Ramone was grinning again. 'You're looking a little freaked out by this.'

Mike wasn't so much freaked out as he was mentally kicking himself for all the times he'd passed up on stories about escaped big cats allegedly roaming the moors. How many of those mysterious sightings had actually been down to werewolves? It would certainly explain why there was no trace of the 'cats' in the morning – they'd gone back to their civil service jobs. Mike could have made his fortune years ago.

'This is crazy,' he muttered. 'I'm not big on conspiracy theories, but this one's going to take some beating. How the hell has this place managed to stay secret?'

'It's not that secret – you managed to find your way here.'

'Yeah, but only because Anna was specifically invited. And even then it was bloody difficult to find. There's an island thirty miles south of here that swears blind this place doesn't exist – it's not on any maps or charts or anything. I know because we got stuck there for four days.'

Ramone shrugged again but didn't answer.

'Aw, hell,' Mike said at last. 'This is too much for me. I going to go to bed and hope it all makes more sense in the morning.' He turned back towards the door. 'Are we likely to get more surprises tomorrow? Anything we should know about in advance?'

'Not that I can think of.' Ramone waited until the man was halfway through the door before adding: 'Apart from the vampires, of course.'

Mike stopped, took two steps backwards and let the door swing shut again. 'What?' he asked.

Ramone grinned broadly at him. 'You got more cigarettes?'

* * *

Some time later, Mike was on his way back to his room, walking slowly as if the weight of the information he'd just learnt was slowing him down. He hesitated as he passed Anna's room, wondering if she was still awake. If she was, this was the sort of thing she needed to know about.

He knocked on her door quietly, but got no reply. She was probably fast asleep by now... Mike checked his watch and saw that it was after one o'clock in the morning. But there was no way he could go back to his room and sleep, not after what he'd just been told...

He knocked louder, pausing to lean his ear against the door. There was no sound from within, so he tried a third time.

He stood out there for nearly five minutes, by which time he'd decided that maybe Anna wasn't easily woken, but other people on the floor might be, and would soon be coming out of their rooms to find out what the goddamn noise was for. He was about to give up when he heard footsteps inside the room.

To his surprise, when Anna opened the door she was still fully dressed, and her brown hair looked messy and windswept. She didn't look like she'd slept either – more like she'd been stood out on the balcony since he'd last seen her.

Mike pushed that aside for the moment. 'Anna, I need to talk to you.'

'Obviously. What the hell's the matter?'

'I just found out something.' He took a deep breath. 'There are vampires on this island.'

To his immense surprise, she burst out laughing. 'Is that so? My goodness, you'd better come in and tell me all about it.'

Chapter 23

When Seth woke up, he was lying on his back staring up at the night sky. He could only see it in patches, broken up by black tree branches that moved a little in the wind. The air was cold and the ground beneath his naked body was even colder, but he was reluctant to move. Those first few moments of waking up after a night out triggered mixed emotions: he knew that he had to get up, and he also knew that it was going to hurt like hell when he did so.

He stretched out his arms and legs, feeling the familiar ache in his muscles. He always promised himself that he would remember to do at least a few stretching exercises before he next changed, but in the event he always forgot or didn't have time. Besides, the walk back to the enclosure would hopefully ease some of the kinks out of his sore limbs.

The thought made him sit up and look around as he tried to work out where he was. He hoped he hadn't run too far from the enclosure, since naked night time walks in the woods was not actually one of his favourite pastimes. Trees stretched out around him as far as he could see, and he couldn't immediately place where he was. Standing up, he saw a glimpse of the dark mountains off to his left between the trees. They were still some distance away, which meant that he probably hadn't run too far.

Seth stretched again, feeling the familiar tired contentment that always came after a change. If he hadn't had important work to do then he would have been quite happy to just remain where he was and rest for a good long while.

He started walking, heading south and trusting to his instincts that he was going in the right direction. The skies had cleared a bit, but the moon had long since set, so it was still pitch black beneath the trees. It didn't bother Seth too much, since even when in human form his night vision was excellent. However, the broken ground made for slow going and he became increasingly aware of how quickly the night was passing.

Eventually he saw the lights of the enclosure fence up ahead, and pushed his way through the last of the bushes. The jeep was parked where he'd left it, and lying on the ground a short distance away was his pile of clothing. He noted with irritation that the three-dozen zombies behind the fence were also exactly where he'd left them, crowded around the fallen corpse. Several of them looked up as Seth strode across the open ground.

Quickly getting dressed, Seth surveyed the walking dead gathered in front of him. They had all shuffled forward now, pressing up against the chain-link fence, and obscuring his view of Ciaran's body. Seth knew that he had to get in there and remove the dead vampire's body, since an unmoving corpse within the enclosure would attract more attention than a moving one. He had been hoping that the zombies would have wandered off somewhere else by now, but once again they'd proved themselves to be completely awkward and unpredictable.

Seth walked along the fence, circling the Portacabins and following the fence onwards for another couple of hundred yards. The dead ones slowly followed him, the more alert ones as usual leading the pack. Seth stopped walking and waited until they had all amassed in front of him, pushing and shoving in their desperation to break through the fence and reach the living flesh on the other side. Then he quickly ran back to his original position.

It had taken the dead ones approximately three minutes to follow him that distance along the fence, so Seth was counting on them taking another three minutes to get back. He would have to move fast, but it should be possible to get in and out of the enclosure in that time.

He quickly snatched up the thick rubber gloves that he had dropped earlier, then scaled the fence. The chain link was easy to grip on to, and he was at the top and then over in a matter of seconds. He dropped to the ground next to Ciaran's inert body.

Seth was careful to glance round and make absolutely sure that there were no zombies lurking unseen anywhere close to him. The last thing he needed right at that moment was a nasty undead surprise. But the only dead ones he could see were the ones grouped together along the fence, who were slowly shuffling their way back towards him. From this side of the fence they looked a hell of a lot closer than they had done before, but Seth put his head down and attempted to ignore them. He told himself that he had plenty of time.

Ciaran's corpse had been torn apart by the zombies, the flesh ripped open all the way down his front and most of his internal organs pulled out and consumed. Seth pulled on the rubber gloves and made a quick check of the internal cavity, making absolutely sure of one thing: that the heart was gone. More effective than a stake, a zombie's teeth had destroyed the vampire's heart completely, and Ciaran was definitely dead. Seth breathed a little easier once he'd made sure of that.

The skin of the face had been partially ripped away, exposing the skull beneath, and one of the eyes was punctured and hung empty like a burst grape. The other eye stared unseeingly up at the night sky. The lips were drawn right back over the teeth in a death grimace that testified to the pain the vampire had suffered in his last moments.

Seth was more concerned at that moment with the arms. When he tried to lift the corpse the mutilated limbs flopped about dangerously, and he shied away from the silver bars that still pinned the wrists and ankles. He dropped the body, realising that there was too much of a risk of accidentally impaling himself on one of the toxic spikes. They had to be removed.

He glanced up quickly. The zombies were still some distance away, moving slowly but steadily in his direction. Seth felt his heart speed up, but forced himself to concentrate on the task in hand. Nothing like a bit of pressure to focus the mind.

His hands shook as he took hold of the first silver bar.

By the time he had removed both of the bars and shoved them quickly back through the chain link fence, the zombies were within fifty yards of him. He almost panicked when one of the spikes snagged going through the fence, and he came within an inch of slicing himself open with the sharpened end. He closed his eyes and drew in a deep, deliberate breath. He had time. There was no need to panic. If it had to, he could always climb back over the fence on his own and lead the zombies away again to buy himself a few more minutes.

With Ciaran's arms and legs free, it was easy for Seth to lift the corpse up and sling it over his shoulder. It weighed a lot less than before, probably because it was now missing most of its insides.

A quick glance told Seth that the zombies were still a good distance away. *Home free*, he grinned to himself.

He had one hand on the chain link fence when he heard the car approaching.

He froze. The noise was coming from not far down the track, and it was definitely headed towards the enclosure. Seth gripped the fence convulsively, his heart skittering within his chest. *Who the hell was coming here at this time of the night?*

He spun round, the weight of the corpse almost unbalancing him. There was nowhere he could hide. He could run to the other side of the enclosure, but that would mean trusting to luck that there weren't any of the dead ones hiding in the shadows there. And besides all that, his jeep would still be parked there, apparently abandoned and definitely suspicious.

Seth's mind scrambled for other options. There was only one that he could think of.

It'll only be one or two people – there's no reason for more than that to be coming out here during the night. It'll only take a second. You've got those metal spikes. There's no-one within ten miles of here that'd hear anything.

His mind seemed to clear instantly, the panic being replaced by smooth, soft calmness. *No problem at all.* He lowered Ciaran's body to the ground, checking to make sure that the zombies were still a safe distance away.

The engine noise was closer now, and as Seth watched he saw the gleam of headlights rounding the corner. He laid the body down and started to stand up.

Just as the headlights washed over him, the dead vampire's hand shot out and grabbed hold of Seth's arm.

Chapter 24

It wasn't like waking up. He opened his eyes to find that the nightmare he was trapped in extended beyond sleep and into the waking world.

The sky and the earth were little more than black and red streaks across his vision. His hands were numb. His whole body was numb. When he tried to lift his arm the muscles felt so stiff that they almost snapped with the effort. Pain edged at his mind, cold and diffuse and as sourceless as it was universal.

Ciaran stared at the night sky and blinked slowly. His black-and-red streaked sight only extended to his left eye – in the other there was only black.

He felt cold but didn't know why. He couldn't work out where he was any more than he could understand how he'd got there. The cold seemed to flow through him like a breeze, touching bits inside his body that it shouldn't have been able to reach. His face felt patchy, as if some spots were cold, others were completely numb, and some were on fire.

The one thing he was sure of was the hunger. It burned through him more completely than the numbing pain or cold, overriding all his other senses. He had never felt it this strongly, not ever.

He could sense something warm and living close by, even though he couldn't see it properly. He managed to turn his head a fraction of an inch and saw the vague outline of a human shape crouched over him. Its features were blurred and unfocused in Ciaran's vision, the eyes little more than smears of red and white against the blackness of its face. But it was alive... and it was food.

Ciaran shot out his hand and grabbed the living shape, closing his fingers around its arm. His muscles didn't seem to respond the way they should have done; it felt almost like controlling someone else's motions. But Ciaran couldn't focus on that thought. All he knew was the hunger.

The thing in his grasp yelled in surprise and tried to jerk away, but Ciaran kept hold of its arm. His fingers had locked and he probably couldn't have let go if he'd wanted to, but his strength was still there. He dragged himself into a sitting position, feeling the coldness slide over and through his insides as he did so. His other hand managed to latch onto the arm of the squirming creature and pull it towards him.

Abruptly his vision cleared a little, as if someone had been shining a bright light into his eyes and had now taken it away. Although it was now darker, the red streaks in his vision faded and became true colours and shapes, and for the first time he was able to focus on the man he was holding on to. Dim recognition flashed through his brain, but not strong enough for him to work out who it was. It didn't matter anyway – as far as he was concerned, the person was no more than desperately needed food.

Something struck Ciaran around the head – probably the man's free hand – but he barely felt it and it didn't stop him for an instant. He yanked the captured arm towards him and sank his teeth deep into the flesh just below the elbow. His fangs missed the main vein, but blood spurted into his mouth regardless. The warmth of the fluid felt like burning in his throat.

In his moment of victory, Ciaran was completely deaf to the screams of the man. He didn't feel the blows that were being aimed at his head, despite their strength. He tugged his head backwards and was rewarded by a chunk of flesh tearing loose between his teeth. A very small part of his mind insisted that his body couldn't accept solid food, but it was overridden by the hunger. Ciaran swallowed, tasting his first solid meal since he'd become a vampire.

Then he lost his grip on his food-source and it escaped from him, staggering backwards across the ground.

Ciaran could see properly now, almost as if the small amount of warm flesh had revived him. His vision was limited and his right side was still in darkness, but he could see the outline of the man as he stumbled away, clutching at his bleeding arm. He could see the panic on his face, the wideness of his eyes, and again something tugged at him; a vague recognition that wouldn't be pinned down.

'...sssssss...' Ciaran's voice managed the sibilance but nothing more. His throat felt as harsh and damaged as the rest of him.

More shapes were moving around him now, but he recognised them as nothing more than walking corpses. They were of no interest to him. The briefest edge of an idea touched his mind, telling him that the corpses were to be feared and avoided, but that made no sense to Ciaran now. He ignored it. The only thing that mattered to him was the still-living flesh, and his attention was fixed on the man in front of him.

The man with the bleeding arm finally turned and ran, sprinting across the enclosure away from the fence. Ciaran struggled to his feet and tried to follow, but his muscles didn't want to respond. He managed two difficult, staggering steps then fell back to his knees. As he stared at the quickly retreating figure and tasted angry defeat, it dawned on him for the first time that there was something badly wrong with his body.

The thought came and went as elusively as the others, and he was unable to work out exactly what was wrong or how things were supposed to be.

Abruptly, his head snapped up. One food source had escaped him, but there was another very close by.

Uncaring of the pain that shot through his leg muscles, Ciaran got to his feet again and turned to face the fence.

There was a jeep parked not far away, its headlights on and shining into the enclosure. It was at an angle to where Ciaran was standing, which was why he was able to see it without the direct light making his vision flare and distort again. He could hear the engine idling, the noise like a beacon drawing his attention even more than the light. And in front of the jeep stood another human.

This face was familiar as well, although less so than that of the first man. A name floated through Ciaran's scrambled mind then drifted away again: another irrelevancy. Ciaran staggered forward, hands reaching out hungrily towards the man.

He was brought up short by the fence. His fingers caught around the chainlink and gripped it with blind instinct, but he couldn't move forward any further. All around him dead bodies were pushing forward as well, shoving him against the fence and pinning him there.

The food was right there, right in front of him, and yet he couldn't reach it. Ciaran tried to scream his frustration, and nothing came out except a hiss of air.

The living man walked towards him, keeping a safe distance from the fence. He seemed to be looking at something, but Ciaran didn't care what it was. The dead vampire gripped the fence tighter, feeling the wire digging into the unresponsive flesh of his fingers.

After a few moments, the man turned away and walked quickly to the jeep. The wheels spun as he turned it around and took off back the way he'd come. Within a minute, the jeep had disappeared around a bend in the road and was gone.

Ciaran closed his one functioning eye, feeling anger and frustration that did nothing to displace the deep, overwhelming hunger inside him. If he didn't feed, he was going to go crazy. His mouth still tasted of blood, but it wasn't enough. He needed more.

He gripped the wire fence so tightly that two of the chainlinks snapped under the pressure.

The other walking dead had backed off now, apparently realising that the chance of food had passed and was now out of their reach. Ciaran remained by the fence, aware of something more than just the hunger now. The fence that blocked his way wasn't that strong, not really. He knew that he was strong – something in his mind told him that there was no way a flimsy section of wire fencing like this could hold him back. There was something wrong with his body, even if he couldn't yet figure out what it was, but he knew that not everything had been taken away from him.

He flexed his fingers experimentally, watching the way they spasmed and almost refused to move as he wanted them to. Then he took hold of the fence again and tightened his grasp.

It hurt this time – a dead sort of pain, like someone squeezing his hand firmly – and he saw the wire cutting deeply into the flesh of his fingers. No blood leaked from the cuts, and the pain was far from unbearable. Ciaran tugged hard and felt a section of the wire tear loose.

With a grim determination that only the dead could have, he pulled at the fence until he had ripped open a section large enough to let him out. Then he forced his stiff leg muscles into action and climbed awkwardly through the fence, ignoring the sharp ends of torn metal that gouged at his skin.

The jeep had disappeared along the dirt track. If Ciaran wanted to find food, then he would have to follow it.

He set off at a slow, steady pace, his one eye fixed on the road ahead. He did not notice or care when the other dead ones slowly began to follow him through the gap in the fence.

DAY TWO

Chapter 25

'Look, I'm just telling you what I saw. Someone was in the enclosure, and he was messing about with one of the alert dead. When he saw me he ran off, but I think the dead one might have bitten him.'

Ehren rubbed at the side of his face with one hand. He couldn't hide the fact that he would rather not have had his sleep disturbed with this news. 'When did you see this happen?' he asked.

'About forty minutes ago. I wouldn't have woken you up if I didn't think it was important.'

'I understand that, but I'm wondering why exactly you were down at the enclosure at this time of night, Ramone.'

The dark-haired man frowned in irritation. 'I couldn't sleep so I went out for a drive. I don't think that's really the issue right now, Doctor Ehren…'

Ehren held up a hand in a placating gesture. 'Alright. So you think you saw someone – '

'No, I don't *think* I saw someone. I saw a man – he looked like he was fighting with one of the dead ones.'

'Did you recognise him?'

Ramone shook his head. 'It was too dark. And he'd run off by the time I got out of the car.'

'But you think he got bitten?'

'I think so. I certainly heard him yell, so I assumed that's what happened.'

Ehren nodded, stifling a yawn. He could understand the man's agitation, but he was also of the opinion that the problem could have waited until a more sociable hour. He would definitely have been a lot happier if Ramone hadn't called him out of his quarters to talk. The hallway of the accommodation block was not the warmest place in the world, and Ehren was beginning to wish that he'd taken the time to put on some shoes before leaving his room.

'Something else,' Ramone added. 'There was a jeep parked off the road, right next to the fence. It looks a lot like someone drove down there, then climbed the fence.'

'One of our people, you mean. Why would anyone do that?'

'Search me. That's pretty much why I came to tell you about it – it doesn't seem like the sort of thing someone would do just for the hell of it.'

'Alright.' Ehren yawned again, covering it with the back of his hand. 'There's not much we can do about it right now. I'll send someone down as soon as it gets light, okay?'

Ramone was already shaking his head. 'Doctor Ehren, if there's a problem down there, then it needs to be dealt with as quickly as possible. If someone did climb into the enclosure and get bitten, then climbed back out again... I'm not saying that that's what's happened, but it's a possibility. A bad possibility. One infected individual loose on this island...'

'Alright, alright.' Ehren held up his hands. 'I understand the risk of that scenario, Ramone. I'll tell you what I want you to do – go down to the main gate and tell whoever's on duty at the moment to lock up. No-one's allowed in without my clearance. If the person you saw *has* been infected and they try to get back in here, we'll stop them at the gate. Then I want a full head count – who's in town, who's out of town, and who if anyone is missing.'

Ramone nodded shortly, even though he'd still not had any sleep so far that night. 'I still think you should send someone to check it out,' he said.

'And I will. I said I would. Pick a couple of people from the first shift, explain the situation and send them out.' Ehren couldn't resist adding, 'Happy now?'

Ramone didn't trust himself to answer that.

* * *

The first shift of the day started about an hour before sunrise. Ramone turned up, fresh from at least four hours sleep, while the staff of the early shift were having breakfast in the main refectory building. He picked out two people and drew them to one side to explain Ehren's instructions. Then he walked them out to one of the jeeps and made sure that they both had rifles and enough spare ammunition with them.

He watched them drive off through the gate and hoped that the bad feeling in his gut was just his own paranoia.

* * *

The gate was barely closed behind them before Graham started complaining.

'You see what you get for being up early? I swear, that's the last time I try and beat Greg to the coffee machine. Look where it's got me. There should be a law against sending us out this damn early in the morning... actually, there should be a law against this time of the morning even existing, if you ask me...'

Irae Roberts sat in the passenger seat and attempted to ignore him. She was no fan of early mornings either, but she preferred to suffer them in silence rather than attempt to fill them with pointless chatter.

'Shut the hell up, Campbell,' she said eventually, when the silent treatment proved ineffective.

'What the hell's wrong with you? Bad night?'

'It's early and it's cold. Is it too much to ask for a bit of peace and quiet?'

Graham took his eyes off the road ahead long enough to sneak a look at her. Even accounting for her usual grouchy state, she seemed particularly uncommunicative today. 'Seriously, Roberts, what's up with you?' he asked in a more concerned tone. 'You don't look great.'

'Oh, thank you.'

'No, really. You didn't have another fight with your little undead boyfriend, did you?'

Irae glared at him. She should have known that his apparent sympathy was just a mask for another cheap dig. 'None of your goddamn business,' she snapped.

'Sorry, I didn't mean that in a bad way.'

'Like hell.' Irae folded her arms, staring out at the silent trees as they drove through the forest. The sky overhead was just beginning to lighten, but in amongst the trees it may as well still have been the middle of the night. Anyway, we didn't even get a chance to argue. He stood me up.'

'Seriously?'

'Yeah. He was supposed to be coming into town to help Seth and Tris out, but then he never showed up afterwards.'

'Geez. I bet you had tickets to the ballet and everything.'

'Drop dead.'

'Well, I know that's how you like your men…'

'Alright then – go fuck yourself. Is that clear enough?' Irae turned away again, wondering why the hell she'd even spoken about it to Graham. He wasn't exactly the most sympathetic person in the world. Maybe it was just because she was mad at Ciaran for standing her up and needed to talk about it with someone.

It wasn't the first time Ciaran had done it either, but Irae had thought that they were past that sort of thing by now. When she said that she was coming up to the mountains to see him then she always did it, so why the hell couldn't he have kept his promise to come see her last night? Irae sighed and shook her head, trying to rid herself of the thought.

They were about ten minutes drive out from the camp now, just approaching a blind corner where the road made a detour around a shingle covered embankment. 'Y'know what I think?' Graham asked, flashing her a grin.

Even if she'd wanted to know, Irae never got the chance to find out. They came around the corner, Graham driving a little too fast because he was safe in the knowledge that there would be no other traffic on the road at this time of the morning, and struck the person that was standing in the middle of the dirt track.

Irae didn't even see him, only heard Graham's startled shout and caught a glimpse of a figure in a red shirt as the front wing of the jeep struck him. There was a sickening double thud as the man was pulled beneath the wheels, then Graham hit the brakes hard, throwing the jeep into a sideways skid. They came to a halt slewed across the track, the engine stalled, the headlights pointed towards the trees on the left.

'What the fuck – ?' Graham stood up in his seat.

Irae stood up as well, craning to see. The man they'd hit was sprawled on the ground, his left arm twisted at an unnatural angle. Even as she watched though, he twitched and then laboriously sat up.

Her sigh of relief turned immediately into a scream.

'It's one of the dead ones!' Graham was already scrabbling for his rifle, which he'd chucked carelessly on the back seat earlier.

The zombie sat up, its white eyes staring unseeingly at the sky. Its left arm had been the part of it that had gone under the wheels, and now it flopped broken and useless at its side. It seemed to be having a problem getting back to its feet.

Irae broke her paralysis and grabbed for the radio under her seat. Before she managed to lift it even halfway to her mouth, she caught sight of something in her peripheral vision. Her breath locked in her throat.

The road ahead of them was filled with the walking dead. Dozens were coming around the corner out of the darkness, slowly converging on the jeep. More of them appeared from the trees on either side of the road, reaching hungrily towards them.

There was no need for the humans to drive any further – the dead had come out to meet them.

Chapter 26

'Campbell!'

Graham had been concentrating on the injured zombie that they'd run down, lifting his rifle to his shoulder and aiming carefully. When Irae grabbed frantically at him, she knocked his aim off and the shot embedded itself harmlessly in the zombie's shoulder, knocking it back to the ground. 'What?' Graham asked angrily.

Then he saw the others.

There were at least twenty of them closing in on the jeep, and more making their way around the corner. Graham's brain froze for a vital second as he stared at the dead ones, unable to understand how the hell they'd come to be there.

The fence has gone down… God no, the enclosure fence must have gone down…

Irae had dropped the radio and grabbed her own rifle, but her hands shook so much that half the rounds fell to the floor as she tried to load it. 'Get us out of here!' she yelled.

Graham dropped back into the driver's seat and fumbled for the ignition key.

Irae managed to chamber a round, lifting and firing almost blindly into the crowd of zombies that now surrounded them. More by luck than judgement it struck one of them in the face, blowing off the back of its head in a spray of rotting brains. Her next shot hit one of the nearest zombies in the chest, not even slowing it down.

She tried to force down her panic, steadying her hands as best she could. It was almost impossible, since the dead ones were within a few yards of them now.

The engine roared into life and Graham slammed it into gear. Too late he realised that the zombie that had been lying in the road a moment ago had finally got back to its feet and stumbled its way towards them. The first he knew of it was when a cold hand fastened around his wrist and teeth sank into his arm.

Graham screamed and took his foot of the clutch. The jeep lurched forward three feet then stalled again. Irae, still standing, almost tumbled out. She only managed to stay upright because someone grabbed hold of her.

She looked down at her rescuer and screamed. The zombie had half its face missing, the skin having been ripped away and the right eye-socket filled with black clotted blood. It grabbed at her, clutching her arms so tightly that the nails dug deeply into her flesh and brought another scream from her throat.

Even in the middle of her hysterical panic, she recognised who it was.

'Oh God… *Ciaran*…'

There was no mutual recognition in what remained of his face. The only emotions there were pain and hunger in equal measures. He pulled her towards him, mouth opening greedily.

She tried to fight against him but he was as strong now as he had always been. His fingers gripped her tightly and would not be shifted, no matter how much she twisted in his grasp. His searching mouth found her throat and his teeth sunk in.

Irae tried to scream again but her breath locked in her chest. She had felt Ciaran's teeth in her neck before now – a half dozen or more times – but always before it had been welcome, and the pain had always been part of the pleasure. This was nowhere near that sensation. Ciaran's elongated fangs tore through her skin, followed by the rest of his teeth, and it hurt more than anything she'd ever experienced in her life.

She shuddered in his grasp and tried to throw him off, but with his fingers embedded deeply in the muscle of her forearms there was no way for her to escape. Ciaran jerked his head backwards and tore out her throat, arterial blood spraying his face.

Graham survived another thirty seconds, punching the red-shirted zombie in the head until he dislodged its teeth from his arm. He grabbed for the ignition key again, twisting it with blood-covered fingers. The engine fired and he stamped down hard on the accelerator.

The sudden movement caused Irae's body to topple on top of him, almost knocking him from his seat. Pinned down by its weight, he couldn't prevent the car from ploughing forward straight into the trees at the side of the road.

It was a small mercy that the impact knocked him unconscious before the first of the zombies could reach him.

* * *

Ciaran stumbled away from the blood-splattered jeep, his hunger for the moment dulled if not completely sated. He had felt some satisfaction beyond hunger as he'd fed on the woman, but his mind was not intact enough to understand why. Right at that moment his new concern was the lightening sky overhead.

Again, he didn't know why it concerned him, but somewhere deep inside of him alarm bells were ringing, warning him that the sun coming up was a very bad thing. He couldn't stay here, he had to…

Had to… what?

He couldn't remember. He didn't know where he was supposed to go or how he was supposed to avoid the sun. All he knew was that he couldn't be here when it rose.

But equally, there was nowhere for him to go. His mind was too messed up to be able to think of where he would be safe. There was still a bit of time before the sun cleared the horizon, but already the lightening sky was stinging his single eye, causing red and white flashes across his vision and making his flesh feel like he was standing too close to a hot fire.

Ciaran stumbled across the dirt track, instinctively heading for the shelter of the trees. Hidden in the shadows there, he found temporary respite from the light of the pre-dawn sun. The same part of his mind that had triggered the initial warning told him that it wouldn't be enough.

Barely aware of what he was doing, Ciaran dropped to his knees and started to scrabble in the dirt like an animal. His fingers were still numb and unresponsive, and it felt like he was trying to work while wearing thick ski gloves. He cut himself on numerous small stones and sharp ends of twigs, but the cuts did not bleed and Ciaran did not notice. He dug with relative ease through the dirt of the soft forest floor, but by the time he had finished the sun was just touching the horizon and the fierce burning in his desensitised skin had returned. If his vision hadn't been more or less redundant by that point, he would have realised that his whole body was visibly smoking, the top layer of skin being singed away by the heat of incipient daylight.

The trench he had dug looked cool and inviting by comparison. Ciaran collapsed into it, no longer even aware of his actions. Some deep survival instinct caused his hands to keep working, pulling in the sides of the trench on top of him, burying himself in a voluntary grave. The cool earth closed over his head, soothing the burning pain.

If he'd had any breath in his lungs, then Ciaran would have sighed in relief.

Back on the road, oblivious to their leader's departure, the rest of the living dead continued to feast. As the sun came up, their two victims shuddered and reopened their eyes, pushing away the now-uninterested attackers and joining their ranks.

With nothing standing in their way now, the army of the dead continued their slow and stumbling but relentless advance towards the distant camp.

Chapter 27

Mike was woken up by someone knocking on his door. For a few moments, in his half-asleep state, he couldn't work out where he was. He'd woken up in so many different locations during the past few weeks. He stared up at the magnolia ceiling and frowned, wondering why he couldn't just be allowed to rest for once.

The previous night he'd sat in Anna's room and listened as she'd told him exactly where she'd been. He'd felt a distinct pang of jealousy that she'd been off consorting with vampires while he'd been left on his own, smoking on the balcony. He'd relayed the information he'd learnt from Ramone, even though a lot of it was now redundant. Anna had sat back on the bed as he'd talked, watching him pace the room, then had fallen asleep somewhere in the middle of one of his hypotheses. Mike had eventually noticed that his audience was paying even less attention than usual, so he'd thrown a blanket over her and gone back to his own room, muttering to himself about the injustice of missing out on actual real-life goddamn *vampires*.

Whoever was outside the door knocked again, apparently patient enough to keep standing out there despite the evident lack of life inside the room. Mike swung his legs out of bed, groaning as his body objected to being forced into movement.

Smoothing his hair down as best he could, Mike opened the door. He found Ramone standing out there.

'Glad you're awake,' the dark-haired man smiled. He looked far too awake for that time of the morning, Mike reflected sourly. 'Sorry 'bout the early start, but Doctor Ehren is wanting to take you guys up to the village this morning.'

'Gah.' Mike rubbed at his eyes, trying to clear the sleep from them. 'Is the village only open in the mornings or something?'

'Not exactly, but we want to be back here long before dark. Don't forget it's the full moon tonight.'

'Oh. Yeah, forgot about that one.'

'You'd be amazed how many people do.' Ramone smiled again, but he looked distracted, as if something was bothering him. 'Miss Martin's already up – she said she'd wait for you downstairs. If you hurry up there might even be a chance of breakfast before we leave.'

The magic word "breakfast" reminded Mike of how hungry he was. 'Okay, you got me. I'll be down in a minute.'

He shut the door and got dressed quickly. He also washed in the cramped little basin, swearing at some length about the temperature of the water, which might as well have come straight out of the North Sea. Mindful of the chill weather, he pulled on a thick, dark blue jumper. Then he picked up his video camera and the spare battery he'd left to charge overnight. He slipped the battery and an extra tape into the zip pocket of his jacket, then hung the camera on its strap around his neck and was ready.

When he got down to the entrance hall he found Anna waiting for him. Apart from her and Ramone, who was standing just inside the front door, no-one else seemed to be about.

Anna gave him a weak smile as he came down the stairs, but he could tell that she still had a lot on her mind. The short night's sleep didn't seem to have done her much good. There were heavy bags under her eyes, which made her look a lot older than usual, although Mike decided against telling her that.

'How did you sleep?' he asked.

Anna shrugged. 'Can't complain, I guess. It's the first night I've had in an actual bed for ages, so that definitely counts for something.'

'Yeah, now if only we could get some hot water in this place – ' Mike was distracted by the front door opening.

Ehren came in, but was immediately stopped by Ramone, who spoke to him quickly. 'There's still been no word.'

Anna was saying something and Mike pretended to listen to her, but was much more interested in the conversation going on behind his back. Although Ramone had spoken in a low voice, his words were still audible.

'Hmm?' Ehren asked, disinterested.

'From Campbell and Roberts. They've not radioed in since they left.'

'How long ago was that?'

'Nearly two hours now.'

There was a pause while Ehren seemed to be considering. 'It's not a problem,' he said in a decisive tone. 'No news is good news, right?' Before Ramone could answer, Ehren walked away towards where Mike and Anna were standing. He smiled broadly in greeting.

Anna managed to return the smile and politely answer his questions about how well she'd slept. Mike could see a hardness in her eyes. She looked like she was going to want answers to her questions soon. Ehren didn't seem to notice anything wrong.

'We've got another visit to make today,' he announced pleasantly. 'To the werewolf village in the north. Now, we want to get moving pretty quickly, so it'd be best to get your breakfast now...'

He was already leading the way out of the building. Anna fell into step next to Mike and elbowed him in the ribs.

'Ow. What?'

'Were you even listening to me just now?'

'Um... no. Sorry.' Mike spoke quickly before she could get mad at him. 'Have you noticed all the stress-lines today? I'm guessing that no-one had a very good night's sleep.'

'That's a shame.' Anna's eyes glittered. 'Oh well, I guess they'll be in the perfect mood to give us information then, won't they?'

* * *

After a functional breakfast in the refectory building, Ehren led them outside to where Ramone's jeep was parked. There was a second, near identical vehicle parked in front of it, and a man with grey-streaked hair sat in the driver's seat. He was dressed in a black longsleeved jumper and was leaning back in his seat, reading a dog-eared paperback. He looked up with habitual irritation as the others approached.

'So why couldn't this have waited till afternoon?' he asked by way of greeting.

Ehren's smile as usual looked patronising. 'There's no point in wasting the whole morning, Brac,' he reasoned. 'Better to get out and see the world than hang around here in camp all day.'

Again, Mike wondered why Ehren was so reluctant to let them explore the human settlement. He decided that question could wait till later.

Brac set his book face down on the passenger seat, open to his page. 'You're the boss,' he said, then added, 'apparently. Let's get moving.'

It looked like they were taking both jeeps, since it would have been a squash getting five people into one of them, and Mike immediately decided he'd rather ride with Brac. After what he'd learned the night before, the man definitely intrigued him. He would have liked the chance to talk with him properly. Unfortunately, Ehren rather swiftly ushered both him and Anna into the other jeep, where they were confined to the back seat again.

Brac started the engine. Mike winced at the amount of noise it made, wondering if it perhaps needed looking at. It sounded louder than the generator that ran the fence.

The two vehicles set off along the dirt track towards the main gate. They passed a few people on the way, but it looked like most people were still in bed – most *sensible* people, Mike amended. When they reached the gate, Brac pulled his noisy jeep to a halt and hit the horn a few times to draw attention to the fact that they wanted to get out of the compound. No-one was manning the gate though, and no-one responded to his beeping. Eventually the man got out and hit a button at the side of the gate that apparently triggered a manual release. The gate was already slightly ajar, as if it didn't close properly, and it shuddered as it swung open. Brac got back in his jeep, casting an irritated look at Ehren as if holding him personally responsible for the gate being unmanned.

Ehren smiled benignly back.

They followed Brac through the gate. Mike glanced backward, watching the gate swing slowly shut. It seemed to get stuck again before it could completely close, but then the jeep turned a corner and the gate was lost to sight.

They headed north, the early morning sun illuminating the trees all around and making the mountains on their left glow. The air felt cool and fresh, as if pollution was something that just wasn't a concern out here. Anna stared up at the mountains, which looked completely different in daylight, and wondered if the previous night had really happened. It seemed so unreal now, like an event that had happened to someone else. At that precise moment, she had about a hundred questions she wanted to put to Doctor Ehren, but couldn't think of where to start.

The road climbed to the top of a small rise. Looking back, Mike had a near perfect view out over the encampment down to the sea, and further south along the curved line of the road to a cleared area that must have been the zombie enclosure. He took the lens cap off his camera and thumbed the ON switch, recording the view and thinking how cool it would look at night with the moon reflecting off the sea. He zoomed in on the main gate of the encampment and thought for a moment that he saw movement there.

His concentration was shattered as Ramone hit the brakes hard. The jeep swerved to a halt in a spray of dirt. The passengers were all thrown forward. Mike, facing the wrong way, couldn't catch himself and hit the seat in front of him hard. He struggled upright immediately, swearing and clutching at his bruised shoulder with one hand and his camera with the other.

The first thing he saw was Brac's car, slewed across the road in front of them. Brac was out of the driver's seat and standing next to it in a defensive crouch. His eyes were focused on the creature that had appeared out of the woods on the other side of the road.

Mike turned, unconsciously swinging the camera round as well. His eyes went wide as he stared at the creature. 'What the flying fuck is *that?*'

Chapter 28

The creature had appeared so suddenly from between the trees that it seemed to have materialised from thin air. It was the size and shape of a very large horse, but the similarity didn't go much further than that. Its coat was jet black, its legs and back so heavily muscled that they appeared deformed. The head on its short neck was elongated and strangely flattened so that it looked almost reptilian. Its ears lay flat against the skull, more like holes than proper ears, and its tail was thin and hairless like that of a whippet. It reared back in surprise, and the passengers of the jeep saw that its teeth were as black as the rest of its body and pointed like needles. Its front hooves were cloven and looked sharp enough to cut a person open.

'*What is it?*' Mike repeated his question urgently.

Ramone stood up in his seat, lifting his rifle in the same movement. 'It's a horse,' he said with apparent calm.

'No it's not!'

'Yes, it is.' Ramone raised his rifle to his shoulder, sighting carefully along it. 'Or it was, about a dozen generations ago.'

The horse-like creature moved forward a few steps, snorting and pawing at the ground. It looked like it had been startled by the noise of the vehicles, but wasn't sure if it wanted to attack or not.

Brac, still keeping the solid bulk of his jeep between himself and the animal, moved backwards. The black creature snorted again, tossing its head and baring its black fangs. Then it seemed to decide against a direct attack, and turned away. It disappeared back into the forest with as much suddenness as it had appeared.

The civilians in the back seat of the second jeep let out their breath at the same time. Mike had kept his camera on the black animal the entire time, watching it through the viewfinder as if that would somehow make it less real and less dangerous. When it retreated out of sight, he slowly lowered the camera.

Unconsciously mirroring the action, Ramone put down his rifle. 'The soil of this island is cursed,' he said, his eyes still on the place where the animal had vanished into the forest. 'Anything dead that is buried in it is spit back out; anything that grows here carries the infection. The animals ate the plants and they changed. Now they mostly eat each other.'

Before either Anna or Mike could respond, Ehren turned in his seat and gave them a slightly pained smile. 'Of course,' he said, 'we don't really use the word "cursed"...'

'Speak for yourself,' Ramone muttered.

Brac, whose vehicle had been a lot closer to the horse-creature than theirs had, came walking over. He looked thoroughly unimpressed. He rested his hand on the hood of the jeep, tapping his fingers on it. 'So,' he said to Ehren. 'You want to carry on, or do you think we should head back?'

Ehren waved his hand in a dismissive gesture. 'It was only a horse, Brac.'

Behind him, Mike made a choking noise. 'Yeah, and Godzilla's only a lizard.'

'We carry on,' Ehren said, ignoring the interruption. 'It probably ran out onto the road by accident.'

Brac shrugged and turned away. 'Alright, but I'm just saying. They're not usually out during daylight hours. I think something might have spooked it.'

'It's the full moon tonight,' Ehren said reasonably. 'All the animals get a bit strange at this time of the month.'

Brac carried on walking, but Mike thought he saw his shoulders stiffen at the comment.

They got started again, driving at a slower, more cautious pace along the dirt track. Mike kept his camera on standby and his finger held over the button, but nothing else came running out of the forest to intercept them. Even so, he kept a close eye on the trees on either side. He was only vaguely aware that when the horse-creature had appeared, Anna had grabbed onto his arm. Although the danger had now passed, she hadn't yet let go.

About fifteen minutes later they came around a long corner and saw the road sloping away in front of them, back down towards sea level. The northern tip of the island appeared to be flatter and less hilly than the south, and also less densely forested. Within half a mile or so, the trees petered out and were replaced with scrubby grassland that stretched out over the gently rolling countryside.

There was no sign of any village. The dirt track wound off ahead without an apparent destination. It didn't look like there was anywhere that could hide a collection of houses, but then the road abruptly dropped down into a natural dip and the passengers caught sight of the village. It was tucked away in a large, ovoid depression that may have been natural, although the sheer rock face at one side of it looked like it had been created deliberately. Even from fifty feet back along the road the houses were all but invisible.

The houses themselves were small and low-lying, appearing at first glance more like shacks than proper, modern dwellings. Mike, watching mostly through his viewfinder again, saw that this wasn't actually the case. Most of the buildings had been built up against the sides of the depression with their sloped, corrugated iron roofs creating continuations of the natural line, and it looked like the buildings extended back into the hillside.

There was a welcoming committee waiting for them, which wasn't surprising since the villagers could hardly have missed hearing the approach of the two jeeps. The dirt track ended in a circular turning area in the centre of the depression, and stood around it were about two dozen people. Most of them were dressed warmly against the autumnal air, but a few were wearing short-sleeved shirts. One grey-haired woman wore a pale blue dress that looked to be woefully inadequate to provide any protection against the weather.

Brac pulled his jeep to a halt and shut off the noisy engine. The woman in the blue dress came forward to greet him as he climbed out.

The others got out as well, Mike taking a moment from videoing to offer Anna a hand, although she brushed the offer away with a minimum of politeness. Brac came over, smiling genuinely for the first time that either Mike or Anna could remember.

'This is Regina,' he said, introducing the woman. 'She's in charge of things here at the village.'

The woman laughed. '"In charge", he says. It makes me sound like I'm the Lady Governor or something.' Despite her greying hair, she did not appear to be that old. Her face was open and friendly, and when she laughed the skin around her blue eyes crinkled. She spoke with an accent that could have been German, although it was too slight to be sure. She also appeared to be completely immune to the cold, because she did not seem to notice the chill breeze that blew across the open ground. The blue dress she wore left her arms bare, but her skin was not even goose-pimpled. 'It's good to meet you,' she said to her visitors, smiling warmly. 'It's been a long time since anyone new has come to the island.'

Brac made the introductions, mentioning Anna's father in passing.

'Of course,' Regina said, smiling as she shook Anna's hand. 'Allister's a lovely man – so much nicer than some of these other scientist types.'

Ehren laughed at that, although Anna had to wonder if it had been intended as a joke.

Mike shook hands as well, then indicated his camera. 'Is it okay if I film around here?' he asked, reasoning that it was only polite to ask permission first. Especially since it had just occurred to him that every person in the village was probably a wolf. He *really* wanted to stay on their good side.

'Certainly.' Regina seemed almost flattered. 'Come on inside though – no point in standing around out here, is there?'

The woman led them towards one of the nearest buildings, with Brac at her side. Ehren and Anna followed, while Mike remained behind for a moment as he videoed a little more. He made sure to smile politely at everyone the camera pointed towards, although he was beginning to feel a little self-conscious. Apart from Regina, none of the other villages had spoken to or acknowledged them. They didn't seem particularly bothered by the presence of the new arrivals, and it seemed to Mike that they'd only turned out in welcome because it was somehow expected of them. Most of them appeared bored or disinterested, and at least one of the children was asleep in his mother's arms.

Mike was just turning away when the thought struck him. *Children.* There were about four or five that he could see, all under the age of ten. Were they wolves too? If they were the sons and daughters of wolves, then was the disease passed on hereditarily? And if not, then why were they here? Surely it couldn't be safe to keep normal children in a village where the rest of the population turned carnivorous once a month.

He was distracted by someone tapping his arm. He turned to find Ramone stood next to him with a young man who looked barely out of his teens. The young man's hair was ginger and badly in need of a trim, and he looked nervous, as if he didn't really want to be there.

Ramone spoke in a low voice. 'Mike, this is Daniel.' The young man nodded in hesitant acknowledgement. 'He says he needs to talk to us.'

Mike glanced behind him towards the house that the others were disappearing into. Ehren had stopped just outside and was looking over with a frown as if wondering what the delay was. 'Sure, what's the problem?'

The young man, Daniel, cleared his throat. 'Um, it's really about the girl. She's Doctor Martin's daughter, yeah?'

'That's right. So?'

'And he's gone missing, hasn't he?'

Mike looked sharply at Ramone. 'No-one's used the term "missing". Last I heard he was just out of town at the moment.'

Daniel looked even more unsure of himself,. 'Yeah… well… I think I've got some information about that. I don't think he's coming back.'

Chapter 29

'What do you mean?' Mike asked the man.

Daniel held up his hands quickly. 'This is just what I've heard, right? I mean, I can't confirm any of this. But Doctor Martin was here, about five days ago, and Ramone says that that's the last you guys have heard of him, and...'

Ramone abruptly silenced him with a quick nudge. Frowning, Mike looked up and saw that Ehren was coming over, his patronising smile fixed in place.

'Are you going to join us?' he asked Mike.

'Um.' Mike glanced at the others, but they kept silent. 'Sure. No problem.'

Ehren led the way back towards the small house that the others had disappeared into. Ramone made no effort to follow them, and when Mike glanced back he saw him and Daniel conferring in whispers. Still frowning to himself, Mike wondered what it was that the young man had been trying to tell him. He felt more than a little irritated that Ehren had stopped him from finding out. He began to think of a valid excuse that would let him – and preferably Anna as well – duck back outside as soon as possible.

As they got closer to the house, Mike could see that it was constructed out of roughly shaped blocks of the same grey stone as the cliff-face behind it. Each separate house had a single doorway with an unpainted wooden door, and there was very little outside decoration. It made the structures look very functional and almost temporary, like no-one who lived here expected to stay long.

Inside, the walls were bare, uncovered stone; the ceiling overhead rounded like a tunnel. Ehren ushered Mike inside the corridor, where he could clearly hear the voices of the others.

Regina was talking with open good cheer to Anna, asking her questions about her home, and what was happening in the news back there. She explained her interest by saying, 'It's very isolated out here. I know that that is the point, but sometimes I miss knowing what is going on in the rest of the world.' Anna answered her questions politely, feeling a little odd at having to think about home and the normal world she had left behind. It felt like she was talking about someone else's life.

As they were led further inside the cramped dwelling, past a heavy iron door that currently stood open, Anna was reminded of the vampire cave she had visited the night before. The fact that the houses here had protective doors and were built far back into the cliff-face made them look suspiciously like bunkers.

The narrow tunnel opened out into a larger area, obviously designated as a sitting room. There were two sofas, both covered with throws that had a rough, hand-finished look to them. A large wooden table would have taken up most of the available space if it hadn't been pushed back against the wall. The main source of light was a pair of mismatched lamps standing on the table, throwing out a warm, homely light. The walls of the room were slightly curved like the inside of a pottery jar, and there were three large bookcases set against them, filled with dozens of books. The doorways that led off from the room were also curved, and covered by beaded curtains. Anna couldn't help but smile, thinking that her original thought had been wrong – the house wasn't a bunker, it was more like a hobbit hole.

Just as the thought came into her head, it was pushed out very swiftly by what was sat on the rug in the middle of the room.

It looked like a dog, but was at least three times as large as any domestic animal that Anna had ever seen. She stopped dead, staring down at it, her mind taking half a second too long to get to the obvious answer.

The wolf looked up at her with curious yellow eyes, but didn't get up. It seemed hugely unimpressed by the presence of the strange woman.

'Oh, I'm sorry.' Regina walked over to the wolf, lifting the hem of her long skirt so that she could crouch down next to it. 'This is Lyell,' she said, stroking the sleek black fur of the animal. 'My daughter.'

Anna blinked. 'Oh. I mean… hello.' She attempted to smile, but it didn't feel very convincing.

The wolf looked up at her mother with a startling human expression of resignation. Regina laughed. 'Don't mind her,' she said. 'She's just a child – a very opinionated child. I adopted her when she was just a baby, and she's been talking back to me pretty much since that moment.'

Cautiously, Anna sat down on one of the sofas. The air inside the house was warm and perfumed with an unusual, spicy odour that tugged at the edge of her memory, like something she associated with a very specific moment from childhood. If it hadn't been for the presence of the unnaturally-sized animal in front of her, she would have instinctively felt comfortable there.

'So, are all the people here wolves then?' she asked. 'The children as well?'

'No, not all the people.' Regina settled herself on the other sofa. Brac sat down next to her. 'About two thirds of us are, and the rest are our families. People come here to visit – to get away from it all – and sometimes they bring their partners and children with them. It's quite safe for them to be here, don't worry. The houses are all designed to be safely sealed during the full moon, just in case.'

The large black wolf on the floor stretched its front legs, yawning widely enough to show off its sharp white teeth. It got to its feet in a lazy motion and padded over towards Mike, who was standing nervously in the doorway with his camera gripped defensively in front of him.

'Oh, don't worry,' Regina told him. 'That's Lyell. She won't hurt you.'

Mike looked up at the woman, then back at the wolf, which was so tall its head was level with his solar plexus. 'Ah. Right. Hi, Lyell...' Cautiously, he held his hand out to her.

The wolf sniffed at his fingers, and Mike fought down the urge to snatch his hand away. Lyell looked up at him with something like amusement in her yellow eyes, then nuzzled against his hand, her tongue lolling out in a wide canine grin.

'I think she likes me...' Mike started to say.

'Lyell!' Regina's voice was sharp. 'Stop that.'

Pouting like a scolded child – a very strange expression to see on an animal – Lyell retreated from Mike and went back to sit on the floor by her mother.

'It's okay,' Mike said quickly. 'I don't mind...'

'It's not that,' Regina said, stroking Lyell's ears. 'Our disease is spread through saliva, so it's not a very good idea to get too close to us.'

'Oh.' Mike resisted the urge to wipe his hand on his jeans. 'Sorry.'

'That's okay, it's easy for us to forget.' Regina looked down at her adopted daughter fondly. 'Lyell spends so much time in this form that she sometimes forgets she isn't actually an animal.' She smiled at Anna then. 'She has a theory, you see. When you're a new wolf, the changes are very painful. At each full moon you are forced into an alternate shape, and it's a traumatic experience. Most of the time an inexperienced wolf will black out completely, at least for the first half a dozen or so changes, and will have no memory of the time they spent in their alternate form. Lyell believes that the more time you willingly spend as an animal, the easier it is to control the change, and the more consciousness you retain when you do change. Certainly she has a remarkable control over it now... although that may be because she has known nothing else during her life.'

Lyell, apparently unconcerned with being the main topic of discussion, curled up on the floor, pinning down her mother's feet, and went back to sleep.

'So...' Anna frowned, watching the animal. 'How old was she when she was changed?'

Regina smiled, but there was a sadness in her blue eyes. 'She wasn't born when it happened. Her mother was still carrying her.'

Anna looked down at the wolf on the floor and bit her lip. 'Really?'

'Yes. We don't know exactly what happened, but it was here on the island, about twenty-five years ago. Lyell's father was a wolf but her mother wasn't, and they had lived here quite happily for a number of years. Then, a few days after the full moon, they were out in the forest and were attacked – apparently by one of the wild animals living here. What we believe happened was that Lyell's father changed form to defend them, but as he was helping them he accidentally scratched his wife. Sometimes the virus can be transmitted that way. Anyway, she was badly injured by the animal and only just managed to escape, although she died shortly after making it back to the village. Her husband never returned home either.' Regina stroked Lyell's neck, making small, reassuring circles with her fingers. 'We were able to save the baby, but apparently the virus had already got into her bloodstream. I've looked after Lyell since then.'

Mike had switched on his camera again and was quietly filming the woman, and the wolf at her feet. He could hear the pain in Regina's voice, although it sounded old and faint, as if it had been touched on so many times that it had worn smooth and lost its sharp edges. Without seeming to think about it, Brac reached out and took the woman's hand, squeezing it gently.

'As I say,' Regina went on, 'that was about twenty-five years ago. This is the only life that Lyell's ever known, which has made her a bit of a strange child. And like the rest of us, she's grown at a delayed rate as well – in her human form, she still has the body of a child.'

Anna caught her breath, glancing down at the wolf again. She couldn't have explained the sudden flash of sympathy she felt for the young girl, except that there was something about her – maybe the look in her golden eyes – that reminded Anna of the girl who haunted her dreams. For the briefest of moments she was certain that she was looking at Amy in an altered form, and it was that thought that made her catch her breath.

If Regina noticed, she didn't comment. 'She's also the only one of us to have never left the island,' she went on. 'Which is – ' The woman broke off abruptly and looked up. Brac did the same, as did Lyell. It looked as if they had simultaneously heard something unexpected.

'What – ?' Anna started to ask, then the door to the small house was thrown open.

Ramone stood framed in the doorway at the end of the tunnel. 'The fence alarm,' he reported.

Ehren was on his feet in a second and headed out of the door. Mike and Anna exchanged a quick look then followed them, Mike thumbing the 'OFF' switch on his camera and slinging it back over his shoulder.

As they emerged back into the dim sunlight, they heard it for the first time. Faint and distant, almost inaudible if they hadn't been listening for it, the rising and falling alarm sounded over the forest.

'What the hell's going on?' Mike asked. Ehren had broken into a run, and Ramone was already in the driver's seat of the jeep, starting the engine. Mike grabbed Anna's arm and dragged her forward. They jumped into the jeep right behind Ehren, a half second before Ramone stepped hard on the accelerator. Dirt flew from beneath the spinning wheels as the vehicle leapt forward onto the track.

'What is it?' Mike asked again, clutching onto the seat in front of him for balance.

'Perimeter fence alarm,' Ramone said tersely as he threw the jeep into the first corner. 'Something's wrong.'

Behind them, the rest of the wolf village were coming out of their houses, glancing at each other nervously. As the noise of the jeep faded, each one of them could clearly hear the distant sound of the alarm, as deeply troubling as any other warning they had ever heard.

Chapter 30

There must have been more boring things in the world than guarding the main gate, but offhand Greg couldn't think of many. He'd been on duty for a little over five hours and had been bored within the first ten minutes.

He reminded himself that there were worst duties to be had first thing in the morning, and at least this one enabled him to watch the sun coming up over the ocean. The air seemed almost unnaturally clear and fresh that far north, and the sunrises were almost always spectacular. It was the one enjoyable thing about morning gate duty, although it couldn't compensate for the cold and the boredom and the rapidly encroaching numbness in his feet.

It wasn't like the gate was even used that much, especially not that early in the morning. Greg couldn't figure out why they even needed someone watching it during daylight hours – surely the people leaving the encampment could open the gate by themselves? So far that morning he had been called on just once, when Campbell and Roberts left, both looking as pleased as him to be on duty that early in the day. Another car had left a few hours after that, but by that point Greg had wandered back to the refectory to get some coffee, so they had let themselves out. Greg had shrugged it off, since officially he was entitled to a ten minute break every hour and unofficially he didn't care very much. He had got into the habit of taking half an hour or so to himself about ten o'clock, which was just enough time for a coffee, a cigarette, and a quick chat with Tris, who was also supposed to be working at that time but very rarely was.

He was now heading back towards the gate, feeling relatively good about the world and not even too distressed that he had another hour to go before he could turn the job over to someone else. Tris had been in a happy, friendly mood that morning, and had made a couple of pointed promises for later that night which had definitely put a smile on his face. He whistled to himself, taking his time to cover the distance between Tris' lab building and the main gate. There was no hurry, especially with Ehren out of the camp for the morning…

Greg stopped short, noticing that someone was standing next to the gate.

Dammit, can't they let themselves out? he thought irritably. Some people would much rather stand waiting for assistance than take a simple matter into their own hands...

It was only when he got a bit closer that he began to wonder why the person was trying to leave the camp on foot. He couldn't remember the last time that had happened... unless it was someone being sent to check the outside of the fence. In that case though, it was strange that the man was dressed in what looked like a smudged grey t-shirt and old jeans, rather than the regulation dark green uniform that most of the encampment staff wore.

Swearing freely to himself, Greg hurried up to the man at the gate, expecting to have to deal with either a moron who couldn't work the gate release button or some officious asshole who would demand to know why the gate was unmanned. Either option was pretty much guaranteed to ruin his otherwise tolerable day.

'Need some help there?' Greg asked when he was a few feet from the man.

If the wind had been blowing in the opposite direction then Greg would have noticed the smell of decay a lot sooner. As it was, he had only a second or so to take in a series of vitally important details – that the gate already stood a foot or so open; that the man was trying to get *in* and not out; and most importantly of all, that the man was dead.

The creature turned towards him, its jaw dropping open in soundless, mindless hunger. Its faltering steps had awkwardly manoeuvred its body through the narrow open gap in the gate, and now it found itself unimpeded, with food standing right in front of it.

Greg let out a shout of surprise and stumbled backwards. The zombie grabbed for him with both hands, its skeletal fingers narrowly missing snagging his jacket. The fact that the creature was missing both its eyes but it did not stop it from lumbering forward, blinding snatching at him.

Moving faster than he had done in many years, Greg danced back out of its reach. The shock of seeing one of the dead ones *here*, inside the fence, had shattered his nerves so completely that it took him several seconds to remember the rifle that was slung over his shoulder. He retreated further, giving himself the space and time to chamber a round and lift the gun to his shoulder.

His hands trembled so much that even at that close range his first shot missed, burying itself in the zombie's shoulder. The creature didn't slow for a moment. Greg forced himself to take the time to aim the next shot, holding his breath as he squeezed the trigger.

The creature's head exploded in a shower of stinking grey matter, and it dropped to the floor.

Greg let out his breath. What the hell was that thing doing here? It must have been what some of the others called a Wanderer – a random person that had come to the island, landing somewhere other than the main camp, who had subsequently died and come back to life. Greg remembered Tris telling him that something like that had happened once, about four months ago, just after she'd arrived here…

His gaze jerked back suddenly to the main gate. Something else was moving there; another figure making its way through the gate. *Fucking hell, another one!* Greg broke into a run, hoping to get to the gate and throw it shut before the dead one could get through, but stopped within a few feet.

There wasn't just one creature outside the fence now. There were a dozen or more, emerging from the forest and pushing up against the gate, searching for the way in.

Greg lifted the rifle again and fired the rest of his rounds into the mass of undead bodies. He saw at least one creature fall, but couldn't be sure whether it had been a true head shot or not. The rifle clicked on an empty round and Greg swore again, his voice thin with panic. He had more ammo, but it was stored in the watertight plastic container next to his post at the gate, and the stumbling dead were now between him and it.

He had a moment of panicked indecision, then made a run towards the fence. There was an alarm there and also an emergency switch that would start up the electric fence.

Extremely conscious of the dead ones that were even now closing in on him, Greg wrenched open the emergency box and triggered the alarm.

This close to the fence the noise was piercingly loud, frying the senses just as effectively as the fear did. Distantly, Greg heard the generator splutter and cough into life, but he didn't stop to listen. He ran, narrowly dodging the grasping hands of the nearest zombies.

All over the camp people were coming out of the buildings, drawn first by the shots and then by the undulating scream of the alarm. Greg made for the closest building, stumbling over the uneven ground in his haste. He could hear the generator struggling to catch – heard it misfire once, twice, three times. Then he reached the building and someone grabbed hold of him, demanding to know what the hell was going on.

Greg recognised Tris' face, but panic and terror had taken away his ability to speak. Irrationally, all he could think of was that five minutes previously he'd been speaking to the same girl, laughing and sharing plans and now… and now…

The generator finally caught and the electric fence buzzed into life. Greg turned to watch, still gripping Tris by the arm.

There were at least half a dozen of the dead ones inside the fence, and more shoving and pushing their way through the gate at every moment. Greg finally realised that something must have happened at the enclosure; that something had gone wrong and the dead ones had all got out, but there were more important things to worry about now. The zombies had unintentionally forced the gate open wider, making it easier for them to stagger through, but the whole structure now had several thousand volts flowing through it.

Greg watched one zombie halfway through the gate as it suddenly froze in its tracks. Its dead fingers were touching the mesh of the gate and although the high charge of electricity couldn't cause it any pain, it at least paralysed its muscles and prevented it from moving. The zombie shuddered spasmodically for several long seconds, then abruptly burst into flames.

Someone inside the camp cheered; several other people screamed. Greg clutched Tris to him with a buzz of elation. There were still a half dozen or so of the dead ones within the camp, but at least no more could get in now...

The burning zombie wrenched itself loose from the fence and staggered forward, still encased in flames. Long past the point where any human would have collapsed and lost consciousness, the dead creature kept walking, oblivious to the pain and the fact that its flesh was being consumed from its bones like wax from a candle. It was aware only that there was food in front of it, and it continued to stumble forward with its burning hands extended hungrily.

'Oh my God...' It was Tris who spoke, her voice choked and harsh. 'They're not stopping...'

Three more of the zombies that touched the fence burst into spontaneous flames, but it didn't stop or slow them either. They continued to shove their way through the gate, in a couple of cases igniting other dead bodies around them. A series of walking human torches came staggering down the slope towards the terrified humans, and still more zombies were coming out of the forest beyond the fence to join them.

'We've gotta get inside.' Greg shoved Tris, trying to get her moving. 'We've gotta hide... get somewhere they can't get at us...'

Tris was crying, but she moved. All across the camp people were streaming back into the buildings, shouts and screams echoing across the open space in counterpoint to the silent dead who inched down towards them like an unstoppable mud flow.

Greg risked one final glance back at the gate. At least one in ten of the dead ones was being caught against the fence and bursting into flames, but the rest were spilling unhindered into the camp, bringing the stench of death with them. It was only when he and the others were inside the building with the fire door firmly shut that he realised they were all trapped.

On one side they had the sea; on the other the electric fence. And in the middle there was them, and the dead ones.

No-one inside the camp was getting out alive.

Chapter 31

'How many shots you got left?'

Greg looked up at the man who, like him, was sheltering underneath one of the wooden desks. 'None. I'm all out.'

'Shit.'

'Oh, that's just great,' someone else added – a blonde woman with mascara streaked down her face from crying. The man's surname was Reid, according to the laminated tag on his pastel blue shirt, but Greg couldn't remember having spoken to him on more than a few occasions. He recognised the woman as one of Tris' friends, but again drew a blank on a name or any other details. It wasn't the most pressing of their problems at that moment anyway.

The building that the four of them were in was little more than a standalone unit, mostly used for storing medical slides and other equipment that wasn't in immediate use. Tris and her friend had been in there filing before the dead ones arrived, and Greg and the other guy had hurried them back inside during the moment of panic when everyone had run for their lives. Now they were all individually doubting the wisdom of that move.

The building had only five rooms, three of which were filled with filing cabinets and spare equipment. The people had taken refuge in one of the free rooms, using whatever furniture they could find to block up the windows and the interior door, and also the outer doors in the corridor. Then they had crawled beneath a remaining table and the recriminations had begun.

'You don't have any spare ammo at all?' Reid asked in disbelief. His face was as white as the lab coat that he still wore. Greg wondered if the man might pass out soon and give them all some peace.

'No,' Greg repeated. 'None. And I'm assuming there's none here either, unless someone's helpfully filed it in one of the other rooms.'

'You think this is funny?'

'Yeah, of course it's fucking funny. We're trapped in a six-by-ten concrete building with a coupla hundred undead outside… no ammo, no way out…

funniest situation I've been in for years, mate.' Greg sat back against the wall, patting his pockets. He found that he at least still had his cigarettes, for all the good that would do him. 'All the defence stuff is stored next to the refectory. I guess Ehren never thought something like this would happen.'

'How exactly *did* this happen?' Tris asked.

'The enclosure fence must've come down or something.' It didn't sound like a very likely explanation, but it was the only one that Greg had been able to come up with. 'Unless someone let them out... and God knows why anyone would want to do a thing like that.'

'Yeah, but... how did they get in *here?*'

Greg covered his guilty flinch with a shrug, then lit a cigarette. He offered them around but no-one else wanted one.

Reid cleared his throat pointedly. 'Weren't you watching the gate this morning, Greg?'

'Yeah. I was on my break when all this happened.'

Reid and the blonde woman both laughed in disbelief; the woman a little hysterically. 'Nice timing,' Reid noted. 'Real nice.'

'Fuck you.'

'Hey, let me ask you this – did you just let those goddamn things in here? Because from the small amount of research I've done on the dead ones, they tend to have problems opening doors and stuff like that...'

Greg sat up, gesturing angrily with his cigarette. 'Look, I don't know what happened, alright? I was coming back from my break and... and... I dunno, the goddamn gate was open, okay? The last sonofabitch that went through mustn't have shut it properly or something... goddamn it, I don't know. But when I got back it was open and one of the dead ones had got through.'

'Just the one?' Reid spread his hands, looking to the girls for back-up. 'You had your gun – you seriously couldn't stop one zombie?'

Greg turned away from him, shaking his head in exasperation. 'I stopped him. But there were a dozen others behind him.'

'And you couldn't get the gate shut before they got in?'

'There were too many of them!'

'And you had a gun! What's wrong with you? If you could've shut the gate before they'd got in, then we wouldn't be – '

Greg got to his feet, shoving the table back against the wall with enough force to make everyone jump. 'Oh yeah, it's real goddamn easy, isn't it? You can just sit there and tell me how easy it would be. I'll tell you this for free – it ain't so easy when you're right there and you've got a dozen of those fucking things trying to take chunks out of you.'

'Right, right.' Reid turned away in disgust. 'Greg Thomas, our first and last line of defence.'

'Alright, that does it.' Greg dropped his rifle to the floor. 'You think you could have done better?' He grabbed hold of the man and dragged him to his feet, ignoring the shouts of the girls behind him.

The sound of breaking glass made everyone freeze, their eyes going fearfully to the barricaded windows. A look of relief passed over every face as they realised the noise came from somewhere outside and their own defences were still intact.

Tris climbed up onto one of the desks, attempting to see what had happened outside. 'Do you think – ?' she started to say, then caught her breath.

'What?' Reluctantly, Greg let go of Reid. The man backed away from him, muttering something. Greg ignored him and climbed up next to Tris, trying to find a crack in the furniture barricade that would let him see out. When he finally put his eye to one he found himself staring directly into the mouth of one of the zombies, which was pressed up against the window with its teeth bared as if it could chew right through the glass. Greg started back and almost fell off the table, swearing loudly.

'Oh my God...' Tris whispered.

Greg stood up, finding a vantage point that let him see out over both the barricade and the mass of zombies outside. It took a moment for his eyes to adjust enough to the chaos outside that he could actually see what was going on.

The building directly opposite, which was separated from them by a stretch of open ground about fifty feet wide, was completely surrounded by the dead ones. They were pawing at the doors and windows, which had been similarly blocked up with furniture. On their own they probably wouldn't have had the strength or the numbers to break through the glass, but unfortunately, one of the burning zombies, so badly scorched that it was little more than a flaming skeleton, had come stumbling into the crowd. It had collapsed within a few seconds, but in doing so it had collided with several of the others and they too had caught light. The flames had spread through the tightly packed, unfeeling bodies, until at least a dozen of the dead ones were blazing like torches.

The fire had not deterred the attack for a moment. The undead had continued to claw at the windows, oblivious to the fact that the flesh was melting from their fingers. Finally, the heat did what their fists had been unable to: the glass in one of the windows shattered, badly lacerating at least two of the nearest zombies.

There were more than enough to take their places. The dead ones reached in through the broken window and clawed at the makeshift barricade, which had been hastily constructed from desks and flimsy filing cabinets. While the cabinets were relatively heat-proof, the desks were not. Within moments the woodwork had begun to scorch and blister under the burning hands that slapped and scratched at them.

Greg and Tris watched as the first flames leapt up around the edges of the window, spreading with alarming speed. For the first time the horrified watchers became aware of the distant screams, coming from the people trapped within the other building. The screams were audible even over the persistent wail of the alarm, and it made Greg's head throb so badly that for a second he was sure he was going to throw up.

An agonising minute passed as the flames grew in size and intensity, and then finally the door to the burning building was wrenched open from the inside. Black smoke billowed out, almost obscuring the doorway from sight. Through the clouds, Greg was just able to make out a shape staggering forward, bent double by the choking effects of the smoke.

Blinded and disorientated, the person had no chance at all against the undead.

Greg turned from the window and shut his eyes tightly, but he couldn't block out the dying man's screams. *No escape*, his numbed mind repeated, over and over. *No escape, no escape, no escape…*

Chapter 32

The jeep skidded to a halt at the top of the rise, almost throwing the passengers out of their seats. Ramone was on his feet in an instant; the others following as soon as they recovered their balance.

It had only been an hour since they had first come over that hill, heading in the opposite direction. At that point, the camp had looked silent and peaceful – a settlement just waking up to morning. Now it looked like a war zone.

There was movement all over the camp, but it was immediately obvious that none of it was human. Shambling figures filled the open spaces, congregating around the white buildings. At least one of the buildings was on fire, as were most of the undead around it, and several other zombies were stumbling about like burning pillars, as unconcerned about the flames as anything else that wasn't food. Thick black smoke hung over everything, making it difficult to assess the extent of the damage.

The fence alarm wailed on constantly.

Mike was the first one to speak. 'What the hell happened?'

Ramone had produced a pair of binoculars from under his seat and was scanning the activity below. 'The fence isn't down,' he said with surprising calmness. 'I can't see for sure, but it looks like they're coming in the main gate.'

'That's impossible,' Ehren stated.

'It's also impossible that the dead ones could have all got out of the enclosure.' Ramone lowered the binoculars to look at the man. 'Right?'

Ehren was shaking his head as if a simple denial would change what he was seeing.

'Where're all the people?' Anna asked. Her eyes were wide as she watched the milling undead below.

'Trapped in the buildings would be my guess.' Ramone kept scanning the binoculars over the camp. 'I can't see anyone. I don't know how the fires have started... unless someone was trying to use it as a weapon. That's not a very smart idea – the dead ones don't burn nearly as quickly as a regular body would.'

'Don't they have guns?' Mike asked him. 'There must be something they can do...'

'All the weapons are in the main store. I'm guessing no-one's got to it.'

'Why not?'

'The only door is outside. From what I can see it's completely surrounded.' He took the binoculars from his eyes and passed them to Mike. Ehren made to take them instead, but Ramone ignored the older man as if he weren't there. 'They've not got any way out of there.'

Even the briefest sweep of the camp told Mike that that was the truth. Every window he could see was blocked up from the inside, and each one had its own crowd of zombies directly outside. In several cases the glass had been broken, but most of the barricades inside seemed to be holding.

'I can't see any people,' Mike agreed, 'but everywhere seems to be sealed up pretty tight. Apart from that building that's on fire...' It suddenly dawned on him that there had almost certainly been people trapped inside when it had started to burn, and his stomach heaved. From that distance it had been almost possible to pretend that what was happening down there wasn't actually real. Almost.

'There're at least a couple of hundred of the dead ones in the camp,' Ramone said, his voice still calm. 'That means the rest are probably still out in the forest.'

Anna glanced around at the silent forest on either side of them. 'How many are there altogether?'

Ramone looked at Ehren, who was still shaking his head.

'Just over three hundred,' Ehren said at last. 'But... they can't *all* be out...'

'Why would two thirds of them be here and the rest of them waiting at home?' Ramone asked. 'Face it – they're all here, where the food is.'

Ehren started to answer but was cut off by Mike.

'Look!' He pointed out towards the distant buildings, forgetting that he was the only one with binoculars. 'Someone's come out of that building!'

'Where?'

'There – far right, second building back from the sea. Heading towards the fence.'

The others saw him then, a tiny figure distinguishable from the others only by the fact that he was sprinting rather than staggering across the open ground. He outdistanced the zombies easily and was far ahead of them by the time he reached the fence. He stopped before he got there, apparently realising too late that the fence was still electrified and there was no escape that way. He took several steps towards the gate, which was halfway across the camp from him. The watchers on the hill could see that there was still a steady stream of zombies coming through that way; more than enough to bar it as an exit.

For several long moments the man stood frozen on the spot, watching the zombies slowly closing in on him like an inescapable wall of death. He backed off and Anna caught her breath, convinced in that instant that he was going to take the option of a quick death and grab hold of the electric fence.

Then the man broke and ran, heading not towards the gate but down the slope towards the sea.

'Where the hell's he going?' Mike asked.

The zombies slowly changed direction and followed the man, but although they had closed the distance a little he was still far in front of them. He ran down to the beach but didn't stop when he got there, instead continuing into the water. He paused briefly, glancing back at the dead ones still in pursuit, then carried on wading into the freezing water.

About ten feet from the shore he turned back in towards the fence and walked up to it without hesitation. The fence there was set on a large concrete shelf above the water, and the man boosted himself up onto it, grabbing onto the fence for support.

Mike and Anna both flinched, but the man stood up, still holding onto the chain link.

'The fence isn't electrified there,' Ramone supplied. 'The electric section ends at that orange marker, out the way of the water.'

Mike watched through the binoculars as the man climbed the fence, reaching the top long before any of the dead ones got within grabbing distance of him. He swung his legs over the top, then started climbing quickly down the other side. Some of the zombies had struggled through the water and were now reaching through the chain link with their fingers, or pushing their faces up against it in a vain attempt to get to him. He climbed halfway down then dropped the rest of the way, pushing outwards so that he fell well beyond the range of the grasping hands. He missed the ledge on the other side and landed in the water up to his knees.

Apparently unharmed, the man waded out of the surf. He took a moment to look at the dead ones crowding the other side of the fence, then turned and walked quickly away into the forest.

'Smart move,' Ramone noted. 'Except for the fact that he's headed south now, which is where all the dead ones have come from.'

'What about the others?' Mike had lowered the binoculars, but the thick, sour taste in his mouth refused to go away. 'What about everyone else that's trapped down there?'

Ramone was frowning as if deep in thought. 'We need guns,' he said at last, then dropped into the driver's seat.

'But I thought you said – ' Mike had to give up on the question as the jeep lurched back into motion. He sat down quickly, pulling Anna into the seat next to him.

Ehren sat down more slowly. His shoulders were slumped as if half the air had been let out of him, and he didn't say a word as the jeep resumed its bumpy journey.

Ramone pulled up a little further down the track, still some distance from where it curved around towards the main entrance. He shut off the engine and climbed out quickly, stopping only to pick up his rifle and a box from under his seat which presumably contained spare rounds.

'There's an emergency store,' he explained. He set off towards the forest on the left hand side of the road without so much as glancing round to make sure the others were following. 'We'd better not go any further in the jeep though – the noise will have the dead ones down on us in a second.'

Mike hurried to catch up with the man, the camera around his neck bouncing heavily against his chest. 'Um, maybe I've missed something,' he said, 'but do we actually have a plan here?'

Without pausing in his stride, Ramone looked round and gave him a smile. 'We're going to play at being the cavalry,' he told him. 'Give those nice folks that're trapped in there a chance to get themselves un-trapped.'

Chapter 33

The trees around the small building had been cut down in a wide circle, but even so the surrounding forest was dense and overgrown. They only caught sight of the building itself when they stumbled through a wall of bushes and abruptly found themselves standing in the open.

Mike helped Anna, letting her use him for balance while she disentangled her leg from some kind of clingy ground vine. *Even the vegetation is hostile here,* Mike thought. It had been a hard fight to push through the undergrowth, and if it hadn't been for Ramone leading the way then he was sure that they would all still be stuck somewhere between the trees.

The building that they had been led to was small and compact, with no windows visible and only one door. The door was made of metal that was already going rusty around the corners, and when Ramone unlocked it with a key on his belt it swung open grudgingly. Even over the continued wail of the alarms from the camp, Mike was sure that the groaning hinges must have been audible for miles around.

Ramone disappeared inside and the others followed him to the door. There were no lights inside the concrete building, and it took a moment for Mike's eyes to adjust. When they did, he saw that the interior consisted of a single, unfurnished room, which was piled high with wooden crates. The crates were stacked on their sides so that they could be opened without having to shift them around.

Ramone flipped the catches on one of the boxes and pulled out from the shadowy interior a rifle much like his own. He passed it over to Mike, who took it without much enthusiasm.

'Go stand outside,' Ramone instructed him. 'We made a lot of noise getting here, and the last thing we need is for any of the dead ones to come investigating.'

'Um.' The rifle felt surprisingly heavy in Mike's hands. 'Okay.'

Ramone gave him a look that might possibly have been sympathetic. 'Have you used one of those before?'

'No,' Mike admitted. 'But I've watched a lot of John Woo movies.'

'Okay. Well, it's like that, but with more aiming.' Ramone took it from him and loaded it with a handful of rounds, then double-checked the safety and passed it back. 'I doubt any of them have tracked this far yet, but you can't be too paranoid. Oh, and aim for the head.'

'Right.' Mike nodded and ducked back outside the building. Anna looked at him with worry evident in her eyes, and he attempted a reassuring smile.

Ehren still hung back, almost at the edge of the cleared area. His shoulders were hunched and he looked more than just worried. His whole demeanour was that of a completely different person to the self-assured and in-control man he had been an hour before.

Ramone came back out into the daylight with his radio in his hand. 'Anyone copy?' he said into it. 'Anyone inside the camp. This is Ramone, anyone alive and with a radio, come back.' He paused, listening to static. 'Anyone at all.'

There was another burst of static, lasting long enough to make Mike's heart sink. Then a voice came through.

'People alive here, over.'

Ramone looked relieved despite himself. 'Good to hear that. Who are you? Over.'

'Greg Thomas. There're four of us here – we're holed up in storage building two. Over.'

'All secure?'

'At the moment, yes. We're…' There was another burst of static before the voice came back. 'There're a whole lot of dead ones around us. We're secure right now but I dunno how long that's going to last. Over.'

'Okay. Just sit tight for now. Anyone else awake down there?'

Another pause, then several more voices answered in quick succession. It was hard to tell over the crackling radio, but all of them seemed calm and collected. Mike was sure that if it were him in the same situation then he wouldn't sound nearly so reasonable.

'Alright,' Ramone said once he'd got positive confirmation that at least a fair proportion of the encampment was still alive and secure. 'There aren't many of us out here, but we've got an idea.'

'You're going to fly in a SWAT team?' someone on the radio asked.

'I'll get back to you on that one. At the moment though, the best we can provide is a distraction until you can all get yourselves a little more secure. Anyone out there got keys for the weapons store?'

He got three positive answers and one slightly hysterical demand as to how exactly they were supposed to get to the store with all the zombies running around.

'We're going to come up to the fence from this side,' Ramone explained.

'We'll try and draw as many of the dead ones away from you as we can. When it's clear, you'll be able to reach the store. Hopefully we'll also give you time to find a good defensible building as well, if you have any doubts about the place you're currently in.'

Immediately the static was broken by several conflicting voices, all asking questions at once. Ramone gave them a moment, then cut them off.

'Also,' he said, 'can anyone get to the radio room? The boat's coming tomorrow morning, but we need to call someone and let them know the situation asap.'

'Uh, that might be a problem.' It was the first man, Greg Thomas, who answered. 'The radio room is currently on fire, over.'

'Shit.' Ramone swore quietly, keeping his finger off the radio button. 'Okay, scratch that. The rest of the plan still stands. If anyone's got any objections, speak now.' There was no answer. He was about to start talking again when a voice came through.

'Did you see Klement?' it asked. 'He got over the fence. Did you see that?'

'Yes, we saw that,' Ramone confirmed. 'If any of you want to try the same, go right ahead. I'd suggest though that you go along the harbour wall and over the fence on the north side – repeat, the *north* side. The forest to the south is likely to be infested with corpses at the present time.'

There was another burst of talking, which again Ramone more or less ignored.

'I'm asking again,' he said then. 'Anyone got a better plan? Speak now.'

There was silence apart from the static.

'Alright then. Give us five minutes. When you hear firing, that'll be us. Wait until all the dead ones have moved from the vicinity before you move. Everyone copy?'

Everyone acknowledged, some more willingly than others.

'See you in hell, folks.' Ramone clipped the radio back to his belt, frowning. 'Maybe we should just leave them to it,' he said, almost to himself, then turned and disappeared back into the building.

Mike and Anna looked at each other for a second. 'I'm sure it'll be fine,' Mike started to say, but Anna obviously had other things on her mind.

She turned to Ehren, her eyes wide. 'Doctor Ehren?' she asked. 'If those things are all over the island, then what about my father? You said he wasn't in the camp at the moment. Where is he?'

'He's...' For a moment, Ehren seemed unable to focus on her. 'He's alright, don't worry about him.'

'How can you be sure?' Anna demanded. 'Where the hell is he?'

Again Ehren avoided her eyes. From inside the building, Ramone made a noise of irritation. 'Don't you think we've run out of time for this?' the man asked.

Ehren heard him. 'Exactly!' he said with a flash of anger. 'We don't have time – '

'That's not what I mean.' Ramone appeared again, his arms full. 'I don't think we've got time for you to keep avoiding the truth. Just tell the girl what she needs to hear and let's get out of here.'

'What?' Anna looked quickly between the two men. 'What do I need to hear?'

Ehren seemed to sag even further. 'I don't know where your father is right now,' he said at length.

'You said he left the encampment – '

'He did. Five days ago.' Ehren hesitated, moistening his lips. 'He left in the evening with one of his colleagues, Doctor Sykes. We... we found Doctor Sykes the following morning.'

Anna remembered the name; remembered what Luca had told her the night before. '*Found* him?' she pressed.

'Dead.' Ehren was staring at a point over her shoulder in a way that made Anna want to grab him and shake him hard. 'We found him out in the woods... we think one of the animals attacked him.'

'A wolf,' Ramone said shortly. 'That's right, isn't it?'

'We're not sure of that...'

Anna finally lost her patience and grabbed the man by his arm. 'And what about my dad?' she demanded. 'Did you find him too?'

Ehren shook his head. 'He's still missing.'

'Missing,' Anna repeated. Abruptly she let go of his arm and covered her face with both hands. She said something else but her voice was too choked for the others to hear it.

'We're still trying to work out what happened...' Ehren said uselessly.

'Why don't you ask Seth?' Ramone asked.

Ehren blinked. 'What?'

'Seth MacColl.' Ramone took in the blank expression on Ehren's face and threw his hands in the air. 'Do you actually talk to anyone at all on this island? Sykes and Martin didn't go out on their own that night. I was talking to one of the wolves at the village. He said that they drove up there and picked up a passenger – Seth. Which makes him the last one to have seen them alive.'

'But...' Ehren shook his head slowly. 'No. He never said anything about that.'

'Is that so? Wonder why that was.' None too gently, Ramone shoved a rifle into Ehren's hands, as well as a carton of rounds. 'Maybe when we catch up with him we can ask, yeah?'

Ehren continued to shake his head in simple denial.

'We'd better get moving.' Ramone picked up a black bag from the floor and slung it over his shoulder. Judging by the weight, he'd obviously taken the time to load it with a few extra supplies from the store. His own rifle went over the other shoulder, and Mike noticed that there was now a sidearm holstered on his belt as well.

Anna was still staring at Ehren, but the look in her eyes was unreadable. Ramone passed the last rifle to her.

'Try to only shoot the things that're already dead,' he suggested. 'Okay?'

Anna took the gun, but didn't answer him.

Chapter 34

'It's been quarter of an hour, where the fuck are they?'

Tris put her hand on Greg's back, but he shrugged it off irritably. 'He said they'd be a few minutes,' she reminded him.

'It's *been* a few minutes. It's alright for them, safe outside that fence – what about us? Who's to say they're not going to just piss off and leave us here?'

Behind him, Reid snorted. 'Oh gee, thanks. Just make us all feel better.'

Greg didn't bother answering. He kept his gaze fixed on the strip of fence that he could see from the window. The undead were still milling around out there, their hands scratching and clawing impotently at the glass. Greg felt a wave of disgust as he looked down on them. 'Stupid goddamn ugly creatures,' he muttered. 'Freaks of nature. I fucking hate them.'

Apart from the dead ones, there was no movement outside. From where he was positioned, Greg could see a few hundred yards of fence and the main gate, which was still admitting a slow but steady stream of the undead. Ever since Ramone's radio message had brought some temporary hope, Greg had been watching from the window intently, anxious for any sign of their rescuers.

'Maybe they're already dead,' he suggested, which drew another sarcastic comment from Reid.

'Hey,' Tris said, looking up suddenly. 'Listen.'

It took Greg a moment to realise what had changed. The alarms from the fence had shut off, and the sudden silence filled the air.

'Have they turned off the fence?' Tris asked.

'I don't think so... the lights are still on. I guess they've just turned the siren off.' For the first time in what felt like hours, Greg was able to hear himself think. He also became aware that he could now hear the dead outside as their hands slapped continuously against the windows.

The silence lasted for several endless minutes, and then they heard the first shots.

'That's them!' Greg stood up on the table, even though it didn't give him any better a view. 'I can't see them, but...'

Several more shots were fired in quick succession, the noise echoing all across the camp so that it was difficult to pinpoint exactly where it was coming from. A moment later though, one of the zombies outside the window turned slowly away, its dead eyes roving across the open space behind it. Then it lumbered away on stiff legs, heading off towards the distant fence.

'Go,' Greg encouraged the creature in a whisper. 'Go, go, go, go, go...'

As the shooting continued, several more of the dead ones turned away from the windows and began to stagger away. They moved with horrendous slowness, making Greg chew his lip in angry impatience. When all but a handful of the zombies had moved off, he jumped down from the table.

'That does it,' he announced. 'There're only a few still out there – I'm gonna start taking down the barricades.'

'Wait, don't go out there!' Tris' voice was panicky, and Greg felt his anger rise at her as well. 'The man said to wait until they were all out of the way!'

'I'm not going anywhere just yet. All I'm doing is shifting some of this stuff out of the way.' He glanced back at her on the way to the door. 'And get down from there. If those things see you looking out then they'll hang around here.'

Tris didn't look happy, but she did as she was told. Greg started moving the piled up desks away from the interior door.

Ten minutes later, Tris risked a glance out of the window and reported that all of the dead ones were some distance away now. Greg stepped out into the corridor and started unblocking the outside door.

'Just be careful, alright?' Tris called. 'Don't go out yet, they haven't gone that far.'

'I'm not stupid, am I? Come on – everyone out here.'

Reluctantly, the other three filed out into the corridor. Reid had unscrewed a metal table leg and was carrying it like a club, and Greg still had his currently useless rifle, but the girls were both unarmed. Greg decided that it probably didn't matter, since they only planned to be out in the open for a few moments.

'Okay,' he said once the outside door was cleared. 'Stick together and move fast, okay?'

The others nodded obediently, which gave Greg a brief warm feeling. He unclipped the key to the armoury storeroom from the loop on his belt, holding it in the palm of his hand, ready. He eased open the door.

The smell of smoke and death were thick in the air outside. Even at a distance, Greg could feel the heat of the burning building on his face, and for a moment he hesitated, held in place by the sudden reality of what they were planning. It would be so much easier to just shut the door and go back to their safe room – let someone else reach the weapon store and play at being a hero.

'Is it clear or what?' Reid said from behind him.

His earlier irritation restored, Greg pulled the door open all the way. There were no zombies in his immediate line of sight, so he stepped outside quickly, waving the others forward.

The others followed nervously, but Greg didn't wait for them. He set off at a run, heading around the back of the burning building, taking the chance that all the dead ones were gone from there. His guess paid off: he caught sight of a few lumbering shapes as he rounded the corner, but they were all a good distance away.

Despite what he had told Ramone, Greg couldn't resist a quick glance into the radio room as he hurried past. Through the shattered windows all he could see was black smoke. No flames though, so there was always a chance that once the smoke cleared the radio equipment would be salvageable. Greg pushed the thought to the back of his mind – at that moment, he had more important things to worry about.

Around the second corner, Greg got a clear view of the top half of the camp. The crowd of zombies looked impossibly large from there, but at least they were all stumbling away from him, towards the fence. Greg could just make out a tiny group of people on the other side of the fence, and see the near continuous muzzle-flashes as they fired dozens of rounds into the approaching horde. They didn't seem to be scoring too many hits, although every now and again one of the zombies would drop to the ground and cease moving, but at least they were doing what they'd said they would – providing a distraction.

When Greg reached the store he found that he'd been beaten to it. Two men were there already and had the door open, hauling out rifles and ammunition and making a large pile on the ground outside. They looked up as Greg came running over, their faces reflecting his own deep fear at being in such an exposed area.

'Here,' one of the men said, indicating the pile of weaponry. 'Grab whatever you can and take it round to the refectory. There's a bunch of us in there – it's a good defensible place, so we're gonna try and get everyone inside.'

Greg chafed at the authoritative tone of voice, but bent quickly and grabbed an extra rifle and several cartons of ammunition from the pile. It was only then that he shook his head.

'No,' he told the man. 'We're not going there.'

The man looked at him, then shook his head angrily. 'Fine, go wherever you want.' He went back to collecting weapons from inside the store.

Tris had caught up with Greg in time to hear the exchange. 'What?' she asked. 'Where are we going then? We're not going back to that tiny storehouse!'

'No, we're not.' Greg pushed a rifle into her hands. 'We're getting out of here. Over the fence.'

'What the hell for? We'll be safe here; we've got guns now...'

'I'm not staying here,' Greg said angrily. 'We're getting out. Come on.' He grabbed her arm and started pulling her away.

'Hey!' Reid and the blonde girl were right behind them, and Greg pushed them out of his way. 'Where the hell are you going?'

Greg didn't bother to reply. He kept hold of Tris' arm and led her quickly away. A backward glance showed him that Reid had gone to help the other two men carry the guns. *Good,* Greg thought. *One less idiot to worry about.*

Keeping between the buildings, Greg made his way towards the sea. Several groups of people passed him, heading towards the store, but he ignored them. He was intent on his own plan now. When he was halfway to the water he realised that it had gone quiet again. The distant sound of shots had abruptly ceased.

Greg didn't stop to worry about what it meant. They were past all the buildings now, with nothing but open ground between them and the surf.

A shout from behind them made both Greg and Tris look back. It was difficult to see through the overlying smoke, but it looked like the people on the other side of the fence had retreated back into the forest. Without that distraction to hold the scant attention of the dead ones, some of them had already turned away in search of another food source, and had spotted the humans scurrying about outside the buildings. It had only taken a couple of the dead ones to start back down the hill, and suddenly all of them were reversing direction. Like a slow-moving wave, the zombies began to return.

Anyone still outside grabbed whatever they could from the store and beat a hasty retreat to the refectory. They were all safely inside long before the first of the dead managed to reach the building.

Greg, however, quickly realised a flaw in his plan. The zombies had been drawn by the shooting towards the fence on the north side, but were now spreading out along it. Although they were still some distance away, Greg suddenly had his doubts that him and Tris would be able to reach the safe part of the fence on that side and climb over before the dead ones reached them.

Still holding tightly onto Tris' arm, he altered direction and started heading along the shoreline towards the southern side of the fence.

'Where are you going?' Tris asked, her voice panicky. 'You said we were going over the fence!'

'We are.' Silently, Greg cursed the woman. She was slowing down, and he was having to practically drag her onwards. 'We're going over this side.'

'But – ' Tris would have stopped walking altogether if Greg hadn't had such a firm grip on her arm. 'The man said that –'

'I know what he said. Look around you – all the dead are in here. I don't care what he said, there won't be any left out in the forest.' Even privately, he would not admit his real reason for changing direction. His brief encounter with the dead ones at the gate had terrified him, and the idea of running the gauntlet past them again made his blood freeze.

Tris gave up fighting and allowed herself to be dragged towards the fence. Behind them, the sound of gunfire resumed, this time coming from within the buildings of the camp, as the survivors began to fight back.

Chapter 35

For a while, it was all going fine.

Mike slowly began to get to grips with the rifle, working the bolt with increasing confidence. He still wasn't hitting very much, but at least he'd stopped flinching every time he pulled the trigger.

To his left, Anna seemed to be having more luck, which was annoying. She still had a strangely distant look in her eyes, and every now and again she took her gaze off the targets and looked over at Ehren, who was standing at the opposite end of the line from her, as far away as possible. She hadn't said a word since they had left the concrete supply building, which Mike took as a bad sign.

Ramone was the only one scoring hits with any frequency. When they'd first got to the fence and set themselves up a way back from it on the safe, non-zombie infested side, he'd told them that their main purpose was to draw all the dead ones towards them. Actually killing them was secondary – 'although, go for it if you like'. They were certainly succeeding at luring the zombies towards them, but only a couple of dozen had been felled so far, and ninety percent of those had been thanks to Ramone. He had also managed to finally silence the wailing alarm by pulling out a handful of wires from one of the fence's control boxes.

Mike had been perturbed at first by his own complete inability to hit anything, but had eventually decided to view it as a progressive training exercise. Gradually he was getting better. At the moment he was focusing his sights on a single zombie – a male corpse wearing jeans and a red shirt with the number "23" printed in white on the front. Mike had hit him three or four times now, mainly in the chest and stomach. Scoring head shots was proving surprisingly difficult. Shooting through the chain-link was also causing a few problems.

He lowered the gun for a moment and shifted his camera, which was hanging from its strap over his shoulder. He'd started it recording earlier, just as they'd come out of the trees in front of the fence, and was trying to keep it pointing generally towards where the action was. *There has to be a record of this*, Mike told himself, lifting the gun again. *This is the most amazing thing ever… and I'm right here, right on the spot to record it all.* He tried to remember the name of the documentary maker who, a few years ago, had videoed an apparent zombie attack up in Siberia… Tyler, Taylor, something like that. The whole thing had been rejected as an elaborate hoax, but the guy who'd filmed it had always maintained that it was genuine. *I always wanted to believe it was real…*

'Try to keep them away from the fence,' Ramone said then, breaking his train of thought. 'I think that might be how the other ones caught fire.'

'Sure.' Mike gave up on the zombie with the 23 shirt, switching his attention to the dead ones closer to the fence. 'Hey, this is harder than it looks.'

'Told you John Woo was full of shit.'

Mike paused to reload. His arms were beginning to ache, and he was sure that there was a bruise forming on his right shoulder from the recoil. 'So, why do you keep a store of weaponry outside the fence?' he asked. 'Is it one of those "just in case" things?'

'Kinda.' Ramone aimed and casually felled another zombie. 'Maybe not this *specific* case, but yeah.'

'Seems like a hell of a lot of weaponry for a small population,' Mike noted.

Ramone laughed quietly. 'Yeah. There're a couple more of those stores on the island as well. One near the main road, and another on the coast, just south of here.' He shot at another zombie, firing a second round when the first one missed. 'That one was left by the military.'

'Is that because of the animals in the forest?' Mike asked, remembering the horse-like monster they had seen briefly out on the road earlier.

Ramone shook his head, but he seemed to be smiling. 'Not entirely, no.' He lowered his rifle for a moment and crouched down, opening the black bag at his feet. He removed one of the boxes of rounds, this one with a red lid, and passed it to Mike.

'What're these?' Mike asked, opening it. The rounds inside looked normal enough when he lifted one out.

'Silver.' Ramone wiped his forehead with the back of his hand, glancing up at the overcast sky. It was just after midday, but it didn't look like it was going to get any warmer or brighter that day.

'Seriously?'

'Uh-huh.'

Mike slotted the round back into its space in the box. 'What for?'

The grin that Ramone gave him seemed genuine. 'Just in case.' He lifted his rifle again. 'Of course, neither the vamps nor the wolves know we keep those.

It was one of the conditions of the truce we have that no-one brings silver onto the island. Right, Ehren?'

Ehren didn't answer; didn't even look at the man.

Anna laughed then, an abrupt, brittle sound. 'So you lot have been stockpiling weapons against them, and they've been killing your men. Nice situation. No wonder shit like this happens.'

Mike started to speak, then closed his mouth. There was nothing he could think of to say to the girl. He could only guess at the strain she was under, wondering where the hell her father was, and not even knowing if he was alive or not. Mike wished that there was something he could say or do that would make it all better, but he knew that there wasn't.

'This was never supposed to happen,' Ehren said then. His voice was so quiet that he might as well have been talking to himself. 'This is exactly what we prepared against...'

'Prepared?' Anna faced him now, unconsciously clutching the gun so tightly that her knuckles turned white. 'The island's overrun with zombies. My father's missing... you've as good as admitted he's probably dead.' Her voice cracked and she clenched her jaw against it. 'The least you could do is admit some fucking responsibility here.'

Ramone had prudently stepped back a little out of the way. 'Miss Martin?' he said calmly. 'With all due respect, you should realise a couple of things.'

Anna was blinking back angry tears. 'What?'

'For one, we have other problems right now.'

'I can see that!' she snapped.

'Also, there's nothing we can do for your father at this time.' Ramone's voice was completely calm, as if he were having this conversation somewhere other than a few dozen yards from a shambling zombie horde, with only a thin chain-link fence between them. 'Even if he's dead... well, that's probably the least of his worries right now.' He touched Anna's shoulder and very gently turned her back round to face the fence. 'We'll deal with it real soon, okay?'

'Don't patronise me,' Anna muttered, but she lifted her rifle again and resumed taking potshots at the zombies.

Again, Mike wished there was something he could add, but Ramone had already said it all. Maybe he had been blunt, but his words were true. Mike couldn't help but feel acutely aware of his own uselessness at that moment.

Several of the dead ones had almost reached the fence now, and Mike concentrated his aim on them. If he couldn't be of any use to Anna, at least he could try and help the people inside the compound.

He sighted on a blonde woman with half her face missing, briefly trying to remember if she was one of the ones they had seen yesterday in the enclosure. It didn't matter. He let his breath out and concentrated on the shot.

The dead woman's head exploded as he pulled the trigger, showering brain tissue over her companions.

'Yes!' Mike yelled. 'Did you see that?' He turned and grinned at the others proudly. 'It's about time I – ' He broke off suddenly, his attention caught by a flicker of movement behind him. Turning, he saw the trees a short distance away rustle as something pushed its way through them.

A zombie stepped out of the undergrowth, its dead eyes swivelling back and forth until finally settling on the humans. It was old, with much of the flesh from its face and arms already rotted away and its shirt and short trousers hanging in tatters, but its eyes seemed almost alive, shining with dull intelligence. It took a step towards them, its arms swinging forward like those of a grotesque marionette.

'Hey, we've got company!' Mike raised his rifle and shot at the zombie, missing by several feet.

'I got him.' Calmly, Ramone took down the dead one. 'Where did it come from?' he asked as the corpse crumpled to the ground.

'Out of the trees. It just popped out over there –' Even as Mike was pointing, another figure emerged from the forest, stumbling on dead limbs through the tangle of undergrowth.

Ramone hesitated, swinging his rifle's sights along the line of trees. 'Why are they coming through the forest?' he asked out loud. 'If they wanted to get to us they would just follow the fence along...'

Mike had stopped listening to him, his already stretched nerves reacting badly to the newly-appeared corpses. He fired several quick rounds at the lumbering zombie, scoring one hit on the creature's chest but missing with all the others.

'We may want to fall back – ' Ramone started to say, and then suddenly the dead ones were appearing like magic from out of the forest.

At least a dozen came in the first wave, tripping over each other in their haste to get out into the open. Their dead eyes rolled frantically, searching for the food that they could sense close by.

Ramone grabbed his bag and started backing away towards the forest. 'Fall back!' he yelled to the others. 'Get back to the road, fast!'

Nobody stopped to question his order. As the undead came spilling out of the woods, the humans broke and ran back the way they had come, angling away from the undead horde that seemed to have come out of nowhere to surround them.

Chapter 36

Although they tried to stick to the path that they had made on their way out of the forest, the undergrowth seemed to have closed up behind them. Ramone led them through the trees at a run, ducking and weaving between the branches. Mike tried to keep up but quickly began to fall behind, having to run with his arms up in front of his head to prevent the springy undergrowth from slapping him in the face. As a result he was running virtually blind and following Ramone by sound and instinct alone. He could only hope that he was still going the right way, and that the others were still behind him.

They came out of the trees so suddenly that Mike almost tripped over his own feet. His hands and arms were scratched in a dozen places and his eyes were watering so much that for a moment all he could do was stand there blinking and trying to work out where the hell they were.

Ramone had led them straight through the forest to the road, avoiding the small clearing with the supply building. He'd angled north in case any more of the dead ones had been lurking in the trees, and when Mike's vision finally cleared he saw that it was a good thing they hadn't directly retraced their steps.

The jeep stood a couple of hundred yards down the road from them, and the roadway around it was now choked with zombies. They were milling about without apparent purpose, but as soon as the humans appeared from the trees the mass of undead slowly turned and began to shuffle towards them.

'They must have followed the road round,' Ramone said, but he was frowning as if working out the likelihood of that. 'Heard the engine noise earlier or something...' He shook his head, dismissing the thought. 'Try and clear a path, okay? Don't hit the jeep. The spare petrol tank's on the back there.'

Mike followed his lead and began shooting at the zombies. Immediately he saw that there were too many of them, and that for every one they put down another two crowded forward to take its place. It seemed impossible that they could clear a safe route back to the jeep, and the thought made Mike's stomach twist. If they couldn't get to the vehicle then their last chance of escape had been effectively cut off and they would be forced to flee on foot. The idea made his hands shake even worse than before and very few of his shots found their marks.

Anna was by his side now, helping them dispatch the dead ones, but Ehren was nowhere to be seen. He had not emerged with them from the forest. Everyone was too busy to be concerned about that right then. The dead continued to surge relentlessly forward, an unstoppable tide that swiftly engulfed the jeep and hid it almost completely from view.

Ramone let out a shout of sudden, helpless anger and started unloading his gun at the zombies with even greater fury, working the bolt so quickly that his hand was almost a blur. He shot down five of the dead ones in a matter of seconds, but he may as well have been throwing pebbles at the sea for all the effect it had. The zombies kept coming, stumbling closer by the second.

Mike knew that they were going to have to withdraw. There was no way the three of them could have taken on the army of the undead, and if they didn't back off soon then they could well find their escape cut off again. Ramone must have been aware of that as well, but there was a look in his eyes that Mike had not seen before. The man's rage was carrying him forward, causing him to continue firing at the enemy even when it was obvious that there was no hope. Worse, he was steadily inching forward as he continued shooting, and the zombies were homing in on him like flies on meat.

Mike turned with the intention of grabbing Anna and pointing out to her that the three of them had to leave, right now. Out of the corner of his eye he saw a figure come stumbling out of the forest to their left and his heart stuttered in his chest. He was already swinging his gun round when he realised that the figure was Ehren.

Torn between relief and anger, Mike started to ask him where the hell he'd been, but he never got the chance. Ramone's shots had become wildly erratic as fury won out over self-control, and he was no longer able to aim with any accuracy. Through sheer weight of gunfire he'd managed to open a passage through to the stranded jeep, but his momentary euphoria was short lived. A careless shot ricocheted off the metalwork of the back of the jeep and ploughed directly into the spare fuel tank.

The explosion knocked all of them off their feet. For a moment Mike was aware only of the heat and the noise and the fact that he was for some reason lying on the ground. He rolled onto his stomach, protecting his camera with his arms until his stunned mind remembered that there were more important things to be worrying about.

Struggling upright, Mike saw that Anna and the two men were also on the ground, although none of them appeared to be hurt. Ramone was already getting back to his feet, the unnatural rage of a moment before fading from his eyes as he saw what had happened. The jeep was in flames, as were at least a dozen of the dead ones in the near vicinity. Several had been too close to the centre of the blast and now lay motionless, and most of the others had been knocked to the ground.

Slowly, the writhing pile of undead humanity began to pull their way back upright. The ones that were on fire paid no heed to the fact. They stumbled forward just as before, occasionally bumping into their companions and causing them to also burst into flame.

'Are you okay?' Mike helped Anna to her feet. The girl looked wide-eyed and stunned, but she nodded. Together they began to retreat hastily up the road.

Ramone stood motionless, a strangely thoughtful look on his face as he stared at the burning wreckage of his jeep.

'Ramone, come on!' Mike yelled after him.

The man finally seemed to shake himself out of it and turned to follow them, apparently now more irritated than anything else. He slung his rifle over his shoulder and broke into a run, quickly catching up with the others.

'Sorry,' he said. 'My fault.' There was no trace of his earlier anger, and he seemed to be back to his usual state of carefully controlled calm.

'It's okay,' Mike told him. 'I'm just assuming you have a Plan B ready for us.' He was still supporting Anna even though she showed no signs of actually needing his help. Ehren was behind him, but none of them had the urge to question him just yet.

Together the four of them jogged away up the dirt track, whilst behind them the tide of undead continued to roll forward in slow pursuit.

'So?' Mike asked after they'd put enough distance between themselves and the dead ones to feel a little more comfortable. 'Do we have a Plan B?'

Ramone dropped the pace to a walk and shrugged. 'I think we're technically onto at least Plan C or D by now.'

'Could we loop back round and try to get back into the camp?'

'I don't know.' Although he still seemed calm, for the first time there was indecision in his eyes. 'We could try, if you want. It probably shouldn't be too difficult to get back to the camp and over the fence, but all the dead ones will be surrounding the buildings in there by now. There's no real way we could break through to them, and then we'd just be right out in the open.'

'So where're we heading?' Mike squinted up the road which sloped upwards away from them. 'Back to the wolf village?'

'I guess so.' Still walking, Ramone began to reload his rifle, then checked the bag to see how much ammo they had left. 'It's going to take a long time to make it there... I guess we'll just have to hope we can make it before nightfall.'

Mike stated to ask why, then his eyes widened. 'Shit,' he said.

'Yep.' Ramone nodded grimly. 'We can probably make it in a couple of hours if we move fast, but it's going to be close. With the full moon tonight, the wolf village isn't my first choice of safe places to be.'

'What would be your first choice?'

For a moment Ramone didn't answer, but then he grinned. 'Back home with a blanket over my head.'

Mike laughed. 'Yeah, that sounds like a good option.'

'Of course, there's one more sunny fact that we've overlooked,' Ramone said then, his mood sobering again. 'The boat's going to be arriving tomorrow morning at the camp. If the people holed up in those buildings are lucky, they'll be able to kill off a fair proportion of the dead ones by then. So they'll either make a run for the boat or at least be able to let the crew know they're there. But as for the fortunate people like us that're stuck outside the camp...' He shrugged. 'We'll have to hope the survivors in the camp are good enough to point out that a well-armed rescue crew needs to come back for the rest of us.'

Mike exchanged a worried look with Anna. 'How long would that take?'

'I have no idea,' Ramone admitted. 'But if we do make it to the wolf village and hole up inside those houses safely, then the dead ones are going to follow us right there. They'll reach the village long before morning, and then we really will be trapped. There'll be no way out until a rescue crew arrives, and that might well be never.'

'Hell,' Anna groaned. 'You make it sound like we've got no hope at all. Why the hell are we even running then?'

'That's not exactly what I'm saying. But I'm not going to start lying about our situation to make us all feel better. The wolf village is the best place I can think of to hide, but anywhere we hole up is going to be a trap, eventually. The dead don't stop, they don't give up, and they can go for months without food. They're not even animals, they're more like machines in that respect. We can run and we can hide, but we can't outlast them.'

'So what the hell do you suggest?'

'I told you, I don't know. We're not exactly burdened with options right now.' He glanced behind them. The army of undead was still in plain sight, stretching out along the road. The smoke from the burning jeep rose in a billowing column, rising to join the general pall hanging over the camp. 'First things first, let's get out of sight of those bloody zombies.'

Chapter 37

The road in front of them sloped upwards gently over a hill, and once they were beyond that the dead ones were out of sight and everyone breathed a little easier. Mike and Anna both paused at the brow of the hill to look back, not at their pursuers but at the encampment beyond the trees. One building there was still burning fitfully, leaking out black smoke into the overcast sky, but the flames appeared to be dying down now. All the undead that had caught fire on the fence had succumbed to the flames and no more human torches wandered the battlefield. Over the still air, Mike and Anna were just able to hear the distant crack of gunshots coming from the barricaded buildings. The camp was too far away for them to be able to judge the effectiveness of the human retaliation, but what was obvious was the size of the zombie infestation. Although no more dead ones were coming in through the gate, each building was completely surrounded by a circle of undead at least ten bodies deep. Around the largest building, which Mike was fairly sure was the refectory, the circle was more like twenty deep.

'Do you really think they'll be able to kill all of them?' Anna asked quietly, watching the milling undead. 'There's so many.'

Mike didn't have any answer, so he just shook his head and turned away.

They walked on in silence for a long while. Already the sun appeared to be dropping in the sky, and Mike wondered how much daylight they really had left. Once the sun disappeared beneath the horizon, their already bad situation was going to get a lot worse.

'So, Ehren,' Ramone asked suddenly. 'Where did you get to earlier?'

The older man looked up, blinking as if he'd been dragged away from a deep train of thought. 'What?'

'Where did you get to? While we were fighting off the dead ones back there, where were you? I thought you'd got yourself lost. Or dead.' He didn't seem particularly upset by the possibility.

'I was just behind a little way.' Ehren's voice was quiet, and he didn't hold

Ramone's gaze for long. 'You left me behind.'

Ramone grunted and kept walking.

Privately, Mike wondered at the change that had come over both the men. All the self-confidence that Ehren had previously displayed had drained away, and he now looked lost and a little confused. Ramone had given up all pretence of deference to him, and it was clear who was in charge now.

The party was halfway down the slope on the other side of the hill, still moving at a fast walk, when Ramone held up his hand and brought them to a halt. Mike and Anna stopped, glancing round nervously. Mike in particular was already a little out of breath, and although he tried hard he was unable to hear anything over his own loud heartbeat in his ears.

Ramone stayed frozen in position, turning his head back and forth to locate the source of the noise he had heard. Finally, the others heard it too: the sound of something moving quickly and easily through the trees on their left side. Ramone quickly shouldered his rifle.

'Another zombie?' Mike asked in a whisper.

Ramone shook his head. 'Too fast. Maybe one of the animals.'

Remembering the horse-monster from that morning, Mike gripped his own rifle tighter and stared at the forest, holding his breath.

The noise from the trees got louder, then abruptly stopped. The brief silence that followed was broken by a short, barking cough from somewhere in the trees.

Ramone visibly relaxed and lowered his gun. 'It's one of the wolves,' he said with relief. Louder, he called: 'C'mon out, we're all friends over here!'

The brush at the edge of the cleared area of ground parted and a figure stepped cautiously out. It was recognisably human, but only just.

'What the hell are you doing here?' the figure asked, and Mike started with surprise as he recognised Brac's voice. The person who came stalking towards them now bore only the most superficial resemblance to the man they'd left in the werewolf village earlier. It looked as if his body had been stretched and bent into a parody of humanity. He walked with a visible stoop, his arms seeming unnaturally long and muscular, reaching almost to the ground. He was naked to the waist, and his entire upper body was covered by a thin layer of coarse grey-black hair. There was something strange about the way he was walking, and it was only when he came closer that Mike realised his legs were jointed differently now, like those of a dog. Mike could only stare. Brac had been turned into something that wasn't human and wasn't wolf, but somewhere in being.

'We've run into a few problems,' Ramone said, answering the question. 'The camp's been overrun by the dead ones, for a start.'

Brac came up to them with a strange, loping stride, then crouched down in roadway. In his altered state it seemed a natural posture. 'Are there any other survivors?' he asked, apparently unsurprised by the information. His voice was pretty much the same as it had been before, but his face was subtly altered. The lower half had been pushed outwards, the nose flattening and the mouth being stretched wider. His unblinking eyes were now a deep amber colour, and the pupils had become black slits. His ears had somehow moved further up his head.

'There's still a bunch of survivors inside the camp,' Ramone told him, 'but they're all holed up in the buildings. We might have joined them, but we had to make a tactical retreat.'

'Where's your jeep?'

Ramone indicated behind them at the thick plume of smoke rising from the hill. 'It suffered a blue-on-blue related incident,' he reported with a trace of annoyance. 'We're reduced to walking now.'

Brac nodded shortly. 'How did all the dead ones get out of the enclosure?'

'That's one of the things we don't know yet. They're right behind us though, so we'd best get moving.'

With another short nod, Brac turned and led the way along the dirt track, keeping pace with Ramone in his half-crouched, loping stride. The others followed them. 'I figured they must be out,' Brac growled. 'I've been able to smell them for some time now. You headed to the village?'

Ramone shrugged. 'Unless a better plan comes to mind.'

'You'd better get thinking then,' Brac said bluntly. 'No-one's getting in or out of the village. Everything's sealed up and they've been ordered not to open the doors until they get the all clear.'

'Who ordered that?'

'Me.' The look in Brac's eyes dared him to question it.

Ramone grunted. 'Well, that's not good.'

'Not for you, no.' The man attempted a smile, but the new shape of his jaw distorted it. 'Like I say, I suspect you need a new plan.'

Ramone stared at the sky for a moment as if seeking answers from the heavens. 'What about you?' he asked then. 'How're you going to get back in?'

'Me? I'm not. Not unless I'm certain it's safe for the doors to be opened again.' His altered face was grim. 'If the situation's as bad as you say, then I'm going to have to take my chances like the rest of you.'

'The situation's that bad,' Ramone confirmed. 'Okay, so we need somewhere safe for tonight, and then we need to get to the boat tomorrow, or at the very least let them know that there are people still alive out here.'

'The first part's going to be difficult enough.' Brac lifted his head and sniffed the air. 'How many of the dead ones are behind you? Smells like a hundred.'

'Y'know, I didn't stop to count.'

'Wait,' Anna said suddenly. 'What about the vampires?'

Ramone frowned. 'What about them?'

'Couldn't we get up to the mountains? They've got that big cavern up there – if we could seal ourselves inside it we'd be safe. Or even better, if we could somehow block off the road behind us…' She trailed off, realising that everyone was staring at her. 'What?'

'How do you know all that?' Ramone asked.

'Oh.' Anna flushed, realising that with the exception of Mike she hadn't spoken to anyone about her excursion the previous evening. 'Well, it's kind of a long story and right now's probably not the time, but I met Luca last night.' Ehren, who had been silent all this time, stared at her wide-eyed. 'Where?' he demanded.

'In the camp. He jumped over the fence and – '

'No! That's impossible!' Ehren seemed outraged by the idea. 'There's no way he could've got inside the fence… and besides, it was in the treaty that he would never – '

'Yeah, yeah.' Ramone cut him off. 'We all know how well your precious treaty's worked so far, Ehren. Hey, maybe if you'd got the dead ones to sign it as well then we could've avoided this whole situation.'

'Anyway,' Anna said hurriedly to avoid an argument. 'If we could get up to the mountains then I'm sure Luca would let us stay there till the morning. They might even be able to come up with a plan to get us out of here.'

Ehren was already shaking his head angrily. 'No. We want nothing to do with those monsters. They've been against us ever since we got here, this is just further proof of that –'

'Shut up, Ehren,' Ramone said. 'I don't hear you making any better suggestions.'

Brac was laughing quietly, although it sounded more like a growl. 'And it's interesting to find out how you really regard your neighbours here, Doctor Ehren.'

'Okay,' Ramone said, coming to a decision. 'Barring objections from anyone except Ehren, we'll go with that idea. We can take the old track and loop back to the main road that way. It should still be clear, and it'll save us having to wade through the forest. We're still probably not going to get to shelter before nightfall, but with the wolves safe indoors we shouldn't have to worry too much. Well, no more than usual.' He smiled without much humour. 'Our biggest problem is going to be if Miss Martin here can't sweet-talk the vamps into letting us in.' He turned to look down at Brac. 'What about you?'

The wolfman blinked his lazy amber eyes. 'Me?'

'Yeah – are you going back to the village? They're going to need to know what's happened.'

'They've already guessed,' Brac said soberly. 'If I don't come back and give the all-clear then they'll know to stay indoors and out of sight. We've always known something like this would happen, ever since you rounded up the dead ones into that enclosure. We're probably better prepared than you.'

Thinking back to the chaos at the camp, Mike was inclined to agree.

'We'll see what the situation is in the morning,' Brac went on. 'But if the village has to stay locked up then they'll manage okay. The wolves are in separate tunnels so they can't do any damage to the others. And there's enough food down there to last at least a couple of months.'

'And after that?'

Brac shrugged his massive shoulders. 'We'll have to hold out for a rescue.'

'Great.' Ramone shifted the bag on his shoulder, glancing back along the road. 'We'd better pick up the pace. The old track's a couple of miles further along.'

Chapter 38

With Ramone and the wolf-man leading, the group increased their pace to a fast walk, and within a matter of minutes Mike began to feel winded. He took a moment to readjust the carrying strap of his camera, shortening it so that the camera hung securely against his chest and didn't bump around so much. With a momentary pang, he wished that he'd left the camera running when the jeep had exploded, but he quickly pushed the thought out of his mind. It was very tempting to start thinking of this whole day in terms of a series of great shots, and he hoped that it was just the stress of the situation making him think like that. Otherwise there was something very messed up with his psyche. He slung his rifle over his other shoulder so that the weight was a little more evenly distributed. Even so, he was becoming very aware of how heavy the rifle was, especially now that they were moving faster. He wasn't particularly happy at the thought of having to haul it round for the rest of the day... but, considering the situation, he decided he'd much rather have it than be without it. Besides, no-one else was complaining – not even Ramone, who was carrying the spare ammunition as well.

It was only a few minutes later that Ramone heard something else moving in the forest and called another abrupt halt. 'What's that?' he asked Brac, since the sound was coming from more or less the same direction as he had appeared from.

Brac made a noise that could have been either a sigh or a growl. 'She's still following me,' he said, and then raised his voice slightly. 'Lyell!'

There was a brief silence, and then a second wolf came out of the forest, her shaggy black head held high. She came bounding across the road like a puppy, her long pink tongue lolling out in a wolfish grin.

'I told you to quit following me,' Brac told her sharply. 'You shouldn't even have left the village.'

Lyell ignored him completely and strolled past, heading straight for Mike and Anna. The young wolf rubbed her head affectionately against them both in greeting.

'I assumed everyone was safely indoors at the village,' Brac explained with a pained expression. 'But she must have slipped out and followed me. She seems to be selectively deaf when it comes to me telling her what to do.'

'Girls are like that,' Mike said, earning him a dirty look from both Anna and Lyell.

'At least I can keep an eye on her this way, I guess,' Brac said. 'Come on, this is going to take forever if we don't keep moving.'

It took them a little over half an hour to reach the track that led to the mountains. Brac had ranged ahead, keeping a lookout for any movement in the forest. Lyell appeared quite content to walk with the humans, occasionally butting her head against Mike's arm as if reminding him of her presence. Mike found it a little disconcerting but decided to keep his opinions to himself. It was weird enough to look at the creature who was leading them and remember that a few short hours ago they had been talking to him in human form. The guy had grown claws and fur and his *ears* had moved position, for God's sake. Mike glanced round at his companions and wondered if any of them were feeling as weirded out as he was.

The track that they turned onto was not even as wide as the dirt road that they had previously been following. It looked barely wide enough for a vehicle to pass through, and the trees on either side had not been cleared away, looming over the road so as to create a tunnel. Just looking at it inspired a feeling of claustrophobia, especially considering what could be lurking in the undergrowth just yards from the track.

'We're going to be looping back on ourselves a little to join up with the main road to the mountains,' Ramone informed them as they paused for a brief rest. 'Hopefully we won't run into any of the dead ones – most of them are in the camp and the rest are following us, so we'll have to assume there aren't too many that will have taken it upon themselves to go wandering around cross-country. But we can't be sure, especially since so far the dead ones haven't been acting in an entirely typical way.'

Brac scratched behind his ear, a gesture that was definitely more canine than human. 'What've they been doing?' he asked.

Briefly, Ramone explained what had happened earlier, when the zombies had circled around behind them and come out through the trees rather than taking the easier and direct route of following the fence. 'Not even the alert ones should've been able to do that,' he concluded. 'I'm hoping it was just a nasty coincidence.'

Brac sat back thoughtfully on his haunches. 'Hopefully. Unless they all got smarter while we weren't looking.'

'They don't get smarter. They can't learn, can't plan, can't change at all except to decompose faster in hot weather.' As always when Ramone spoke of the dead ones, there was a thread of disgust and anger in his voice. 'The only thing I can think of is that a few of the alert ones used to be residents of the island. I'll admit that it's bloody tenuous, but if they had any kind of residual memories left...'

Ehren spoke flatly, without looking at any of them. 'The dead ones don't have memories. That part of the brain is completely dead and inaccessible. They don't retain memories.'

'Yeah.' Ramone's tone was hard. 'So you keep saying.' He turned away and started up the track.

The others followed him again, Brac loping ahead as a scout and occasionally disappearing into the bushes on either side of the track. Mike glanced back at Ehren, who continued to trail behind like a sullen child. His face looked even paler than before, and the fast pace was obviously taking its toll on him. Mike found it difficult to summon up much sympathy for the man though.

Within half a mile the ground began to slope gradually upwards, and through the occasional gap in the tree cover the walkers were able to see the mountains rising up in front of them. The closeness of the trees on either side stifled conversation and stretched nerves even closer to breaking point. Mike began to jump at every small noise in the forest, and when Lyell bumped her head against his arm he almost yelled out loud. Judging by the way that the young wolf did it several more times in the next few minutes, she seemed to find it funny.

'How long have we got till nightfall?' Mike asked at last.

Ramone checked his watch. 'Two hours, maybe a little more. Anyone want to stop for a break?'

'Yes,' Mike said immediately. 'Please.'

'Alright.' Ramone smiled a little, unslinging the bag from his shoulder. 'Five minutes, people.'

Brac came wandering back to join them as they sat down on the ground. 'The whole forest smells like death,' he reported irritably. 'It never smells good at the best of times, but this is ridiculous. I'm worried we might walk straight into something before we're even aware it's there. By the way, there's a stream not far off if any of you need a drink.'

It had just occurred to Mike that he was getting more than a little thirsty. Wearily he pushed himself back to his feet. 'Which way?' he asked.

'Hang on.' Ramone held up a hand to stop him, then rooted around in his bag, coming up with a large metal canteen. 'Use this up first,' he told Mike. 'It's not a great idea to drink the water here, unless you're really desperate.'

Brac grinned, displaying pointed front teeth. 'Never did me any harm.'

'Obviously.' The man returned the grin, then turned back to Mike. 'Yeah, no offence to the local inhabitants, but the soil here causes the dead to come back to life, and eating the plants has mutated all the local wildlife, so you'll forgive me if I'm not quite willing to trust the water supply just yet.'

Brac shrugged lazily. 'Your choice.'

Ramone tossed the canteen to Mike. 'Go easy on that, it's got to last at least until we reach the mountains.'

'And what makes the water up there safe to drink?' Brac muttered to himself.

Mike took a drink. The water tasted heavily of chlorine, but it was still welcome. He passed the canteen along to Ehren, who took his share hurriedly, as if he was suffering from thirst more than the others. The doctor handed the canteen back with obvious reluctance.

Taking advantage of the break, Mike sat back and lit himself a cigarette, offering one to Ramone as well. His cigarettes had got a little crushed in his pocket, and he wished briefly that he'd brought his camera bag with him so that he could have put all his excess stuff into it. What with the spare tapes and battery for the camera, plus the two bulky cartons of ammo that he'd been given, the pockets of his jacket were beginning to feel definitely overstuffed. But his camera bag was in his room back at the camp, and it occurred to him then that he might never be able to retrieve it.

'Shit,' he said aloud.

'What?' Anna asked. She looked like he'd surprised her out of a deep train of thought.

'I just realised – all of my stuff's back in the camp.'

Anna stared at him, then started to laugh.

'Shut up, it's not funny.' Mike couldn't help smiling himself. 'I mean, my passport's there, and my wallet... all my money, my house keys... even if we do get out of here I'm not going to be able to get on a plane back home, and even if I somehow do manage *that* then I'm still going to be locked out of my goddamn house.'

Anna covered her mouth with one hand, her eyes sparkling. 'You worry about the most random things.'

'Hey, it beats the hell out of worrying about whether we're going to get eaten alive or not, or if – '

Lyell suddenly leaped to her feet, a growl rising in her throat. She stood rigid, staring at something in the trees to their left, something out of sight to the rest of them. Her ears were laid back flat against her sleek head.

Ramone was immediately on his feet as well. 'What?' he asked.

'The dead,' Brac answered in a growl. He stepped forward, walking on all fours with his nose raised to smell the air. 'Somewhere real close...'

Chapter 39

'We gotta move – ' Ramone made a grab for his bag, and just as he did so something came crashing out of the trees.

Mike only got the briefest impression of the creatures, but he knew at once that they were more of the dead ones. He didn't stop to wonder where they'd come from or how the hell they'd managed to sneak up on them through the dense undergrowth. Instant panic flooded him and he was on his feet at once, scrambling out of the way and trying to grab hold of the rifle over his shoulder. The straps had tangled together and the gun was snagged against his back, resisting his frantic attempts to free it.

The zombies spilled out onto the track, five of them, falling over one another in their haste. Their rotted hands grabbed at the humans, lurching for them with mouths agape. More followed close behind, not hesitating for a second before grabbing at their victims.

Anna had been closest when they appeared, and two of them immediately got hold of her arm. Screaming, Anna hit one of them in the face with the butt of her rifle, breaking its jaw but failing to loosen its grasp. The second zombie dug its nails in and dragged her towards its waiting mouth.

Lyell saved her. The young wolf sprang forward, knocking down both of the dead ones and tearing at them with claws rather than teeth. Her heavy paws stove in the skulls in the space of two heartbeats.

Ramone grabbed hold of Anna as she staggered back and quickly dragged her to safety. At such close range he didn't even bother using his rifle against the dead ones, instead drawing a hand gun from the holster at his side. In another second three more of the dead ones were on the ground, each with a neat bullet hole in their foreheads.

Obeying panic rather than sense, Mike's first instinct had been to run, and he'd stumbled back along the track in the direction they had come. By the time he realised that the others were retreating the opposite way, more of the dead ones had come crashing out of the trees, and with a fresh sense of panic he saw that he was being swiftly cut off from his friends. He heard Ramone yelling to the others to fall back: there were too many of the dead ones for them to handle at such close quarters. They couldn't fight their way back to where Mike was.

Lyell and Brac, still in his half-wolf form, were holding back the zombies with a certain amount of success. Using only their elongated claws, the pair of them were systematically ripping apart the dead ones. On human opponents the wolves would have been able to best them all within moments, but the dead ones ignored even the most horrific of mutilations and continued staggering forward. Several times the wolves narrowly avoided the snapping teeth of the undead.

Brac finally backed away, so swiftly that he almost collided with Mike behind him. He was breathing hard from the fight, and his furred body was splattered with blood and gore. 'Where did they come from?' he demanded, his voice a barely recognisable snarl. 'I don't understand how –'

'The others –' Mike pointed out, waving frantically up the track towards where the rest of their party were quickly disappearing from sight.

'I know.' Brac hung back from the fight for a moment, assessing the situation. 'We'll have to cut through the forest. Lyell!'

The female wolf was intent on ripping apart a zombie that had grabbed hold of one of her legs, and she gave no indication of having heard.

Dropping onto all fours, Brac let out a short, angry bark. Lyell immediately responded, withdrawing her claws from the twice-dead carcass. She jumped clear of the tangle of dead with easy agility, dodging their grasping hands as she ran over to Brac. Her forelegs were matted with blood, but there was a wild kind of exuberance in her amber eyes.

'Follow me,' Brac growled at Mike. 'We're gonna have to move fast, so stay as close as you can.'

'Sure.' Mike's heart was in his throat, and it was all he could do to stop himself from bolting back down the track. His eyes were fixed on the undead creatures that were still slowly spilling out from the gap in the trees. *Holy shit, where are they all coming from?*

'Go!' Brac sprang forward, shouldering his way into the dense forest on the other side of the track from where the zombies had appeared.

Mike ducked his head and followed at a blind run, holding up his arms to protect against the branches that whipped back into his face. He was aware of padding footfalls behind him as Lyell plunged into the forest as well. Sharp twigs tore at his hands and clothing, the larger branches slapping at him hard enough to bruise and batter his skin. It was all he could do to keep his eyes open and his legs moving fast enough to keep pace with Brac in front of him. The fear in his heart doubled as he realised that every step was carrying him further away from Anna and the others.

Brac swerved to the left and Mike followed him, unable to see anything but a grey-black blur of motion in between the brown of the branches. His feet kept snagging on roots and low-lying branches, and a dozen times he almost went sprawling in the mud. Irrationally, he found time to wonder whether, if he fell, Lyell would stop for him or just keep running straight over his head.

He was so busy concentrating on not tripping over that he almost ran straight into the back of Brac when the wolf-man pulled up short. For a second Mike didn't know what had caused him to stop, then suddenly dead hands were snatching at him from out of the undergrowth.

Mike yelled out loud as one of the zombies staggered into him, its hands locking hard onto his shoulders and its ragged nails digging into his flesh. He registered that the corpse was old, the flesh having disintegrated almost entirely from its skull and its eyes shrunken and discoloured deep in the eye sockets. But it was just as strong as any of the other dead ones. It forced its human victim backward under its grip.

Staggering under the assault, Mike was too surprised by the suddenness of the attack to react with anything but sheer instinct. He grabbed for his rifle, this time managing to swing it round to the front of his body and jam the barrel up neatly underneath the zombie's jaw. His finger snatched at the trigger.

Nothing happened. The zombie leaned forward, its dead mouth gaping wide. Belatedly Mike realised that the safety was still on, and it took an agonising second for his fingers to find the switch. By that point the zombie practically had its teeth in his neck and he could feel its dry, dead breath on his face.

Somehow he managed to flick the safety off and find the trigger again, his hands functioning a lot better than his brain. He barely had the presence of mind to close his eyes as he pulled the trigger.

The noise of the gunshot was so loud and so close that it almost ruptured his eardrums. Mike staggered backwards, losing his footing and sitting down hard on the ground. The corpse collapsed with him, its skull a bloody pulped ruin. The steel grip on his shoulders abruptly relaxed as the body tumbled forward, knocking him onto his back and pinning him down.

Mike tasted blood in his mouth and prayed that it was his own. His ears were ringing and all the breath felt like it had been knocked out of him. The corpse that was sprawled over his ribcage was crushing his lungs. He tried to shove it off him and his fingers sank deeply into the shattered brain case. He jerked his hand away in revulsion, squirming and kicking at the body until finally he was free.

All around him was chaos. The dead ones seemed to have appeared from everywhere at once, more bodies emerging from between the trees each moment. Brac and Lyell were fighting them off, but they were hampered by the fact that they didn't dare use their teeth on the infected flesh. For every zombie they felled another two came scrambling over it, reaching for them with skeletal fingers. Relentlessly the two wolves were being forced further and further back.

Wiping the gore from his face, Mike hurriedly raised his rifle and fired at almost point blank range at the dead ones. He was still so deafened that he didn't hear any of the shots, but managed to put down a handful of the undead creatures, until he too was forced back.

Unexpectedly he stepped back too far and bumped against Brac: glancing round he realised that all three of them had run out of room and were now pressed in against each other with the dead ones all around.

'What now?' Mike barely heard his shouted words in his own ears. Another zombie made a grab for him and he shot it through the head with his last round. Hastily he began to reload, his shaking hands fumbling the task.

Brac hesitated, staring around to try and find a spot where they could break through to safety. On all sides they were cut off by the undead. Maybe if it were just him and Lyell then they could have used their speed and strength to put down enough of the zombies to escape, but not with Mike as well…

His gaze turned upwards. The trees all around were massive and old, most with huge spreading branches that interlocked with those of their close-pressed neighbours. Many of the branches were relatively low, and if a person could somehow clear the first ten feet or so and pull themselves up to the lowest of them then it would be relatively easy to climb up well out of the way.

'Up!' Brac instructed Mike.

'What?' Mike was unable to hear him.

'Up the tree! I'll boost you.' When Mike realised what was being said he started to object, and Brac bared his teeth at him in an angry snarl. 'Just move! We can get out of here, you can't!'

Mike nodded quickly and threw his rifle back over his shoulder. Brac tore through a pair of zombies that were crowding in on him, then grabbed hold of the man. Behind them Lyell provided a semblance of cover, viciously ripping and tearing at the other zombies.

The nearest tree had several sturdy branches hanging just a couple of feet above head height. Mike was able to grab onto one of them by stretching up, but he lacked the necessary upper body strength to pull himself up onto it.

Brac ducked and took hold of Mike's legs in both arms, hoisting him up effortlessly. His claws tore into the fabric of the man's jeans. Behind Brac a one-armed woman came stumbling out of the trees, her once-white t-shirt heavily stained with black blood. She made an ineffectual grab for Brac and he kicked her away, following up with a vicious one-handed swipe across the midsection that ripped open the zombie's chest cavity. It collapsed to the ground with its rotten guts spilling out around it.

'Up,' Brac commanded again, pushing Mike skywards.

Straining with the effort, Mike pulled himself onto the branch. Quickly he hooked his legs around it and sat up, untangling himself from the straps over his shoulders. Looking down from his vantage point he was able to see the next attack coming, but was unable to do anything but shout a futile warning.

The woman that Brac had just disembowelled had somehow got back to her feet, heedless the loops of intestine that tangled around her ankles. She grabbed hungrily at Brac, who had half-turned away in order to help Mike. He saw the danger and spun back, lashing out with his claws. The zombie had hold of his shoulder and was falling forward. She managed to sink her teeth deep into the flesh of his ribcage.

Brac howled with pain and struck out with his claws, striking the creature so hard in the throat that its spine was severed and it was practically decapitated. It collapsed to the ground as Brac doubled over in pain, clutching at his bleeding side.

'No!' Finding his balance, Mike managed to lift and steady the rifle, and was able to take down another zombie that was advancing on the injured wolf-man. The shot found its target but the recoil nearly knocked Mike from his perch, and for one heart-stopping moment he thought he was going to fall.

Below him, Brac's howl of pain turned into a harsh snarl. His face began to stretch and elongate into a muzzle. Thicker fur sprouted along the length of his body. He turned his glowing eyes up towards Mike, waving for the man to climb up higher. 'We'll come back for you!' the wolf-man said in a cracked, barely human voice.

Then, dropping to all fours and with blood matting the fur of his flank, Brac dodged past his attackers and managed to break through to the trees beyond. Lyell bounded after him and the two were instantly swallowed by the forest.

Mike stared after them, certain in that one terrible instant that they would never come back and that he was all on his own. The zombies seemed to have forgotten his presence and were busy swarming after the departed wolves, tripping over their fallen comrades.

Mike didn't have time to feel glad about the fact, because something suddenly grabbed at his leg. With a yelp of fear, he looked down and saw that at least one of the dead ones hadn't followed the others. The corpse had hold of his leg with one skeletal hand, and was trying unsuccessfully to secure a grip with the other. Mike kicked viciously at its head, panicking as the dead fingers closed tighter around his ankle.

He kicked it twice more in the arm, finally knocking the creature loose. It fell back, its jaw snapping angrily at its lost meal. Mike quickly pulled his legs back up out of reach, then stood up on the branch, holding on tightly to the main trunk of the tree.

His first instinct was to shoot the creature, but he realised that the gunshot would bring others straight to this spot, and then he really would be trapped. He had to do as Brac had said and stay put; climb higher and pray that the wolves would manage to draw the zombies off somewhere they could fight them successfully. And that they would then come back for him.

Keeping his eyes on the zombie below, Mike carefully climbed up several more limbs of the tree. It would have been easy to climb even further, but it occurred to him that when and if the wolves came back, he ought to stay somewhere that they would see him. The idea of being left up in that tree with a hungry zombie at the bottom until he died of exposure or got so weak that he dropped from his branch... no, he didn't like that idea. It wouldn't come to that of course – not so long as he still had a gun with him – but he still shuddered at the thought.

Making himself as comfortable as was possible, Mike set his back against the tree trunk and searched his pockets for his cigarettes. They weren't there. He realised that they must have fallen out during the fight, and a quick survey of the muddy ground below revealed something square and white which could well have been the packet.

Mike swore quietly. Then he disentangled his camera and switched it on, using the viewfinder to zoom in for a closer look. Yes, those were indeed his cigarettes, fifteen feet down and as unreachable as the far side of the moon. A quick glance up at the sky also told him that it was soon going to be dark, just to add to his problems.

He pressed the record button, then zoomed out slowly from his lost cigarettes and panned over to the thwarted zombie shuffling around a few feet away.

'I'm not at all happy about this situation,' Mike said aloud.

Chapter 40

Nightfall.

The sun had sunk beneath the horizon, leaving only a pale smear of whitish-orange behind in the west, and Andreas Klement had no idea where he was.

It had seemed like a good idea at the time – escaping from the buildings and making a run for the fence before the entire army of the undead had gotten into the encampment. As soon as his feet had hit the ground on the other side of the fence he had told himself that it had been the only sensible option. The others inside the encampment were doomed; there was no way they could have held off the dead ones forever. He had been the first to run, and he wondered if anyone else had got the same idea. Certainly no-one had followed him over the southern side of the fence.

But then, as he'd headed south along the coast away from the camp, he'd heard gunshots behind him, and he'd started to question whether he'd made the right decision. Somehow the survivors in the camp had made it to the arms store and were fighting back against the zombies.

Klement had hesitated, wondering if he should head back, but finally had decided against it. All the dead ones were at the camp, either inside or very close to it, and it would be suicide for him to go back there unarmed. So he had continued heading south, cutting into the forest when the wind had picked up in the late afternoon and he had started feeling the cold.

Now he couldn't shake off the feeling that he was hopelessly lost.

Almost as soon as the sun started to go down, it became so dark within the forest that Klement was barely able to make out the ground beneath his feet. A dozen times he lost his footing and stumbled heavily, on one occasion slipping on a patch of mud and ending up flat on his back and badly winded. He'd picked himself up and continued staggering through the forest, both arms held up in front of him in futile protection against the whipping branches. He was deaf to any sound except his own harsh, laboured breathing, and the crashing footsteps that he made.

About twenty minutes previously he had seen a small rise through a gap in the trees, somewhere up ahead. He'd changed direction to head towards it, in the vague hope that from the top he might have been able to see where the camp was. As soon as he'd plunged back into the thick undergrowth he'd almost tumbled into a dry streambed that was deep and wide enough to practically be called a crevasse. It had taken Klement far off course to find a way across it, and by the time he'd got to the other side he could no longer be sure that he was still heading towards the rise.

That seemed increasingly unlikely now. For a start, the ground had begun to slope downhill. The man hesitated, wondering whether he would be better off backtracking. It didn't take him long to decide, since it was so much easier to follow the path of least resistance. The undergrowth seemed to have thinned out as well, although the trees were still as closely packed as ever. He justified his choice of path with the fact that the ground could possibly be sloping down towards the coast. Once he found the coast, he would be able to get his bearings. He stopped for a moment and tried to listen for the sound of distant surf. He couldn't hear anything, but that didn't necessarily mean anything, since the sea had been virtually flat earlier that evening.

After another ten minutes of walking, Klement tripped on an exposed tree root and tumbled to the ground again. His hands and arms were already scratched and torn, and he swore loudly several times. His voice seemed to echo through the silent forest.

He started to pick himself up, then decided against it. It was time for a break anyhow. He twisted round so that he was sitting on the cold ground with his back to the large tree whose root he'd tripped over. He drew his knees up to his chest and wrapped his arms around them, suddenly aware of how cold it was out there. While he'd been moving it hadn't been so noticeable, but now that he'd stopped he was freezing. His thin jacket offered very little protection against the night air. He wondered if it was cold enough for him to die of exposure out there, but rejected the idea – not because he didn't believe it but because he could not imagine something like that happening to *him*. He would get very cold, sure, but it wasn't like it was *that* close to winter or anything. When the sun came up the following morning he would be semi-frozen but still alive, and in the daylight it would be a million times easier to find his way.

If that had been the only factor then he probably would have found himself a dry, sheltered place among the trees roots and tried to keep warm until the morning. But Klement was becoming worried that he wasn't alone in those woods anymore. All of the dead ones had to be around the camp, far to the north of him... all common sense told him that, but for some reason he was no longer sure. Some deep-seated instinct was urging him to keep moving.

Over and over, he silently questioned how the hell this could have happened.

The whole situation seemed impossible, irrational. The humans controlled the zombies, kept them contained, studied them and kept them in a continuous state. There was no way they could have got out. Klement sat there and bitterly reflected on the fact that he'd been studying the dead ones for months and yet, when it came right down to a moment like this, he didn't know the first damn thing about them. Now he shuddered to think of the hundreds of corpses that were somehow loose from their confinement and hungrily seeking the flesh of the living.

Eventually he pushed himself to his feet and continued walking, still heading downhill. It occurred to him that even if this particular slope didn't lead to the coast, then it would almost certainly lead into a valley where there'd be a stream or a river that he could follow. Plus he could definitely have used a drink of water by that point. His throat felt like it was on fire.

It was only after he'd been walking for several more minutes, watching his feet all the time through the increasing darkness, that he realised there was another noise out there that he couldn't possibly be making himself. Another set of footfalls, keeping pace with his own but definitely *not* his own. Klement stopped walking immediately, his head coming up as he glanced quickly around.

The forest was silent again. No, maybe not quite silent: the wind must have picked up. There was a soft shushing noise, like the sound of the treetops being stirred in the breeze. It wasn't a loud noise, and it seemed peculiarly isolated, because when Klement turned he thought it was coming from a point about twenty feet off to his left.

Klement stood frozen for the space of maybe five heartbeats, listening to the shushing noise that could have been the wind in the trees, or could equally have been the sound of something slow and heavy dragging its feet across the leaf-covered ground. He realised that it was moving towards him, not increasing its pace even though it must have heard him pause.

Fresh panic hit Klement, and he turned and bolted through the trees. He didn't know if one of the zombies had followed him or if it had just been lurking nearby and sensed him, but he knew that if there was one then there were bound to be others. He ran like a man possessed, the tree branches whipping at him with renewed frenzy, his feet catching and skidding on the unseen ground.

He thought he heard a crashing noise behind him but didn't even glance back. As long as he kept moving, as long as he kept on his feet, then he could stay ahead. The dead ones were vicious and dangerous and inhumanly strong, but they were slow and if he could just stay far enough ahead...

Something was wrong. Klement could hear the footsteps clearly now, the shuffling and heavy tread that immediately marked out a zombie. But the noise was *right behind him*, and it was gaining on him, as if the creature with its lurching stride was somehow able to outrun the human.

Every muscle burning with the effort, Klement put on a burst of speed, leaping over half-hidden obstacles as some long-dormant instinct took over and guided him with a speed and agility he'd never before possessed. He was dimly aware of the footsteps falling back behind him and hope flared within him, and then suddenly the creature speeded up as well. It covered the intervening distance in the space of a few brief seconds and smashed into Klement's back.

He tumbled to the ground and rolled, his elbows and knees striking painfully against exposed tree roots. He landed on his back with his head spinning and his lungs so cramped and winded that each breath was sucked in with a painful gasp. Through a break in the trees directly above him he caught a glimpse of the stars, and then something had hold of him.

It grabbed his right arm, dragging him viciously across the uneven ground. Fingernails that were more like claws dug deep into his soft flesh and made him cry out. The cry echoed in the silent wood and was heard by no-one. Klement felt himself being lifted, catching another brief glimpse of the stars overhead before they were blotted out by a shadow that loomed over him. Cold, stale breath washed over his neck a moment before sharp teeth tore into it, ripping out his jugular and ending his life in a flash of agony.

The creature sank its face into the wound, guzzling the blood and flesh in a desperate, greedy attempt to stem the pain within its own body. The warmth of the blood flowed through its body, making its crazed brain reel but doing nothing to push the pain away.

Its mouth full of blood, the creature moaned with anguish. Always before, the blood had healed it; had been the one thing that could make everything better. Human blood, resisted for so long, had been the ultimate cure.

No longer.

Ciaran raised his bloody face to the darkened sky and howled in pain and frustration.

Chapter 41

He heard the howls from a long way away, but somehow he knew that they were ultimately meant for him.

His skin had been burning for hours now, from very soon after he'd been bitten. It had alternated between deep, burning pain and aching numbness, and it had spread upwards with alarming speed.

Seth knew that he was dying.

In his mind, he had played over and over again the moment when it had all gone so wrong for him. If that jeep hadn't appeared at exactly the moment it had… if he'd had just a few more minutes to make sure that Ciaran had really been dead…

It didn't matter. All of his calculations had been so far off the mark that none of it truly mattered any more. The fact that Ciaran's body had reacted to the zombie virus when all the tests had indicated it wouldn't was proof of that. And now the bastard vampire had passed on his sickness to Seth and infected him as well.

Several hours ago the flesh around the bite had begun to blacken, followed by rapid loss of sensation in his fingers. He was able to trace the passage of the virus through his body by the areas that had started to sicken and die first. Because of the healing abilities that his lycanthropy gave him, the process was a lot slower than it would have been in a regular human being. When night began to fall Seth was still alive. By that point he didn't necessarily see it as a good thing.

Also, the change had been pulling hard at him, getting stronger and stronger as the night crept closer. Eventually he'd been unable to hold it off any longer, especially as the pain of his dying arm continued to claw at him. He'd started to change to his animal form in the faint and desperate hope that somehow it might push the infection from his body. Other injuries and illnesses had been healed in the past by letting the change have full control, but none of his lab tests had ever tried forcing out the zombie virus. It had never occurred to him as a possible situation.

As Seth very quickly discovered, the change had not rid him of the invading virus. It somehow made it worse.

He couldn't stop the change once it was started, and before it was halfway through he had blacked out from the sheer agony. When he finally came back to himself it had been all he could do to lie still and breathe in and out. It was nearly an hour before he was even able to lift his head and observe the damage that had been done to his body. His skin had sloughed off almost completely, hanging in tatters from his bleeding carcass. Thick hair had sprouted, apparently growing straight out of the pulpy muscle, and his hands had twisted into almost useless claws. Walking, once he'd finally mustered the strength to drag himself to his feet, was nothing short of torture. It was no consolation at all to him that the feeling had been restored to his deadened nerves, especially since his body was rotting from the inside out. He could smell it clearly; taste it in his mouth. He had to clench his teeth against it.

As the sun set, Seth had realised that he was likely to stay in his current state for some considerable time. He didn't know why the virus that had infected him had taken effect so quickly and then seemed to stabilise without actually killing him. He guessed that it had to have something to do with his lycanthropy. And when he heard the howling in the distance he somehow knew that it had to be Ciaran, and that he too was alive and in pain somewhere.

Good, Seth thought through the swirling redness in his mind. *He deserves this. He deserves to be in pain, in undying pain. I don't.*

Seth was on his feet now, pacing his way with agonising slowness back towards the north. He had fled south after he'd been attacked, running as far as he could before collapsing amongst the trees. Now he began to retrace his steps, walking on all fours in a kind of shuffling limp, unable to think of much else apart from the pain.

When he finally made it back to the zombie enclosure and begun to hobble his way around it, he found time to wonder where all the dead ones had got to. It was only when he got right back to the road and discovered the massive hole in the fence that he realised what must have happened there.

In the dirt a few meters away from the break in the fence was one solitary zombie. Its back had been broken at some point in the past and it was unable to walk, forced to drag itself along by its fingertips. It had managed to inch itself this far along in pursuit of its comrades, its useless legs ploughing furrows in the soft ground. Seth stood over the creature and looked down at it in disgust. Even in his own condition he was unable to feel any pity for the crippled undead monster that continued to squirm its way forwards in search of food. It paid no attention to Seth, and he realised with a shock that it must not have been able to sense that he was still alive. The stench of putrefaction coming from his own body was confusing the zombie into thinking that he was just another one of the undead.

Angrily, Seth brought his forefoot down hard onto the creature's head, shattering its skull. His rage momentarily pushed away the pain, and he shook his foot to get rid of the clinging brain fragments. Then he turned and began to hobble off along the road that led back to the camp.

There was no doubt in his mind that Ciaran was still alive – in a sense – and that he had been the one who had torn through the fence. Seth also knew where the vampire would have headed: towards the single source of food on the island.

And where Ciaran had led, the other dead ones would have followed.

Chapter 42

On the edge of waking, Mike thought he heard someone calling his name from a great distance. He opened his eyes groggily, blinking several times as he tried to orientate himself. He found himself sat upright in an enforced and not particularly comfortable position, his arms and legs wrapped around the trunk of a large tree. It took him several moments to remember where he was and why he was clinging onto the tree like grim death.

It was fully dark now, the sky overhead studded with stars. Through a gap in the swaying branches, Mike could see the edge of the full moon, fat and glowing with shocking brightness. The wind had picked up a little, moving the tops of the trees in a constant, shifting whisper of noise, and he thought that maybe it was that which had woken him. He didn't remember falling asleep, and wondered if he'd passed out from delayed shock or something.

Then someone below shouted his name again.

Awkwardly, he twisted so that he could stare down at the ground. He gave himself a flash of vertigo as he was reminded how high he had climbed prior to accidentally falling asleep. Twenty feet below, three people were staring up at him from the ground, and the sight made relief flow through Mike's body.

'Oh, thank God,' he whispered to himself, recognising Anna's face immediately.

'Mike!' Anna yelled up at him again. 'Are you alright?' Ehren and Ramone were with her as well, the latter keeping a close eye on the forest all around. It took Mike a moment longer to realise that the movement he could just make out in the shadows at the foot of the tree was Lyell, still in her wolf-form.

He tried to wave to them, but his arms felt like they were welded to the tree trunk. 'I'm fine,' he called down, his voice hoarse. 'How are you?'

'Never better.' Anna was smiling with sheer relief. 'How did you get up there?'

'It's kind of a long story.' Cautiously, Mike peeled his right arm away from the tree. It felt like it had been moulded there by the cold, and it hurt to move it. 'Ow,' he added, flexing his frozen fingers painfully.

'Can you get down?'

'That's a good question. Probably.' Carefully, Mike moved his other arm, and then his legs. All of his limbs had cramped painfully in place, and even the smallest of movements set off flashes of pins and needles. From the base of his spine down to his knees, where he'd been sat on the unforgiving branch, he was completely numb. 'What the hell happened to you guys?'

'We had to get far enough away from the dead ones so that we could pick them off without them overwhelming us. It took longer than we expected, but I think we got them all.'

Her words reminded Mike of something, and he looked down quickly. 'Hey – there was another one around here... watch your backs...'

'It's okay, we got it.' Anna indicated something on the ground that Mike couldn't quite make out, but he assumed it must have been the zombie that had been waiting at the foot of his tree.

'Oh good, now I can get my cigarettes.' He shifted off the branch and began to pick his way slowly back down the tree.

'Do you need a hand?' Anna called, although there wasn't much she could do to help. It wasn't as if she could climb up there and carry the man down.

Mike shook his head. 'I can manage.' In truth, it was a hell of a lot harder coming down than it had been coming up, not least because his fingers were refusing to grip properly and his body felt so stiff and sore that every movement was an effort. Plus he'd had the added benefit of three years worth of adrenaline pumped into his system at once when he'd come up the tree.

'Lyell found us a few minutes ago,' Anna told him. 'We came back looking for you, but we wouldn't have found you without her...'

'Where's Brac? Is he with you?'

There was a silence below. 'We've not seen him,' Ramone said at last. 'We figured he was with you.'

'He was, but he ran off. Led the zombies away from me.' With a certain amount of difficulty, Mike managed to get back down to the thick branch that was closest to the ground. He paused, trying to work out the best way to get down the last eight or so feet.

Ramone asked suddenly, 'What happened to your leg?'

Mike glanced down and realised with some surprise that there was a long gash on his right calf. He frowned, trying to remember exactly how it had happened, but he had no memory of injuring himself. The tear in his trousers was almost four inches long, and the cloth around it was dark with dried blood, indicating that the cut must have been pretty deep and bled quite a lot. He had no idea when it had happened, but he suddenly had an uncomfortable flash of memory. Remembering Brac with his clawed hands grabbing his legs and lifting him into the tree... Brac with hands covered in undead blood...

He realised then that Ramone had a look of growing suspicion on his face, and the rifle under his arm was no longer pointed at the ground. It wasn't aimed exactly at him, but it wouldn't have taken much of a movement to put it there.

As casually as was possible, Mike shrugged. 'I caught it on one of these branches,' he said. 'I was in a bit of a hurry coming up here.' He sat down on the branch and then lowered himself to the ground, concentrating hard on what he was doing and trying to ignore the itching feeling that had suddenly developed between his shoulder blades.

'Are you sure?' Ramone asked.

Anna must have caught the tone of his voice because she put a hand on his right arm. 'Hey, what are you doing?' she asked him, frowning. 'You heard what he said.'

Ramone didn't answer.

'Come on, he just caught it on the tree.' Very deliberately, Anna pressed down on Ramone's arm, forcing him to lower the rifle. 'Look for yourself, alright? That's a cut, not a bite. So just calm down, okay?'

Mike dropped the rest of the way to the ground and took a moment to dust himself down and then examine the cut on his leg. He was very aware of the eyes of the others on him as he did so. The cut looked long and deep and was crusted over with dried blood, and as soon as he saw how bad it looked he also realised that it hurt a great deal. He hadn't noticed it before over the general aching of his body, but now, as he flexed the muscle of his calf, he felt it tingle with pain. Anna was right: it was definitely a cut rather than a bite, but the question remained – what exactly had he cut it on? The sick sensation in his stomach didn't improve when he remembered the zombie that had grabbed his leg as he'd climbed the tree, clutching at him with its ragged fingernails. Had that been his left leg or his right? He couldn't remember.

'Yeah,' he said, straightening back up and attempting a smile. 'That hurts a lot.'

Anna crouched down to look at the wound. 'Are you able to walk on it?' she asked.

Mike tried a couple of experimental steps. It was uncomfortable, but not impossible. 'I can walk,' he affirmed. 'Just don't ask me to sprint anywhere, okay?'

'Hopefully it won't come to that.'

Nodding, Mike turned away and looked down at Lyell, who was crouched in the shadows. Now that he was on the ground he could see the corpse that had earlier tried to grab him, and which the young wolf had apparently eviscerated just recently. Cautiously, he held his hand out to Lyell.

The young wolf looked up at him with her unreadable amber eyes, then slowly got to her feet and butted her head against his hand.

'Thanks,' he said. 'You saved my life.'

Lyell abruptly turned away, and Mike's insides twisted again. She had come back, but Brac hadn't. What had happened to him?

'We'd better get moving,' Ramone said. 'The vamps will all be awake by now, so – '

He was interrupted by Lyell, who let out a whine. The others looked at her hurriedly, but it did not seem like it was meant as a warning. Instead she was stood at the edge of the trampled area of ground around the tree, looking back at them calmly.

With a start, Mike realised that she was standing at the spot where Brac had disappeared into the trees, and he knew then what she was telling them. 'We've gotta go that way,' he said.

'What for?' Anna asked.

'We've gotta find Brac.' Without bothering to explain further, he turned and started to follow the young wolf, pausing only to retrieve his battered and crushed packet of cigarettes from the ground and shove it back into his pocket.

Chapter 43

'So what happened?' Ramone asked as they pushed their way through the forest. 'What happened to Brac?'

'He got hurt during the fight,' Mike told him. 'It was my fault – he was getting me out of the way when one of the zombies bit him.' He looked over at Ramone. 'Will he be all right? I mean, will the virus affect him, since he's a wolf and all?'

The man shrugged and glanced backwards at Ehren, who as usual was trudging along in silence behind them. 'What's your opinion, Doctor Ehren?' he asked, his tone half-mocking. 'You're the closest thing we've got to an expert here.'

Ehren didn't even bother looking up. In the darkness, his face looked even paler and his eyes seemed strangely sunken, as if he were shrinking gradually away. 'I don't know,' he said, his voice hollow and flat. 'Doctor Sykes was working on a theory before... before.' He paused, running his tongue over dry lips. 'We were never sure whether any of the afflictions could be passed between species, but Doctor Sykes was working on preliminary research on the subject. He was mainly looking at the link between the vampires and the lycanthropes – whether the diseases were compatible, or if having one gave you immunity to the other. Certainly he theorised that a vampire could never catch lycanthropy, since that virus requires the victim to be alive in order for it to work. He couldn't conclusively rule out it working the other way round though.'

'What about the dead ones?' Mike asked.

'Nothing affects them – their bodies are already dead and decomposing. But their virus is incredibly powerful... I can't remember if Doctor Sykes ever really considered the effect it would have on other species. It's the only virus that kills off the host without retaining any of the higher brain functions at all. Lycanthropy leaves its host alive, taking over the body only on occasions, and the vampire virus causes the body to die but keeps it intact and perfectly preserved. The virus that the dead ones carry is the most potent – it destroys the mind and the body, and it's the easiest to transmit to humans…'

'That doesn't really answer the question, y'know.'

'The answer is that I don't know.' Ehren raised his eyes from the ground and held Mike's gaze for a moment. 'I can tell you that it's possible. There's no real reason why such a powerful virus wouldn't affect a lycanthrope, but it's never been tested so I just don't know. Theoretically it could even affect a vampire, since we've tested the virus on flesh that's already dead, and it can move through dead cells quite easily …'

Up ahead, Lyell let out a strange, whimpering howl.

'Come on.' Ramone hurried them forward.

The sick feeling inside Mike's stomach got a hundred times worse as he followed the man between the closely packed trees. He knew before they even reached the place where Lyell was waiting for them that Brac was dead; that they were too late to help him.

Ramone stopped and swore quietly. Mike pushed past him, dreading what he was going to see but having to look nonetheless. Then he stood and stared, wondering what the hell he *was* seeing.

The shape on the ground looked like a pile of unconnected body parts, stacked together and slick with viscous blood. A very thin amount of moonlight shone down through the overhead branches, illuminating patches of the scene in perfect detail but leaving others in darkness. A thin, almost skeletal arm projected from the middle of the mass, splayed outwards with the fingers clutching at the ground so hard that the nails were buried deep in the soil. An illuminated portion of leg appeared to have been partially skinned, thick chunks of the hairy flesh having sloughed away to reveal blood-streaked fat and muscle beneath. Over everything hung the almost palpable stench of rotting flesh.

Mike took several steps towards the pile of body parts, then his legs seemed to give out and he dropped heavily to his knees. *Oh shit, shit, shit, shit,* a voice whispered inside his head. *This is my fault…*

Lyell whimpered again, and then the pile of body parts shuddered and drew breath.

'No…' Mike's voice died as soon as it reached his lips. He stared in horror at the body on the ground, suddenly seeing is as a body and not just a jumble of disconnected parts. The limbs were twisted and contorted, the shadows obfuscating the fact that they were somehow still joined to the main trunk. It was only when the whole moved and the moonlight shifted that the mess on the floor revealed it to be something that was still clinging to life.

The skeletal fingers dug into the ground convulsively as another shudder racked the body. A shaft of moonlight fell on the face as it painfully changed position, and the eyes opened. They had been gummed shut by blood that was oozing from a row of deep, seeping red sores on the left side of the face. In the elongated muzzle, the lips were drawn back, revealing blood covered teeth. The incisors were chipped, as if they'd been round together forcibly. The mouth opened but no sound came out except a thin gasp of air.

Mike couldn't comprehend what had happened to the man. It seemed impossible that any disease could have had such a rapid effect, disintegrating the flesh off the bones in places while leaving other parts of the body strangely untouched. A shudder of revulsion ran through him, and he had to close his eyes.

He opened them again when he heard Ramone step forward and click the safety off his handgun.

'What – ?' It took two attempts for Mike to make his voice work. 'What are you doing?'

Ramone had refilled the clip with silver bullets, and now he was moving to stand directly over the dying man on the ground. He didn't answer the question.

Painfully, Brac rolled his eyes so that he could watch the man approaching. Once he saw what was happening he lowered his head back to the ground with an exhalation of air. His hand continued to clutch at the ground, scratching deep furrows in the soft earth.

'Wait.' Mike wasn't sure if he spoke out loud or not, but it didn't matter. Carefully, he inched forward on his knees until he was close enough to reach out and grasp the man's hand.

'Get back,' Ramone warned him. 'You'll get infected.'

'Shut up.' Mike didn't move or look up at him. 'This is my fault.'

The skeletal hand closed around his own, clutching onto it with a strength that came close to crushing Mike's fingers. Brac's eyes flicked open again, focusing with difficulty. For a brief moment, Mike thought that he saw gratitude pass through the man's eyes before they eased closed again. As soon as eye contact was broken, Mike was able to shut his own eyes as well.

There was a deafening gunshot, and Brac's hand convulsed violently once, then relaxed and lay still. Mike let go of it and opened his eyes with trepidation.

Brac's head had been mulched by the shot, fragments of skull and brain matter splattered across the ground. The previous illusion of the body being merely a pile of disassociated parts was restored, and it was once again possible for Mike to look at it and pretend that it hadn't until recently been a living person.

Behind him, Lyell howled mournfully; a thin, painful sound. Mike wasn't sure if he could stand up yet, so he shuffled backwards on his knees. His searching hand found the soft fur of Lyell's neck, stroking it in gentle and comforting circles until her quiet moaning ceased.

Then Anna touched his shoulder and asked him if he was okay, and he let her help him to his feet. Lyell remained where she was, lying down on the ground beside Brac's corpse with her head resting on her paws.

Ramone had put the gun away and was standing off to one side, well out of the way. He wasn't surprised that neither Mike nor Anna looked at him as they came over. 'We've got to move,' he said quietly. 'We have to get out of these trees and up to the mountains as fast as possible.'

The others nodded, silently turning to follow him. Mike glanced back at Lyell, but although the wolf raised her amber eyes towards him, she showed no sign of coming with them.

Feeling mentally and physically wrecked, Mike turned away and left her behind. If it hadn't been for Anna's presence at his side, silently supporting him, chances were that he would have stayed there in that blood-splattered clearing as well.

Chapter 44

It felt like they had been walking forever through the dark forest. The slowest part of the journey had been trying to find their way back to the track that they had left earlier. Once they were there and the ground was relatively level again the going became a lot faster, and there was less need to watch where every single step was placed. Even so, it took them the best part of an hour to finally make it to the main track that led up to the mountains.

Everyone breathed a little easier as soon as they were out from underneath the oppressive overhang of trees. The full moon cast enough light that the main track was clearly illuminated, with everything thrown into silver highlights and midnight black shadows. The fact that the group of walkers once again had a certain amount of open space between them and the dark wall of trees on either side of the track made everyone feel less anxious, since it reduced the chance of anything else being able to sneak up on them.

Mike walked to one side of the others, giving himself a little distance and a little time to think. He badly needed to get things sorted in his mind. Even Anna had given up walking beside him after he had continually shrugged off her attempts at support and conversation.

His left leg still hurt and he limped as he walked, acutely aware of every twinge of pain that ran through it. He couldn't stop himself from thinking about it, and every few seconds he came close to stopping to check whether it was okay… and whether there had been any changes to the state of the wound. In his mind he was sure he could feel the stinging and itching getting worse, and could imagine the flesh around the wound blackening and beginning to rot, just as it had done with Brac. But he kept walking and didn't stop to check, because he was scared to draw attention to himself. He plainly remembered the look on Ramone's face when the man had thought Mike had been infected. He was still watching him now, out of the corner of his eye.

The group walked in silence with Ramone leading and Ehren bringing up the rear, as usual. Apart from the soft sound of the wind in the trees, the forest was unusually quiet, and they encountered no other nasty surprises. It was difficult to estimate time, and when Mike glanced at his watch he was surprised to find that it wasn't nearly as late as he'd thought. It also occurred to him that it was at least twelve hours since he'd last eaten, and although he had absolutely no appetite at that moment he was feeling a little light-headed from lack of food. They had shared out the last of the water from Ramone's canteen when they'd reached the main track, and Mike wondered when they'd find another source of water.

They rounded a bend in the road and the trees abruptly dropped away on both sides. The road curved up in front of them through irregular, rocky land, sloping gradually upwards into the foothills. The mountains loomed vast and black above them, still some distance away.

For Anna, it seemed like a week or more had passed since she'd been there last, even though it had only been the previous night. She stared up at the moonlit mountains and hoped to hell that Luca would be able to help them.

'Watch yourselves,' Ramone told them. 'They usually have lookouts watching the road, so they're going to know we're coming. We'll just have to hope they're feeling friendly tonight.'

The others followed him along the track that wound upwards through the first gentle hills. The last of the trees quickly fell away, and Mike glanced back at the dark forest, not sorry in the slightest to be leaving it behind.

Because of the way that the road twisted and turned through the low hills it was impossible to see very far ahead, and the anxiety that had been alleviated by leaving the forest soon returned. As they climbed higher the track began to curve around the first of the peaks, so that they were walking with a steep slope dropping away on one side of them. They all became acutely aware that if something attacked them, they didn't have anywhere to run to except back the way they had come.

Several times Ramone motioned them to stop, and each time they froze in their tracks, their eyes anxiously searching the road ahead and behind, as well as up the steep slope to their right. Each time there was nothing there, and they cautiously resumed their slow trek.

They were just approaching a pass where the road disappeared into darkness for a considerable distance when Ramone called another halt. 'My vote is to stop here,' he said quietly. 'They must know we're here, and I for one would much rather wait for them to come to us than wander blindly up there in the dark.'

'Do you have any torches?' Anna asked him.

'No. There were a couple on the jeep, but it didn't occur to me to pick them up. I didn't expect us to be out this late.'

'So we wait here?'

'That seems like the best plan. We could use a rest anyway.' Ramone unslung his bag and dumped it on the ground. 'Stay alert though, we don't want – '

Someone stepped out of the darkness behind him, as smoothly as a portion of shadow detaching itself from the main body. Ramone had just started to sit down and he jerked back upright, swearing loudly.

'Sorry,' the shadow said. 'Didn't mean to make you jump.' It stepped forward, both hands out to the sides in a peaceable gesture. Anna saw that the right hand was twisted round so that the palm was facing away from them.

'Come out where we can see you.' Now that Ramone was back on his feet and had his rifle pointed at the new arrival he automatically took charge of the situation again.

'Sure thing.' The man came towards them, smiling pleasantly. He was tall, with white-blond hair and sharp, Nordic features. Anna had recognised him as soon as she'd seen his deformed arm, but it took her a moment to recall his name.

Ramone was quickly scanning the darkness behind the vampire. 'You alone?' he asked.

'Ah... no. I didn't think it'd be wise to walk around out here on my own.'

A flash of movement alerted Mike to the fact that someone was behind him. He spun round and found two people standing in the road barely three feet away: a man and a woman, standing completely at ease as if they were just out for a moonlit stroll. The female smiled at the shocked look on Mike's face, and he saw that her top incisors were pointed and sharp.

The breath caught within his throat, and without really meaning to his hand instinctively dropped to the camera around his neck. He quickly switched it on and hit the record button, shifting so that it was pointed in roughly the right direction. It was only then that he realised he should really have taken his cue from Ramone and moved his rifle into position instead.

Ramone hadn't taken his eyes off the blond vampire. 'Anyone else?' he asked.

'Nope, that's us.' The smile never faltered. 'Now, how about you tell us what you're all doing up here.'

Anna spoke quickly. 'We want to see Luca. There's a problem at the camp.'

'No kidding. We can hear that from here.'

'So you know what's going on then?'

'Educated guesses, mostly.' The vampire shrugged. 'We figured there was either some major catastrophe or you humans were having a blackout party and forgot to invite us.'

'Listen – we're all really tired and we've been walking for hours. Can we please come up and speak with Luca?'

'That's not possible, I'm afraid.'

'What?' Anna glanced round at the others, and at the vampires behind her. 'Why not?'

'He's not here at the moment.' The pleasant smile had changed to something more malicious. 'Which means that you'll just have to deal with us instead. Sorry 'bout that.'

Chapter 45

Anna realised they were in trouble. The two vampires that had somehow got behind them were moving closer step by step, although they only seemed to move when no-one was looking, closing in on them like magic.

She turned her attention back to the blond vampire, who was still smiling at her in a way that made her even more nervous. She was holding onto her rifle tightly, but hadn't yet had the presence of mind to aim it at the vampire in front of her.

'You're... Tyr, right?' The name had finally come back to her. 'We met last night.'

The vampire inclined his head. 'That's right. And you're Anna Martin, and you've brought along Doctor Ehren and that monkey he's trained to drive a car. I don't recognise the jumpy guy with the camera though.'

Anna didn't dare look round to see how the others reacted to those comments. 'Tyr, we really need to talk to Luca.'

'I told you, he's not here.'

'Then where the hell is he?'

'Out there somewhere.' Tyr shrugged vaguely. 'Him and Jason left to find out what the hell you humans are doing. I told him not to bother.'

'We *really* need to talk to him,' Anna repeated, a sick sense of dread developing in her stomach. 'Can we come up and wait until he gets back?'

The vampire folded his arms across his chest, the twisted one lying palm up. 'Go back and wait in the forest,' he suggested.

'The forest's filled with the dead right now. We've been running from them all day. Please. We just need to talk to Luca.'

'He's. Not. Here,' Tyr repeated slowly. He stepped towards her, the smile fading from his face. 'And this road is officially closed to humans. Just turn yourselves around and get back to the mess you've created.'

Before he could get too close, Ramone blocked his way, his rifle raised to chest level. Tyr turned his head to look at him with a slight frown creasing his smooth forehead.

'Alright now,' Ramone said calmly. 'Your point is taken, we'll get off your mountain. We're leaving right this second. Okay?'

Tyr smiled again, but didn't move back. 'So what exactly *is* going on down in the forest?' he asked instead. 'How did you humans manage to fuck up so badly that the dead ones all got out?'

'It was nothing to do with us.'

'Oh no, of course not. Doctor Ehren just set up the enclosure and filled it with every dead body he could find and called it a great step forward for science. You mess with the natural balance and then you wonder why it all blows up in your face. You've brought this situation on yourselves.'

Ramone smiled slightly. 'Y'know what? I agree with you.'

'That's good. So what you need to do now is go back to overseeing your destruction of our home. Maybe once you're all dead this island can go back to belonging to the monsters.'

Anna spoke angrily. 'You can't just send us back out there! This isn't our fault!'

'Yes it is, and yes we can. Bye now.'

'Come on.' Ramone took hold of her arm and began leading her backwards. 'Let's get out of here.'

One of the other vampires, a wide-built man with a shaved head, spoke from behind them. 'And what about Ciaran?' he asked. He had a strong American accent.

Ramone glanced at him, then back to Tyr. 'Ciaran?'

'One of our younger people,' Tyr said. 'He went into the camp yesterday night to help out your scientists. He was supposed to have been gone an hour, but he never came home.' When Ramone started to answer, Tyr held up his hand to silence him. 'If you don't mind, I've had enough of talking to you, monkey. I believe Doctor Ehren is in charge, so he should be the one answering.'

Ehren looked up, his eyes widening. 'I – I don't know. I don't know anything about that.'

'You honestly expect me to believe that you would let one of us come into your precious camp without you being informed about it? No, you know perfectly well. So tell us where he is.'

'I swear, I don't know…' Ehren shook his head nervously, his eyes a little wild. 'Wait… wait. Seth. Seth said that he was bringing someone in last night.' He attempted a weak smile. 'I – I've no idea who it was though. I don't think he told me…'

'How very careless of him. So Ciaran was at the camp last night, in the care of one of your employees. And where the hell is he now?'

Ramone interrupted. 'If he didn't come home then he'll still be at the camp.

He'll be in one of the safe houses, and he'll probably be as secure there as anywhere. But I can tell you something for nothing – I'm fairly sure Seth's gone missing as well. I saw someone this morning, down at the enclosure, and I'm increasingly convinced it was him. He was messing about with the dead ones, and one of them bit him. Then he ran off. That was right before everything went tits up out there.'

Anna was staring at him. 'Why didn't you tell us that?' she demanded.

The smile was returning to Tyr's face, although it was even less pleasant than before. 'Ah, yes. Of course you should have been told about that, Miss Martin. You deserve to know as much as possible about your father's murderer.'

'*What?*' Anna rounded on him. 'What the hell do you know about it?'

Tyr shrugged vaguely. 'More than you'd expect. Unlike Luca, I actually know most of what happens on this island. I know that you should never have bothered coming here, because there's nothing for you to find. Your father is dead. On the plus side though, we can arrange to reunited you with him.'

As soon as the words were out his mouth something came rushing down the side of the mountain, ploughing into their group at high speed. None of them saw it coming; even as it snatched Ramone off his feet they saw nothing but a black blur of motion. By the time Anna managed to shout a warning, Ramone had already been slammed to the ground hard enough to break two of his ribs. He skidded across the rough track with the dark shape on top of him, coming to rest only inches from where the edge of the road dropped away into darkness.

Anna screamed, and then someone grabbed hold of her, pinning her arms to her sides and crushing the air out of her lungs. The rifle was plucked almost carelessly from her hands. A face pressed itself against her neck and a female voice whispered, 'Don't fight, sweetheart.'

Behind her, Mike had a moment of sickening disorientation as something struck him hard in the face, spinning him round. He stumbled and was only vaguely aware of hands taking the rifle out of his hands. Then someone grabbed and caught him, yanking his head violently to one side. He blinked and found himself staring out at the others, about ten feet from where he'd been stood a moment before. The shaven-headed vampire was behind him, one arm wrapped around his chest, the other hand twisted in his hair and holding his neck tightly exposed.

Ehren was the only one who had not been grabbed, although Tyr had taken his rifle away with a single, negligent movement. He had also picked up Ramone's handgun, which had fallen to the ground. He turned it over in his hands, popping the clip. 'I see,' the vampire said. 'So much for your promise that you wouldn't keep supplies of silver bullets on this island. Well, maybe if that part of our agreement is null and void, then so is the rest of it.'

The vampire holding Mike laughed softly and tightened his grip on the man's hair. Mike tried again to pull free, but the effort brought stinging tears to his eyes. He felt something brush against his neck and he caught his breath. Two tiny sharp points pressed very gently against his skin.

'Tyr,' Ehren said. For the first time in many hours his voice held some of the old calm and control. 'We're not your enemy. I'll admit, this is a bad situation that we've got here on the island, and I'll also admit that it's our fault. But we've got to work together if we want to get through this. The dead ones are a problem to us all; we've got to – '

Tyr held his finger up to his lips and shushed him. 'Okay, Doctor Ehren,' he smiled. 'You've made your very valid point. Kristoff.' He looked over at the vampire holding onto Mike. 'Go right ahead.'

Mike felt warm breath on his neck and realised that the vampire behind him was laughing again. Then the warmth turned to sudden sharp pain as two needle sharp teeth slid through his skin. He gasped and tried to jerk away, but Kristoff held him in place with no apparent effort. Pain shot through Mike's body as the teeth sank deeper, warm blood welling up to spill out into the vampire's mouth.

'No!' Anna struggled to get free of her attacker, kicking ineffectually at her shins. She could do nothing but watch as Mike's eyes grew wide with pain and shock.

Tyr shot out his hand and caught hold of Ehren by the front of his shirt, drawing him forward. His twisted right arm grabbed the man's neck and turned the head to one side. 'Human blood,' the vampire said in a low whisper that was almost a growl. 'It's been so long...' He leaned forward until his mouth was only a half-inch above the exposed flesh.

Mike's eyes rolled up into his skull and his knees began to buckle.

Tyr's lips drew back and he inhaled deeply, drawing the scent of warm human skin deep into his lungs. The smell of heat, and fear, and life... and...

The vampire jerked his head back with a snarl. Something beneath the warm smell of contained blood. *Death.*

Tyr swung round towards Kristoff. 'Stop!'

Kristoff lifted his head, blood smeared across his chin. His eyes took a moment to focus, as if he'd been completely lost in the moment of feeding. His face quickly filled with anger at the interruption. 'What?' he demanded.

'Don't drink from these ones!' Tyr ordered, his hand still gripping Ehren's throat. 'They're infected.'

Chapter 46

Anna twisted her head so that she could see Tyr. *'What?'*

Kristoff looked down at Mike, his eyes widening.

'We're not infected!' Anna said hurriedly. 'What the hell are you talking about?'

Tyr angrily silenced her with a wave of his hand. He pulled Ehren towards him, bringing their faces close together. *'Death,'* Tyr spat. 'You smell of death, Doctor Ehren. You've been infected.'

Ehren didn't reply. Tyr grabbed the sleeve of the man's shirt and yanked it up, revealing a piece of cloth that had been hastily tied around the forearm. The cloth was stained darkly with dried blood.

Anna's eyes went wide. 'No,' she whispered. 'No, this is a mistake.'

'No mistake.' Tyr's sharp ears had heard her. He tore the bandage from Ehren's arm, revealing the crescent of bruised and bleeding teeth marks. The flesh around the wounds was red and inflamed, clear fluid oozing from the edges.

The vampire who had been holding Mike abruptly dropped him and stepped away, letting him fall heavily to his knees. Blood flowed freely from the wound in Mike's neck as his head lolled forward. He remained swaying there for a long moment, then toppled to the ground.

'No!' Anna struggled against the vampire holding her. 'Let me go! Mike!'

'Tyr!' Kristoff wiped convulsively at his mouth and spat out bloodstained phlegm. 'What about this one? Is this one infected?' There was a trace of panic in his voice as he stared down at Mike's motionless form.

Tyr released his grip on Ehren's shirt, then in the same motion drew back his fist and hit him hard in the face. The man's head snapped back and he sat down hard on the ground, his hands going to his nose. Tyr had already turned away, kneeling beside Mike. He touched his fingers to the blood leaking from the man's neck, then smelled it carefully.

An agonising second passed before the vampire shook his head. 'No, he's clean.'

The look of relief on Kristoff's face was immense. 'Can I finish him, then?'

'Sure.' Tyr stood back up. 'If you've not lost your appetite.'

Behind him, Ramone was still pinned to the ground, the pressure on his chest causing spots to appear before his eyes. He could barely focus on the vampire who was sat on him; unable to get little more than a vague impression of size and shape. His rifle was crushed against his chest and there was no way that he could get it free, but it wasn't the only weapon available to him. When Tyr had yelled at Kristoff to stop feeding, the vampire pinning Ramone down had turned to see what the hell was going on. Ramone had used that opportunity to work his left hand free and reach down to the objects hanging from his belt.

It took several painfully long moments for him to work one loose, but once he did, it was an easy matter to dislodge the pin. He closed his hand tightly around the metal cylinder, keeping the detonator held down.

'Hey.' His voice was weak, and on the first try the vampire didn't hear him. 'Hey,' he said again.

The vampire snapped his attention back to him. 'What?' he hissed.

'You know what a flash grenade is?'

The vampire stared at him, then at the object in his hand, and then he went very still.

'They're great fun,' Ramone told him in the same painful whisper. 'Wanna find out?'

The vampire shifted, baring his teeth.

'Get off me,' Ramone ordered.

Very carefully, the vampire got off him and backed away, his eyes never straying from the grenade in the man's hand. 'Tyr!'

Tyr turned and saw Ramone on his feet. 'What – ?' he stared to ask, then he too saw what the man was holding. 'What are you doing?' he demanded.

'Telling you to back away, right now.'

'Or what? You'll blow us all up?'

Ramone grinned viciously. 'Flash grenade. It'll stun the hell out of humans for about a minute, but I've always wondered – what do you reckon a magnesium flare would do to you motherfuckers?'

'If it's non-lethal to you useless creatures, what the hell do you expect it to do to us?' Despite the confidence of Tyr's tone, Ramone could see the look of doubt in his eyes, and he made him smile even wider.

'No idea,' he shrugged. 'But maybe we'll get a chance to find out. Exactly how bright a light do you reckon you could withstand, Tyr?'

The vampire's silence was all the answer he needed.

'All of you, back off,' Ramone said. 'Over there where I can see you.'

Reluctantly, the female vampire let go of Anna and stepped away. Immediately Anna ran to Mike's side, kneeling beside him.

Mike was lying face down on the ground, unmoving. Blood was streaming from the two puncture wounds in his neck, and when Anna shook his shoulder he did not respond. Panic blossomed inside her and she rolled him onto his back. His eyelids flickered briefly, showing that he was at least still alive.

She pressed her hand down over the twin holes to try and stop the bleeding. Mike's skin was slick with warm blood and despite her putting pressure on it the bleeding did not seem to slow.

From behind her, someone laughed. 'You might as well give that up, girl,' Kristoff said. 'He's going to bleed to death real fast.'

'Anna.' Ramone's voice was as calm and authoritative as always. 'Find my bag. In the left hand pocket there's a first aid kit. Look inside and find the bag with the red label.'

The bag was just out of her reach, and Anna had to take her hand off Mike's neck for several vital seconds in order to grab it. She dragged it over to her side and put her hand back over the wound. Her insides twisted as she saw that blood was pooling rapidly underneath Mike's head. It took her only a moment to find the first aid kit and the small bag inside.

She tore the vacuum-sealed bag open with her teeth. A small, moist piece of cloth dropped out.

'Press it over the wound and hold it in place. It's soaked in coagulant; it'll counteract the saliva.'

Anna did as she was told, pressing the square piece of spongy fabric against Mike's neck. Almost immediately it became soaked with blood. She touched Mike's face and again the eyelids fluttered, but his skin had gone deathly pale and he still did not respond.

The vampires had backed off a short distance, but didn't show any signs of moving further. 'So, let me get this straight,' Tyr said then. 'If that device *doesn't* kill us buts knocks you all unconscious... where exactly would that leave you?'

'That's the fun thing about taking risks,' Ramone told him. 'You just don't know how they're going to work out. Now, we're leaving, and you're not going to stop us, and –'

'*What has happened here?*' a voice demanded from behind them.

Ramone almost dropped the grenade in surprise, swinging round and taking his eyes off the other vampires.

'Luca!' Anna cried in relief.

The black-haired vampire stood in the centre of the road, his dark eyes burning with rage. He stepped forward, his gaze fixed on Tyr. He completely ignored the humans.

'What is going on?' he asked again, his voice cold with anger.

Ramone answered him. 'We came up here looking for protection. Which turns out to have been a bit of an optimistic hope.' Now that he knew who was behind him, he turned his attention back to the other vampires, who had not moved.

Luca pointed his finger at Mike. 'Which one of you did this?'

Tyr held up his hands, his smile mocking. 'Don't know nothing about that, boss. He was like that when we found him.'

'It was him!' Anna spat, pointing at Kristoff with her free hand. 'They attacked us... he was going to kill Mike. They were going to kill us all.'

Tyr shrugged. 'That's an over-exaggeration.'

'Alright.' Luca stepped in front of the humans so that he was standing between them and the other vampires. 'All of you – get back to the cave. Now.'

All of them except for Tyr began to retreat. The blond vampire did not move, instead continuing to face Luca with the same slight smile on his face.

'Tyr,' Luca said. 'I told you to move. I will settle this argument with you in private. Not now.'

'No argument to settle, boss. I was just protecting your territory in your absence – as instructed.'

'I never instructed *this*.' Luca took another step forward, closing the distance between them. 'Tyr... you remember the last time you tried something like this? Didn't your last master punish you enough?'

'You're not my master,' Tyr said, the first trace of real anger creeping into his voice.

Anna was still kneeling on the ground, transfixed by the exchange, and she nearly screamed aloud as someone touched her shoulder. She looked up and realised that it was Jason, the young vampire who had driven her up to the mountains the night before.

'Come on,' he said. 'I'll carry your friend.'

Reluctantly, Anna let go of Mike and allowed Jason to lift him into his arms. Mike mumbled something incoherent, but didn't awake. The flow of blood from the puncture wounds had slowed to a sluggish trickle.

'Get them inside,' Luca instructed him without looking round.

Tyr cleared his throat. 'Y'know, that's not such a great idea.'

'Is that so?'

'That's so. Because that one – ' Tyr pointed with his twisted right hand. ' – is infected. He's been bitten by one of the dead ones.'

Slowly, Luca turned his black eyes towards Ehren, who was still sat on the ground where he'd landed after being struck. The bite mark on his arm was very obvious in the silver glow of the moonlight.

'You see?' Tyr spread his arms. 'I was just looking out for the welfare of your people, as you asked me.'

'Quiet.' Luca's eyes were unreadable as he stared down at the man. 'Jason – take the others inside. Doctor Ehren will have to remain here.'

'*What?*' Anna demanded incredulously. 'You can't leave him out here on his own!'

'We can't allow him inside either.' Luca shook his head slowly. 'I'm sorry.'

Ramone had finally lowered the grenade, taking a moment to shakily re-insert the pin and disarm it. To be on the safe side, he discarded the device over the side of the road and stepped away from the edge quickly. Better to be safe than sorry.

Wiping his damp palms on his jacket, he stepped forward. 'It's okay,' he told the others. 'Ehren won't have to stay out here alone. I'll stop here with him.'

Ehren raised his eyes towards him.

'After all,' Ramone said calmly, 'someone's going to have to put him down before he turns.'

Chapter 47

'Wait!' Anna had hold of Ramone's arm, refusing to let go. 'What are you going to do?'

Ramone gave a heavy sigh. 'Look, just take your friend inside, okay? He's the one you should be worrying about.'

'But...' She looked between him and Ehren, who was still sat silently on the ground. She dropped her voice to a whisper. 'You're going to *kill* him?'

'Would you rather do it instead?'

Anna stared at him, unable to find an answer.

'Listen.' Ramone's voice was unusually soft and gentle. 'Go inside. Look after Mike, don't let him out of your sight. And stay close to Luca – you'll need his protection. I'll be inside in just a few minutes. Try real hard not to think about it, okay?'

Anna opened her mouth, then closed it again. She dropped her gaze and silently nodded.

'Here.' Ramone passed her his handgun, the one that Tyr had been forced to give back to him. He'd checked to make sure it had a full clip of silver bullets. 'I'll feel better if you have this.'

Anna took the gun and attempted a weak smile. 'That won't really protect us, will it?'

'No,' he admitted. 'Like I say, it's just to make me feel better about you guys going in there without me.'

'Thanks.' Still avoiding meeting his eyes, she turned away and hurried after Jason, who was carrying Mike as easily as if he were a child.

Ramone waited for a long moment after they had all disappeared into the darkness further up the track. Then he turned back to Ehren. 'So,' he asked. 'How you feeling there?'

Ehren stared up at him but made no attempt to reply. Now that Ramone knew what to look for, he could clearly see the changes that had affected the man. The flesh of his face was discoloured and seemed to sag loosely from his bones, his eyes deeply sunken in their sockets. Ramone wondered how the hell he hadn't noticed it before, and cursed himself for his inattention.

Ramone sat down cross-legged on the road in front of the man, placing himself a certain distance away. 'When did this happen?' he asked. Getting no reply, he shrugged. 'Let me see… there weren't that many times we lost sight of each other. When we were cutting through the forest from the fence back to the road – was it then?'

A hesitation, then Ehren nodded.

'That would be…' Ramone checked his watch. 'Hell, eight or nine hours ago. You're a lucky son of a bitch to still be alive after that amount of time, aren't you? What's the normal reference range? Six hours? Seven?'

'About that, yes,' Ehren said quietly.

'And yet you're still up and walking around. God. If we were back at the camp you'd be your own number one test subject. Nine hours and still with complete motor function.' Ramone laughed and shook his head. 'That's pretty amazing, don't you think?'

Ehren shifted his position. Over the past few hours he had begun to notice that if he stayed in the same position for too long his muscles and joints all cramped up. The sensation was steadily getting worse. 'I know what you're going to do,' Ehren said then. 'And I can tell that you're not going to make it easy for me.'

'Make it easy for you? To be honest, I can't see why I should.' Ramone pointed an accusing finger. 'You could have turned at any point in the last five hours. If that had happened and we hadn't been prepared, you could have killed one of us. And even now, you still wouldn't have told us if those goddamn vampires hadn't sniffed out the fact that you're already dead. I am in no mood at all to make it easy for you.'

'Fine. That's fine.' Ehren tried to get to his feet, but his legs may as well have been made of lead for all the effect it had. He fell back onto the hard ground with a groan. He tried to say something else but his breath had escaped.

Ramone watched without emotion as the man tried again to move his legs. He knew that it was a fruitless struggle, because the blood had already ceased to flow to those extremities. 'Must be interesting for you,' he noted. 'After all your study, to finally get to experience it for yourself. How many of the seven stages have you been through so far? Are you up to acceptance yet, or should I give you a while longer?'

Ehren leaned back against the stone behind him and closed his eyes. He was silent for a long moment, consumed by the sickening feeling of sensation being leached from his limbs. Every breath he took was slow and painful, as if parts of his lungs were no longer working properly. 'This is about James,' he said eventually. 'Isn't it?'

Ramone didn't answer him. He was staring out over the forest, his face betraying no sign of what he was thinking.

'I always knew you must hate me for that,' Ehren went on, his eyes still closed. 'I know you think that we should have killed him, but... he was already dead. You know that. He wasn't alive, he wasn't conscious, there was nothing left of the person he'd been. There was no need to kill him, because he was already dead.'

Ramone spoke without looking round. 'Can you prove that? For definite, one hundred percent prove that there was no consciousness?'

'The test results were always there, if you'd wanted to see them...'

'I've seen your tests. You've proved that sometimes the dead can feel pain, will back away from fire, and that some are smarter than others.'

'That doesn't mean that...'

'You've proved that some of them still recognise their own names.'

Ehren opened his eyes, staring up at the dark sky. 'Out of one hundred and fifty-seven tests, it was suspected six times, and proven conclusively only once. It was rare, very unusual, the result of a very specific set of circumstances...'

'Did you run that test on James?'

Ehren licked his lips. His tongue felt cold and dry, like a lump of pumice that had somehow been grafted into his mouth. As he ran it slowly over his lips he could feel the areas where there was no nerves left alive in his flesh, the little numb spots that would rapidly spread outwards. The constant fear that had been with him since the moment he'd been bitten surged briefly, and he had to force it back down. 'It was part of the standard series of tests,' he answered at last.

Ramone laughed very quietly. 'Even at a time like this, you still do all you can to avoid a direct answer. So what was the result, Doctor Ehren?'

'Negative. There was no response at all.' Ehren exhaled painfully. 'There was nothing left of him,' he said again. 'And no need to kill him... except to make yourself feel better.'

Another silence descended on them. Ramone took a moment to pull his bag across to him and open it up. He dug out another handgun to replace the one he had given to Anna, and quietly popped in a full clip. Ehren continued to stare up at the sky, trying to remember what the sunset had been like that evening. He had known at the time that it was his last, and yet he still couldn't recall how it had looked.

'Did you ever consider,' Ramone said suddenly, 'that maybe the dead respond to the person speaking, not just to the sound of their name?' He shook his head, not really expecting an answer. 'What about faces? Did you ever try to see if they responded to familiar faces, anything like that? Maybe some of them would have responded to that, rather than to their names.'

Ehren coughed painfully. His chest felt like it was burning up from the inside out. 'There wouldn't have been a response,' he whispered. 'There aren't any residual memories… nothing like that. Consciousness leaves at the moment of death, and the memories become inaccessible at that same moment. Any intelligence or recognition is… something we can't explain. Something outside of residual consciousness. Even if the information remains in their heads, they can't use it for anything… can't access it. Some of the lights get left on when we leave… that's all.'

Ramone listened as the man's voice faded. Ehren had closed his eyes again, his breathing becoming more laboured by the moment. He was still alive, but both of them knew that it was a matter of minutes, not hours.

'I think it's time.'

Ehren stirred but didn't open his eyes. Ramone went over to him and slid his arms behind the man's shoulders with strange gentleness. Carefully, he sat him up.

'Ehren, wake up.'

The eyelids flicked, and Ehren slowly opened his eyes. 'What?' he asked. His voice was nothing more than a cracked whisper now, filled with pain.

'Wanted to see if you still recognised your name. Also, it's time.'

Ehren's eyes rolled. 'Why… wake me? Couldn't you have just…' Another coughing fit interrupted him. Ramone waited patiently until it had run its course. 'Couldn't you have just shot me while I was unconscious?' he managed.

Ramone smiled without humour. 'I'm not big on shooting people in their sleep. Sit up and look out at your empire one last time.'

There wasn't enough living flesh left in Ehren's body for him to support himself, so Ramone propped his limp form up against the stone behind him. The moonlight cast its silver glow over the entirety of the forest below, illuminating it with eerie beauty. Ehren could still see, although his vision had dimmed a great deal. The island looked peaceful, serene.

'This… is all my fault…' he managed to say.

'Is that some kind of deathbed repentance?' Ramone asked. He had got to his feet and was holding the gun in his right hand. 'Well, I hope it helps.'

Ehren didn't have the strength to say anything else. He closed his eyes and moved his lips in silent prayer.

He heard the gunshot, and then a moment later opened his eyes to wonder why the hell he was still alive.

Painfully, he looked up at Ramone. The man had put the gun away and was standing there with a strange smile on his face.

'Y'know,' Ramone said, 'I think that maybe you're going to die tonight, but perhaps it shouldn't be the end of things for you.'

Ignoring the feeble protests of the dying man, Ramone stooped and took hold of Ehren under the shoulders, lifting him up. The man was a dead weight, and it took a lot of effort to get him off the ground. Ramone grunted in pain – some of his ribs were definitely broken. Awkwardly, he half-carried and half-dragged Ehren towards the edge of the track where the slope dropped steeply away into darkness.

'You have a nice unlife now, Doctor Ehren.' Smiling, Ramone lay the man down and began to roll him towards the edge. 'Maybe if you're lucky you'll break your neck on the way down.'

'No…. pl… ssss…'

'Too late. Goodbye now – I'm sure I'll see you in hell.' With a final shove, Ramone pushed the body onto the slope, standing up to watch as it rolled and bounced with increasing speed down the side of the mountain.

He stood there for a long time after it disappeared from sight before he finally turned and resumed walking back up the track.

Chapter 48

The first thing Mike was aware of as he came awake was the burning pain in his throat. He coughed, attempted to sit up, and felt someone pressing him back down.

'It's okay,' Anna's voice said. 'Lie still.'

'Gah.' His throat felt like it was on fire, and another coughing fit just made it worse. Blearily he opened his eyes and saw Anna's concerned face staring down at him. 'Oh.' It hurt to talk as well, and the word came out as a croak. 'Hey, I'm not dead.' The fact surprised him.

'No, you're not. Although you did scare the sweet hell out of me. Please stop trying to move.'

'Sorry. Where are we?' From his limited viewpoint, Mike could see that he was inside a house of some kind, lying on a fairly rudimentary bed. He could just see the edge of a window, and outside it appeared to be pitch black.

'Inside the vampire cave.'

'*What?*' Without thinking, Mike tried to sit up again.

'Will you quit doing that? It's alright – Luca saved us. He brought us in here.'

'Really? Well, not wishing to sound ungrateful, but I'm still gonna have words with him about his choice of friends...'

A second voice spoke. 'I'm already aware of the poor choices I make.'

Mike turned his head as much as he could and found that Luca was sat at the other side of the small room. 'Oops,' he said. 'Sorry.'

'It's alright, I completely understand.' The vampire leaned forward, his black eyes deep and serious. 'In fact, it should really be me apologising. This should never have happened, and I'm sorry.'

Mike lay back down and closed his eyes. 'I can't believe he bit me,' he muttered. 'That absolute bastard. Hey, is my camera okay?'

Anna rolled her eyes. 'Yes, it's fine.'

'What about me, am I fine?' His eyes suddenly opened wide, his hand going to the wound on his throat. 'I'm not going to... y'know...'

'You're quite safe,' Luca told him. 'Our... affliction cannot be transmitted through a simple bite.'

'Thank fuck for that. No offence, of course.'

'Of course.' Only Anna saw the haunted look that passed through the vampire's black eyes.

'So,' she said quickly to cover the moment. 'Where did you go this evening, Luca? Did you see what's happening at the camp?'

'No, we never made it that far. Jason drove us, but about halfway to the camp we were attacked.'

'By the dead ones?' Anna guessed.

Luca shook his head slowly. 'Not exactly. It was one of the animals that live in the forest, but... I can only guess that it had been bitten by the dead ones. It had become like them. It tried to attack us as we were driving, and destroyed our jeep in the process. I have a feeling that we were lucky to get away. We didn't want to risk carrying on on foot, so we turned round and got back here as fast as we could. We saw quite a few more of the dead ones on the way back, but we were able to evade or kill them.' He leaned forward again, his brow furrowing. 'It's strange that they're so widespread though. The whole forest is filled with movement, and I don't quite understand it. Really, the dead ones should all have followed one another to the encampment. Them spreading out like this is too... rational.'

Anna nodded. 'We were wondering about that as well. When we were in the forest we kept running into isolated little groups of them... and they were appearing out of nowhere. No warning, no noise, nothing like that. Like they were deliberately trying to head us off. It was really scary.'

'Strange. I don't understand that at all.' Luca looked over at Mike, who seemed to be about to drift back off to sleep. 'You should get your friend to eat and drink something before he sleeps again. Otherwise he'll feel a lot worse when he wakes up.'

'Great,' Mike complained. 'Feeling worse than this is just what I need.' The mention of food had made him realise that he was absolutely starving. The burning in his throat was at least partially due to thirst.

'There's food in the other room,' Luca told them. 'Nothing special, I'm afraid, and you'll have to cook it yourself.' He smiled a little. 'None of us have had much practice at cooking in recent years.'

'That's fine.' Anna smiled at him. 'It's great, in fact. Thank you, Luca.'

'The least I could do.' The vampire stood up. 'I've got to go, but Jason is right outside if you need anything.'

After he had gone outside and closed the door, Mike carefully sat himself up. 'Wow-eee, I can't believe you can sit there so calmly and talk to a vampire like that. A real vampire, for God's sake! I must say he doesn't really look the part... t-shirt and jeans? Not greatly inspired. Shouldn't it be more, y'know, leather and lace? Something a teeny bit more gothic?'

'I'm glad your sense of humour's feeling better,' Anna remarked. 'You want food?'

'Yes. Yes, I most definitely do.'

'Then shut up and be a good patient.' Anna stood up and walked through to the adjoining room, which contained a roughly-finished table and a small larder, and not much else. The vampires obviously didn't cater for guests that often. There was a small camp stove on the table, and the larder was stocked with piles of cans and dried goods, many of them out of date. Anna pursed her lips and rummaged around in the cupboard, digging out the basic essentials of a meal and stacking them on the table.

From the other room, she could hear Mike getting up slowly from the bed. *Fine*, she thought. *If he doesn't want to listen to advice, that's just fine with me.* She pulled a chair up to the table and tried to figure out how to light the paraffin stove.

'Need a hand?' Mike was standing in the doorway, leaning heavily on the doorframe.

'Yes, in fact. Grab a chair and sit down and you can start opening cans for me.'

With only a minimum of complaints, Mike did as he was told. He sat down opposite her and pulled a couple of cans and the opener towards him. 'So you and Luca are friends then?' he asked, struggling with a can-opener that seemed to be mostly held together by rust.

'I only met him last night.'

'Yeah, but... well, he stopped us from getting chomped just now, so I'm guessing that he counts you as a friend. Right?'

'I don't know... I guess.'

'He's certainly got that "vampire angst" thing going on though, hasn't he?' Mike laughed. 'Ooh, moody.'

Anna didn't laugh. 'Yeah. Well, he's got problems to sort out, hasn't he?'

'What problems?' Mike's smile faded as he saw the look on her face.

'The problem that four of his people attacked us. Apparently it means he now has to do something about Tyr.' Anna shook her head. 'I don't think he's happy about that at all.'

'Geez, how much did I miss while I was out?' Mike finally managed to force open a tin of beans. He was so hungry that he ignored the fact that Anna had got the stove lit, and instead just dug into the can with his fingers. The cold beans were possibly the best thing he had ever tasted in his life.

'Don't eat with your hands,' Anna scolded him. 'You don't know where they've been.'

Mike froze with his fingers halfway to his mouth. A few hours ago he'd accidentally stuck his hand into the shattered brainpan of a zombie. He stared at his bean-covered hands in horror.

'Relax.' Anna laughed. 'We cleaned you up while you were asleep.'

Mike grunted and shoved the tin across the table to her. He wiped his fingers on the front of his jumper. 'Is that where Luca's gone?' he asked. 'To deal with the blond psychopathic guy?'

'I think so. If you want anything with your beans you'll have to open another tin.'

Mike fidgeted in his seat, torn between his desperate hunger and his equally desperate curiosity as to what was going on outside. Finally he picked up the can-opener again with a sigh.

As they ate, Anna told Mike what had happened earlier when Luca had intervened and saved them from the other vampires. 'Ramone was trying to drive them back with a flash grenade,' she added, 'but even if he'd managed it then I don't know what we would have done. I don't think we could've carried you down from there, and you weren't in any state to walk.' She stared at her food rather than at him. 'So if Luca hadn't turned up when he did I'm fairly sure we would've been screwed.'

'Uh-huh.' The beans tasted even better now that they'd been cooked. Mike was concentrating on eating and was trying hard not to focus too much on what Anna was saying, because he kept getting chills up and down his spine. He remembered clearly being bitten by the vampire, and the idea that he could easily have died was something he didn't want to dwell on. 'I owe him then,' he said at last 'I owe him really big.'

'Yes, you do.'

Mike finished the last of his food and pushed the plate away. 'Why the hell does Ramone carry around stun grenades with him? That man has everything, it's not fair.' He looked around as if suddenly realising the absence of half of their party. 'Hey, where did him and Ehren go anyway?'

'Ah. That's kinda... difficult to explain.'

'Can you make it short?' Mike was already standing up from the table and hurrying back through to the other room to get his camera. 'I wanna get out there and find out what's going on with these vampires.'

'Mike...'

He heard the tone in her voice and turned back, his heart dropping. 'What?' he asked. 'Where are they?'

'I think you'd better sit down.'

Mike did as he was told.

Chapter 49

The doors that led to the inside cavern hadn't been closed yet, although there were two vampires stationed in the tunnel before it. Ramone walked past them both without acknowledgement, silently relieved that neither of them tried to stop him. He hoped that that meant things were still relatively calm inside the cavern, and that Mike and Anna were okay.

He passed through the doors and down the sloping ground towards the semi-circle of houses that marked the newest edge of the ancient underground city. In the centre of the semi-circle the large, stylised electric lamp was lit, giving a warm glow to the area around it. Apparently the lamp was kept lit at all times, despite the fact that the vampires did not need it to see by. It was one of their idiosyncrasies – like the fact that they built human-style dwellings that they also had no real use for.

A small group of people was standing underneath the strangely shaped lamp, and as he got closer Ramone picked out two of them as Anna and Mike. He was pleased to see that the third was Jason, who had obviously been placed there by Luca as protection. Jason was one of the few vampires that Ramone felt he could trust, although he couldn't give any concrete reason as to why. Just gut instinct.

'Are you okay?' Anna asked as soon as he got close. Her eyes were large with concern, and for a moment Ramone felt almost guilty that he didn't feel half as bad as she obviously did.

'I'm fine,' he told her. 'It's all done.'

Anna bit her lip and nodded. Ramone happened to glance up at Mike and saw the look in his eyes. Unlike Anna, the man was obviously wondering if Ramone had been the best person to take care of Ehren. Mike was now the only one apart from himself who knew about James.

'Where's everybody else?' Ramone asked, looking round.

Jason nodded towards the back of the cave. 'Down there. Luca's dealing with the others… at least, that's what he was planning on doing.'

'Great. Internal disputes are so much fun to get involved in. Should we go along and lend moral support?'

Jason grinned. 'Moral support involving magnesium flare grenades?'

Ramone shrugged. 'Sure, if necessary.' He looked at the others. 'Are you two okay to come with, or do you need to rest?'

'I'm not resting,' Mike said immediately. 'I'm full of beans and caffeine.'

'We're fine,' Anna confirmed. 'I want to know what's going on.'

'Alright.' Ramone took a moment to dump his bag in front of one of the houses. After a quick think, he also left his rifle behind, although he kept the handgun strapped to his side. Silver bullets would do little to the vampires apart from piss them off, but he wanted to have the gun with him. He motioned to Jason. 'Lead on.'

The vampire led them through the maze of buildings, towards the back of the vast cavern. Although most of the houses were identical in design and they were all made of the same dark grey stone, some were obviously a lot older than others. Several had collapsed in on themselves, and many more had no roofs. Lights still burned in a few, but the further back into the cave they went, the fewer lights showed, until they were walking in almost complete darkness. Despite the fact that they were underground, the sheer size of the cavern began to give Mike a sense of agoraphobia, and he spent a lot of time staring at the ground and trying not to think about the fact that the black sky above was in fact a solid roof.

'Ramone?' he asked after a bit.

'Hmm?'

'I was wondering – why exactly are you carrying around stun grenades?'

'Oh. That. They're not actually flash grenades,' Ramone said blithely. 'They're regular grenades. But that probably wouldn't have scared off the bloodsuckers, so I told them they were stuns.'

Mike stared at him. 'That was a *real* grenade?'

'Yeah, what of it?'

Mike started to say something, then gave up and shook his head. 'Never mind.' He figured it probably wasn't polite to get picky about the man's methods.

They reached a place where the houses encircled a rough area of ground, forming a natural amphitheatre. A single dim electric light at one side illuminated the scene, and the humans all stopped as soon as they reached its glow. All around the depression in the floor were dozens of vampires.

Many were standing or crouching at the edges of the rough area, but the majority were perched on the flat roofs of the surrounding buildings. It was impossible to accurately guess their number, because so many were partially or totally concealed by the shadows, but there must have been at least fifty and probably a lot more.

'Your human friends are here,' someone noted, his voice clearly audible in the silence.

Two figures were standing in the centre of the depression. Even at a distance and in the dim light, it was easy to pick out that one was tall and blond and the other was shorter and dark-haired. In fact, Luca looked surprisingly small and slight next to Tyr, and his pale face was the only part of him that was clearly visible in the darkness. He didn't seem bothered by the humans arriving.

'You were the one who involved them in this,' Luca said. 'They have a right to bear witness.'

'They have no rights at all,' Tyr spat. 'They're busy destroying our island, and they almost brought the infection right in here.'

Mike's camera whirred quietly as he switched it on, holding it at waist height. It was difficult to get the focus right because of the poor light, but he wanted some kind of record of this.

Several of the vampires heard the whirring sound and immediately turned towards him. 'What are you doing?' Tyr demanded.

'Um...' Mike would have backed away if his legs hadn't frozen at that exact moment.

Luca took something out of his pocket, turning it casually in his hand. It was too dark to see what it was, but suddenly a thin beam of light stabbed out from it. The watchers realised that it was a very small pocket torch.

The effect on Tyr was immediate. The thin beam hit him on the arm and he yelped in pain, darting out of the way. Luca turned the torch off again.

'Ultraviolet light.' Even in the darkness it was obvious that he was smiling. 'I'd recommend that you pay attention to me, Tyr, and not to anybody else. I have no wish to hurt you like your last master did.'

'That's good.' Tyr was still rubbing the burnt spot on his arm. 'Because you're not going to get the chance.'

None of the humans saw what happened next. The two figures seemed to blur and an instant later Tyr was on the ground with Luca holding him down. They could only guess that the blond vampire had initiated the attack, but he was definitely getting the worst of it now. Luca held him down with little apparent effort, one knee on his chest and the other one pinning down the right arm.

Tyr snarled and tried to throw him off, but Luca drove his knee down hard into his rib cage. There was an audible crack as the ribs fractured, and Tyr's cry of pain died into a gasp.

Luca was talking in a fast whisper, but neither Mike nor Anna recognised the language. They saw Tyr shake his head, defiant despite the pain in his chest. Then Luca used his free hand to turn on the torch again, and Tyr's frantic efforts to escape redoubled.

The hiss of burning flesh was audible even over his screams. Anna bit her knuckles hard but couldn't turn away, transfixed by what was happening.

Very deliberately, Luca ran the wavering light over the neck of the blond vampire. The flesh puckered and smoked, the blood underneath boiling with the heat. A vein swelled grotesquely, then cracked and burst, spewing blood across the blackening skin.

Luca clicked the torch off. 'You will not disobey me,' he said in the same calm, deliberate voice. 'And you will not feed off humans, ever again.'

Tyr's lips moved but no sound came out. His blue eyes were unnaturally wide and showed too much white, as if he were about to go into shock.

'Just nod,' Luca suggested. 'I'll take that as your surrender.'

Slowly, Tyr moved. The muscles of his neck stood out like burnt cords with the effort it took, but he somehow managed to shake his head. *No.*

Luca switched on the torch again and moved it with the precision of a surgeon around the jawline. Tyr struggled against him, but his strength seemed to be fading fast. Still no sound emerged from his throat apart from a tortured hiss of air. It occurred to Anna with a shudder that the ultraviolet light must have damaged his voice box.

In the whole cavern there was no sound except for the hiss of light burning skin, and the fading breaths of the vampire. Not one of the silent watching figures made any move to stop what was happening.

Again Luca stopped and sat up, his smooth face betraying no emotion. He asked Tyr something in that other language, but got no reply. 'Come on, Tyr,' he said then in English. 'Just say it, or I'll burn out your eyes.'

The blond vampire was still for so long that Anna was sure he wasn't going to answer. But then somehow his lips moved.

'...*sorry*...' he managed to whisper.

Luca smiled very slightly and got up. 'You two,' he ordered, indicating a male and a female vampire standing nearby. 'Seal him up.'

They did as they were told at once. It was only when they got near Tyr's motionless body that Anna realised Luca had picked two of the vampires who had attacked them earlier. They moved quickly, showing no signs of defiance anymore; only fear. They picked up Tyr as if he weighed less than nothing and carried him away.

Luca turned to face the vampires all around. '*Go,*' he ordered, and every figure melted into the darkness.

Chapter 50

They suddenly became very aware of the silence in the vast cavern. The vampires had all vanished into the darkness in a matter of seconds, moving as soundlessly as the shadows around them, and the humans were left alone. Even Jason had disappeared from their side.

Mike slowly lowered his camera, glancing at the others. Anna had her knuckles pressed to her mouth, and she had gone very pale. It was more difficult to tell what Ramone was thinking, as his expression was as impassive as ever.

Luca came towards them, putting the small torch carefully back into his pocket. 'Are you okay now?' he asked.

Surprisingly, the question was directed at Mike, who wondered why the hell he was being asked. Then he remembered the wound on his throat, and his hand went to touch the bandage that covered it. 'Yeah, I'm fine,' he said, forcing a smile. 'Just... y'know... um. I've never seen anyone killed by a pocket torch before.'

'I didn't kill him,' Luca said with a shake of his head. 'He's just very weak now, and he won't be able to heal until he feeds again. Which is not likely to be for a long while.'

'Why not?' Anna asked.

'I've ordered him to be sealed up in his house. He won't be released until I say so.'

'And when will that be?'

'When I say so.' His tone was hard, as if he were annoyed by her questioning him. 'Follow me, I'll show you where you can sleep tonight.'

As the vampire turned away, Mike gave Anna a questioning look, but she seemed just as taken aback by Luca's abruptness as him. Not daring to ask anything else, they fell into step behind him as he led the way back through the maze of grey stone buildings.

Ramone didn't seem to share their reluctance, and moved forward so that he could walk beside Luca. 'It's almost midnight,' he said. 'If we can get a few hours sleep we should be awake before dawn. Then we can make plans for leaving.'

'It wouldn't be wise to leave the cavern, even after the sun comes up.' Luca's voice was still hard, and his accent was more pronounced than usual. 'You'll have to stay here until we can assess how much damage has been done to the island.'

'You'd let us stay here in the cavern during the day?' Ramone was greatly surprised.

'The others won't like the idea,' Luca admitted, 'and if I could see any other way then I wouldn't even suggest it. But I cannot allow you to go back out into the forest. You'll have to remain here.'

Ramone nodded slowly. 'I understand the danger, believe me I do. But the boat will be arriving tomorrow morning, and if we can't let them know that we're here then the chances are they'll leave and never come back. They'll take the people from the camp and then just abandon the island. And,' he added, 'it's not just us. The wolves are holed up in the village, and if they don't get the all clear from Brac then they're going to stay like that. By the time they figure out he's not coming back then the dead ones will have invaded the village. It's really urgent that we get to the mainland and bring in people who can help sort out this situation.'

Luca looked at him. 'You want to bring *more* of your kind here?'

'Yes. We fucked things up, so we've got to help deal with the consequences. I know some people on the mainland who'll be able to help.'

They walked in silence for several minutes as Luca seemed to consider this. 'I don't like the idea,' he said at last.

'Neither do I,' Ramone admitted. 'Even in daylight, it's going to be extremely hard to get back to the camp. And we'll have to pray that when we get there the people in the camp will have killed enough of the dead ones to let us get through to the boat.' He glanced back at Mike and Anna, his dark eyes thoughtful. 'Of course, there's no point in risking all of our lives, so maybe these two could stay here under your protection.'

'What?' Anna objected. 'No!'

'Why not?'

'Well... because...' Anna realised she couldn't actually think of a valid argument. 'You can't just leave us behind...'

Ramone turned his back on her. 'We can talk about it later,' he said to Luca. 'You've got other things to worry about, I'm sure, and we all need to sleep. I'll be awake before dawn so we can talk then. Okay?'

'Alright,' Luca agreed. He was obviously not in the mood to discuss things now.

They walked in silence the rest of the way, taking a slightly different path

206

to the one they had followed on the way in. Luca led them up the sloping side of the cavern to a place where the houses were more widely spaced. One large, low-lying building stood by itself, with at least thirty feet between itself and the closest neighbours. There was an electric light above the door, and more lights showing from each of the thin, slit-like windows.

'This is the nearest thing we have to guest accommodation,' Luca told them. 'There's enough space for the three of you, and you'll be able to secure the door.'

'From outside or in,' Ramone noted, examining the heavy bar that could be placed across the outside of the door. 'Convenient.'

Luca shrugged but didn't comment. 'I'll send Jason back as well, so if you need anything you can ask him. I'll speak to you later.' Without even looking at either of the others, he turned and started walking away back the way they had come.

Anna in particular was distressed, because she would have liked to speak to him. It made her hurt inside to see his attitude changed so completely, and to have him ignore her like that. She watched him as he retreated into the darkness, then reluctantly followed the others into the house.

Inside, the building was not as spacious as it had appeared from the outside, mainly because the walls were built of very thick grey stone. There was one main room with another roughly finished table and a selection of mismatched chairs, and three smaller rooms leading off from it. The interior doors all stood open and Anna could see that two of the rooms contained low camp beds, while the third looked like a very basic bathroom. She could tell just from a cursory glance that there was no such thing as running water in the vampire cavern.

Ramone inspected each of the rooms in turn, taking note of the windows that were far too narrow to allow anyone to get in – or out – through them. 'I call this room,' he decided, picking one of the bedrooms at random.

Mike was too tired to argue. The events of the day were fast catching up on him, and he was only now realising how exhausted he was. Even the short walk across the cavern and back had made the muscles in his legs tremble. He went into the second bedroom and collapsed on the nearest bed. 'Ohhh,' he groaned. 'I'm *so* tired…'

Anna followed him in and sat down on the other bed, her expression distant.

A moment later, Ramone appeared at the door. 'I've got to go get my bag. Will you two be alright here?'

'We're fine,' Mike told him without bothering to look up from his crashed position. 'So long as I can sleep I'll be happy.'

'That's good. Are you okay?' he asked Anna, who was still looking a little vacant.

'I… yeah.' The girl managed a smile. 'I'm okay. Just a bit…' She sighed, then shook her head. 'So much has happened… and seeing Luca like that…'

Ramone shrugged as if the vampire's behaviour hadn't surprised him in the slightest. 'He's got a lot on his mind, I guess. I'm just amazed he offered to let us stay here during the day.'

'Why?'

'Are you kidding? Letting a group of armed humans wander around in here while most of the vamps are asleep? Granted some of them would still be awake, but even so, it'd be one hell of a risk.'

'So he really must trust us,' Anna suggested.

Ramone smiled without humour. 'I don't think it's trust.'

'No?'

'Think about it for a moment – you saw what he just did to one of his own kind. Imagine what he'd do to us if we pissed him off.'

Anna just stared at him. 'But… we're his friends…'

'That would make absolutely no difference. His own species will always come first, don't forget that.' He moved to the outside door. 'Get some sleep. I'm going to get my bag.'

The building was very quiet once he'd gone. Anna remained sat on her bed, staring down at the ground as she tried to put her thoughts into some semblance of order. Across the room from her, Mike shifted awkwardly onto his back, propping his head up on the solitary pillow. His neck was hurting a lot, and he hoped that Ramone would have some painkillers in his bag of tricks. He stretched out his left leg, remembering his other injury of the day. He hadn't had a chance to check how it was looking.

He glanced over at Anna, but she was staring at something that only she could see. Trying not to draw attention to himself, Mike sat upright and rolled up the shredded leg of his jeans. There was a fresh bandage around his calf, and someone had indeed cleaned the wound up. Peeling the bandage off, he saw that it didn't look so bad now that the dirt was gone. It was difficult to tell whether there had been any change, but at least it didn't look infected. He was phenomenally grateful for the fact.

He retied the bandage and settled back onto the bed. He picked up his camera from the floor and rested it on his stomach. Switching it on, he noticed that the battery was almost flat. Fortunately he still had the spare one in his pocket, as well as an extra tape. He decided to change both, now that he had a quiet moment, but first he rewound the current tape a bit, flipping out the small view screen at the side of the camera.

The footage that he'd taken a few minutes earlier flashed up on the screen. The picture wavered in and out of focus because of the bad light, and the sound through the internal speaker was faint and tinny, but he was pleased to see that it was possible to make out what was going on. He watched again as

Luca played the light of the torch over Tyr's face, and he had to marvel at the way such a simple thing had done so much damage.

'Turn that off,' Anna said angrily.

Mike looked at her in surprise. 'What? Why?'

'It was bad enough to sit through it once, I don't need to be reminded of it again. Okay?'

Shrugging, Mike turned down the volume but didn't switch off the picture. 'After everything that's happened today I'm surprised that *this* weirded you out. Didn't you think your pretty vampire would be capable of something like that?' He laughed. 'You know he kills people for food as well, right?'

Anna turned away from him and lay down on the bed. 'You're not funny.'

'It wasn't supposed to be funny.' Mike glanced up at her, frowning. 'What's up with you?'

'What's up with me? How can you even ask that? After everything that's happened today, and… and what Tyr said about my father…' She suddenly found that her eyes were full of tears and she had to stop talking.

Mike switched the camera off and sat up. 'Shit, I'm sorry. I didn't even think…'

Anna turned her face into the thin pillow. 'And everything is my fault,' she moaned.

'Hey, come on…' Mike crossed the room and sat down on the edge of her bed, putting his hands gently on her shoulders. 'How could it be your fault? Don't be silly.'

'I brought us here, didn't I? I dragged you here and now we're trapped and you almost died, and – ' Another sob choked her and for a moment she couldn't breathe. 'All I wanted,' she said with forced slowness, 'was to see my dad again. And now I'm too late to even do that.'

Mike rubbed her shoulders softly, waiting until her muffled sobs subsided. 'It's not your fault,' he said quietly. 'Of course it's not.' He stroked her hair, unable to think of anything else to say. 'Go to sleep, okay? Things will be better in the morning.'

Anna laughed into her pillow. 'That's a lie, isn't it?'

'Yeah, but it's an optimistic lie. Go to sleep.' Mike gave her shoulders a squeeze and then went back to his own bed. He lay down, trying not to think about what the morning would bring.

DAY THREE

Chapter 51

In the encampment it was unnaturally quiet. The generator had spluttered and died shortly after midnight when it ran out of fuel. Everyone had become so used to the noise at night that they barely noticed it anymore, and without it the silence seemed oppressive. The only sound to be heard outside was the soft shushing that could have been the wind in the trees or the distant surf on the shore. The survivors knew differently though. The quiet, almost gentle sound was that of dozens of corpses moving continuously against each other as they searched for a way to get at the people inside.

On top of the flat roof of the refectory building, the sound was clearer and even more disconcerting. A man was sat up there on a cheap plastic chair, which he had laboriously hauled up through the skylight so that he could sit facing the sea. He was wrapped in a blanket made of yellow packaging foam, pulled tightly around his body so that only his face was showing. The foam was scratchy and not very comfortable, but it provided a good deal of protection against the cold night air. He had spent the last several hours staring at the black sea and trying to block out the hushed sounds of movement from all around the building.

At least the lights in the camp were still working, since they were powered by a different source to the main fence. From where he was sat, Reid could see the lights shining brightly from several windows, despite the fact that the other buildings were now unoccupied. All the survivors of the camp were sheltered together inside the refectory, and none of them had thought to turn out the lights in their previous hiding places before they left. Reid wondered how long the stored power from the solar panels would last. Probably not long with all these lights burning.

Throughout the afternoon, the people had been taking turns at going up to the roof and play target practise with the dead ones around the building. They had managed to thin out the undead crowd considerably before the encroaching darkness had convinced them to give up for the night. Now there were fewer than three-dozen zombies milling around down there. Reid was the only person who had remained on the roof after the sun had gone down, keeping watch on the horizon and silently praying for sunrise. The cold kept him awake and he preferred the open air to the cramped atmosphere inside the building. Most of the people were asleep by now, but some were still awake and determined to keep the arguments going.

Reid pulled the makeshift blanket tighter around his shoulders. What did it matter anyway? There was nothing anyone could do about what had happened. Did it really make any difference whose fault it was? Chances were they would never know how the dead ones had got loose. The people downstairs should just be grateful that they were still alive, and should quit going over and over the same ground in an attempt to make some sense of an impossible situation.

A quick headcount earlier in the evening had revealed that at least twenty people were missing, and unless they were still hiding out in one of the other buildings or had managed to get over the fence and into the forest, then they were almost certainly dead. Reid briefly turned his eyes towards the dark forest, wondering if the people who had escaped over the fence were still alive out there. Maybe they were the ones who had made the right decision after all... at least they weren't trapped here with those undead creatures surrounding them.

He reminded himself that that was a stupid way to think. The situation was bad, but it wasn't critical. The survivors were secure inside their building, and all they had to do was last out a single night until the boat arrived. When the sun came up they would be able to clear away the remaining dead ones from around the building and then...

He was facing away from the main gate, his gaze wandering over the black, moonlit sea. He did not see the figure that appeared from out of the darkness under the trees and stepped through the gate. The first warning he got was the faint sound of steady footsteps approaching over the rough ground.

Frowning, he turned in his seat. The footsteps were slow but regular, with none of the dragging hesitancy that characterised the way the dead ones walked. In the faint light, it took a moment for Reid to pick out the figure that was now walking purposefully across the open ground towards the refectory. His heart leaped as he realised the person had to still be alive, because nothing dead could move with such steady confidence.

Reid stood up, his blanket dropping unnoticed to the floor. He hurried to the edge of the flat roof, planning to shout a warning. It seemed impossible that the person might not have noticed the dead ones crowded around the building, and yet he didn't slow for a second. He was heading right for them. What was going on?

The figure stepped into a patch of yellow light that shone from the window of one of the buildings, and Reid got the answer to his unspoken question. The man was dead. The skin covering half of his face was deathly pale, while the other half had been torn away to expose the skull underneath. Tattered remains of a black t-shirt failed to cover the vast gaping hole in the abdominal cavity. His arms were streaked with mud as if he had pulled himself up from his own grave. One of the eye-sockets was empty, but the look in the other eye made Reid back away from the edge of the roof. Even in the most alert of the dead ones, he had never seen such a look of absolute rage.

The dead man didn't pause as he strode up to the other zombies. None of them paid him the slightest bit of attention, even when he roughly shoved them out of his way. One stumbled and fell against him and the man angrily wrenched at its arm, tearing it from the socket. He stepped past the corpse, the burning gaze of that single eye fixed on the building in front of him.

Reid didn't dare move. The idea of the dead man noticing him made his blood freeze. The creature couldn't possibly have got to him up there, but even so... Reid shuddered as the man threw another zombie out of his way. Nothing dead should have had that much strength, it just wasn't possible...

He had to warn the others. He knew he had to, and yet the fear kept him frozen in place. He did nothing but watch as the dead man forced his way to the front of the building.

The main doors had been locked and barricaded from within with as much furniture as could be found. Reid knew because he'd helped to do it. Even the combined weight of all the dead ones out there had not been enough to push them open. The dead man stepped up to the double doors, drew back his fist and punched a hole right through the two-inch wood.

Inside the building someone screamed. The man punched another hole through the door, then grabbed the splintered edges with his bare hands and pulled, ripping the wood apart as if it were little more than paper. The other dead ones crowded behind him, anxiously pushing forward as they sensed the food within.

More people were shouting now, and gunshots rang out as someone began firing through the barricade. Watching from the roof, Reid saw the bullets strike the dead man in the chest, knocking him backwards but not slowing him down for an instant. One of the zombies behind him caught a round in the head and dropped to the ground, but the others simply trampled forward over its body.

Within seconds the door was in pieces and the dead ones were stumbling through, their hands tearing at the barricade inside. Reid leaned out over the edge, trying to see what was happening. More of the survivors were firing at the zombies, using up the last of the ammunition in a desperate attempt to force the dead ones back.

The screams suddenly intensified and Reid knew that the barricade had been breached. He jammed his hands over his ears, even though nothing could block out the screams from downstairs. In his mind's eye he could imagine the undead man tearing into the living with the same strength and fury that he had demonstrated a moment before on the dead ones.

Reid sank down on the cold stone roof, squeezing his eyes shut and drawing his knees up to his chest. Part of his mind was screaming that he needed to go down there and help the others fight back, but a colder, more rational part was pointing out that he didn't even have a weapon. Going down there now would be suicide; there was nothing he could do to help any of them...

The skylight in the centre of the roof banged open with such force that the glass shattered into pieces. Reid started in surprise, cowering backwards against the raised edge of the roof. It was impossible, the dead ones couldn't have known he was up there...

A black shape lifted itself from the square hole, pulling itself up with death-like ease. It rose to its feet, the silver moonlight glinting off the exposed bone of its forehead.

Reid tried to stand; failed. There was nothing he could use as a weapon; nowhere he could go except over the edge of the roof. If he'd been able to stand then he might have risked the twenty foot drop to the ground, but he remained paralysed, his back pressed against the low wall.

The dead man took a step forward and smiled. The expression was horrible on the ruins of his face. Blood ran down his chin and coated his arms up to the elbows in testament to the destruction he had caused downstairs. There was just enough of his mind left to savour the look of absolute terror on the trapped human's face.

Reid saw the elongated fangs in the mouth of the undead man, but didn't realise what it meant. He was unable to do anything but watch as his death approached him.

Chapter 52

The forest was even darker and more overgrown than it had been during the day, but as Anna stopped beneath the branches everything seemed unnaturally highlighted with a silver glow. She picked her way with ease over or between the tangled branches and leafless bushes. Every time there was a break in the trees she would see the mountains rising up behind her, black and silent against the night sky. The full moon over the peaks bathed them in harsh silver light.

She knew it had to be a dream, because the little girl was leading her. Anna could just see her outline, maybe a dozen feet ahead, moving through the thick forest as if it were as insubstantial as mist. Her black hair was little more than a darker shadow occasionally flecked with silver. The forest stretched out forever around them, and the vast mountains never seemed to get any further away. The moonlight gave everything a diseased, sickly tone, and Anna felt cold and afraid, aware of the darkness around her.

The girl was leading her somewhere... or possibly she was forcing Anna to follow. When the girl turned and looked back, the shadows hid her face and made her eyes look like black, empty sockets. It was the first time that Anna had ever felt afraid of the little girl who inhabited her dreams. She was deeply scared, but she couldn't be sure if it was fear of the girl or fear of the place that she was being led to.

'Where are we going?' She didn't know if she asked the question aloud or not. 'Amy? Where are you taking me?'

The girl stopped walking, waiting for her to catch up. The silver-tinged shadows moved restlessly around her. 'We've got to find him,' she answered.

'Find – ? Is he *here*?'

'Yes. Somewhere.' The girl turned and resumed walking, leading her onwards through the forest.

'They... they told me he was dead.'

'You promised me you'd find him.'

Anna didn't need to see the girl's face to know that her eyes were filled with tears, and she flinched at the accusation. 'I know… I'm sorry…'

'Why does everyone leave?'

Even though it was only a dream, Anna felt guilt overwhelm her.

The forest around them evaporated as suddenly as if it really had been made of mist. Anna saw that they were now in the cleared area of ground just before the electrified fence that encircled the main camp. In her dream the land had only recently been cleared, and the ground underfoot was thick with slushy black ash. It clung unpleasantly to her feet as she hurried forward, trying to keep up with the small girl.

She didn't realise what was happening inside the camp until she reached the main gate. There was a body caught in the wire of the gate, and as she approached it shuffled to face her and snapped its jaws hungrily. Anna stepped quickly out of its reach. Its arm had got tangled up in the wire and it was unable to free itself. Moving carefully around the zombie, Anna stepped through the gate.

The ground inside the fence was slushy and dark as well, but when she glanced down she saw that it was not ash but blood that clung to her feet. Gingerly, she kept walking, noticing that the girl who was leading her seemed to glide over the crimson ground, the hem of her white dress remaining pristine.

Anna's gaze was drawn to the buildings that protruded from the bleeding ground like broken teeth. The moonlight cast swirling shadows around the bases of the buildings, and as she came closer the shadows split and reformed into the shape of the dead ones, milling restlessly around. They paid no attention to the little girl or to Anna, allowing them to pass like ghosts through to the largest of the buildings.

The interior was packed with bodies.

All of them were dead, and most of them weren't moving. Even as Anna watched, one of the corpses shuddered and pulled itself upright, rising into its unlife and casting about for food. It found none, because there was no life left in the whole of the encampment.

In the centre of a large room, a circle had been cleared amongst the bodies, and in the middle of the circle sat a lone zombie. It was leaning forward, its arms braced against the floor as if it were in deep pain. Its entire body was coated with a layer of viscous blood, its dark hair hanging in dripping rat-tails over its face.

As the two girls entered the room, the zombie looked up. It had only one eye and half its face was missing, but it was unmistakably smiling.

Around them, the dead were suddenly coming back to life. Although the undead outside had not been aware of the humans before, they definitely sensed them now.

In panic Anna grabbed the little girl's hand. It felt cold and damp, as if it belonged to one of the corpses.

The room went dark and they were back in the forest, but still Anna couldn't stop herself from screaming. The moon had gone and everything was pitch black. She could still feel the girl's cold hand in her own, and she also knew that something else was there. She could hear it breathing in the darkness very close by. She screamed again and it echoed uselessly in her ears.

'It's okay, it's okay – don't scream.' The girl's voice was distant, a lot further away than the harsh breathing. 'He's here. You promised me you'd find him and he's here!'

Anna could barely draw breath to answer. 'Amy!' she yelled. 'Where? *Where?*'

The darkness closed in until it was almost suffocating. Just as she was forced into wakefulness, Anna heard Amy screaming for her grandfather.

* * *

'Anna! Wake up, what's wrong with you?'

Mike was shaking her and she hit out at him, the tatters of the nightmare still wrapped around her mind. He caught her hands and held onto them until her eyes snapped back into focus and she stopped screaming.

'It's okay, it's okay,' he repeated to her. 'You're alright, don't panic. It's okay.'

Her throat felt sore from screaming and there was a dark pressure behind her eyes like the start of the biggest migraine in the world. She stared at Mike and then abruptly burst into tears.

'Hey, it's alright.' Mike put his arms around her shoulders and held her tightly, feeling her body shuddering against his. 'What the hell was that? Are you okay?'

'I... no.' Anna shook her head, her voice choked by tears. 'No, something's happened.'

'What? What's happened?'

Ramone was standing in the doorway, roused from sleep by the screams. 'Is she okay?' he asked.

'I think so. Just a nightmare... right, Anna?'

Anna kept shaking her head. 'No... no, it was *real*... I saw it happen...'

'Okay, okay. Just calm down and talk to me. Okay?'

Slowly, Anna got herself under control. When her breath stopped hitching she pulled away from Mike and looked him directly in the eye. 'We've got to go,' she told him as calmly as she could manage. 'Something's happened at the camp. Something really, *really* bad. Everyone's dead.'

The two men exchanged a glance. 'Anna – ' Mike started to say.

'*No.*' She cut him off forcibly. 'I saw it happen. Something is in the camp and it's killed all the people. We have got to leave *right now...*'

'Anna, it's still the middle of the night, we can't leave. Listen – it was just a bad dream, that's all. With all the shit we've been through I'm not surprised you're having nightmares. But that's all it was...'

'Let go of me.'

Mike hadn't realised he was still holding her arm, and he relaxed his grip. 'C'mon, please...' he tried again.

'Mike, shut up.' Anna looked up at Ramone, her eyes red-rimmed but determined. 'Go get Luca,' she told him. 'I need to talk to him about this.'

If Ramone had any opinions he kept them to himself. He picked up his jacket and turned to Jason, who was standing just inside the front door, unnoticed by the others. Together they disappeared outside.

Anna shut her eyes and drew in a shuddering breath. She knew that it had been more than just a bad dream; knew with a deep, painful certainty that what she had witnessed had been true. She wished that Mike believed her, but he continued to stare at her with worried eyes. It didn't matter. Luca would believe her.

'Anna...'

She shook her head. 'No, Mike. I know what I saw and it wasn't a dream.'

Hesitantly he took her hand. '*What* did you see?' he asked.

'Death.' She closed her eyes again. 'Everyone in the camp is dead. There's something there that's worse than the zombies, and it killed them all. And –' Her voice wavered again. 'And my dad's still alive out there. Somewhere.'

Chapter 53

When Luca reached the building, Mike was standing outside the front door. 'She told me to wait out here,' he said, concern obvious on his face. 'I tried to talk to her, but she won't listen to me...'

Luca nodded shortly and went into the house, closing the door firmly behind him. Anna was sat on the edge of her makeshift bed, her hands folded in her lap. She was fully dressed and had her jacket on, as if ready to leave right that moment. She looked up as Luca came in, and he saw at once the tension behind her eyes.

'We have to get back to the camp,' she said as soon as the door was shut.

Luca came into the room and sat down on the other bed. 'Why? What's happened?'

'Something is there, something other than the dead ones. It got into the refectory and killed everyone. I saw it.'

'How did you see it?'

'I...' She hesitated for the first time. 'It was a dream. But I know it wasn't just a dream; it was real. All of it is really happening, or has already happened.'

'I'm not doubting you,' Luca said, 'but how are you so sure that it was real?'

Anna was silent for a long moment, staring down at her hands while she tried to decide what to tell him. 'There's a girl,' she said at last. 'I see her in my dreams now and again, and... I know that the things she tells me are real. She's been in my head for about eight years now.' She smiled weakly, aware of how crazy she must sound. 'At first she was just a baby, but she's older now. She's been growing up with me.'

'Who is she?'

It was the first time that Anna had ever spoken to anyone about Amy, and it felt like a betrayal or a weird invasion of privacy to be telling it to a stranger. 'She's not a real person, if that's what you mean,' she said slowly. 'It's difficult to explain, but it all started when I was a teenager. I found out that I was pregnant…' She dropped her gaze. 'I was just a kid myself… anyway, I lost the baby at about six weeks. Fortunately, I guess.' Another weak smile. 'A while after that that I started having the dreams.'

'How long afterwards?'

'About eight months,' Anna admitted. 'I figured out pretty quickly that it was just my mind going slightly nuts – part of me was aware that by that point I should have had my baby, and it affected my dreams. I figured it was quite normal to be dreaming that I'd had a baby. A little girl. Amy.'

Luca was silent, waiting for her to continue.

'That's about all there is to it.' Anna sighed. 'I don't dream about her very often now – maybe three or four times a year, at most. But I'm always kinda aware that she's around.' She tapped her finger to the side of her head. 'Up here. And sometimes she tells me things, like the night that my mother died…' She broke off, shaking her head as if to clear it of the images there. 'I sound insane, don't I?'

Luca smiled gently. 'It doesn't sound so insane to me. Perhaps you should bear in mind that very few people would seriously believe that *I* exist. So I'm not about to argue with you about the possibility of ghosts or anything else.'

'Thank you.' Having Luca believe in her lifted a weight from Anna's shoulders. 'I'm glad you don't think I'm crazy.'

'No more so than anyone here. So, tell me – what exactly did you see happening at the encampment?'

In the same careful, deliberate tone of voice, she told him what she had already told Mike about her dream. When she was finished she waited for Luca to speak, knowing that whatever he said, she would still have to leave.

'What did he look like?' Luca asked at length. 'The creature you saw.'

'He looked like the other dead ones. Half his face was missing, and he was covered with blood. But he wasn't dead… well, not like the others are dead. He could still think and move like he was alive.' Anna shuddered as she remembered the way the creature had smiled at her, its face filled with evil intent.

Luca was frowning. 'That does not sound like any of the dead ones on this island.'

'Are you sure? Maybe it was something Ehren was messing around with… I don't know, an experiment or something?'

'Tell me,' Luca said suddenly. 'What would the creature have looked like in life?'

Anna frowned, trying to picture the undead creature without its covering of blood and gore, and with its face still intact. 'I'm not sure… quite tall… mid-length hair… it was kinda difficult to tell though. And he had – ' She broke off as a clear memory of the creature's smile came back to her. She hadn't taken it in before, but the creature had elongated fang teeth. Anna blinked several times to try and resolve the mental image and work out whether it was actually true or if her mind had just invented the fact.

'I've seen something like it before,' Luca said quietly. 'A decade ago, up in the far north of Russia. A creature that was like the dead ones, only stronger and faster and smarter. I saw it with my own eyes before its former master destroyed it.'

'What the hell was it?' Anna asked, although she was afraid that she already knew the answer.

'One of us. A vampire, infected with the virus from the dead ones.' Luca got to his feet. 'Last night I took one of our people to the camp to help Doctor Ehren with his tests. He didn't return, and we figured that he'd stayed the day in one of the safe houses at the camp. He's done it a few times before, so we weren't worried. But I guess the dead ones must have found him…' He trailed off, the expression in his dark eyes grim.

'We've got to get to the camp, haven't we?'

'I don't know.' Luca shook his head. 'If that is Ciaran down there – or the creature he's become – then I doubt there's anything that any of us can do. You said yourself that everyone there is almost certainly dead already.'

'Okay, but what about the boat? We've got to be there in the morning otherwise no-one on the mainland will know what's going on here. If the people in the camp are all gone, then we're the only ones left.' Saying it aloud made her feel cold all over. 'We have to be there when it arrives.'

Luca stood in thought for several long moments, his expression unreadable. Anna waited silently, despite the urgency she felt.

'Alright,' Luca said at last. 'Come outside and we'll talk to the others.'

Anna stood up quickly and followed him from the building.

Mike had been talking quietly to Ramone and Jason, and he looked up as Luca stepped outside. 'Is she okay?' he asked, his concern still obvious.

'I'm fine,' Anna told him shortly.

'We need to make a decision,' Luca said. 'Some of us are going to have to go to the camp and confirm what's happening, and wait there for the boat.'

'What?' Mike's eyes widened. 'But that's insane! Suicidally insane, not just the regular kind.'

'It has to be done.' The tone of Luca's voice made it clear that he wasn't changing his mind. 'If any of you want to leave this island then we'll have to do it.'

'I'm going,' Ramone said at once.

Luca nodded. 'And I'm coming with you.'

'Well, no offence,' the man said, 'but we've got less than five hours before the sun comes up. There's no way you'd be able to make it to the camp and back before then, especially on foot.'

'If we can get to the camp then I can go into one of the safe houses. You could use my help out there.'

'Luca.' It was Jason who spoke, and he was frowning. 'I'll go instead of you. You've got problems here... I don't think you can leave.'

'Yes, I can.' Luca smiled very slightly. 'You're going to be in charge while I'm gone, Jason. There won't be any further problems.'

Jason started to object further, but fell silent at the look Luca gave him. He nodded, not looking particularly happy.

'And we'll stay here, right?' Mike asked Anna hopefully.

Anna just shook her head.

Chapter 54

They stopped just inside the large doors that sealed the cave off from the outside world. Luca gave a few last instructions to Jason, while Ramone sorted through his bag, planning to redistribute some of the items among their small group. He had bandaged up his broken ribs, but they were still giving him a lot of pain. Anna was staring out over the vast cavern with a distant look in her eyes, and Mike wondered what she was thinking. What she was *seeing*.

'I thought Luca was going to talk you out of this,' he said to her, attempting a smile.

'Why would he have done that?' Anna didn't bother to look at him, and her tone was as distant as her gaze. 'He believes what I saw is true.'

Mike decided not to reply to that. Instead he lifted his video camera and checked it over for damage. Yesterday's trek through the forest hadn't been easy, and personally he was surprised that the camera had survived as well as it had. Apart from a couple of scratches in the outer casing and a chip missing from the plastic lens cap there was no real damage. Mike had changed both the battery and the tape earlier, storing the used ones carefully in the zipped-up interior pocket of his jacket. Wanting to check that the new tape was working, he removed the lens cap and switched the camera on, idly filming the silent vampire city. It was too dark to be able to see much, but the soft glow of the irregularly placed lights illuminated enough.

'Why are you doing that?'

Mike shut off the camera quickly, a reaction made automatic by years of close calls with authority figures. He looked up and found that it was Luca who had asked the question. 'Sorry,' he said hastily. 'I was just...'

'It's okay, I wasn't telling you not to.' The vampire smiled. 'I just wondered why you were doing it. Who are you planning to show that tape to?'

'I... well, I've not really thought that far ahead. I don't know.' Mike frowned. 'To be honest, I have no clue who I'd show it to. No-one would believe it, for one thing. Obviously if you don't want anyone to see it then I promise I won't...'

Luca waved it away. 'You can do whatever you want, it's not my concern. I was just curious.' He indicated across the cavern with a lazy sweep of his hand. 'There are very few humans who have ever seen this place. It interests me to think that a permanent record of it will exist in the world. It's just a shame that we don't have more time, otherwise I might have been able to show you some more of the cave system... it runs underneath practically the entire island, as far as we can tell. No-one's really explored it.'

'Why not?'

Luca shrugged. 'We think that's where the monsters come from.'

Ramone spoke then. 'Are we ready to move? We've not got that much dark-time left.'

'We're ready,' Luca confirmed.

'Good. Here.' Ramone stood up and passed handguns to Mike and Anna, along with extra ammo. 'I'm sick of carrying this stuff myself, and I figure it'll do more good if you guys have them to hand. Mike, yours holds twelve rounds; Anna, you've got eight. Try not to use them all at once, okay?'

They both nodded, and Anna put her gun into the pocket of her jacket. Mike's pockets were already filled with ammo and the spare tapes for his camera, so he rather self-consciously tucked the gun into the waistband of his jeans.

'Check that the safety's on if you're gonna do that,' Ramone recommended.

Mike hurriedly did so.

Picking up the now lighter bag, Ramone looked the others over. They were carrying their rifles as well as the handguns now, although it was noticeable that Anna handled hers with much more confidence than Mike. Neither of them looked ready to go back outside and face the undead, but then very few people would. If Ramone had had any say in the matter then he would have insisted that they stayed behind in the cavern... but he also understood their reasons for not doing so.

'Alright,' he said. 'We'll stick to the main road and move as fast as possible. For God's sake keep your eyes and ears open – I've had more than enough of the dead ones creeping up on us. Especially since it's technically impossible for them to do that.'

Mike raised his hand. 'Isn't this the same plan we had when we were coming up here?'

'Yes, but this time it's in reverse. Next question?'

'If the dead ones are leaving the camp,' Luca said, 'then they could well be following the road this way. We'll probably walk right into them.'

'I've already considered that happy possibility, thanks. But we're gonna run into them sooner or later, so if anyone's got a better plan I'm still open to options.'

Anna spoke, her eyes still distant. 'There's not many of the dead ones left. Maybe twenty or thirty. The people at the camp killed the rest.'

'Good, that changes our odds to slightly less than suicidal, which is an improvement.' Ramone turned towards the door. 'Let's get it over with.'

Luca opened the vast wooden door, moving it with ease despite its obvious weight.

'Good luck out there,' Jason said to him.

'Thank you. If I'm not back before sunrise then I'll be back first thing tomorrow night.' Luca held the door as the others filed through, and then pulled it shut behind them. The tunnel beyond was in utter darkness, and the humans had to feel their way along the rough wall. Even after they'd passed the bend in the tunnel and could see the exit there was still very little light.

Outside in the cold night air, Mike realised why. The full moon had set below the horizon, and without its illumination the whole island was blacked out. The road that led down the mountain was almost impossible to pick out.

'Now I really wish I'd salvaged some flashlights,' Ramone complained. 'This is going to slow us down.'

Luca smiled. 'You can have this, if you like.' He produced the small torch from his pocket and passed it to the man. 'I'd thank you to keep it away from me though.'

'Thanks.' Ramone laughed quietly. 'Okay, we'll lead the way; regular humans stay behind us. Try not to wander off the edge of the road, there's a pretty long drop.'

In the pitch darkness, Mike and Anna had very little choice but to stay right behind him. The thin, yellowish-white circle of light cast by the small torch was very little help at all, and after a few minutes Ramone switched it off in irritation. 'Thanks, but no thanks,' he said to Luca. 'We'll probably be better off relying on your night vision.'

'Alright, but I refuse to accept responsibility if you do accidentally step off the edge.'

The two spoke quietly, their voices belying the tension underneath. Both of them knew that once they got down from the mountain and back under the trees then it would be even more difficult to see anything, and the trees all around could be hiding a multitude of surprises.

They moved as quickly as was possible in the difficult conditions, but it still took them longer than expected to reach the forest. When they got there, Ramone called for a brief halt, swearing to himself as he checked the glowing dial of his watch.

'Stay in the centre of the track,' he told them in a whisper. 'Move fast but keep as quiet as you can. No talking. If you see anything that looks even slightly dead – present company excluded – let me know about it before you start taking pot-shots. Any loud noises will announce our presence for five kliks all around. Everybody say, "sir yes sir".'

The others repeated it, Luca smiling as he did so.

'Good. Let's go.'

It was difficult to tell in the poor light, but Mike thought that there was a shine to the man's eyes that was slightly unnerving. 'You're enjoying this, aren't you?' he asked as they started moving again.

'Me?' Ramone glanced back at him. 'Why would I enjoy heading straight into vicious chompy death?'

'I don't know, but you are. You're grinning right now, aren't you?'

A pause. 'Maybe.'

'Look, if you're going to freak out on us, at least give us some warning...'

'Hey, I've been fighting dead ones for years. Worry about yourself first, alright?'

Mike fell silent for a moment, then frowned. 'Wait... you told me last night that you've only been on this island for a few months...'

Ramone held a finger up to his lips. 'Shh. No talking now.'

Reluctantly, Mike bit his tongue. They walked in silence along the track into the forest.

It was impossible to judge time and distance as they walked, since every minute felt like an eternity when stretched out by nerves. Mike kept scanning the close-pressed trees on either side, and a dozen times he thought he saw something there. He began to feel light-headed and wished that he'd had more than a scant few hours sleep. He also alternated between wanting to move faster and demanding they stop for a break. He badly needed a cigarette.

The pad of gauze on his neck was irritating him so he pulled it off as he walked. His fingers probed the two small holes underneath. The skin was puffed up and probably developing into a massive bruise, but the wounds themselves had scabbed over. He wasn't impressed at how much two small puncture wounds could hurt.

He had no idea how long they had been walking when he heard a faint noise from the forest off to his left. 'Stop,' he hissed to the others.

Ramone was at his side in an instant. 'What's wrong?'

'You hear that?'

All the others listened, but even Luca shook his head.

'Seriously?' Mike could hear the whisper of sound quite clearly. He pointed towards the trees. 'There. Don't shoot,' he added quickly, as Ramone had already started to lift his rifle. 'It's okay... I think it's...'

The black and silent trees seemed to part like water as a tiny, dark shape emerged from between them. The shape hesitated for a moment, then crossed the track quickly, heading directly for the small group.

'Lyell.' Even before she was close enough to see, Mike knew it was her. He dropped to one knee and held his arms out to her, incredibly glad to see her alive.

The young wolf looked at him with her orange eyes, then allowed him to put his arms around her shaggy neck. He pulled her close, aware of the musky smell of her fur and the fact that all the muscles in her body were trembling. She licked his neck like a puppy.

'It's okay,' he murmured. 'It's going to be okay now.' The words were to reassure himself as much as Lyell.

Chapter 55

Mike ran his hands over the rough fur of the young wolf's back. 'Are you okay?' he asked. 'Are you hurt?' In places the thick fur was heavily matted with dried blood, but he couldn't find any spots where the skin was broken.

Lyell pulled away so that he could see her face, and the look in her eyes plainly asked why he should care.

'I… I was just worried. That's all.' Mike managed a smile. 'So, you're okay?'

He would've sworn that she smiled at him, if a wolf had been able to smile. But he knew that she was okay, and a load lifted from him. He let go of her and stood up.

Ramone was looking at him strangely. 'She's alright?'

'That's what she says.'

'Yeah, about that. I don't know if you've noticed, but she's a wolf and wolves don't talk out loud. How do you know she's alright?'

'I… well, she looks fine. Right?'

Ramone obviously wasn't in the mood to argue. 'Fine. Can we just get moving? I'd quite like to – '

He was cut off abruptly by an echoing gunshot. Everybody flinched, eyes darting around for the source of the sound. A second and a third shot quickly followed, and Mike realised that they had come from some distance away.

Ramone pinpointed the sound before the rest of them. 'That way,' he said, pointing off to their right. 'Not far.'

'Someone else is still alive,' Luca said.

'Apparently so.' Ramone looked at the others. 'I don't want to leave the road,' he said then. 'Leaving the road is a bad idea. But I guess someone else is out there, and if they're shooting then they're in trouble. Any votes for carrying on regardless?'

No-one spoke.

'That's what I figured.' Ramone hefted his rifle. 'Okay, stay close to me.'

He set off in the direction of the shots, and the others followed close behind him. As soon as they entered the forest the trees closed behind them like a curtain, completely sealing off the road from view. Lyell ran alongside Mike, brushing against his legs as they dodged between the close-packed trees, the heavy branches slapping at their faces. Mike felt his heart in his mouth as he ran, scared to death to be back in this zero visibility situation. Even more so than before they were running blind, and he panicked at the idea of getting separated from the others.

There was another series of shots, sounding so close that Mike instinctively ducked. Someone screamed, and it was cut off abruptly. Mike spun round, but Anna was right behind him and she was alright, her face a pale, frightened shadow in the darkness.

'Keep down!' Ramone hissed from somewhere in front of them. They heard him edging forward through the undergrowth. 'Hey!' he called in a louder voice.

There was a tense silence that lasted several long seconds. Then a voice called back. 'Someone there?'

'Yep, several someones.' Ramone sounded relieved that his query hadn't attracted any panicked shots, and he moved forward slowly. 'And we're all alive so please don't be shooting us.'

Almost before the words were out of his mouth, several more shots were fired, and everyone hit the ground. Mike heard Ramone swearing.

The voice from ahead called again. 'There're dead ones all over! Where the hell are you?'

Cautiously, Ramone got back to his feet and pushed forward, keeping his head down. Hitting the ground like that had done no good at all to his damaged ribs, and he kept one hand pressed to them. 'We're over here, coming right towards you…' Without warning he stepped out of the trees and into a small clearing, almost stumbling. He hadn't realised how close he was to the person who was shooting, otherwise he would have been a lot more cautious. A figure spun towards him and Ramone quickly held up his hands. 'Alive, don't shoot!' he yelled.

'What the hell are – ?' the man started to ask. A shape came staggering out of the undergrowth on the other side of the clearing, its dead hands grabbing for him.

Ramone was faster than the other man, lifting his rifle and shooting the dead one cleanly through the head. The corpse dropped to the ground in mid stride. Quickly, Ramone scanned the rest of the clearing and saw movement at the far end. He stepped around the man, lined up his shot and took down the other two dead ones that were busy pushing their way through the trees.

'Is it just you here?' Ramone asked the man, walking quickly around the clearing. There were no other signs of zombies, but he saw several unmoving corpses on the ground. 'Hey, fella?' There wasn't any answer from the man. 'Anyone else with you?'

'I – ' The man's voice wavered, and Ramone guessed that he was in shock.

'We heard someone scream. Who was it?' As he circled back round the clearing, Ramone found the others waiting where he had left them. He waved them forward. 'Watch the perimeter,' he told them. 'I can't see any other dead ones, but don't trust my word for it.'

The man hadn't moved from his spot in the centre of the clearing, and for the first time Ramone paused to take a good look at him. The man's face was almost unnaturally pale in the darkness, and his eyes were far too wide. He was definitely going into shock. He clutched a rifle to his chest, his hands as bone-white as his face. Ramone recognised him then as one of the guys from the camp.

'Greg?' he asked. 'That you?'

The man blinked as if surprised by the question. It took several attempts for him to get his voice working. 'Yeah. Yeah, it's me.'

'What're you doing out here? You alone?'

The man frowned, then slowly shook his head. 'I think she's hurt.'

'You think – ?' Ramone stared at him. 'Who? Where is she?'

'She's… over there…'

Ramone ran across the clearing. He had stepped over a woman's body there a few moments ago but he hadn't even glanced down at it, assuming that it was just another of the dead ones. Now he found her again and knelt on the hard ground. 'What happened?' he asked the man, but as expected got no answer.

The girl was lying on her back, and her eyes were wide open. As Ramone leaned down towards her he heard the fast, panicky sound of her breathing. He touched her neck to locate a pulse and felt something warm and liquid under his fingers.

'What the hell happened?' he demanded again. 'Anna, come here. The rest of you watch out for more of the dead ones.'

Anna was at his side in a moment, although she didn't know what the hell she could do. In the darkness it was difficult to see where the girl had been hurt, but she was definitely bleeding profusely from somewhere. Faint silvery starlight highlighted a ragged wetness that seemed to extend from her neck most of the way down her chest.

'They came out of nowhere,' Greg said suddenly, his voice thin with residual fear. 'We were resting here and they all just appeared. Oh God, is she okay?'

Ramone was still trying to determine the size of the wound. 'Did she get bit?' he asked. There was no reply from the man, and Ramone lifted his head to look at him. 'Hey – Greg. Answer me.'

'What?'

'Did one of those things bite her?'

Greg was shaking now, and he stared about with wide eyes. 'I dunno what happened,' he said with sudden urgency. 'Everything just went crazy – we were shooting at them but they were all around... and... and...'

'Shit.' Ramone used both hands to tug the girl's thin jacket out of the way. The flesh underneath was a pulped red mess, but it didn't look like a bite mark.

Anna sucked in her breath. 'What?' she asked.

'This is a gunshot wound.'

Chapter 56

Ramone unslung the bag from his shoulder, dumping it next to Anna. 'First aid kit,' he said tersely, shrugging off his jacket. 'Not sure how much use it's gonna be though.' He folded the jacket and pressed it over the red mess that had once been the chest of the young girl.

'It was an accident,' Greg said from behind him.

Ramone didn't bother to look up. 'I don't doubt it. Accidents happen all the time. Anna, put pressure here.'

Anna did as she was told, holding down the folded jacket. Within a matter of seconds the thick material became damp with warm blood. She glanced at the girl's face, saw the eyes wide and staring but able to focus. 'It's okay,' Anna told her, trying to maintain that eye contact. 'You're going to be alright. Just hang in there.' She looked up at Greg. 'What's her name?'

Ramone answered first. 'Trisha. Tris. She works in the vamp lab. A lady bacteriologist.' He had found a disposable syringe in the first aid box and was filling it from a small glass bottle.

'Alright.' Anna wondered if she vaguely recognised the girl, but it may as well have been from another lifetime. 'Tris – don't worry, okay?' The girl was at least still conscious and able to focus, but her eyes were showing far too much white around the edges.

Luca appeared beside them, kneeling down and taking one of Tris' hands. The girl turned her wide eyes towards him and a strange look came over her face. Her mouth started to form his name.

'It's okay, Trisha,' Luca said. 'Don't try to talk.'

'You know her?' Anna asked.

Luca nodded. 'She's been up to the mountains a few times.'

'Hold still,' Ramone instructed. He had rolled up the girl's sleeve and carefully slid the needle into the crook of her arm. 'That should numb the pain for her...'

'Wait.' It was Greg who spoke, although the others had all but forgotten his presence. 'You're one of the vampires, right?' He gestured at Luca with his rifle, apparently forgetting that he was still holding it.

Warily, Luca looked up. 'That's right, I am.'

The jacket was now soaked through with blood, despite the continued pressure. Ramone shook his head. 'She's bleeding from something major, I don't think – ' He broke off as Tris convulsed under their hands, and they had to fight to hold her down.

Greg was still looking at Luca, biting hard at his lower lip. 'She's gonna die, isn't she?'

'Do I look like a doctor?' Ramone snapped. 'I'll let you know, alright?'

'But you can help her.' Greg's statement was directed at Luca.

The vampire frowned. 'Me?'

'Sure. You're a vampire – you can turn her as well, and then she'll be okay. Right?'

Luca's face went very smooth and blank. 'Greg – ' he started to say.

'It'd work though, wouldn't it?' Greg was still holding the rifle, and now it was no accident that it was aimed at Luca. 'It'd save her.'

Luca took a moment before replying. 'It would heal the damage, yes.'

The injection of morphine seemed to be taking effect, and Tris abruptly relaxed, her muscles going slack. Her breathing slowed, becoming calmer but still dangerously shallow, and it seemed like the bleeding was slowing as well. Ramone was worried that could just mean she was running out of blood to lose. 'Greg,' he said over his shoulder. 'If you want to make yourself useful then get your ass over here and help. Quit acting like a fucking retard.'

Greg didn't move. 'She's going to die,' he said to Luca. 'But you can save her. Do it.'

'I can't.'

Greg cranked a round into the breach. He was still holding it at waist-height, but at such close range it wouldn't matter. 'Do it,' he ordered. 'This is loaded with silver mercury points, so don't think you'll be able to walk away from it. Do it, now!'

Anna started to get to her feet and Greg shifted his stance so that he could cover all of them at once. His eyes had gone even wider, like he was right on the edge of snapping.

Suddenly, Tris grabbed at Anna's hand, pulling her back down. It seemed incredible that she had even the smallest amount of strength left, but she dragged on Anna's arm until she was close enough to speak.

'*Don't...*'

Anna took her eyes off the man with the gun for a moment. 'What?'

'Don't let him do it.' There was an urgency to Tris' words, despite the fact that her lifeblood was rapidly draining away. 'Don't let him...'

Greg steadied the rifle on Luca. 'Do it.'

The vampire shook his head. 'She said no. She doesn't want it.'

'She doesn't know what she's saying! Look at her, for fuck's sake – she doesn't know what she's saying…'

'I think she does,' Luca said calmly.

Tris' head had fallen back, her skin so pale that it looked like bleached paper. She kept shaking her head, over and over. 'Don't let him… please don't… please don't… I don't want to…'

Anna tried to calm the girl, but she kept on shaking her head even as her voice cracked and faded to nothing. 'Don't want to… don't wanna be… monster… don't… please…'

'Last chance,' Greg said. 'Do it right now or I kill you.'

Luca looked at him coldly. 'Maybe what Tris really needs is you at her side right now, before she dies.'

'I can be at her side once you've changed her, goddammit! I mean it, this is the last time I'm gonna ask you –'

Ramone spoke. 'You can quit asking now, Greg. She's gone.'

'No!' Greg hefted the rifle to his shoulder, his aim shaking violently. 'You can still do it, right? It's not too late…'

Luca shook his head, his black eyes cold and empty. 'It's too late. It was too late from the moment you shot her, Greg.'

Greg's face seemed to crumple in on itself. 'No,' he said again, but it came out as a choked sob. 'It's not my goddamn fault!'

He screamed in anger, and pulled the trigger.

Luca, halfway to his feet, twisted out of the way. Even his agility wasn't able to save him. He felt the shot hit; felt the explosive silver round detonate on impact. His mind registered the damage and knew he'd been hurt bad even before the pain began. The echo rebounded around the clearing and through his head as he hit the ground.

The first shot was followed an instant later by a second, as Mike, standing forgotten on the far side of the clearing, raised his pistol and shot Greg through the head.

It was all over so fast that for a moment the others weren't sure exactly what had happened. The two shots were so close together that the second sounded more like an echo to the first. Ramone was on his feet almost before Greg's body had collapsed to the ground. He ran to Luca.

Anna was still holding onto Tris' now-limp hand. The double gunshot had frozen her in place like a startled animal, and for a long moment she could do nothing but stare in shock at the scene in front of her. She'd been focusing so totally on Greg and Luca that she hadn't even seen Mike draw out his handgun. None of them had seen it.

'Oh my God… Luca…' Finally, she forced herself to her feet and ran over. Ramone knelt beside the vampire. 'Are you okay? Where did it hit?'

Luca turned slowly onto his back so that Ramone could see the damage. The bullet had caught him in the upper arm, not far below the shoulder, and had left a gaping wound nearly five inches wide. It had fractured the femur, and Ramone could clearly see shards of white bone mixed in with the pulped red flesh. In a normal human, he guessed that the shock alone would probably have been fatal. Swearing, Ramone took off his belt and looped it around the top of Luca's arm as a tourniquet. The bleeding appeared to be quite slow and sluggish, but he did it anyway, not knowing what else he could do.

'Are you okay?' he asked again, ignoring the stupidity of the question.

Luca nodded. His face had gone even paler than normal, a faint crease appearing on his forehead as if he couldn't quite understand what had happened. 'It hurts,' he said, his voice distant. 'It's been a long time since I've been hurt.'

Anna took hold of his hand, but Luca waved her away weakly.

'I'm okay, go check on your friend,' he instructed.

Anna glanced round. Mike had sat down carefully on the hard ground, his face oddly blank and unreadable. He laid the gun down next to him, then placed his hands in his lap. Anna got up quickly and went to him.

Ramone shook his head. 'I don't know what to do about the pain,' he told the vampire. 'I've got more morphine, but – '

'It won't work. My metabolism is too fast.'

'Figured. Will you be able to heal this? It don't look too good, but it's not bleeding much.'

'I don't know.' Apart from the slight frown, Luca was giving no outward sign of his pain. 'This has never happened to me before... it was silver, so I don't know how difficult it'll be to heal. Maybe hours... more likely days.'

'Your arm's out of action till then, in that case. If you can't heal that sort of thing fast then you're fucking lucky that you didn't get hit in the chest or anything.'

Luca nodded, and his black eyes momentarily clouded with pain. 'I know. I know.'

Chapter 57

Mike stared down at the body on the ground, which was leaking blood from the circular hole in its skull. It seemed peculiarly unreal, even after everything else he had seen in the past two days. He was vaguely aware that Anna was crouched next to him and that she was speaking, but it was difficult to concentrate on her words. He forced himself to close his eyes so that he wasn't staring fixedly at Greg's body, and then it was a little easier to focus.

'Come on. Snap out of it.'

He heard her that time and opened his eyes. Anna was caught off balance by how suddenly he looked up at her. 'I shouldn't have done that,' he said.

'What?'

'I shouldn't have done that,' Mike repeated. 'Luca's okay, isn't he?'

'He – ' Anna blinked, then glanced behind her. Ramone, who was close enough to have heard the question, gave her a terse thumbs-up. 'He's fine,' she said. 'And you did fine too… shit, you probably saved all of us…' It was only when she took hold of his hand that she realised hers were shaking too. 'Are you okay? Can you get up?'

Mike thought about it for a moment, then shrugged carefully. 'Probably. But I'd quite like to just sit here for a while, if that's alright.'

Anna's smile was relieved. 'That's fine. You just sit and take it easy, okay?' She squeezed his hand, then let go.

As she stood up, Mike closed his hands into tight fists. He hadn't noticed before, but his fingers were tingling from the sharp recoil of the gun.

Something warm and furred brushed his shoulder from behind, then Lyell nuzzled against his arm. He looked up just a little and saw that her orange eyes were filled with concern. If his hands hadn't been shaking then he would have reached up and stroked her neck, but as it was he just let her lie down on the ground next to him, her body warm and soft and comforting.

Anna went to Ramone's side to help him patch up Luca's arm. 'Is he really okay?' she asked quietly.

'I'm fine,' Luca answered for himself with some annoyance. 'I'm pretty sure I don't need this much attention.'

Ramone had found a roll of bandages in the first aid kit and was using them to bind and pad the wound. 'Is that so? Well, you'll forgive me for not taking a chance on you bleeding to death.' He glanced up from what he was doing to give Luca a quizzical look. 'Can that actually happen to you, incidentally? Bleeding to death?'

Luca shook his head. 'Not as such. If we lose enough blood we become very weak and unable to move. Then if we can't get to a safe place before dawn…' He shrugged his good shoulder.

'Then you go poof up in smoke.' Ramone smiled, but it was more than a little strained.

'Pretty much, yes.'

'Let's hope you don't start haemorrhaging any time soon then.' He found a fallen branch on the ground nearby and broke it in half, using the two pieces of roughly straight wood to splint the arm, wrapping the whole thing in another layer of bandages. He tied the ends of the last one off, looking at it critically. 'I never was any good as a field surgeon. Friend of mine used to swear by duct tape to hold any bandage in place. Mind you, he was practically hairless all over. Can you sit up?'

'I think so.' With a little help, Luca pulled himself into a sitting position. His expression went very blank as he did so, as if he were forcibly concealing his pain.

Ramone used another long strip of cloth bandage to form a rudimentary sling. 'It's not pretty but I'm hoping it'll do the job. Check it before you go to sleep in the morning. If it's still bleeding then leave it in place, but if it's not then loosen it. I know what you guys are like for healing foreign objects into wounds.'

'Thank you.' Luca ran his fingers over the white bandage, his eyes appearing distant and subdued. Ramone wondered if shock affected vampires the same way it affected regular humans.

'We'd better get back to the road.' Carefully, Ramone and Anna helped Luca to his feet, then looked around at Mike. 'Are you two ready to move?' Ramone asked.

Mike nodded, although he looked like he would have been quite happy to stay sat where he was for a little longer. He got up and Lyell stood as well, still pressed against his legs protectively. Before they followed the others back into the trees, Mike reluctantly picked up his gun from the ground.

Ramone led them back the way they had come, moving as fast as was possible in the difficult conditions. They hadn't gone too far into the forest, so he didn't expect it to take more than a few minutes for them to return to the road. But ten minutes later they were still pushing through the trees, and Ramone started to feel worried. It was impossible to tell if they were following exactly the same route that they had come in by, but even so it shouldn't have taken them so long to get back.

He felt something brush his legs and glanced down. Lyell was there, staring up at him with those deep amber eyes. Ramone stopped walking. 'What's wrong?' he asked her.

Lyell turned and set off into the trees at a ninety-degree angle to the way they'd been walking. Ramone frowned, then followed her, glancing back to make sure the others didn't get lost.

The trees parted and they were back on the road.

'What the hell?' Ramone turned and stared at the forest as if an answer could be found there. 'We can't have got *that* lost...'

'What's the problem?' Anna asked him. 'We're back, aren't we?'

'Yeah, but...' Ramone was shaking his head in denial. 'We went in a straight line from there to here. How the hell did we get so turned around that we were walking parallel to the road?'

'These things happen,' Luca suggested.

'Not as often as you'd think.' The man seemed very put out that he'd got disorientated. 'It's like every time we set foot off the road we get lost. And if you stop to think about it, how come Greg and Tris were so close to the main road and yet not actually on it? They must have been out here for hours. Why hadn't they found the road?'

No-one had an answer for him.

'Something's fucked up about this island,' Ramone voiced his opinion. 'I swear it's messing with our heads somehow.'

'How exactly would that work?' Anna asked, eyebrows raised.

'I have no idea. But it's a possibility. And that disturbs me.' Ramone looked along the road. 'Let's keep moving.' He motioned the others forward.

They walked in silence for some time, each of them deep in their own thoughts. Mike especially lagged behind, unresponsive to anything around him, even Lyell at his side. He wasn't thinking of anything; he was barely seeing the ground in front of him. It was some minutes before he looked up and found Luca silently keeping pace with him.

'I need to say thank you,' the vampire said at length.

Mike shrugged awkwardly, not in the mood to talk. 'That guy mostly missed you anyway.'

'Yes. Mostly. And you made sure that he didn't get a chance of a second shot. At any of us.'

'Yeah, well.' Mike tone was noncommittal. 'I guess I wasn't thinking about that at the time. I still shouldn't have done it.'

'If you say so.' Luca's voice was soft, impossible to take offence at. 'But personally I'm glad you did. This might not be much of a life that I have, but

I'm quite attached to it.'

Mike glanced at him. 'Are you okay?'

'I'm not sure.' Luca looked upwards at the pale stars overhead. 'No. No, I'm not okay.'

'Does your arm hurt?'

'Hmm?' Luca blinked, as if he'd forgotten the injury was even there. 'Oh. No, not really. It's something else. Something Trisha said… just before she died.'

'Uh-huh?' Mike couldn't bring to mind anything the woman had said, but then he hadn't been listening to her.

'I've known her for some time now. She was one of the first people that Ehren brought over here, and she's always worked with us. With my people. I thought…' He sighed and shook his head so that his black hair fell over his eyes. 'I never realised what she truly thought of us. Even when she was moments from death, she turned down the chance of life if it meant being infected with the same virus as us. If it meant becoming a monster.' His mouth turned down at the corners. 'I know others see us like that… see *me* like that. Even the people here on the island; even some of the wolves.' He laughed bitterly. 'You know something is wrong with you when even the wolves look down on you as a freak and a monster. But Trisha… she always smiled at me. I thought she accepted us. And it hurts a lot to know how she really felt about us all this time.' He shook his head again. 'To have someone die rather than live like you. That hurts a lot.'

Mike didn't know what he could say to that. 'I'm sorry… I didn't realise.' Suddenly he felt bad for obsessing over what he'd gone through, without thinking about any of the others.

'It's alright.' Luca was again staring at the pale stars, his head tilted back. 'I've had a lot worse things said about me. I've been alive for a long time, and I think I can live through a few hurtful words.' The vampire smiled then, although his black eyes were still empty and impossible to read. 'Anyway, I didn't mean to get into all of this. All I really wanted to say was thank you for saving my life. It means a lot to me that you thought it worth saving.'

Mike tried to shrug it off. 'Sure. Anytime.'

Luca lowered his gaze again, then frowned. 'Hey,' he said, pointing into the darkness of the road up ahead, 'do you see that?'

Chapter 58

At first it was difficult to see anything in the darkness. Mike squinted but was unable to make out any movement, and on impulse he lifted his camera and took off the lens cap. Looking through the viewfinder, he zoomed in to the spot that Luca was pointing at. He thought he saw part of the shadow shift and take a few steps towards them. The focus on his camera promptly went and he zoomed back out to try and refocus.

'I see something,' Mike said in a whisper, 'but I don't know what the hell it is.'

'Me neither.' Ramone stared into the darkness. 'It's big though, bigger than the dead ones.'

'One of the animals?'

'Could be. We're not that far from the camp though – the main junction is just up ahead. It could have come from the camp.'

Mike glanced at Anna. 'Is it – ?'

The girl shook her head. 'It's not the thing I saw,' she told him. 'That looked like a man.'

The shape in the darkness came a little closer and Mike saw that she was right. Whatever the creature was, it was definitely not humanoid. It was walking on all fours, but even so its head was as high as their chests. In the dim starlight its skin appeared to be covered in something dark and liquid. As it slowly approached Mike caught the strong, overpowering reek of dead flesh.

'It *must* be one of the animals,' Luca whispered. 'Like the one that attacked me and Jason… it looks…'

'Dead,' Ramone finished for him. 'You're right, the dead ones must have got it.' He lifted his rifle. 'Okay, drop it.'

He fired at the creature, and a moment later Mike and Anna joined him. At least one of the shots found its mark because the creature staggered back. It let out an angry, guttural hiss.

Ramone hesitated, knowing full well that the dead ones couldn't make any sound. 'What – ?' he started to ask.

The angry hiss turned into a full-throated growl, and then the creature sprang forward. Huge, curved white teeth glinted in its mouth as it ran at them with shocking speed.

'*Run!*' Mike grabbed Anna and dragged her off the road. He looked back and saw Luca and Lyell darting for cover on the other side of the road, but Ramone stayed put, his rifle steadied against his shoulder as he lined up his next shot.

'*Get out of the way!*' Mike yelled at him.

The man wasn't listening. He calmly took aim and fired three more shots at the beast even as it came charging out of the darkness towards him. Two of the shots connected, thwacking into the dead meat of the creature's shoulder but not slowing it at all.

The others could only watch as the undead beast slammed into Ramone, the two bodies crashing to the ground and rolling over and over in the dirt.

'*No!*' Mike ran back onto the road, discarding his rifle in favour of the handgun again. He fired at the creature, but wasn't sure if the shots connected or not. He heard a snarl and saw Lyell launch herself into the air. She came down on the back of the creature, tearing at the bloody flesh of its back with her claws.

Ramone was still trapped underneath the monster, pinned by its weight. He was trying to fight his way out, his arms raised in futile defence. Mike saw the gleam of white teeth as the creature's head came down, closing on the upraised arms. It snapped and ripped at them.

Mike kept firing until the hammer clicked on an empty round. The huge beast shuddered, raising its bloody mouth in an angry howl as it attempted to throw off the wolf on its back. Anna ran forward and shot at it as well, hitting the beast in the chest and neck. Black blood splattered from the wounds and for a moment the creature faltered, stumbling under the assault. It reared up on its hind legs and twisted round, its jaws snapping viciously at Lyell until she was forced to retract her claws from its flesh and jump clear.

Growling harshly, the monster turned and ran back the way it had come, limping on bloody paws. It vanished into the darkness as quickly as it had appeared.

'What the fuck was that?' Mike's voice was high and almost hysterical. 'What the *fuck* was that?'

Behind him, Ramone was attempting to sit up. Anna dropped to her knees beside him, her heart in her mouth. She had assumed that the man was dead, or at least very badly injured. She put her hands on his shoulders to try and push him back down.

'No!' Ramone jerked away from her, his arms cradled against his chest.

Anna could see where his t-shirt had been shredded, thick red blood welling up and soaking through the fabric. 'Don't touch me!' the man hissed. 'Keep away!'

'It's okay, we'll help you…'

Anna reached for him again and Ramone rolled out of the way, heedless of the pain it caused. 'Don't touch me!' he said again, his voice hoarse and angry. 'I'm infected, don't you understand? Keep away from me.'

Helplessly, Anna held out her hands to him. 'Please, just – '

Ramone shook his head, his teeth gritted. 'Keep back, or I'll kill you. I swear to God, you touch me and I'll have to kill you.'

'Don't be stupid…'

Ramone managed to get into a sitting position. He drew his knees up to his chest, protecting his mutilated arms. His shoulders shuddered with pain, and he put his head down to hide his face from the others. 'I'm not being stupid,' he said, his voice calmer. 'I'm being rational. I'm infected and if you touch me then you'll get infected too. Just… don't. Okay?'

'What the fuck was that thing?' Mike asked again.

'One of the wolves… I think.' Ramone didn't lift his head. His breath was laboured. 'It must have got bitten by the dead ones… and the viruses must have had a fucked up reaction. Same as with Brac.' He could feel the numb tingling in his arms that would wear off all too quickly. He didn't dare even try to flex his fingers. And he knew that whatever conflict of viruses had been in effect within the deformed beast were now working their way into his own bloodstream. He drew his knees up tighter to his chest and closed his eyes.

Anna looked at the others, not knowing what she could do. She edged closer to the injured man, but didn't dare touch him after what he'd said. Her vision blurred with tears as she saw the blood leaking from the deep wounds and dripping steadily onto the ground.

Then Lyell started growling again and everyone looked up in fear, expecting the nightmarish creature to have returned. But Lyell was facing the other way, back along the road in the direction they had come from.

'Now what?' Mike asked.

Luca was scanning the darkness. 'There,' he said at last. 'Dead ones.'

'What?' Mike couldn't see anything. 'Where the hell did they come from? Why are they behind us?'

'They must have come out of the forest after we passed.' Luca didn't sound very certain.

'Great. Fuck this for a laugh.' He moved towards Ramone. 'C'mon, we've got to get out of here.'

'I see about half a dozen,' Luca said. 'Maybe it'd be best to dispose of them now so that they're not following us anymore…'

Mike hesitated. 'I don't know… yeah, you're right. Plus we don't really want to go running towards that wolf-thing again.' He untangled his rifle from the other straps over his shoulders. 'I'm not a great shot though.'

'Wait.' It was Ramone who spoke. He had lifted his head, turning it just enough so that he could see what was happening. 'I've got a better idea. One which involves you guys actually staying alive.'

'Hey,' Mike objected. 'I think I can take them.'

'There'll be more behind them. Look, the sun's going to be coming up real soon and you lot have to get to the camp. I'm obviously not going with you.' He unfolded his legs enough that he could free one of his arms. It hurt like hell to move, but he was able to reach the handgun at his side. It took a lot of effort to get his fingers to close on it. 'So you guys go ahead, and I'll make sure you're not followed.'

'No...' Anna reached for him again; drew back at the look he gave her. 'We're not leaving you...'

'Sure you are. I'm gonna sit here and watch you do it.'

'You can't get all of them,' Mike said. 'They'll kill you.'

A ghost of a smile formed on Ramone's lips. 'Nah.' His other hand was working loose one of the smooth metal cylinders from his belt. 'They won't do that.'

Anna stared at the grenade, shaking her head in mute denial.

The dead ones were approaching, discernable shapes in the darkness. 'Mike, there's a chain around my neck,' Ramone said. 'Take it with you and show it to the guy on the boat.'

Carefully, Mike reached out, slipping his hand under the collar of the man's t-shirt. His fingers found the slim metal chain and drew it out, bringing with it a pair of dog tags. He lifted it over the man's head and held it up, realising that the tags were coated with blood.

'There's a name on there,' Ramone told him. 'The guy on the boat will know where to find him. He'll sort all of this out – just find him and tell him what's happened. Okay?'

There was nothing Mike could do but nod.

Lyell cautiously approached Ramone, whimpering softly and butting at his leg. Ramone pushed her away with his elbow. 'Get off me,' he murmured. 'Stupid puppy.' The wolf ignored him, laying her head on top of his knees. Ramone sighed. 'Take care of these retards, alright?'

Lyell made a small noise in her throat, and the man took it as an affirmation.

The dead ones were stumbling closer now, their dragging footsteps muffled by the loose dirt of the road. Although they were still a fair distance away they were close enough to make Mike nervous. He took hold of Anna's arm, pulling her to her feet. The girl moved limply, as if the life had drained from her body, and for a moment it seemed like her legs would not support her weight. Mike kept her upright with difficulty.

'We can't leave him…' Anna whispered.

Ramone looked up irritably. 'Why are you still here? You can help me most by being as far away as possible in three minutes time.'

Mike began to lead her away. 'I'm sorry, man,' he said to Ramone.

Ramone said nothing. He sat and watched as they walked away, and he silently urged them to move faster. He flexed his fingers around the grenade; felt blood leaking down both of his arms and his chest as well. He took a deep breath and shuddered at how much it hurt. More broken ribs. His mouth tasted of copper.

Painfully, he turned himself round so that he was facing the dead ones. His hand shook as he raised the gun towards them.

Some distance away along the road, Mike looked back as he heard the first of the gunshots. He hurried Anna forward, desperate to get her as far away from there as possible.

They managed to get around two bends in the road before they heard the grenade detonate.

Chapter 59

By the time they reached the place where the road split, Anna was barely able to walk. At every other step she faltered and on several occasions would have fallen if Mike hadn't been holding her up. It was as if the cumulative effect of the past two days had caught up with her all at once, and her energy was almost visibly draining away by the minute. Having to leave Ramone behind had obviously been the last straw for her shattered nerves.

Mike didn't feel much better, but he forced himself to keep going more for the sake of the girl than for himself. All of his muscles ached, and exhaustion threatened to pull him down. He kept glancing back, refusing to believe that Ramone was really gone. The man had led them this far – what the hell were they going to do now that he was gone? None of the small group was capable of taking his place at that moment. Luca was injured, and Anna's former strength seemed to have deserted her. Mike could feel a heavy coldness in his stomach, knowing that the wolf-thing that had attacked them was almost certainly waiting up ahead, along with the rest of the dead ones and whatever the fuck it was that Anna had seen at the camp.

At the junction in the road, Mike called a halt and let Anna rest. She sat down, covering her face with trembling hands. Her eyes were red-rimmed from silent tears. Luca sat down next to her and hesitantly put his uninjured arm around her shoulders in a comforting gesture.

'We can't do this,' Mike said quietly. To the right, the road headed south, while straight ahead it disappeared around a curve that Mike knew led back to the main gate of the camp. They were so close that Mike imagined he could smell the cloying stench of smoke and dead flesh hanging in the air. He shook his head and fumbled in his pocket for his cigarettes.

Luca was staring at the sky, the only one of them who could detect the imperceptible change of light that marked the first edge of dawn. He estimated that there was little more than an hour before the sun would start to rise and burn his skin, and he privately wondered if there was any way he could be in a safe place by that time. His arm tightened around Anna's shoulders and he knew that he couldn't desert the humans, maybe not even if it meant his own death. He wondered if Lyell shared the same sentiment. The young wolf certainly seemed to have no intention of leaving Mike's side.

'There's no way,' Mike went on, speaking mainly to himself. 'Whatever that thing was, we can't fight it. No way.'

'Regardless of what it used to be,' Luca said, 'now it is just another of the dead ones. It will die just as easily as the others if you shoot it in the head.'

'We tried. You saw us try. I swear I hit it at least a couple of times.' Mike lit his cigarette, noticing that it was the second-to-last one in the crumpled pack. He had two or three spare packs – some unpronounceable and unfiltered brand that he had picked up in Narvik on the way there – but they were in his bag back at the camp, presumably lost forever. He shook his head to rid himself of the irrelevant thought. 'It was too strong for us. And I'm too crap at shooting.'

'We still have to try though.'

'I don't know.' Mike shook his head again. 'This is impossible. If Ramone couldn't survive this, then how the hell can we?'

'You've survived this far.'

Mike laughed bitterly. 'I should be dead about fifty times over. Look at the state of me.' He indicated the wounds on his neck and his leg. 'I don't deserve to even be here. First Brac, and now Ramone... everyone else is dead. Why am I still here?'

Luca didn't answer him, his unreadable black eyes still staring at the sky. 'The wolf that attacked us,' he said after a long moment. 'I think I know who it was.'

'You do?'

'Yes. Ramone was telling me that yesterday morning he saw someone down at the enclosure of the dead ones, and that he'd become convinced it was that boy Seth. The one who worked at the camp.'

Anna raised her head, just a little. 'You think that was him?' she asked, her voice still sounding strained. 'That creature?'

'I don't know. I can't be sure, but...' The vampire shrugged. 'Instinct tells me that it was. I think I would recognise Seth out of all the others wolves on this island, even in that state.'

'How come?'

'Because... probably because he is the only one of the wolves I have never trusted.'

Anna shifted, drawing away from him a little so that she could see his face. 'What do you mean by that?' she asked.

'I've heard stories about him,' Luca said bleakly. 'Some from the other wolves, but mainly from Tyr, who would never tell me where he'd heard them.

I trusted his opinion, so I watched Seth as closely as was possible. I wanted to find out whether he really was a danger to us.'

'A danger?'

'He has an irrational hatred about us vampires.' Luca smiled without humour. 'Or maybe not quite so irrational, judging by some of the stories. But as far as I'm aware he never actually did anything to us here, so I've got no proof. Just my suspicions.'

Mike had been listening to the vampire, and realised with irritation that his cigarette had been burning down unnoticed. 'So what were these stories?' he asked. 'We've been hearing shit about this Seth guy ever since we got here, but no-one will tell us anything straight. When we met him he seemed alright.'

'That was my first impression as well. He seemed young and nervous but not... unstable. All of the wolves have a certain amount of trauma in their lives, even the ones like Lyell who were born with their condition. Within those sort of boundaries, Seth seemed almost normal. I found it very difficult to connect him with the stories I had been told.'

Lyell lay down on the ground, her ears pricked up as she listened.

'Apparently,' Luca went on, 'something happened to Seth some years before he came to live here. He was attacked by a group of vampires... I don't know for certain what the circumstances were leading up to the attack. Tyr was happy to make a few guesses. Anyway, the vampires took him from somewhere and kept him captive for some time; at least a couple of weeks and possibly longer. They found it amusing to cut him and watch how long it took him to heal, and when they got bored of that game they started using silver knives so that the cuts would not heal so fast, and would leave scars.'

Anna shuddered, but Mike only frowned.

'But,' Luca said with a shrug, 'if he really did harbour that much ill-will towards us then he kept it well hidden. I have watched him very closely, and as far as I can tell he's never done anything.'

'Are you sure it's true then?' Anna said. 'I mean, no offence, but couldn't Tyr have been wrong? Or even making it up?'

'He had no reason to do that. The vampires who did it were friends of his.' He smiled then, without humour. 'That's one of the reasons Tyr dislikes me, actually. After he told me those stories, I went and had a few words with his former friends. Even among us monsters there are still lines that should not be overstepped.'

Anna started to ask what exactly he had done to them, then decided she probably didn't want to know. 'Why didn't you tell Doctor Ehren about this?' she asked instead.

Luca's eyes were bleak. 'If Seth ever harmed one of my people, then there would have been no need to speak to Ehren about it. I would have dealt with it myself. But after watching him all this time I'd more or less convinced myself that he was no danger to us.'

'Yeah, well.' Mike finished his cigarette and dropped the end to the ground. 'That's as may be, but he sure as hell is a danger to all of us now. And personally I don't think we have much of a chance against him.'

'We've got to get back to the camp,' Anna reminded him. 'The boat will be arriving soon.'

'But it won't be much good to us if we're dead, now will it? It's suicide to go walking in there, we all know that.' He shook his head. 'The guys on the boat will just have to figure it out for themselves. It won't take a genius to realise something's wrong here. Or maybe we could cut through the forest and find our way to the coast… maybe signal the boat from there…'

'Fine.' Anna pushed herself to her feet. 'Give me those tags you took from Ramone.'

Frowning, Mike dug into the pocket of his jeans and pulled out the silver chain, lifting it up so he could read the tags. He'd wiped the blood from them, but it was still difficult to see the carved words in the poor light. He made out a name and a six digit number that could have been a date of birth, and underneath that the inscription, "Ch. 22". 'What do you want them for?' he asked Anna.

'I'll take them to the boat myself. You go off and find the coast and shout at the boat or whatever you want to do, and if you're lucky maybe they'll hear you before the dead ones do.'

'Hey, come on…'

'No. Just shut up.' Anna's eyes blazed with anger, and Mike knew that she was completely serious. 'I'm going to reach the boat and if that thing in there is Seth then I'm going to kill him myself. And I'll do it without your help.'

Stung by her words, Mike closed his fist around the dog tags. 'That's harsh, Anna.'

'I don't care.' She held out her hand. 'Just give them to me, okay?'

Angrily, Mike turned away. 'Fine. Whatever. Let's go die and get it over with quickly, shall we?'

The others followed him, but Mike didn't look back. He set off towards the main gate of the camp, trying hard not to think about what waited for them there. The dog tags felt warm against his palm, and he wished desperately that Ramone was still alive so that he could have taken the lead and got them through this. Because Mike was convinced that he couldn't do it himself.

Chapter 60

It was getting harder and harder to walk, but Ramone had come too far to give up now. Each step was more difficult and more painful that the last, and he had to force himself onwards along the deserted road.

It seemed like a long time since he'd detonated the grenade. Up until the exact moment that he'd pulled the pin, he'd been ready to sit there and let it take him and the half-dozen dead ones around him into oblivion. He had shot as many of them as he had been able to, but finally the tremor in his hands had proved too much and he'd had to give up and let them close in on him. It was only when he'd removed the pin that he'd suddenly realised he was terrified.

Ramone hadn't been prepared for that feeling. He'd never before considered that death would scare him.

He'd struggled to his feet, dropped the grenade and run, dodging between the dead ones then throwing himself to the ground at the last possible moment. The explosion had torn apart all of the zombies as if they had been made of paper. Ramone had glanced back just once to reassure himself that none of them would be following him, then he had got back up and started walking along the road. The wounds on his arms were still streaming blood and he hurt in dozens of places, but he was still alive. As he walked, he tried to work out why.

By the time he reached the place where the road divided, he had figured it out.

He should have headed for the camp; should have gone after Anna and Mike and tried to help them, but he knew that in his weakened state he would be no use at all. And he had thought of something else that he could be wasting his last few hours of life on.

Holding his arms folded across his chest to try and minimise the bleeding, Ramone turned and headed south, towards the enclosure that had until recently housed the dead ones.

The sun must have been touching the underside of the horizon by the time he rounded a corner and saw the enclosure in front of him. He wondered briefly how the others were faring, but his mind was fogging and it was difficult to concentrate on any one thought. The virus was affecting him a lot quicker than it should have. He could only suppose that it was something to do with it having been mixed and contaminated with the wolf virus. He was glad that he had not met any more of the dead ones on the road, because he doubted that there was enough energy left in his body for another confrontation.

Bad karma, he thought. *This is because of what I did to Ehren... bad karma, it always comes back to get you...*

Now that his goal was in sight his pace flagged, and for the first time he stumbled. He drew in a deep breath, grateful that his lungs were still working okay. Other parts of his body were already going numb – not just the tingling numbness of cold or shock, but the paralysis of nerve ends as they steadily died. It would not be long before his muscles started to freeze up and his body slipped quickly into death.

He walked across the open ground, glancing around instinctively in case any of the dead ones were still lurking there. All seemed to be quiet though; the same unnatural quiet that had always hung over the enclosure. There was never any birdsong or animal noise near that place. The whole area was dead and deserted.

The temporary cabins were directly in front of him, not more than a hundred yards away. Ramone kept his eyes fixed on them as he hobbled forward, refusing to think about how far that hundred yards seemed now.

By the time he reached the cabins, his vision was definitely beginning to fade and darken at the edges. He stumbled forwards and caught himself against the side of the nearest cabin. He felt the coolness of the metal against his palm and three of his fingers, but the rest of his hand was too numb to feel anything. He flexed his hand and saw only half of it respond.

Death by inches, by centimetres... creeping slowly over you and taking away your body one tiny piece at a time. So this was how the others had felt. Maybe this was how all death felt.

Should've held onto the grenade.

Slowly, Ramone pulled back his hand and tried to close it into a fist. It didn't go very well. He leaned against the metal wall and slid his way along, around the rear of the cabin towards the back door. Taking it one step at a time.

Finally, he reached the reinforced door and his hand found the keypad that operated the locking mechanism. The front entrance, the one that led to the viewing area, was secured with heavy bolts, but this door was not for general access. He didn't know the combination for the keypad – had never known it, since Ehren had never seen fit to share it with him. Ramone took a moment to steady himself, drawing his dwindling strength together. He lifted his rifle and used the butt of it to break the lock. It took only two blows for it to shatter, but the effort left the man exhausted. He let the metal door swing open inwards and leaned heavily against the outside wall.

Despite his exhaustion, he couldn't help but feel angry at himself. He'd stood and stared at that lock so many times in the past, but he'd never had the balls to just smash it. And after all of that, it had broken so easily. Why had he waited till now to do this?

He must have closed his eyes for longer than intended, because when he opened them again, the tops of the trees were framed against the lightening sky. He tried to move and found that his feet had gone numb. When he pulled his way through the door it was like he was walking on huge, unresponsive blocks of dead flesh... which by that point was probably true. He could barely feel the metal frame of the door under the fingers of his left hand. He knew he had to hurry before his muscles packed up for good.

Spasms in his chest and stomach told him that his organs were in the process of shutting down as well. He tried to ignore it, even when the pain rode up so high that it threatened to overwhelm him. *Just a few more steps now.*

The second door was right in front of him, but this one was secured with nothing more serious than a double set of manual bolts. He awkwardly shifted his rifle to this left hand, then drew back the bolts. He knew that the occupant of the cell would have heard him coming by now and would be waiting just inside the door in mindless anticipation. Ramone steeled himself, then pushed hard against the door, throwing it open inwards.

As he'd hoped, the sudden movement caught the cell's occupant by surprise and knocked him back. It gave Ramone a precious few seconds to get inside. In his weakened state it almost all came apart when he stumbled on his dead feet and came close to falling.

Somehow he remained upright and so was able to fend off the first attack by the dead one inside the cell. Ramone swung his rifle and more by luck than design caught the creature squarely on the side of its head, knocking it down for a second time.

Ramone fell back against the wall, his lungs heaving painfully. His vision swam, the enclosed room dimming almost to black before coming slowly back to him. The faint dawn light coming through the single barred window and the open door were just about enough for him to see what was going on.

He watched as the creature that had once been his friend James dragged itself back to its feet. The dead eyes rolled in their rotten sockets, showing no trace of recognition at all.

'Hey, buddy,' Ramone said, his voice weak. 'Sorry I took so long.'

The dead one was upright and moving forward again, its skeletal fingers reaching for him. Its jaws worked hungrily but no sound came out. Ramone dropped his rifle to the ground and drew his handgun, but did not try to halt the creature's approach.

The zombie fell on him like a starving man, its teeth automatically seeking out his throat even as its fingers closed on his shoulders. The long nails pushed into his flesh. Ramone gasped in pain as the teeth tore through the skin of his neck, and then warm blood flowed down his chest. He knew that James' teeth had unerringly found the main artery.

Ramone felt the teeth slice through the meat of his neck and then pull back with a chunk of flesh locked between them. But because his body was already half-dead, he felt only a fraction of the pain he would have if he had been fully alive. Even so it was agony and he almost fell to his knees. Through blurring vision he saw the dead one lift its head; saw the red wetness of its mouth and the ragged convulsions of the decayed muscles in its throat as it swallowed.

Ramone had been careful to keep his right hand clear and unimpeded during all of this. He raised it now, bringing the gun up to rest against the creature's head.

James didn't even notice. Ramone tried to speak, but something was wrong with his voice.

He pulled the trigger and watched James' head snap backwards as if jerked on a string. The death-grip on his shoulders released and the body crumpled, finally realising that it was supposed to be dead.

Ramone fell back heavily and knew that he was dying too. His legs would no longer respond – the only reason he was still upright was because they had locked in place when he'd been attacked, and he couldn't make them relax again. He could feel blood running freely down the front of his shirt, but could do nothing about it. There was no way he could even lift his hand to check what the damage to his neck was, although he knew it was severe. His main artery had been torn, and he was very quickly bleeding to death.

But it's not death, his mind reminded him. *You won't die, not for real. You'll keep on living, just like the rest of them out there...*

His eyes turned painfully up towards the window, through which he could just see the pinkish light of sunrise. *This doesn't have to be the end, y'know... life is life... if you're still up and walking then what the hell difference does it make...?*

Ramone shut his eyes and groaned, then forced the stiffening muscles of his right arm to respond. Painfully, he lifted the gun towards his own head.

It still took a lot more courage than he'd expected to put the barrel under his chin and his finger on the trigger. His last thought was one of deep terror that the living death had gone too far and that the muscles of his hand would not respond.

He never got the chance to feel relief that they did.

Chapter 61

As their diminished group rounded the corner, the main fence loomed up in front of them. It was a black shape against a sky that was just beginning to lighten as dawn approached. Beyond the fence, a few faint points of light picked out the buildings where the interior lights still burned, running off the last few drops of stored solar energy. Mike strained his ears but couldn't hear a single sound from anywhere in the camp, and didn't know whether that was a good or a bad sign.

Anna pushed in front of him as they approached the gate. Her heart was pounding in her chest, but a strange calm overlaid her mind. She was less scared now than she had been in her dream, as if she were simply living through something that had already happened. Mike said something in a whisper to her, but she ignored him.

A figure by the main gate swung towards them. Anna walked forward calmly, and as she got closer recognised it as the zombie she had seen there in her dream. Its arm was caught in the wire of the fence, its attempts to free itself having twisted the wire deeply into the decaying flesh. The dead one pulled futilely at it, its free arm stretching to reach the girl. Its red shirt bore the number "23" in white on the front, but it was all but obliterated now by globs of blood and dirt. The scene was so much like her dream that Anna found herself glancing down to see if Amy was there, leading her onwards. Instead she found Lyell at her side.

Mike looked at the trapped zombie in disgust, reaching for his gun.

'No,' Anna said quietly. 'We don't want to draw attention to ourselves. Leave it.'

Reluctantly, Mike nodded then followed her as she stepped around the dead one. Its bulging eyes followed them, its mouth working constantly. Mike kept glancing back at it, feeling his skin crawl at the idea of leaving one of those things behind them.

Together, they moved in silence down the sloping road that led to the white buildings. The scant light from the few windows was still more than had been available in the forest, and the humans were able to find their way with relative ease over the uneven ground. Lyell ran a few steps ahead of them, her paws making no noise, and she cast her head back and forth constantly to sniff out anything that lay ahead.

'I don't see anyone,' Mike whispered.

'They're here somewhere,' Anna told him. 'They must still be here.'

They got to within fifty feet of the nearest building when a deep growl came out of the darkness ahead. Everyone froze in place, the sound raising the hairs on their necks. It sounded like it came from practically on top of them, but Mike could see nothing at all either ahead or behind them.

'Steady,' Anna murmured to him, then cautiously crept forward again.

Mike followed her, his heart beating so fast that he felt like it would rupture at any moment. He desperately wished that he could be somewhere else at that moment – anywhere at all, so long as it wasn't there.

As they inched their way onwards, they came around the first building and got a clear, unobstructed view into the centre of the encampment. Mike heard Luca swear softly in some language that wasn't English as he took in the scene before them.

* * *

It had taken Seth entirely too long to find his way back to the camp. He had hobbled on broken and bloody paws for hours along the rough dirt track, his mind fading in and out of consciousness. Twice he had come back out of the red fog in his brain to find that he had wandered off the road and was pushing through the thick trees instead. And then when he was so close to the camp that he could almost smell it, he had faded out again and it was only the sharp fragrance of living human flesh that had brought him back to himself. His bloody feet had carried him in the wrong direction, along the track that led to the mountains; some unconscious part of his brain directing him there.

He had seen the humans there on the road and the violent, overpowering hunger had filled him. It forced him to run at them when at another time he would probably have thought twice. He had been blind to everything except the need to devour the warm flesh and blood in the hope that it might somehow ease the fierce pain within his own body. He hadn't even realised that the humans were shooting at him; was unaware of the bullets striking his already mutilated and bleeding body. He had come so close as well, so close to tearing out the throat of that pathetic man that he'd pinned to the ground. His body shivered again at the thought of it, and another spasm of agony shot through him. The humans had shot him full of silver. He could still feel the bullets burning deep within his flesh. The pain had brought him to his senses, and he had escaped. Now he almost wished that he had not run; that he had stopped to feed and ease his pain, even if it had meant his death.

But he had run, and he had finally found his way back to the camp that he had left under very different circumstances twenty-four hours ago. Back then he had been in control and on the verge of one of the greatest moments in his life. Now he was a crippled, rotting misrepresentation of the creature he had once been. And as he limped into the camp, he caught sight of the person who had caused all of his problems.

Ciaran was crouched on the ground in front of one of the white buildings. His face was still a ruin of dried, bloody material, and the remains of his shirt hung in tatters over the empty chest cavity. His arms were coated with fresh blood, and as Seth watched he dug his fingers into a female corpse that lay on the ground in front of him. He pulled out a handful of stringy entrails, transferring them to his mouth. All around, the dead ones milled about or fed on other bodies that were sprawled across the ground. Seth felt the hunger turn over inside him again, and a low growl rose in his throat.

The noise was enough to make Ciaran look up. His one eye focused with difficulty, and Seth saw the flash of recognition there... and the hatred that went with it.

Ciaran stood up, the dead muscles in his legs protesting loudly at the movement. He had been in the camp for several hours, and was certain now that none remained alive within the perimeter fence. The red mist still clouded his mind, making it difficult for him to think straight, but it felt clearer now than it had before. At first there had only been the hunger; the deep, desperate need to fill his body with the flesh of others. Now his hunger had faded to a level where he could almost ignore it, and in its place he felt his anger rising again. It intensified a hundredfold as he saw the creature standing in front of him.

He knew it was Seth. Some part of his brain was aware enough to recognise the man who had tortured him and left him to be eaten alive by the undead. Within his own skull, Ciaran laughed loudly, knowing that Seth was infected with the same virus as he himself was. He hoped that the wolfman was suffering just an equal amount.

Seth hobbled forward, his growling becoming louder. The claws that protruded from the twisted stubs of his feet were stained black with his own clotted blood and the mud of the road, but they were still long and curved and could have ripped a human to shreds in moments. His teeth were permanently bared in a vicious snarl, the lips having sloughed away with the rest of his skin.

Ciaran had no weapons except for the bare hands which had already torn apart a dozen or more people that night. As he moved forward, circling around the wolf, he was dimly aware that he also had the advantage of speed – Seth moved as if each step were an agony, and he stumbled as he tried to turn to follow Ciaran's movement. Ciaran could no longer feel most of his body, although he was aware of it moving, like an organic machine that responded to his every unspoken command. He had lost the finesse and delicacy of his former life, but he was still faster and more agile than the wolf-creature.

Seth made the first move, darting forward on clumsy feet with his mouth wide. Ciaran stepped out of his way, grabbing at the wolf's neck. He missed, his numb fingers closing instead around a projection of flesh that had once been an ear. It was slick with viscous blood, but Ciaran dug his nails in and twisted. The lump of flesh and gristle tore loose.

The wolf screamed, a shockingly human sound. He spun round. The teeth snapped together, closing on Ciaran's hand before he could snatch it back. Two fingers and the glob of bloodied flesh disappeared into Seth's maw. Ciaran struck at him with his other hand, landing a blow that was hard enough to crack the jawbone. With a grunt of pain, Seth let go of his hand but immediately snapped at the arm instead. The brutal teeth closed around the elbow and crunched through the bone, but Ciaran wrenched himself free and staggered away.

Seth swallowed the mouthful of flesh that he had won, even though it tasted putrid and diseased. Then he turned and made another lunge at the vampire, hatred blinding him to the searing pain of his own body.

As the wolf struck at him, Ciaran caught hold of its leg with his one functioning hand. A sharp twist rewarded him with the crack of a fractured bone and another scream of pain.

The two combatants were unaware that they were being watched by human eyes. A little way up the hillside, Mike and Anna stared in horror and revulsion at the two creatures intent on ripping each other apart. Luca was muttering to himself, his words harsh but incomprehensible. None of them noticed that Lyell had crept away into the darkness.

They also did not notice that although Seth and Ciaran were too preoccupied with each other to have smelled their presence, other creatures had. As the fight continued, a dozen undead faces slowly looked up from the fallen bodies they were feasting on and stared into the shadows, sensing fresh food.

Chapter 62

'This is not good.' Mike stared down at the two undead creatures. 'This is so not good.'

'Just keep quiet,' Anna told him in a whisper. 'If they want to fight with each other then it's better than them fighting with us, right?'

'Sure. Maybe they'll kill each other and leave us alone.' Mike tone was not hopeful.

Luca was shaking his head, his face even paler than normal. 'That's Ciaran down there,' he whispered. 'I've got to help him...'

'I think he's a little beyond your help now,' Mike pointed out. 'He's already dead, there's nothing you can do for him.'

'Yes, but...' Luca said something harsh in that other language. 'I cannot stand here and watch him get torn to pieces.'

It seemed like he was about to go walking towards the fight, so Mike caught hold of his arm. 'There's nothing you can do,' he repeated, ignoring the look that the vampire directed at him. 'Besides, he seems to be holding his own at the moment anyway.'

Mike appeared to be right. Ciaran was staying continually out of range of Seth's teeth and claws, circling around and forcing the wolf to use his dwindling energy to follow. With one of his front legs out of action, Seth was moving even slower, and again and again Ciaran took advantage of the fact, striking hard at the wolf with pummelling fists and tearing nails.

'So what's the plan?' Anna asked. 'Just stay here and watch until they're both dead?'

'Sounds good to me,' Mike replied. 'Beats the hell out of any of the alternatives I can think of.'

Luca didn't seem happy, but he didn't break loose from the grip Mike had on his arm, even though it would obviously have been no effort for him. He chewed on his lower lip as he watched the fight. 'I don't understand – ' he started to say, then abruptly stopped. 'Wait, I think there might be trouble.'

'Where?' As soon as Mike spoke, he saw what Luca meant. The group of zombies that had been milling around outside the building had one by one turned and started shuffling in their direction. 'Shit, we've been spotted.' He let go of Luca and lifted his rifle.

'I don't see that many,' Anna frowned. 'There must be others still inside that building.'

'Well, they'll be here soon enough.' Mike sighted along his rifle, letting out his breath. 'So much for stealth,' he muttered to himself, then squeezed the trigger.

His first two shots went wide and he forced himself to calm down and focus on aiming. The next one hit a zombie in the side of its head, spraying brains over the one directly behind it. Anna joined him, standing at his side. By unspoken agreement, they took one side of the wide street each, taking down each zombie as it staggered slowly towards them.

Mike paused to reload, glancing round to see what was happening with the two undead monsters. They were still fighting, the wolf having maimed the vampire with a lucky strike that had taken a large chunk out of the left thigh. Either they had not spotted the humans or they were too concerned with each other to care.

Even as he watched, Mike saw the wolf stagger forward, bloodstained teeth flashing. Ciaran attempted to back up out of the way, but his damaged legs responded too slowly. His foot caught on one of the bodies on the ground and he fell. Seth was on him in a second, almost before the vampire hit the ground. Curved teeth flashed down with unerring accuracy to sink into the soft flesh of Ciaran's throat.

'*No!*'

Mike looked up in surprise. It was Luca who had cried out, and he was sprinting away in the direction of the fight.

'Luca!' Anna yelled after him.

Luca either didn't hear or wasn't listening. He kept running, dodging between the remaining dead ones with frightening speed, at times moving so fast that the humans were hard pressed to follow him with their eyes. At one point a zombie stumbled into his path, its hands grabbing automatically at him. Luca didn't even pause in his stride. He swung his free arm at the dead one, his fist connecting with its face so hard that the skull collapsed inwards as if it were made of paper.

'What the hell's he doing?' Mike asked aloud. 'The absolute *idiot...*'

Anna started moving forward as well, a few steps at a time, still concentrating on shooting at the dead ones. There was an urgency to her actions now – Luca may have been able to slip through the dead ones easily but she could not follow him unless the corpses were out of the way.

Mike saw what she was doing but was reluctant to do the same. They were a good distance from the dead ones where they were; close enough to have them in range, but far enough away to be out of immediate danger. If Luca wanted to go running to the aid of someone who was far beyond saving then he could do it alone. For Mike and Anna to follow him would have been suicidal.

Mike lost sight of Luca among the remaining dead, and went back to focusing on lining up his shots properly. Out of the corner of his eye he was aware of more of the dead ones spilling out of the building and shuffling their way towards them. He silently prayed that Anna had been right in her estimate and that there weren't many more zombies left.

The rifle shots were deafening to his ears, but when he paused to reload Mike clearly heard a howl of triumph. He looked up and saw Seth standing over Ciaran's body. The vampire-creature lay motionless on the ground. Seth's teeth had managed to sever the spinal cord with that last bite. As Mike watched, Seth lowered his huge, bloodied jaws and lifted Ciaran's head in his teeth, the last few strands of flesh stretching taunt then snapping wetly. The creature that had once been a wolf crunched down hard on the skull, splintering it into pulpy fragments.

Completely in the throes of his triumph, Seth swallowed the foul-tasting brain matter, not caring that his stomach twisted and rebelled at the vile substance.

He had been so caught up in his battle that he hadn't for a moment registered the shots that were being fired behind him, nor the shouts of the humans. He hadn't noticed the dead ones staggering away towards the new source of food. His scarred brain still could focus on nothing but the mangled remains of Ciaran. Even though the flesh was rotting and inedible, he had the urge to tear into it again, to rip it to pieces and devour as much as he was able. To destroy it completely, and make sure that the vampire would never rise again, in any shape or form.

It was only then that he raised his head and saw the man coming towards him.

Seth couldn't focus properly, his eyes being covered with a film of dirt and blood. He couldn't dislodge it since he no longer had any eyelids. He could make out the general shape of the person; got an impression of black hair and a pale, death-like face. His first thought was that it was one of the walking corpses, wandering into his line of view. But a moment later his sluggish brain realised that the figure was walking too quickly, with too much determination, and that he was headed straight towards him. It appeared that the man had only one arm, a pale blur of cloth covering the other shoulder and half of the chest.

Seth growled, sniffing the air automatically but catching no scent. His senses had all died along with his body, and he could smell nothing at all, not even the putrefaction of his own flesh. But some other sense was working, and he knew that the man was not dead, and yet not alive either. Another vampire. If it had been possible, Seth would have grinned.

Luca saw the beast raise its head towards him. Close up, with the orange light from the nearby building spilling over it, it looked even more shocking than before. One of the front paws dangled uselessly, the bone obviously broken. The head was grossly misshapen, the jaw misaligned and one side of the muzzle appearing crushed, presumably where one of Ciaran's blows had landed. It looked as if the whole creature had been fashioned out of raw meat and then left to decay, the flanks covered by coarse hair matted with black blood. The stench was unbelievable, and had Luca hesitating in his tracks.

The growl rose into a snarl. Luca stepped back a pace, his hand tightening around the heavy piece of wood that he had picked up off the ground a moment before. He felt sick as he saw what remained of Ciaran's body; anger and guilt over the fact that he had been unable to save him. It was Luca's fault that Ciaran had come to the camp last night, and it was his fault that his life had ended this way. Now he could do nothing but avenge the man he should have protected.

The wolf-thing staggered towards him, limping on its three paws. It seemed impossible that the creature could still be moving, let alone be ready for another fight, but Luca caught a glimpse of the madness in its eyes. The monster would continue to fight until it was no longer able to move even a single muscle.

Luca did not wait for it to attack. He stepped forward and swung the piece of wood with his good arm. There was enough force behind it to have put a hole in a solid wall, and if it had connected with Seth's skull it would have crushed it like an egg.

But Seth dodged out of the way, letting out a roar of pain as he accidentally put weight onto his broken front leg. Anger boiled through his mind and he leaped forward, teeth aiming for the vampire's throat. He missed his target by inches, his jaws shutting on empty air. The momentum caused his body to collide with Luca and knock him off his feet.

Luca rolled and came back upright. He struck again at the wolf's head. The heavy wood glanced off the beast's shoulder instead, cracking the bone and also splintering the wood.

With a roar of pain, Seth spun towards him, his huge head smashing into Luca's chest like a battering ram. Luca was thrown backwards and smashed his head against the wall of the building. He tried to push himself upright but then his legs buckled and he spilled to the ground. He did not get back up.

Chapter 63

'What the hell is happening?' Mike demanded, looking around wildly. The dead ones were still pressing in on them but Anna kept steadily moving forward, pausing every other step to take down another zombie. Her eyes kept flicking towards Luca, and she continued to ignore Mike.

He gave up trying to get answers from her and put all his concentration into hitting the dead ones. For the first time he was actually doing quite well. Almost fifty percent of his shots were on target, and he was thinning out the ranks of the undead with surprising speed. *Ramone would be proud*, he thought bitterly.

He heard Anna suddenly gasp and looked up. It took him a moment to focus on what she had seen, and another moment to realise what was happening. Luca was on the ground, unmoving. Mike saw the wolf-creature hobble towards him and immediately swung his gun round.

He emptied the rifle at the beast, but the distance was too great and none of the shots found their mark. The creature didn't even look up at him; just continued to stalk towards the fallen vampire. Mike fumbled for more ammo, spilling a carton from his pocket. 'Shoot it!' he yelled at Anna.

The girl was already moving. 'We've got to get closer!' She started to run, heedless of the dead ones that immediately changed course to surround her.

'Fuck!' Mike swore viciously. He managed to reload his rifle and tried to take down the last few of the dead ones as quickly as possible, but he was terrified that he would hit Anna by accident and most of his shots went wide.

He was distracted by a blur of motion next to the building. He glanced round and his heart seemed to freeze within his chest.

A dark shape had come running out of the shadows and launched itself at Seth. Mike caught a glimpse of black fur and knew it had to be Lyell. She threw herself onto the back of the larger beast, digging her claws into its flesh just as she had done when it attacked them before. The wolf-creature let out a howl of anger and pain and reared up on its hind legs.

That was it for Mike. He gave up on the rifle and drew his handgun instead, charging down the slope towards the dead ones. There weren't more than half a dozen left now, and he killed two of them at point blank range, darting out of reach of the others. As he ran, he thought he saw Anna dodging past the two wolves and running to Luca's side, but then something happened that made him skid to a halt.

Another wolf had appeared, apparently from nowhere. This one even larger than Seth and had black fur streaked with grey. Mike had a sudden flash of Brac in his wolf form... but Brac was dead, and Mike had no idea who this could be.

The grey wolf circled around Seth then struck out at him with a huge forepaw. Seth was trying to dislodge the young wolf from his back and didn't appear to even realise that the other was there. The swipe caught him across the flank, peeling off a long strip of rotten flesh. Seth tried to turn, tripping over his own damaged paw and almost losing his balance. Lyell clawed at him, ripping at the back of his head with one paw while clinging to his shoulders with the other.

Mike was so intent on the fighting wolves that he didn't realise the remaining dead ones had turned to follow him. The first warning he got was when one grabbed his shoulder. Mike yelled in surprise and spun round. He jammed his gun up underneath the zombie's chin and blew the top of its head off. The last few dead ones were right behind it, and Mike picked them off quickly, aiming and firing automatically. When the last one dropped he turned full circle, making sure that no others were sneaking up on him. Finally he turned his attention back to the wolves.

He was just in time to see Seth stagger under Lyell's weight and collapse to the ground, his injured legs unable to support him any longer. The grey wolf had torn bleeding chunks out of his body in a dozen places, and the last swipe of his claws had taken out Seth's throat, leaving a ragged black wound that was so deep the white gleam of spinal bone was visible within it. Still Seth attempted to fight, his jaws snapping weakly at the two wolves.

Mike ran closer, his gun raised. The grey wolf heard his approach and turned to face him. Mike hesitated under the fierceness of that gaze, but then the wolf stepped back a pace. Cautiously, Mike edged closer.

Seth saw him coming and tried to raise himself up, but his other front leg had been broken at some point during the fight and would not bear his weight. His teeth were bared in a permanent snarl, but the growling now sounded thin and pained. He was unable to close his mouth properly. Black, clotted blood dripped from his jaw to pool on the ground beneath him. Both eyes were filmed with dirt, giving them a blind, staring cast.

Mike lifted his gun and fired directly into the creature's head. He kept firing until the magazine was empty and Seth's skull was a shattered ruin.

Then he took the magazine out and tried to reload it, but his hands were shaking so much that he couldn't do it. He closed his eyes and took several deep breaths to try and steady himself, then realised that all he could smell was dead meat.

Behind him, Anna had been trying to wake Luca up when the grey wolf had appeared. She sat frozen in place, one hand still resting on Luca's chest, staring with wide eyes at the wolf. Now she slowly got to her feet.

'Is Luca okay?' Mike asked over his shoulder. He got no reply and turned to look at her. 'Anna?'

The girl stepped past him without a word, her gaze fixed on the second wolf.

Mike was more worried about Luca. The question of where the grey wolf had come from could wait till later as far as he was concerned. He knelt down beside Luca and touched the vampire's neck, feeling for a pulse. He held his breath, unable to feel anything. 'C'mon Luca,' he muttered, shaking the vampire by the shoulder. 'Wake up.'

Luca's head lolled to the side and Mike saw that his black hair was matted with blood. Mike's heart turned over, even though he knew that head wounds bled a whole lot so it probably wasn't as bad as it looked. But he had no idea what damage a blow to the head would do to a vampire...

Even as he thought it, Luca's eyelids fluttered open.

'Oh, thank God.' Mike smiled with genuine relief. 'Tell me you're okay.'

'I...' Luca blinked slowly, his black eyes focusing with difficulty. 'Yes. I'm okay.' He frowned, then screwed up his eyes. 'The sun... it's nearly morning.'

Mike glanced upwards. Possibly the sky was getting lighter, but if so then it was so slight a change that he would not have noticed it himself. 'It's okay, we'll get you somewhere safe. You hit your head pretty hard – you sure you alright?'

Luca lifted his hand and touched the back of his head, frowning again as his fingers touched the fresh blood there. Carefully, he sat up, tilting his head to one side then the other experimentally. 'I think so,' he said at last. 'Groggy. But alright. Where's Anna?'

'Over there,' Mike said. He looked towards the girl and saw her approaching the grey wolf. She was holding her hand out to him as if she couldn't quite believe that he was real.

'I dreamt about you,' she said in a whisper. 'I knew it was you.'

The wolf backed away a couple of steps, keeping just out of her reach.

'I knew it was you.' Anna smiled, her face lit with happiness for the first time in many weeks. 'Amy told me. I knew you hadn't left us.'

The wolf held his ground this time and let her touch his neck, her fingers stroking lightly over the greying fur. He had dark amber eyes like Lyell, filled with something deep and troubled.

Abruptly he backed away again.

'Wait…' Anna started towards him. 'It's okay…'

The grey turned and started to run back towards the main gate, covering the ground in a fast loping stride.

'No!' Anna ran after him, but there was no way she could catch up. 'Come back!'

The black wolf kept running, pausing only briefly just before he reached the gate. He glanced back once, then turned and disappeared into the forest.

'Wait!' Tears ran freely down her cheeks as Anna stumbled on the rough slope. 'Please come back, please don't leave! *Dad!*'

She got halfway to the gate before tears overcame her and she collapsed on the ground. She remained there sobbing until Mike caught up with her and gently helped her back to her feet.

Chapter 64

Luca had gone into one of the smaller buildings, and when Mike came back with Anna he appeared in the doorway. 'There's a safe-cellar in this one,' he told them. He was shading his eyes with his hand, even though the sky had not lightened that much and the sun would not be rising above the horizon for a while yet.

'Will you be okay there?' Mike asked.

The vampire nodded. 'They were designed for situations like this.' He smiled slightly. 'Well, maybe not exactly like this, but you know what I mean. I'll stay here today and return home this evening.'

'We'll check around here,' Mike promised. 'Make sure there aren't any more of the dead ones lurking about.'

'Thank you. I appreciate that.' Luca retreated a few steps into the darkness of the building, as if the meagre light outside was hurting him more than he'd admit. 'Anna, are you okay?'

The girl's eyes were red from crying, and the sorrow in her face was almost painful to see. She mutely shook her head, devoid of words.

'Come here.' Luca held his good arm out to her. 'Let me talk to you.'

Anna did as she was told, moving like a sleepwalker. Luca took her hand and drew her into the interior of the building.

'I've gotta do something,' Mike said. 'Bye, Luca.'

'We'll meet again, my friend.' The vampire smiled at him. 'It's been good to know you.'

'Sure.' It was difficult for Mike to smile in return. 'See you around then.' He turned and walked away, back towards the building that was surrounded by felled corpses.

Inside the windowless supply building, Luca put his arm around Anna, pulling her towards him. She didn't resist, leaning into his body and laying her head on his shoulder. He could feel the tension in her shoulders; the faint tremor that revealed the torment inside her.

'We haven't got much time,' Luca said softly.

Anna nodded. 'Let me stay here,' she said then. 'I can't leave, not now. I've got to stay and find him. Let me stay here with you, please? I'm so tired… I'll just sleep right through the day, then tonight I'll go looking for him. Please… let me stay.'

'Anna… you can't stay.'

'Why not?' She pulled back so that she could see his face, her eyes shining with some of her former defiance. 'We've made it; we got past all the dead ones. The boat will be coming soon and Mike can go on it alone. He can tell them what happened; he can go get help. He doesn't need me with him.'

'I think he does.' Luca tightened his arm protectively around her shoulder. 'And I also think he won't leave without you.'

'What? Why the hell not? He doesn't need me to hold his hand.'

'No, but he won't leave you behind. If you stay then he will as well.'

'Don't be stupid.' Anna frowned as she said it. 'He doesn't owe me anything…'

'Listen, he followed you here; he's been beside you all this time. Half the time the only reason he kept going was to help you. He won't leave you now.'

'Yes he will. Everyone leaves.' She blinked back fresh tears. 'Everyone always leaves me. Why would he be any different?'

Luca shook his head. 'I don't know. But I know that he won't go unless you go with him.'

'I *can't* go! Don't you understand? That was my father – he's still alive and he's been turned into something else. I've got to find him.' Tears were spilling down her cheeks again. 'Why did he run away from me?' she asked, her voice breaking. 'I came all this way to find him… and he ran away.'

'You have to understand, Anna – he's been through a lot. It is not an easy thing to adjust to and he's probably terrified. He's had no-one to help him through this or explain what's happening… and the first full moon is always very difficult. He was probably barely aware of what he was doing – a lot of the wolves black out when they change for the first time. And if he *was* aware… well, he was more than likely scared to death of how you'd react.'

Anna wiped at her eyes with a shaky hand. 'I just wanted to help him…'

'*I* know that and *you* know that, but think about what your father must have thought. In his eyes… he's a monster. He hasn't had time to come to terms with that yet, let alone think about how anyone else will react.'

'I still can't believe he ran from me.' She leaned her head on Luca's shoulder again, suddenly grateful for his support. Part of her was aware that his body was cool to the touch – a lot cooler than it should have been. She pushed the thought away. She didn't want to think about him not being human, not at that moment. 'This is like a nightmare,' she murmured. 'How could this have happened? It's all the fault of that bastard Seth… he did this…' She pressed her face into the cloth of Luca's t-shirt, trying and failing to hold back the tears.

'It's okay…' Luca stroked her hair. 'It's over now.' He lifted his head, squinting against the increasing light of the sky outside. He could feel the skin on his arms beginning to tighten, as if already feeling the heat of the unrisen sun. 'Anna, I have to go.'

'Please,' she said again, not raising her head. 'Please let me stay with you.'

'I'm sorry.' Gently, he let go of her and stepped away. 'I've got to go.'

In the centre of the room was a hinged trapdoor made of a single piece of heavy wood reinforced with steel edging. Luca crouched down and grabbed hold of the metal handle, lifting the door with some effort. It was obviously as heavy as it looked, and Anna doubted that she would ever have been able to move it herself. The smell of damp earth rose from the opened door, and Anna moved forward so that she could peer inside. The area under the floor was little more than a deep crawlspace, probably no more than four feet from floor to ceiling and lined with unfinished concrete. Luca jumped down into the hole then turned around to face her. The level of the floor came up to his chest.

'It's not exactly five star accommodation,' he smiled, 'but it's safe. My people have stayed here many times before, so don't worry about me. Okay?'

'I'll try.' Anna managed to return the smile. 'I still don't want to go.'

Luca reached up and took hold of her hand. 'It'll be alright,' he promised. 'I'll see you again.'

Anna nodded, accepting it as truth. 'Thanks, Luca.'

Luca get go of her hand, then knelt down in the crawlspace and pulled the heavy door down over him, sealing himself tightly within the concrete tomb. Anna held her smile until he disappeared into the darkness, and then she let it crumble. She crouched down on the cold floor and pressed her hands against the wooden door, imagining that she could still feel the coolness of his body under her fingertips. She didn't want to think about him lying down there in the dark, so deep in sleep as to be effectively dead. For a brief, irrational moment as she lifted her head she hated the sun.

It was several long minutes before she stood up and walked back outside, and by that time a thin sliver of orange sun had cleared the horizon. She stared at it until her eyes hurt, trying to remember the last time she had stopped to watch a sunrise.

Down the slope a little way, she saw Mike dragging something along the ground. She watched him without much interest, wondering what he was doing. Eventually, she wandered down towards him.

The plastic container that Mike had found in one of the supply buildings was marked as containing kerosene, and he assumed that it had been for use in the generator. It was also a lot heavier than he had expected, and it was taking a lot of effort to drag it across the uneven ground. He stopped to rest, wondering how much strength he really had left in his body. He felt impossibly tired and sore, not to mention thirsty and hungry. Now that they appeared to be out of danger, it was as if everything had caught up with him at once, and he wanted nothing more than to lie down in the dirt and sleep forever. The warmth of the rising sun on his back was the only thing that kept him going.

He glanced up and saw Anna approaching, and quickly went back to dragging the heavy container. He had wanted to get this done before she came back, but it was taking longer than he'd expected.

Finally, he got the container level with the pile of flesh and broken bones that had once been Seth. The creature was even more unrecognisable now in the light of day, the legs skewed at odd angles and the head a pulped ruin. Mike removed the screw cap from the container and tipped it up, splashing the contents over the body. The thick, choking smell of kerosene fumes filled the air, making his eyes water. He tipped out half of the fuel, covering the body completely, then put the cap back on tightly and dragged the container well out of the way.

'I'm not convinced he's dead,' Mike explained to Anna, grimacing. 'And I'm not going to feel happy until I'm absolutely sure.'

Anna nodded but said nothing.

Mike picked up a splinter of wood from the ground and dipped it in the spreading kerosene puddle, then stood well back. He used his lighter to set fire to the splinter, turning it between his fingers to make sure it caught light evenly. Then he tossed it towards Seth's body.

The fuel ignited more violently than he'd expected, and he and Anna had to back quickly away from the sudden intense heat. They stood together and watched the fire reduce the body to ashes.

Mike's camera let out a whirring noise and he glanced down at it, realising with surprise that the lens cap was not on. Lifting it up, he saw that the whirring had come from the tape having reached the end and automatically stopped. He must have knocked the camera at some point and started it recording, and it had run through an entire hour-and-a-half tape. He couldn't remember the last time he had checked the camera or switched it on, so he couldn't be sure when it had started going. He was too tired to think about it now. Carefully, he ejected the tape and placed it in the zip-up pocket inside his jacket, along with the first one. *One hell of a video project*, he thought to himself. *What I did on my weirdest holiday ever...*

'Is Luca okay?' he asked.

'Yeah, I think so.' Anna still didn't feel like talking. She kept glancing behind her, back at the silent forest. 'He's sealed up in that building... I guess he's okay.'

'I wonder where Lyell went.' The young wolf had disappeared at some point after the fight, but Mike hadn't seen her go. He felt bad about that, because he had wanted to say goodbye to her. He hoped she came back before the boat arrived. 'Y'know, I think I might go check out the accommodation building… it looks intact, so maybe our stuff is still up there.' It seemed insane to think that his bag might be sat up on the bed in his room, exactly where he'd left it twenty-hour hours previously. He would have been happy to get his passport back though.

Anna nodded again, her thoughts far away. She paid no real attention to Mike as he wandered off, her gaze focused on the semi-circle of sun that was slowly inching its way over the horizon. If she concentrated hard, she could just make out the tiny black speck in the middle of the sea, silhouetted against the flame-coloured sky. She knew that it was the boat, and that in another hour or so it would be at the docks and she would have the job of explaining to the captain exactly what had happened to the island. One more hour to remain on the island; to enjoy the absolute peace of a silent world.

She flexed her right hand and felt the palm grow warm, as if a small child was holding it with trust.

Behind her, a little way up the slope, Mike paused to light the final cigarette in his pack. He was about to discard the empty packet then changed his mind, putting it back in his pocket. It had survived this far, after all. He glanced back and saw Anna staring fixedly out over the sea, and he wondered what she was thinking. He sighed then, knowing he would have to talk to her soon.

He shouldn't get on the boat. God, he wanted to – he wanted to be as far away as possible from this place. And if Anna was going then he had to go with her. He couldn't desert her now, not after everyone else in the world had.

But he shouldn't get on the boat. A few minutes earlier, he had checked the wound on his leg to see how it was looking. Now he had to work out how he was going to tell Anna that it had somehow healed to a faint pink scar in the space of a few hours.

THE END

+ Bizarre Film + Cult Icons + TV Nostalgia +

Have you got the taste buds for the more **unusual**? Are the High Street Magazines starving you of substance, and instead forcing upon you the world of Fast Food, Gossip, Fashion and mundane Celebrity Culture? Sick of looking at Anorexic A-Listers with cellulite?

Want something more lean, tasty, and occasionally down-right bizarre?

Stop buying takeaways and feast on-line with our delectable British Baked recipe....

Serve: **Monthly**

Ingredients

2 Fluid Oz. Of **Film News**
A Pinch of **Classic TV**
Liberally added **Bizarre** Flakes for taste.
Some specially selected **Iconic Interviews** (check sell by date.)
A Sprinkle of fat Elvis Jokes......

Instructions

Just take the ingredients..... **And Cream**

WWW.ANDCREAM.COM

I scream...
You scream....
We all scream for...

And Cream

HAMMERHEAD: A SUMMER OF MASSACRE
GARRY CHARLES

Edward Craven wasn't born into a normal family. He was raised to be an animal, a hunter and a feaster of human flesh.

Four vacationing university students are about to stumble into his territory. They are about to discover why the town of Blackwood is deserted and they learn the true meaning of death as, one by one, they face their predator....

HAMMERHEAD

Prepare for slaughter.

ISBN: 978-0-9550314-8-9

£7.99

"Shaun Hutson turned up to eleven"- Garry Charles

FILTH KISS
C J LINES

Set against the backdrop of rural England in the 1980s, "Filth Kiss"is a dizzying plunge into the nightmarish heart of depravity.

A man's body is found in the river Severn.

Two brothers return to the village of their childhood to pay last respects to a father they barely knew.

Broadoak never changes. The same shops sell the same homemade trinkets. The same tongues wag behind the same closed doors. The same souls seek salvation at the bottom of the same pint glasses. The same shadows move along the same streets after closing time. The same malevolence waits to awaken once more.

As they fight off their own demons, the brothers discover that the evil within is nothing to be afraid of; what's coming for them is far, far worse.

ISBN: 978-0-9550314-5-8

£7.99

HEAVEN'S FALLING: ASCENSION
GARRY CHARLES

When Virgil Kain was murdered, the last that he expected was to awake mere hours later in a hospital bed.

To add to his confusion he is told that he should not be dead, that the future of the realms of Heaven, Hell and Earth are dependent on his survival.

God has a job for him.

In the search for his killer, he is forced to team up with a transgender demon and Satan herself, but will they be enough to stop......

Heaven from falling.

ISBN: 978-0-9550314-0-3

£11.99

HEAVEN'S FALLING: REDEMPTION
GARRY CHARLES

It is time for Kain to face the ghosts of his past and make amends for his actions, but he will soon discover the redemption he seeks comes at a price.

Limbo has fallen.

The once great city a ruin of its former glory and the after life is hanging by a thread.

Gods and Demons alike are running scared as an all powerful enemy prepares to destroy all that is.

Kain, Lucy and Damien are only at the start of their long quest, a journey that will lead them to Eden and beyond.

ISBN: 978-0-9550314-1-0

£15.99

THINGS FROM THE PAST
STEVEN DEIGHAN

Another collection of shorts from Steven Deighan brings a scare to whoever may read it's pages.

People may be drawn to the cover at first, but we assure you that what lies inside, is pure quality, pure horror and pure excellence.

Artwork by Ian Simmons.

ISBN: 978-0-9550314-3-4

£7.99